nancy thayer

A NANTUCKET
WEDDING

a novel

2019 Ballantine Books Trade Paperback Edition

Copyright © 2018 by Nancy Thayer
Reading group guide copyright © 2019 by Penguin Random House LLC
Excerpt from *Surfside Sisters* by Nancy Thayer copyright © 2019 by Nancy Thayer

Originally published in hardcover in the United States by Ballantine Books, an imprint of Random House, a division of Penguin Random House LLC, in 2018.

This book contains an excerpt from the forthcoming book *Surfside Sisters* by Nancy Thayer. This excerpt has been set for this edition only and may not reflect the final content of the forthcoming edition.

ISBN 9781101967119
Ebook ISBN 9781101967126

Printed in the United States of America on acid-free paper

randomhousebooks.com
randomhousereaderscircle.com

2 4 6 8 9 7 5 3 1

Book design by Mary A. Wirth

Title-page image: © istockphoto / Ali Looney

For Charley

I want to hold your hand

acknowledgments

Here I sit, once again, in my aerie on Nantucket, all alone (Charley's downstairs), while the wind howls and the rain falls and for the first time in my thirty-three years here, we have dolphins swimming in our harbor.

I spend so much time alone, writing. When I'm not writing, I'm thinking about fictional people. So I'm enormously grateful to the real people who keep me sane and happy.

Especially in the winter, Nantucket is a small town, and really, it is out of a storybook. Hugs and smooches to Tricia Patterson, Gussie Manville, Sofiya Popova, Alexandra LePaglia, Katie Hemingway, Joann Skokan, Ive Nakova, Curlette Anglin (aka The Orchid Whisperer), Jan Dougherty, Mary and John West, and Deborah and Mark Beale. I'm very grateful to the charming and capable Christina Hall of Nantucket Island Resorts, who helped me envision the wedding in my book.

Special thanks to Jeff Lee, who bid an astonishing amount at the Safe Harbor for Animals auction so I would use the names Charlie and Henry in this book, and then brought his two gorgeous Labradors to meet me. They impressed me so much that they jumped right in as characters.

Nantucket is fortunate to have its own bookstores, and again and always, thanks to Wendy Hudson, Wendy Schmidt, Laura Wasserman, Christina Machiavelli (I really want to use her name in a book!), Dick Burns, and Suzanne Bennett. Many thanks to bookstores everywhere, and of course, to libraries, who make it possible for everyone to hold a book in their hands.

Sometimes I leave the island and go to the big city, and wow! The energy there is inspiring! I'm grateful to my incomparable editor, Shauna Summers, and my dynamite team at Ballantine: Gina Centrello, Kara Welsh, Christine Mykityshyn, Maggie Oberrender, Lexi Batsides, Hanna Gibeau, and Stephanie Reddaway, and Madeline Hopkins. I know I'm blessed to work with Kim Hovey. Enormous thanks to Meg Ruley, Michael Conroy, and Christina Hogrebe at the Jane Rotrosen Agency.

I send my love and thanks to off-islanders Jill Hunter Burrill, Martha Foshee, Toni Massie, Sara Manela, Julie Hensler, Lisa Winika, Tommy Clair, and Sam Wilde and her Fantastic Four.

Finally, but really firstly, because these are friends I communicate with every day, thank you—heart heart heart flowers smiley face—to my Facebook friends. Thank you for being my readers.

a nantucket wedding

Praise for Nancy Thayer

A NANTUCKET WEDDING

"[Nancy] Thayer's latest Nantucket confection does not disappoint. . . . [*A Nantucket Wedding*] is a Nancy Meyers film in book form and should be recommended accordingly."
—*Booklist*

"As the chaos in the Gladstone home increases in tandem with summer temperatures, the reader can't help but wonder if Alison and David's relationship can survive the heat. A delightful beach-town tale about family relationships and second chances."
—*Kirkus Reviews*

"Thayer proves once again that she is a master of the perfect beach read. . . . *A Nantucket Wedding* is a compelling drama [in] an idyllic Nantucket setting. With strong characters with real, relatable problems, fans will no doubt enjoy her latest and want to add it to their reading collection."
—*RT Book Reviews*

SECRETS IN SUMMER

"Full of rich details about life on Nantucket, this breezy tale is at once nostalgic and hopeful. . . . The story is filled with sweet moments of unlikely female connections. An easily digestible, warmhearted tale of eye-opening friendships."
—*Kirkus Reviews*

"Thayer's beachside novel brims with themes that women's-fiction readers love, and the plot skims important issues—infidelity, fear of commitment, grief—while maintaining its focus on Darcy's personal growth and the intergenerational friendship between the four women."
—*Booklist* (starred review)

THE ISLAND HOUSE

"Thayer's latest should be filed under a Best Beach Reads of 2016 list. . . . The characters are complex and their struggles and concerns feel real. . . . Thayer has a really wonderful ability to showcase the meaning of family."
—*RT Book Reviews*

THE GUEST COTTAGE

"Smart and entertaining . . . The combination of summer-at-the-beach living and a second chance at love will prove irresistible to fans of women's fiction."
—*Booklist*

"A pleasant escape to a state of mind in which rebuilding a life is as simple as pitching an umbrella and spreading out a towel—everything is better at the beach."
—*Kirkus Reviews*

NANTUCKET SISTERS

"Thayer obviously knows her Nantucket, and the strong sense of place makes this the perfect escapist book for the summer, particularly for fans of Elin Hilderbrand."
—*Booklist*

"Thayer keeps readers on the edge of their seats with her dramatic story spanning the girls' childhood to adulthood. This wonderful beach read packs a punch."
—*Library Journal*

SUMMER BREEZE

"Nancy Thayer is the queen of beach books. . . . All [these characters] are involved in life-changing choices, with all the heart-wrenching decisions such moments demand."
—*The Star-Ledger*

"An entertaining and lively read that is perfect for summer reading indulgence."
—Wichita Falls *Times Record News*

ISLAND GIRLS

"A book to be savored and passed on to the good women in your life."
—SUSAN WIGGS

"Full of emotion and just plain fun, this novel is delightful."
—*Romance Reviews Today*

BY NANCY THAYER

A Nantucket Wedding

Secrets in Summer

The Island House

A Very Nantucket Christmas

The Guest Cottage

An Island Christmas

Nantucket Sisters

A Nantucket Christmas

Island Girls

Summer Breeze

Heat Wave

Beachcombers

Summer House

Moon Shell Beach

The Hot Flash Club Chills Out

Hot Flash Holidays

The Hot Flash Club Strikes Again

The Hot Flash Club

Custody

Between Husbands and Friends

An Act of Love

Belonging

Family Secrets

Everlasting

My Dearest Friend

Spirit Lost

Morning

Nell

Bodies and Souls

Three Women at the Water's Edge

Stepping

BALLANTINE BOOKS
NEW YORK

one

Alison had no trouble spotting her younger daughter in the crowd milling around the ferry's blue luggage racks. Felicity was the one who looked like an 1890s Irish peasant. She wore a flowing skirt undoubtedly made from an Indian bedspread, a lace blouse, a brightly colored shawl, and Birkenstock sandals. And dangling beaded earrings and maybe a dozen multicolored bracelets. And a backpack made out of what looked like corn husks.

Even so, she was lovely. Her dark blond hair tumbled down her back and her sweet face was heartbreakingly beautiful.

"Mom!" Felicity embraced Alison tightly, swiftly, then drew back and did a little dance. "Can you believe it? Look, Ma, no kids!" Felicity laughed. "I'm awful, aren't I, but you know I've never been away from them for three days. I'm not sure I can walk without holding someone's hand."

"Hold my hand," Alison suggested and led her daughter to her SUV. "Do you have luggage on the rack?"

"No, I've got everything in my backpack. Clean underpants, a toothbrush, and a bathing suit."

Alison opened the hatch so Felicity could stow her backpack, and then they buckled themselves in and headed for David's house. "How was the trip?"

"Oh, Mom, it was divine."

Alison had worried when Felicity said she was taking the slow ferry, which took two and a quarter hours to cross Nantucket Sound. The fast ferries took only an hour but cost more. Alison assumed it was a matter of expense. Noah kept Felicity on a limited budget, which was why Felicity's clothes were all from thrift stores, which Alison knew was her daughter's preferred way to shop. Felicity was a great believer in resisting the powerful draw of consumerism. If Felicity's half-sister, Jane, ever had children, she'd probably dress them in Chanel, but Jane swore she was never having children.

In the passenger seat beside her, Felicity was in full flood. ". . . so I bought a beer—a beer! In the middle of the day! And took it to the upper deck, outside, and settled in one of the seats looking out to sea. I leaned my head back and soaked in the sun. It was so heavenly, so peaceful." Felicity burst into laughter. "And, Mom, a guy tried to pick me up! Seriously—and I think he was just out of college. I couldn't tell him I'm an old married woman with two kids, I was afraid it would embarrass him."

Alison glanced over at her daughter. "Well, Felicity, you are only twenty-eight. And with your gorgeous hair, and, um, the way you dress, you look like a college student yourself."

"Mom, you're crazy. I have bags under my eyes and I've gotten all pudgy. Still, it was so sweet, talking to this guy. Okay, flirting with this guy. He wants to get together for a drink tonight, but I said I was here to visit my sick mother. I'm sorry, I don't want you to be sick, but I needed to pretend this visit was a real crisis so I couldn't possibly get away." Felicity laughed again. "How's Jane? Is she here yet? Did she come by private jet?"

"Stop it. Jane is flying but not by private jet. She said she'll rent a car and drive to David's house."

"Oh, good. I didn't bring my laptop or even a pad of paper, because I'm sure Jane brought hers, so when we plan your wedding, she'll keep a list of what we have to do."

"It won't be all wedding talk. It's going to be such a treat, having both of you together again."

"Yes, because it was always a pleasure before," Felicity muttered and automatically apologized. "Sorry, I don't mean to be snarky. But it's strange, don't you think, how different I am from Jane? Maybe it's nurture, but I blame it on nature. I mean, Alice is seven now, and actually? She's so much like Jane. She needs a lot of private space. I think it's hard on her, having to share a room with Luke—"

"But, Felicity," Alison protested, "your house is enormous. You have four bedrooms."

"I know, but Noah thinks the kids will bond better if they sleep in the same room. Also, he doesn't want them to be spoiled when so many children in the world hardly even have houses."

Alison wanted to ask why it was, then, that Noah had purchased such a huge house. The cathedral ceiling in the living room held a fourteen-foot evergreen at Christmas; Noah had to climb a ladder to decorate it. But she bit her tongue. She didn't want to be disapproving before they even arrived home.

"Alice is bossy," Felicity was saying, "and Luke, well, Luke is a maniac. So much energy!" She sagged, fake-pouting. "I miss those little guys already." Immediately she rallied, smiling at Alison. "But this is going to be so much fun! The three of us together again. Oh, my gosh!"

Alison laughed at her daughter's enthusiasm. She steered the Jeep between tall rose of Sharon bushes and up David's white shell driveway, and there, in front of the house, stood Jane, leaning against her rented dark green Mini Cooper convertible. She wore a lightweight gray silk pantsuit and Manolo Blahnik stilettos. On the ground next to her were a small Hermès suitcase, her purse, and her briefcase. Her briefcase? For two nights and a day and a half on Nantucket?

"Jane! You're here!" Felicity jumped out of the Jeep, raced over to Jane, and clutched her in a rib-breaking bear hug. Jane wrapped her arms around her sister and rolled her eyes at Alison over Felicity's shoulder.

"It's real. The three of us are really here together!" Felicity crowed. "And look at this house! Wow, Mom."

"Yes, it's wonderful, isn't it? Wait till you see the view." Alison held the door open. "Come in. Look around. Go upstairs and choose any bedroom you want—except the master bedroom, of course. I'll pour some iced tea."

"Do we need snacks?" Felicity asked, talking more to herself than to the others. "Probably not, we don't want to spoil dinner and I did have that bag of Fritos on the boat. Oh, man, it is *outrageously* satisfying to eat Fritos without the children fighting for them or Noah acting like I'm eating toxic chemicals."

"I'll bring out a bowl of grapes," Alison said.

She leaned against the refrigerator, eyes closed, just listening to her two daughters chatting away as they went up the stairs. It had been a long time since the three of them had been together like this, and she wondered if they could make it through this weekend without some spat or disagreement and hurt feelings. When Alison looked at her grown, capable daughters, it was as if she were seeing living Russian matryoshka dolls, the façade holding a memory of each stage of their development, down to the smallest, youngest infant, still residing within.

Her girls had never been close, and Alison felt responsible for that. True, they did have different fathers. Alison was married to Flint when she had Jane—she'd married Flint *because* she was pregnant with Jane.

Jane had always been a loner, a reader, a prickly little perfectionist with her straight brown hair held back with a headband. Her arguing abilities were astonishing; no wonder she became a lawyer. She was always a levelheaded, straight-A student, never once crashing the car when she learned to drive (Felicity had dented it a few times), and—as far as Alison had ever known—never once falling into the depths of a tumultuous adolescent love affair. It wasn't that guys didn't pursue Jane. She was attractive, but aloof. *Elegant.* She was tall, lean, with naturally arched black velvet eyebrows over her hazel eyes. She was smart, no genius, but ambitious and hardworking enough to make all As and get accepted to Harvard and then Harvard Law.

Four years younger than Jane, Felicity was the adored daughter of Alison's second husband, Mark. Mark had tried not to show any preference in his treatment of the girls, and he'd succeeded. If anything, he let Jane have her way far too often. But he couldn't help the way his eyes softened when he looked at Felicity, who had the blue eyes and blond hair of the LaCosta family.

Felicity, Alison had to admit, *was* adorable. From the moment she'd toddled across the floor, babbling with glee, Felicity was happy and friendly and girly and sweet. As she entered her teens, she chose lace and ruffles, pale pink and baby blue, short flippy skirts, and multicolored friendship bracelets (which she and her friends made themselves, of course). In high school, she'd had lots of friends. And boyfriends. Felicity had been the drum majorette for her high school's marching band. She'd been prom queen her senior year. She'd attended the University of Vermont, married Noah right after graduation, had two babies, and become what Jane sometimes called "the little wifey."

Now Jane was a lawyer in New York, and so was her husband, Scott, although they worked for separate firms. They rented an upscale apartment on West Sixty-Fifth and went backpacking in Costa Rica and river rafting in Utah. Their lives were crazy busy and stressful and completely adult. Alison wasn't sure how she felt about Scott. He was so quiet, restrained, locked up. He was probably perfect for Jane.

Alison wasn't sure how she felt about Felicity's husband, Noah, either. Noah was an idealistic man, brilliant and ambitious. Straight out of college, he'd started a company selling organic drinks with catchy, healthy names. Now, Noah was trying to make "green food," alternative protein foods made, as far as Alison could tell, basically from kale and beet juice. Alison wished him well, although she worried about the stress he carried with him and how exhausted he always seemed.

Noah and Felicity's two gorgeous, funny, good children were the lights of Alison's life. The children adored their father—when they saw him, which wasn't often, since he worked at the office late into the night and on weekends. Alison did her best to feel fond of him and to smooth Felicity's life in little ways—buying her a nice new SUV for driving around with her children, or taking them on a Disney vacation.

But she couldn't wave a wand and make things perfect for Felicity; and, as David reminded her, Alison had her own life to live.

And she was living a wonderful life.

She'd never dreamed, after Mark's death six years ago, that she would love again. Of course her love for David was quite different from her love for Mark. Mark had been the love of her life. They'd been married for nearly twenty-five years, and after his sudden death, after the shock and the bitterness of grief, and the support of her friends and the days of mourning with her daughters, after the tedious legal work of life insurance and the will, after the months spent with other widows joining together to relearn the movements of normal existence, Alison had finally settled down like a swan without her mate, understanding that even with his loss, the nest that was her life was a lovely creation. She took a job as a receptionist for a dental group and became friends with the staff. She was busy, helpful, and grateful for each daily pleasure. She had her two daughters, her beloved grandchildren, her comfortable house, happy memories. Many friends. Many pleasures. She could go on.

And on she went, if not happily, at least gratefully, for almost six years. She hadn't been prepared last June, when she visited a friend on Nantucket, to meet David Gladstone. The love of his life, Emma, had died after a long illness four years ago, and David had never planned to marry again. Like Alison, he had a busy, if lonely, life.

When Alison and David met, at a simple summer cocktail party, it was as if the moment they stepped out onto the patio, they boarded a train that would speed them into lives they'd never anticipated. For one thing, the first miraculous, surprising, joy-making thing, there was the *chemistry*. Right from the moment their eyes met, a physical attraction reawakened them to the joys of the body. Who knew that a woman could experience adolescent sexual hunger in her fifties? Right there, in the midst of perhaps two dozen other people, men and women in light summer colors, wineglasses in hand, canapés floating by on the caterer's trays, right there, right then, *Boom!* David introduced himself. Alison shook his hand. They couldn't stop smiling at each other. Alison heard herself laughing softly in a feminine way she'd thought she'd forgotten. She practically cooed like a dove at the man.

"Would you like to leave this party and join me for dinner?" David had asked.

"Oh," Alison had said. "Yes. Yes, I would."

They'd departed without saying goodbye, like a pair of teenagers sneaking away from their parents. David took her to Topper's, the poshest restaurant on an island blessed with posh restaurants, and while they feasted on lobster washed down with an icy champagne, they talked. Their conversation told them much about one another, but the hours they spent together told them more.

Alison quickly learned that David was a man of action, not of contemplation. He was a man of hearty appetites. He was only a few inches taller than her, but he had a wrestler's shoulders and arms, so the extra weight he carried looked good on him. He was more en-thusiastic than elegant—when he laughed, his entire body shook and others around him, overhearing that wholehearted laugh, found themselves smiling. David loved to eat and drink and travel. He loved to dance and make puns and tell jokes and swim in the ocean no matter how cold it was. He was a successful, well-educated man who over the course of his life had worked for and then become the CEO of a popular skin-care line called English Garden Creams. At sixty-three, he was wealthy and planning to retire, even though he still enjoyed the complicated responsibilities essential to manufacturing and selling a fine product. He liked his employees, the challenges, the rivals, the achievements. He enjoyed the work.

His hands were big and elegant. Alison was mesmerized by his hands—how would they feel on her body? She imagined he'd be an enthusiastic lover. And he was.

They both lived in the Boston area, and for three months they spent every free moment together. They attended art gallery openings and concerts. They sat in front of the fire on rainy days reading books. They went dancing and spent the next morning in bed with the Sunday papers. They made each other laugh. They reminisced about their spouses and consoled each other for their losses. They fit each other like two halves of a Fabergé egg.

They met each other's children. First, David took Alison to the Boston's Top of the Hub to meet his daughter, Poppy, and his son, Ethan, both in their late thirties, both with all of David's charm. Ethan, who lived an easygoing life as a gentleman farmer in Vermont, had been delighted to see his father with a new love interest. Poppy, not so much. She was married with two children and was in line to take over English Garden Creams when her father retired. And Poppy was ambitious. Alison could almost read her practical thoughts like a ticker tape running across Poppy's sapphire blue eyes: *New woman, marriage, retirement, the business will finally be mine!*

That encounter had been cordial if not delightful, so Alison and David considered it a success. Soon after that, Christmas arrived, held that year in Alison's house in a Boston suburb. Her oldest daughter, Jane, and her husband, Scott, traveled up to stay with Alison for the holidays. Felicity lived in the Boston suburb of Arlington with her two small children and her husband, Noah, so of course they came for Christmas. David stopped by for a drink that Christmas evening and met Alison's small clan. He brought presents for Jane and Felicity—beautifully wrapped gift packages of English Garden Creams products—toys for Alice and Luke, and handsome bottles of Scotch for the men. He also brought champagne for them to share. That evening was great fun.

In January, David asked Alison to marry him and live with him in Boston and wherever else he was. And really, since they were together every morning and night and weekend, it was silly for Alison to retain a house that she scarcely even saw. Alison had sold the home she'd lived in for years, with Mark and the girls, and then with Mark when the girls grew up and got married, and finally, alone, in the years after Mark died. She put some family furniture and china into storage and placed the money from the sale of the house into money market accounts and wrote a will dividing all her assets between her two daughters in the event of her death. She was surprised at how free she felt when she said goodbye to the house. It had become for her a place of mourning and loneliness. She happily moved into David's large apartment on Marlborough Street in Boston, and now here she was, hostess and chatelaine of his gorgeous Nantucket summer house and about to marry David in the most fabulous party of her life.

Today, Alison reminded herself, she had her daughters with her for the weekend in David's beach house. She wanted to savor each moment.

"MOM!" Felicity burst into the kitchen. "This house!"

Jane followed more quietly. "It's stunning, Mom."

"I know," Alison agreed. "Let's go out on the deck so you can enjoy the view."

They sat at the round wooden table on wooden chairs softened by cushions—another David touch, this comfort. Steps led down the deck to the tangled mass of wild beach roses and razor-edged beach grass. A well-trodden sandy path wound through the shrub-

bery down to the golden beach and the deep blue ocean, today rolling calmly toward shore.

"This is heaven," Felicity cooed, resting her feet on another
chair and pulling her skirt up to her hips to allow the sun to tan her
legs. "Are you so thrilled, Mom?"

"I'm thrilled to be with David. The beach house is wonderful,
but it's David who makes me happy."

Felicity eyed Jane. "You look fabulous, Jane. How are you?"

"I'm good. Scott's good. And you look great, too, Filly."

"I do?" Felicity glowed at her sister's compliment. "I don't feel
like I look great. I'm so exhausted from the children, I never get
enough sleep, I haven't lost my baby weight, and my breasts are all
saggy from nursing."

Alison laughed. "Oh, darling! You look beautiful."

"So, Mom," Jane said, "when do we get to hear about your plans
for the wedding?"

"After dinner. I've got quite a special show organized." She
wanted her daughters to have some time alone together to talk, so
she said, "But first, I need to go buy a few groceries. I thought you
two might like to take a long walk on the beach."

Jane looked at her watch. "Sure, yes, if we have time."

"We've got all the time in the world. David is in Boston, so it's
just the three of us, and I've already made an enormous salad and I
thought I'd grill some salmon—"

"Oh, Mom? Um . . ." Felicity blushed. "Instead of salmon,
could we have, maybe, steak?"

"But, Filly," Jane said, "you're a vegetarian!"

Felicity was bright red. "Actually, it's Noah who's the vegetarian. He doesn't want me to cook beef or pork or lamb in our kitchen.
And of course, he's absolutely right, we do need to think of the animals. But sometimes . . ."

"I'll go to Annye's," Alison suggested. "Their meat is from cat-
tle that drink champagne while they lie there listening to the *Pach-
elbel's Canon*. They never know a thing."

"Oh, Mom! You act as if I'm demented! And I'm not," Felicity protested. "It's just that—only for the time I'm here—I'd really enjoy eating some meat."

Alison kissed the top of her daughter's head. "Good. I'm off. You girls have a walk on the beach." She rose, biting back a laugh. "And I'll pick up some bacon for breakfast tomorrow."

two

After Alison left, an awkward silence fell between Jane and Felicity. Jane looked at her watch. "I suppose it's too early for a drink."

"It absolutely is! We're going for that walk on the beach first. And I want to hear all about you and Scott and the glamorous life you're leading, and you can hear all about my children." Felicity pushed her chair away from the table and stood. She held out her hand. "Come on, Sis, let's get our feet in the sand."

They went, single file, down the wooden steps to the yard and along the path between the wild, fragrant beach roses. Jane had changed into flip-flops, which she kicked off and positioned next to Felicity's Birkenstocks, and together they stepped onto the cool sand. The ocean was lazy today, rolling up to the beach with a sigh.

"What a spectacular view," Jane said.

"Lucky Mom," Felicity replied, immediately adding, "and David's lucky, too, to be loved by her."

Jane tilted her head and scrutinized her sister. "Am I crazy or do you look sad?" Immediately, she worried that she'd been intrusive. She couldn't remember one single time when she and Felicity had talked intimately. As they grew up, Jane had called Felicity a lightweight, and Felicity had called Jane a drudge. Jane knew that underneath her disdain for Felicity's silliness bubbled a thick layer of jealousy. Felicity was so pretty. The world was so easy for her! She didn't make the grades Jane did, but lucky Filly, she didn't *care* about grades. Now, after over a decade of living apart, she and Felicity hadn't kept in touch. They saw each other at Christmas or Thanksgiving or when they got together for their mother's birthday. Recently they'd begun to text about their mother's wedding and this visit to Nantucket. But maybe Jane had gone too close too fast. Jane began, "I don't mean—"

"No, it's fine. I'd like to talk. I need to talk. I don't think I'm *sad*, exactly," Felicity said. "Maybe only tired. Come on, let's walk." For years Felicity had considered Jane a coldhearted intellectual snob, but she had always valued Jane's advice. Jane was so much more shrewd and judicious than Felicity.

They headed west, stepping into the cold breakers, shrieking as the waves splashed their ankles.

"It's just hard," Felicity admitted. "I love my children, and I want more children, and I do love Noah, but he's always working and when he *is* home, he's tense and frantic about some problem at work, and really all he does is zombie-out in front of the television. We haven't had any time together, just the two of us, for months." She shot a warning glance at Jane. "This doesn't mean *you* can be critical of him."

Jane nodded. "Understood. And if it's any comfort, that's a lot like Scott and I are on weeknights. Work can be exhausting."

"Being a mother is exhausting, too!" All their lives Felicity had lived in the shade of her sister's brilliance. Jane was a *lawyer*. Felicity was just a mother. Felicity wanted to say, *You're too coldhearted to understand what being a mother means.* She forced herself to swallow her words. She wasn't going to ruin this weekend for her mother with arguments and insults.

Jane took a deep yoga breath. Felicity was always dramatic when she thought she'd been insulted. She'd toss her head and stride from the room, slamming the door behind her. Calm, rational Jane had always felt superior to Felicity when it involved an argument.

Jane slung a friendly arm over Felicity's shoulders. "I'm not saying it's not. Just being an adult can be draining. I'm on your side, Filly, don't misinterpret everything I say. I meant that most evenings Scott and I collapse in front of the television, too, and I'll bet we eat takeout most evenings."

"Noah wouldn't stand for that. He doesn't even like delivery pizza."

"Wow." Jane studied her angelically beautiful baby sister, the princess of everything always, and experienced an odd sensation: she wanted to make Felicity feel better. She lowered her voice and confided, "If you want to talk about sex, let me tell you, the passion has certainly faded between Scott and me. I don't mean we don't love each other, but we've been married for seven years now, and sometimes on Sunday mornings we make love, but to tell the truth, I'd rather sleep late."

Felicity bent to pick up an angel-wing shell. "I know." She took a moment to inspect her find and gather her thoughts. "I *do* know. Noah and I were wild for each other when we first met—well, that's why we had to get married so quickly. I got pregnant almost right away, before we'd even had time to get to know each other. But we *were* in love."

"Were?" Jane asked.

"Are. We still are. And I read books, Janey, I talk to friends, I know that the years when you have babies are hard on a relationship, and if you add the stress Noah's under with his company . . ."

"So you still love Noah."

"Of course! I'll always love him. And I respect what he's trying to do. His work is enormously important. I know that, and I support him in all the ways I can. And we *do* have sex, and it's lovely. Just not like it was when we met."

"Well," Jane mused philosophically, "nothing lasts forever. Everything changes. So you don't have crazy monkey sex but you have two beautiful children."

Felicity smiled. "You're right, Janey." She gave her sister a spontaneous sideways hug. "And what about you?"

"What do you mean?" Jane bent to pick up a small rock and toss it into the ocean.

"You know what I mean. Do you still think you won't have any children?"

Jane tensed. She wanted to talk about this with someone, but it was hard to say the words. Jane had always been the straight-A, smart, achieving older sister. Felicity had always been the beauty. If Jane confessed her problem, she would seem less than perfect. Plus, she wasn't completely sure Felicity could keep a secret. And yet, something about the high blue sky and vast azure water opened her heart. Right now, here, with the sunlight all around her, she could trust. She *would* trust.

"Sometimes, Filly, I do wish I had a child—"

Felicity shrieked. "Oh my God!"

"Settle down. You're overreacting. I only said *sometimes*."

"But this is HUGE!"

"I know. But I only started thinking about it . . ." That was a white lie. She'd been thinking about it constantly for months.

"What does Scott think?"

"He says no. Absolutely not."

"What are you going to do?"

"I don't know. I shouldn't have brought it up. I'm not totally there yet. I might change my mind."

"Oh, Jane, it would be so wonderful—"

"Really. I don't want to talk about it. Not another word."

Felicity clamped her hands over her mouth and staggered in and out of the waves, pretending to struggle to keep from talking.

"You goofball." Jane linked arms with her sister and turned her around. "Let's go back to the house. I could use some sunblock."

"Me, too. I'd forgotten how bright the sun is near the water."

For a while they walked in a companionable silence, the sand warm beneath their bare feet, the waves whispering as they reached the shore.

"This is nice," Felicity said. "Being with you. Here." She yawned a huge jaw-cracking yawn. "I could lie down right on the sand and fall asleep."

"You should take a nap when we get back to the house," Jane suggested.

"A nap! In the middle of the day! That would be the height of luxury." Felicity laughed. "To tell the truth, having a nice long nap right now, without anyone wailing for me or crawling into bed and kicking my stomach—"

"Noah kicks you in the stomach?" Jane asked jokingly.

"No, silly! I meant Luke. He doesn't *mean* to kick me, but he's only five, he's trying to snuggle. Oh, and I do love my snuggle bunnies. Sometimes they climb in bed with me and the three of us cuddle like bears in a cave."

"Where's Noah?"

"Oh, he gets up early. He works even on Saturdays. I wish he wouldn't but I know how much he wants his company to be a success." Sounding wistful, Felicity added, "He does cuddle with us on Sundays. Or, I should say, the kids cuddle with him. They're always so excited to have time with him, they just adore Noah, and they're both *fascinated* by his bristly morning beard. Luke will touch it and cry, 'Ow!' and they all laugh like crazy."

"That sounds wonderful." Jane dropped her sister's arm and began the single-file trek back through the low shrubbery up to the house.

In the kitchen, Jane filled a glass with artesian water from a bottle. Felicity, who thought such luxuries were wasteful, filled her glass from the tap at the sink.

Footsteps came from the hall.

"Mom?" Felicity called.

"Probably not," someone said, and then a tall and inordinately handsome man walked into the room.

Both sisters gawked. He was tall and broad-shouldered, with a look of easy strength. Blond-haired, blue-eyed, he had a smile that would charm the birds off the trees. He wore jeans and a navy-blue and white striped rugby shirt and carried a duffel bag.

"You must be Jane and Felicity. I'm Ethan Gladstone, David's son."

"Golly," Felicity blurted. "You're handsome! And I can say that because I'm an old married woman."

Jane shot her a wry glance, knowing that Felicity expected Ethan Gladstone to reply that she didn't look old enough to be married. If a male was around, Felicity flirted.

Jane stepped forward, holding out her hand. "Hi, Ethan. I'm Jane, and my old married sister here is Felicity."

Ethan shook her hand.

Lightning streaked up Jane's arm, sparking through her torso.

What was *that*? Surprised and embarrassed—of course no one could see what she felt, but her body had just gone radioactive—Jane pulled her hand away, saying defensively, "And I'm an old married woman, too."

Ethan's mouth quirked in a sideways smile. "Ah, too bad. Because I'm a free man."

Behind Jane, Felicity sighed. "Of course you are," she said.

"Does Alison know you're here?" Jane asked. She couldn't help herself, she was speaking in her lawyer voice, her instinctive protection against all sorts of weaknesses. She tried to tone it down a notch. "I mean, I don't think David will be down for the weekend."

"I know. I didn't plan to come, but a friend called. He's putting his boat in the water and wants me to help. So here I am, and don't worry, I won't be in your way. I'll sleep here, but the only sustenance I'll ask for is a cup of coffee in the morning, and I know Alison makes great coffee."

"Um, is one of the bedrooms yours?" Felicity asked.

Bed, Jane thought. *Ethan in a bed.* She knew her face was now fire-engine crimson.

"Not really. We all just pile in wherever we can. You two should take the rooms with the water view. I've seen it plenty of times."

"Oh, that's so nice of you," Felicity gushed.

Ethan tossed Felicity a careless smile and turned to leave the room. "I'll put my bag in one of the bedrooms, and then I'm off for the day and most of the evening. See you all later." He shot a glance at Jane and did not smile. Instead, he looked curious, questioning. Then he shook his head and left the room.

The sisters heard him whistling as he went up the stairs two at a time.

"Good grief," Felicity whispered.

"You're married," Jane reminded her sister.

"And so are you!" Felicity shot back.

"We can't just stand here drooling."

"I know, but seriously, wow."

Jane tried to collect her thoughts. "You're going to take a nap, right?"

"I don't know," Felicity said, hugging herself. "I don't think I could sleep now with him here. In a bedroom. Near my bedroom."

"Well, we've got to *do* something," Jane insisted in a whisper. "What would we be doing if he hadn't arrived?"

"Arguing, of course," Felicity teased with a grin.

"Oh, ha-ha." Jane's emotions were all over the place.

The front door slammed. Alison called, "Darlings! Come help carry in the groceries." When her girls appeared in the front hall, she told them, "More groceries in the car, Felicity. Steak and bacon. Here, Jane, take this, it's a heavy bag."

"Ethan's here," Felicity said.

"Oh, good. He's lovely. Is he staying for dinner?"

"I don't think so," Jane answered, lifting the bag from her mother's arms. "This *is* heavy. What did you buy?"

"A little of everything. It's such a luxury to have both of you here with me, and I want this weekend to be something special."

"I think I've just had a special moment," Jane murmured.

"I think I had the same one," Felicity said, grinning.

"They say it's always better at the beach." Jane nudged her sister.

As her daughters unpacked the groceries, Alison set the steak in a long glass dish to marinate in olive oil and crushed garlic and red wine. Hearing her girls laughing with each other filled her heart. Alison could relax. Jane and Felicity *were* adults. They had husbands, families, work, their very own lives. It would be brilliant and not so impossible if they got along this weekend. Alison wanted to tell them all about David's plan for an amazingly romantic wedding, and David's children and grandchildren, and how much she was hoping they could all be, just for a while, one big happy family, like all the families on Christmas cards.

Had they ever been one big happy family? Yes, Alison thought, they had. She knew that no one was happy all the time, and it would be unreasonable for her to expect her daughters to be without their own worries and fears, but her daughters were so different in every way—what they liked to eat, how they dressed, what they read, how they played—it had been impossible to please them both at once. Still, the years of her marriage to Mark, Felicity's father, had been golden for them all.

Her daughters had their own families now. Alison was free to focus on David, to enjoy life, to accept with pleasure the remarkable gift of love which fate had brought her way. She told herself to get her mind off her daughters and focus on the approaching summer.

She heard whistling and knew that Ethan was coming downstairs.

three

Felicity and Jane shared a look.

Ethan walked into the room. When he saw Alison, he broke into a huge, gorgeous smile.

Their mother smiled back. "Ethan!"

Together the sisters stood like statues, staring as their mother so casually threw her arms around Ethan and hugged him.

"Sweetie, I'm so glad to see you."

Jane and Felicity exchanged glances. *Sweetie.*

"We're having steak!" Alison announced. "And I bought a nice red wine and some new potatoes and asparagus and maybe Felicity will make her fabulous chocolate 'mouse.' That's what we've always called it since she was a little girl."

Felicity knew she was blushing. First of all, it was way too much responsibility, making a dessert for this man to eat. She'd worry with every teaspoon that something would go wrong. Second, she hated that her mother made her seem so childish, so silly.

"Sounds great, Alison, but I've got to go help a friend with his boat. We'll grab a hamburger later."

"Well, tomorrow night, then," Alison said.

"That's a plan." Ethan waved. "Have a good night, ladies."

Then he was gone.

As if she hadn't noticed their giddy smiles, Alison announced, "I thought we'd eat early tonight. That way we can talk about the wedding and plan the summer and maybe watch a movie together."

"Oh, perfect!" Felicity dumped the new potatoes into a colander and rinsed them in the sink.

"Let's have a drink on the deck. It's still a bit cool in the evenings, so we'll need sweaters. Jane, can you set the table and open the wine? We'll eat in the kitchen. It's just us, the dining room is too big, and it will be too cool to eat outside. Let's forget making the mouse, Felicity. I'd rather have you sit and talk. We can have fruit."

As Felicity rinsed the asparagus and snapped off the tough ends, she couldn't help but notice what a great kitchen David had. Granite counters, Wolf gas stove and Sub-Zero refrigerator-freezer, and . . . "Mom, is the kitchen floor cork?"

"It is. Isn't it heaven to walk on? And if we drop a dish, it won't break, and cork is resistant to mold and mildew, brilliant for the island."

"It's so warm, and the colors echo the wood in the chopping block. Did you choose it?"

"No, Emma did, a few years before she died."

Felicity dried her hands on a hand towel in colors that coordinated with the pale cream and soft foam green on the kitchen walls. "Do you feel funny, working in this kitchen where David's first wife worked?"

Alison laughed. "You have no idea how grateful I am Emma was such a wonderful decorator. You know me, I can't get my mind to settle on things like wallpaper and rugs. Oh, I suppose if the kitchen had been ancient avocado, I might have done something, but fortunately I don't need to."

Jane was laying out the striped linen placemats and napkins. "So you don't feel jealous *at all*?"

"Truthfully, not at all." Alison washed her hands and squirted hand lotion from the bottle next to the sink. As she rubbed the lotion into her skin, she leaned back against the counter. "Remember, I had all those good years with Mark. I wouldn't trade my memories for anything. And I'm glad David was happy with Emma. He knows how to make a marriage work."

Felicity pounced. "How?"

Alison put back her head and laughed. "Oh, honey, if only I could tell you in one quick and easy sentence! Janey, pour the wine. Let's sit on the deck for a while."

They sat at the round wood table, moving their chairs to face the water.

"So beautiful," Felicity said. "The way the colors change as the waves ripple."

"How much of the year will you and David spend here?" Jane asked.

"Not so much, at least not together. He's turning his business over to his daughter, Poppy, and that's an enormously complicated process. So until he's out from under it all, I'll be down here more than he will. When he's free, fully retired, I imagine we'll be here a lot. Summers, definitely. Plus the fall is an unsung glory here, so I assume we'll stay through October. And we'll want to be here some Christmases—and you girls should come, too, at least for the Stroll. Your children would love it, Felicity. Winter? I think we'll travel, take a cruise. Come back here in April for the Daffodil Festival."

"Gosh," Felicity said. "You and David have made a lot of plans."

Alison chuckled. "*I've* made a lot of plans. David is so invested in his company. I think he's finding it difficult to let go. I'm trying to slow him down, stop him from working so hard, get him to enjoy life. Smell the roses. No one knows what tomorrow will bring—"

"Carpe diem," Felicity said. "Seize the day."

"Um, yes," Alison responded in a meditative tone, "but that's not what I was going to say. I think I want more to simply *be there* in the day. *Seizing* sounds aggressive to me, almost hostile." Alison took a deep sip of wine and gazed out at the water. "Yes," she murmured, as much to herself as to her daughters. "Be there in the day."

"I like that," Jane said.

"You know," Felicity mused, "I think motherhood makes me seize the day. Or really it's the other way around. The day seizes me. The moment I open my eyes, I'm right *there*. Fixing breakfast, making coffee, finding someone's lost sock, looming over my children like an ogre to make sure they brush their teeth, driving Alice to school, trying not to have a wreck while Alice and Luke are fighting over an ancient jelly bean that popped up in the car's backseat, and I'm trying to get Luke to stop kicking the back of my seat and look at one of his books . . . then I get to the grocery store and Luke vomits all down the cart and his clothes."

"Oh, Felicity!" Jane cried. "That sounds so hard!"

"That's just the beginning of the day." All at once, she burst out laughing. "Two Saturdays ago, I had the flu but the kids were fine and crazed with energy so I put coats on them and pulled a coat over my pajamas and staggered out into the fresh air so they could run around the yard, using up their excess energy. Then the UPS man, who is really a hunk, drove up to deliver a package. He was all tall and tanned and muscular and young, and he nodded at me and said, 'How ya doin', Mrs. Wellington?' And I thought, that's who I am, *Mrs. Wellington,* the crazy version. And as he drove away, I wanted to raise my arm in the air like Scarlett O'Hara in *Gone with the Wind,* and shout, 'As God is my witness, I'll never leave the house without combing my hair again!'"

Alison laughed. "Oh, Lord, I remember those days!"

Jane said soothingly, "Oh, Filly, you know you're beautiful no matter what."

Felicity snorted. "Yeah, well, Ethan clearly thinks you're the beautiful one."

"What?" Jane and Alison asked in unison.

"It's true," Felicity said. "When Ethan was in the kitchen, he couldn't take his eyes off Jane. I might as well have been a chair."

"You're crazy," Jane said.

"Not crazy," Felicity protested and tears began to well in her eyes. "And I don't blame him. You've got a fabulous haircut and you're thin and toned and so all that. I've gotten all saggy and maternal. I should buy some of those 'mom jeans' Tina Fey jokes about."

Jane and Alison exchanged worried glances.

"Oh, sweetie," Alison said. "That's not true at all."

Jane rose from her chair and bent over Felicity and enclosed her in a warm hug. "I think you're just tired."

Felicity sniffed. "Sorry I'm so pathetic. You're right. I am tired."

Alison rose. "I think it's time we grilled the steak. Jane, will you take over at the grill? I've coated the asparagus in olive oil and kosher salt, so when you turn the steak, put the asparagus on." She gathered up the wine and her glass. "Felicity, would you bring the other glasses in? I'll toss the salad."

Felicity was grateful that her mother didn't comment on her outburst. Wryly, she admitted to herself that Alison had seen plenty of Felicity's meltdowns before. On the deck, gathering the glasses, she paused to let the aroma of grilled steak seduce her. Her mouth watered. Sometimes it sucked, being a vegetarian.

Back in the house, her mother said, "Toss the potatoes in butter in that bowl over there, the blue and white striped one."

At last they all sat down to eat. Felicity said, "I'm sorry, but would you mind?" Without waiting for answer, she sang, "Thank you for this food this food this glorious glorious food and thanks to the animals and the vegetables and the minerals that make it possible. Amen."

"Lovely, darling," Alison said.

Jane said nothing, but at least she didn't roll her eyes or snort.

For a while, they all focused on the meal, so aromatic, so succulent, so satisfying. They served the salad last.

"So," Jane said, "want to talk about your wedding, Mom?"

"Good idea," Felicity said. "What's your vision?"

"My *vision* . . ." Alison's mouth trembled with suppressed laughter.

"Start with your dress," Felicity prompted.

"Let her tell it her own way," Jane said to her sister.

Alison was smug. "Actually, girls, David and I don't have a *vision,* but we do have some plans. Let me explain. David married Emma in a big church wedding. I never had that, not with either of your fathers. You know I was pregnant when I married Flint, so it was a rather sober event in front of our parents with a justice of the peace. And then, when I married Mark—" She put her hand to her throat, as if to ease it. "Well, we got married quietly then, too. We just went to the clerk of the court. We paid strangers to be our witnesses, they have people waiting for that purpose." She cast an apologetic look at Jane. "We didn't want to make a big deal of it because—"

"Because you had an affair with Mark and left my father." Jane's words were clipped.

Alison held back a sigh. She'd been over this many times before with Jane and Felicity, and she wasn't going to take them all down this prickly memory lane again.

"SO!" Alison clapped her hands like a delighted child. "I told David I want our wedding to be *fabulous.*"

Alison watched her daughters exchange surprised looks. She knew exactly what they were thinking: *Mom, fabulous?* Alison was attractive, but she was more maternal than remarkable. She was generous and reliable and loving and sweet.

"I mean a fabulous *party,*" Alison amended. "A sort of celebration of life and love with our families and our friends."

"Please don't tell me we're all going to stand in a circle holding hands and singing 'Kumbaya.'" Jane groaned.

Alison laughed. "Don't worry. David isn't a 'Kumbaya' kind of man." Alison stood up and stretched. "Let's go in and get comfy on the sofa. David had the computer synced to the TV in the den and we can check out the dresses and see what you like."

"Well, you know, Mom," Jane said, taking the bottle and her glass and following her mother, "I'm not sure you can manage *fabulous* when your wedding is in September. These events take lots of preparation and research and time—"

Alison settled on the cozy sofa in the den. "It's all right, Janey. It's all set."

Both daughters collapsed next to her as if Alison had hit them behind the knees.

"What?" they cried.

"David and I have been seeing each other for almost a year, and during that time, I've gotten to know his friends and he's come to know mine. We're all . . . I guess *mature* would be the right word. We've been through a lot. We've been married before. So we thought this time we would have a wedding that is really a spectacular party. But neither David nor I have the skills it takes to organize a party—"

Felicity piped up. "We could help you with that!"

"That's sweet of you, honey, but his assistant, Heather, has it all under control."

"'His assistant, Heather'?" Felicity echoed.

"Cool," Jane said. "Tell us more."

Alison smiled. "Outside of town, off on a quiet road, there's the poshest hotel on the island. The Wauwinet. It fronts a gorgeous beach and the end of Nantucket harbor, so it's very private."

As she talked, Alison picked up the remote control and a video of the venue drifted across the wide screen. "They've got an amazing restaurant, Topper's, and if any guests want to take a drive around the island, they've got BMWs we can use, and kayaks and a gorgeous boat to take us on a tour of the island. So David and I made up our guest list, and he's taken the hotel for the second weekend in September. The weather will still be won—"

Felicity frowned. "What exactly do you mean, 'he's taken the hotel for the weekend'?"

"Well, sweetie, I think it's pretty clear. He's reserved all the rooms and the restaurant and hotel property for the weekend. Friday through Sunday nights."

Felicity looked wide-eyed at her sister. "Jane, David must be rich."

Jane said, "He is. I know."

"How do you know?" Felicity looked suspiciously at her mother and Jane, as if they'd been keeping a secret from her.

"I googled him," Jane said.

"Smart." Felicity brightened.

"I know." Jane straightened. This was her element. "David Gladstone's parents came from England when David was a boy. They built a successful business from making and packaging British-named soaps and lotions: English Garden Creams. They supply the most elite hotels and department stores with face, hand, and body lotions and anti-aging creams and lip balms, all beautifully packaged. David Gladstone, I'm sorry to say, is not a billionaire. But he is a millionaire several times over. He has substantial holdings in real estate all over the country. He pays his taxes on time. He is widowed and has two grown children, Ethan and Poppy. Poppy is married and has two children. Both Poppy and her husband, Patrick, work in the corporate offices in Boston. Ethan is divorced, with a nine-year-old daughter. He lives on a large property in central Vermont where he manages a staff who keep horses and hens, hold summer camps for city kids, and grows, among other things, flowers to be used in researching new products for English Garden Creams."

"Goodness," Felicity said. "You're certainly thorough."

"And you girls can relax. No worries, as everyone says now. Heather will be taking care of most of the details. She's sent Save the Date cards to our friends, and she's working with Brie at the hotel about the food, the flowers, that sort of thing. And she's on island often to personally check on things. She and her husband have a house on Nantucket."

"Wow," Jane said softly. "How posh, Mom."

"It's not because we're too busy or not interested in it all, we are," Alison said. "But David is still managing his company, and I want to put all my energies into creating a perfectly wonderful summer for you and for David's children. And our grandchildren, of course. I want to focus on making everyone happy. I want to make this house so welcoming, so warm, that my family and David's get to know each other. So we can be, really, one big happy family. I want to sit on the deck with an iced tea and watch Alice and Luke play with Daphne and Hunter. I want to watch Noah and Scott and Patrick and Ethan play poker here on a rainy day. I want you girls and David's daughter, Poppy, to watch silly romantic movies with me, all snuggled together on the sofa."

"That's so sweet, Mom," Jane said, adding, "and maybe a bit unrealistic?"

Felicity asked, "Okay, but what about your wedding gown? And our gowns? We are attendants, aren't we? Could Alice be your flower girl? Luke could be the ring bearer!"

"We'll have to talk. Poppy has little ones, too," Alison said. "I've chosen my gown, and I've got a computer file of possibilities for you two to study. When you've decided on one, we'll have Anya fly in with the dresses and make all the necessary alterations."

"So you're not exactly following a normal wedding planner calendar," Jane said.

"No, I'm not," Alison replied smoothly. "Why should I? David and I are doing it the way we want to."

"I can't believe you live like this," Felicity said.

"David has worked very hard for his financial success," Alison reminded her daughters. "We're old enough to want to spend our time the way we want. So! Let's look at the possibilities for your dresses."

Jane expected to see gowns on hangers, but no, models wore the gowns, turning at a click of the remote to display the back and sides. Alison's gown came first, a strapless bodice of ivory satin with a knee-length ruched satin skirt and a lace shrug she could take off later for dancing.

"Wow, Mom, that's so—wow!" Jane exclaimed.

Alison laughed. "I know. Not like my usual under-the-radar style."

"This is so weird, Mom," Felicity said. "It should be the mother helping the bride pick her dress."

"Well, darling, *my* mother is dead. You're so busy with the children, and I didn't want to make Jane travel from New York just to watch me try on clothes." With a level glance at Felicity, Alison said, "Anyway, I don't think you and I would have the same taste. And I knew what I wanted—a short skirt, because I've still got good legs—"

"You've got killer legs," Jane agreed.

"And the color makes it not so virgin-bride-ish, and the ruched skirt adds a bit of fabulous, don't you think?"

"You'll look amazing," Felicity agreed.

"Now let me show you what I'm thinking for you two."

She clicked the remote. Felicity of course burbled over the pastels with Little Bo Peep wide-skirted shapes. Jane preferred the sleek form-fitting black, but both her mother and Felicity refused to consider that. They all liked the strapless dresses that echoed Alison's but were shorter, the hem falling a few inches above the knee—Alison's daughters had killer legs, too. Felicity chose pale pink, Jane, a darker rose. Because Alison's jewelry would be the diamond earrings and necklace David had given her, Felicity demanded at least a little bling for her and Jane. So they added a sparkling ornament at the waist. They would all wear their hair up and glittery earrings.

"What's David going to wear?" Jane asked.

"A tuxedo with a cummerbund that matches my dress. Ethan and Poppy will be his attendants, and David knows the details of what I'm wearing—although he hasn't seen the dress, of course."

"What about Poppy? What is she wearing?"

Alison took a moment to gather her thoughts. "I've emailed Poppy about the gowns. I sent her the video file showing her the dresses I've just shown you. She hasn't responded."

"That's rude," Felicity said.

"I don't know, Felicity, maybe she hasn't had time. She's working and she has two children and a husband, so she must be wildly busy."

"Have David tell Poppy to get on the stick," Jane said.

"No, honey. I want to work out some kind of relationship with Poppy. She's coming down next weekend, and I can talk with her then. And Anya is good to go on any alterations on any gown Poppy might choose." Alison stood up. "Now. Red grapes and movie time!"

They ate dessert while watching Kate Hudson and Anne Hathaway in *Bride Wars*. They tidied the kitchen together, talking about weddings and gowns with seven layers of tulle until Alison said, "Time for bed, girls. We've got a big day tomorrow."

The sisters shared a smile. How many times had their mother spoken those exact words to them? They kissed their mother's cheek and dutifully went up the stairs.

four

Jane brushed and flossed her teeth and brushed her hair and washed and creamed her face and rubbed lotion into her hands. She'd already changed into the tank top and boxer shorts she slept in. In her room, the bed with its sumptuous Frette linens waited, the bedside table piled with magazines, books, and a crystal carafe of water and a glass, in case she woke in the night and was thirsty. From the antique dresser, a light, sweet perfume drifted from a vase of fresh flowers.

It was all so . . . sensual. *Too* sensual. It was so unsettling. This evening had been *strange*.

Probably, Jane decided, flicking off the bathroom light and crossing the room to her bed, she'd simply had too much to drink. Felicity certainly had. She'd confessed she seldom drank so much, as if that wasn't obvious. She'd almost stumbled up the stairs to her bedroom. Jane followed, waiting to catch her if she fell, but Felicity made it to her bed, where she did fall, wham, like an axed tree, onto her bed. Immediately she was asleep and snoring. Jane took a mohair throw from the back of an armchair and laid it over her sister.

Now Jane slid into her own bed, and she was completely awake. She usually mentally composed a list of duties to be performed the next day and somewhere along the way she fell into sleep. But tonight she couldn't wrench her mind into its reliable categorizing. Frivolous thoughts flashed through her brain—if she didn't have her hair cut for the next three months, it could be twisted up and held with a dazzling clip—she was glad her mother was at last having a romantic wedding—should she get a tan, would that look good against the deep rose dress? And why was she so agitated about this anyway?

She gave up, turned on the bedside lamp, and reached for one of the books on the bedside table. Oh dear, it was a bodice ripper. A bare-chested man held a curvaceous woman wearing a dress much like some of the bridesmaids gowns they'd seen. They were on a beach or in a boat, whatever, blue water rippled in the background beneath a sky blazing with light. The man's black hair was as long as the woman's blond locks, and he had abs like no real man Jane had ever seen. She touched her finger to the man's chest, as if she could feel—

"Oh, for heaven's sake!" she said and tossed the book facedown on the bed. Had she lost her mind?

Whatever, she wouldn't get to sleep this way. Throwing back the covers, she slid her feet into flip-flops and crept out of her room and down the stairs. She'd racewalk down the beach. That would tire her out.

The moon wasn't quite full but large enough and close enough to cast the world into shades of silver. No wind blew, so the waves quietly slid up to the shore and away, making sighing sounds. Jane was slightly cool in only her tank top, but she knew as she walked that she'd warm up, so she pattered down the steps and through the wild roses to the beach.

The frothy white curls of the waves made her think of some of the wedding gowns she'd seen on the slide show. As if all brides wanted to look like a princess on their wedding day. Ridiculous, really.

Jane had never bought into that whole fantasy. First of all, she was well aware that no matter how gorgeous the wedding, at least half of all marriages ended in divorce. There was no ceremony for divorce and women certainly didn't look like princesses by the time Prince Charming had morphed back into a frog. She didn't see any sense in spending thousands of dollars on one event when that money could be used toward an apartment in the city.

For their own wedding, Jane and Scott had decided to put some money toward a trip and go low on expenses for the actual marriage ceremony. After all, Jane's stepfather had died, unexpectedly of a heart attack, in January. The three women were still mourning. It hadn't seemed right to throw a festive ceremony in that same year. Jane and Scott had just finished law school and passed the New York bar. They chose to be married by a justice of the peace on a bright April morning in a conference room at the Logan airport Hilton in Boston. That made it easy for her mother, sister, and friends from the Boston area to attend. Her best friend, Lisa, and Scott's best friend, Brendon, came from San Francisco and D.C. to be witnesses. They all enjoyed a privately catered lunch after the ceremony. Jane and Scott flew out that afternoon, to L.A., where they picked up their rental Jeep and drove to Death Valley.

Jane's friends had shrieked when she'd told them she was honeymooning in Death Valley.

"Those words don't belong in the same sentence!" Lisa had said.

"Scott and I love hiking," Jane reminded them in a serene and reasonable tone of voice. "Death Valley is a hiker's paradise, with endless canyons and hills made of minerals so they're streaked turquoise and rose. We'll see coyotes and ravens and salt plains and snowcapped mountains. Plus," she added, knowing this would win her friends over, "we'll be staying at The Oasis at Death Valley. Google it. It's luxurious, a green oasis in the middle of the desert.

We'll hike all day or swim in the pool or play golf or horseback ride, and if we're exhausted at the end of the day, we'll get massages."

"Still," Marcy said, "it doesn't sound very romantic."

Jane had shrugged. "Scott and I have lived together for two years. I've seen him clip his nose hairs. He's put up with me when I'm PMSing. We don't need fantasy. We want to hike."

"Still weird," Lisa had concluded.

Jane had enjoyed the honeymoon immensely. Every day she felt stronger from hiking, and in spite of sunscreen, she got a fantastic tan, and she never thought about work—how could she, when she was in such an unworldly landscape? Maybe she and Scott hadn't made love as much as they should have, but again, they'd been together for two years, so the bloom was off the rose, and besides, they hiked or rode horseback every day and were completely bushed at night. And now that she remembered it, Scott—typical male—had refused to wear sunscreen, and gotten a painful sunburn on his arms and legs. For several days he couldn't stand to have Jane touch him.

And look, their marriage had lasted. They were filling in all the right boxes in their plans. Once they'd bought an apartment in the city, *then* they would travel in more exotic places. Bali. Tokyo. She wanted to see the opal caves in Australia.

But recently, suddenly, unexpectedly, Jane had started wishing for something more than all the opal caves in the world.

She wanted to have a baby.

Maybe more than one.

A few months ago, she'd been astonished to find this craving unfolding within herself, like a dormant plant opening so wide it took up all the room in her heart and could not be ignored. She wanted a child. Or two. She caught herself pausing at the windows of baby-clothing stores, smiling at young mothers carrying their babies on their chests. She wanted the tiny white onesie embroidered with a duck, the wraparound garment that held a baby close to her heart— she wanted to carry a baby in her body and to give birth even if it did make her scream in pain.

She had forced herself to wait for months before discussing this with Scott. She didn't want to talk about something so huge, so life-changing, without giving it serious thought. She had never been moody. She'd never been fickle in her decisions or her actions, and she understood how women's hormones could cause temporary insanity. She'd forced herself to study glossy sites about hiking trips in the four corners of the world, and nothing had called to her, but the moment a mother came down the street pushing a stroller, Jane's eyes were pulled irresistibly to the sight of the baby—and when she saw the child, her heart melted.

Finally, she'd brought up the idea to Scott, after first marshaling her arguing points as if preparing for a court case, because she knew her husband well. He hated change. She'd expected a battle. It hadn't been a battle so much as a kind of tantrum on Jane's part and a quiet, adamant, sustained lack of interest from Scott. Scott simply remained politely unwilling to engage in an argument, certain that Jane would wear herself down and subside in exhaustion.

And for a while, she did subside. She allowed Scott to remind her of the pleasures of their chosen life, not just by getting tickets to the best seats at the biggest plays and concerts but also by spending a day with her touring the charter school in the Bronx and talking with the real children whom they were supporting with their financial donations. She waged her own silent war by accepting every invitation from friends with children—rosy-cheeked, giggling tots who made an appearance before being gently taken to bed by the babysitter or nanny.

Her efforts had been in vain. Scott was firmly planted in his decision; she could not coax or seduce or cajole him even to consider her desire.

Now she pushed the thought away and listened to the waves splash against the sand as she returned to David's house. She still wasn't tired, so she decided to enjoy a beer and sit on the deck for a while.

"Hey."

"Oh!" Jane jumped at the sound of Ethan's voice. He was sitting on a lounger, beer bottle in hand, looking toward the ocean.

"Nice night for a walk," Ethan said. He wore a T-shirt and board shorts and his feet were bare.

"Or for stargazing," Jane answered, intending to slip past him into the house.

"Join me," Ethan invited. He held up another cold beer.

"Wait. How did you do that? Produce a beer out of thin air?"

Ethan laughed. "I'm lazy but I'm smart. I brought a cooler out with ice and a few beers in it."

"Oh. Well, thanks." Jane accepted the beer—their hands touched lightly—and stretched out on the lounger next to him. "Ah. This is brilliant. But what, you were planning to sit out here drinking beer all night?"

"I've certainly done it before," Ethan said. "But no, I came out with the beer because I saw you walk down to the beach."

Jane worked hard to keep from choking on her sip of beer. She cleared her throat. "So you couldn't sleep, either?"

"That, and also I thought it would be nice to get to know you."

His words made her go hot all over. She was glad it was too dark for him to see her blush. *Mom and David!* Jane thought, rather desperately trying to catalog his words in a nonpersonal file. *Ethan is family, kind of.* "Oh, right. After all, we're going to be kind of step-siblings."

Ethan laughed. He had a nice, low, soft laugh. "Maybe not step-siblings at our age. I think there's probably a sell-by date on that."

"All right, then, we can be friends." Jane liked attaching a nice neutral term to her relationship, not that she *had* a relationship, with Ethan.

Ethan laughed. "Let's shake on it."

He turned sideways on the lounger and extended his hand. Jane had no choice but to do the same. His hand was warm, calloused, larger than hers.

She lifted her eyes to meet his and they remained holding hands. It was too dark to see much, but she *felt* something in his gaze that stopped her breathing.

She pulled her hand away. She inhaled deeply as she resettled in her lounger.

After a moment, Ethan faced the ocean. He took a long drink of his beer. "Okay, friend," he said. "Tell me about yourself."

"I'm a lawyer," Jane said. "My husband, Scott, is, too. We rent an apartment in Manhattan and we're saving to buy. We usually take a couple of vacations a year, hiking. We like to hike."

"Wow," Ethan said softly. "That's a lot of *we*'s."

A spot of anger kicked her in the chest. "Okay, why don't you tell me about yourself the way you think it should be done."

"I didn't mean to criticize," Ethan told her. "That just sounded like you were filling out a questionnaire. I do know you're a lawyer. Dad told me. So that might explain why you're guarded."

I'm not guarded! Jane thought. She tightened her lips to keep from saying the words out loud. That would be just too childish. "No, really," she said, putting a little silk in her voice, "tell me about you." *And I'll be able to tell if you're lying, because I googled you,* she thought.

Ethan gazed out at the ocean. "I'm fortunate. My family's wealthy—I'm sure you know that. My life is disjointed, all over the place, literally. I have a farm in Vermont, and I'm there most of the time, but I'm divorced, with a daughter, Canny. She's nine, she lives with me, she's the center of my world. What else? I like adventure, but I'm also kind of a coward, not a good combination. I like surfing in Australia and hang gliding in Norway and ballooning out in Arizona. I own a red Lamborghini that can hit over two hundred miles an hour, not that I've ever gone that fast. I have a Harley, too."

Jane laughed. "Ah, you're the rebel in your family, the bad boy."

"But I'm *not* bad!" Ethan protested. "All summer and fall, I host a group of inner-city kids from the Bronx. A new group every week. I teach them to ride horses, to dig potatoes, to make bread. Plus, I help the family business by growing flowers, new varieties, for experimental new products."

"You make bread?"

"I do. Have you ever made bread?"

Jane laughed. "I hardly have time to make my bed." *Bed? I had to say bed?* "I mean," she rushed on, "we have a wonderful bakery right on our block. We're both so busy we don't really have time to cook."

"Making bread is an experience everyone should have once. It connects you with what's real. Simple, basic ingredients, the kneading and shaping, the magic of how it rises, and then you take it warm from the oven, crusty outside, you break it open and it's soft and yielding as the butter melts into it . . ."

Jane felt like she was having sex. "You make it sound so . . . physical." She meant sexual, but no way would she say that.

"It is physical. Spiritual, too."

"I'll have to try it sometime."

"How about tomorrow? I could give you a lesson in making bread."

Tomorrow, Jane thought. The sun would be shining tomorrow. They'd be in a brightly lit kitchen full of practical objects instead of reclining in the moonlit sea salt air.

"Okay." She tipped back her beer bottle and chugged the rest down. "I'll see you tomorrow." She stood, still caught in some kind of spell. "I'll rinse the bottle and put it in recycling," she said, sounding like her normal self again. For a moment, she thought her body wouldn't obey her and move away into the house. Then a strange shiver went through her, and she was okay.

"Good night," she called as she stepped into the kitchen.

"Sweet dreams," Ethan told her.

five

Felicity opened her eyes. It was eight-thirty. Sun flooded the room.

"Oh, no!" She sat up straight, her heart racing.

Then she remembered, in a wash of pleasure, that she was here on Nantucket, with her mother and sister, and without Noah and the children. Her heart twinged when she thought of her darling babies tumbling around on her bed while she tried to squeeze in a few more moments of simply lying down. But that particular sadness didn't last long. She reminded herself that Noah was there to take care of the children, *his* children, and that would be a marvelous treat for the little ones, to have a full day of special time with Daddy.

She sank back into the pillows. She sort of wanted to go back to sleep. Sleep was so precious to her these days, it was like entering a very exclusive spa. But the sun was so bright, and a delicious silence filled the room. She allowed her eyes to drift from the blue and white chair by the closet to the mirror bordered with seashells over the dresser to the mermaids singing on the Claire Murray rug lying on the shining, polished pine floorboards. It was luxurious.

Unlike the house she and Jane had grown up in. An elderly Victorian in the Boston suburb of Lexington, the house had been spacious and filled with so much stuff it would often be impossible to say what color the sofa was, not that they'd cared about that. Alison had cared about comfort, so new, fake, deeply plush Oriental rugs were piled on top of threadbare antique Oriental carpets and sagging but soft sofas and armchairs were everywhere, waiting for friends, children, or pets to sink into their animal hair–covered depths.

Felicity had loved their house and the life lived in it. People were always coming in and out, settling at the kitchen table for tea and cookies or wandering out to the garden with a glass of wine while Felicity and a friend climbed up to the tree house her father had built. Only as she began her own family and tried to keep some sign of sanity in her busy house did she realize how much seemingly effortless work her mother had done to keep them all clean, well fed, and on time to every scheduled event. She had assumed her mother had enjoyed making cupcakes for school sales and sweeping the kitchen floor every day and doing loads of laundry . . . she was *still* sure Alison had loved the laundry bit. When it was sunny Alison had carried a wicker basket of wet sheets, towels, tablecloths, and hand towels outside and pegged the linens onto the clothesline, humming as she did. And when she'd brought the linens in, she would say, every single time, "I *love* the way laundry smells after it's dried in the sun."

The smell of bacon snapped Felicity right back to the present. She jumped out of bed and hurriedly dressed.

In the kitchen, Felicity found her mother at the stove and her sister and Ethan huddled over a laptop on the kitchen table.

"Good morning, darling," Alison called.

"Good morning, everyone," Felicity said, scooting past the long pine table to stand at the glass doors and gaze at the view. Sparkling blue water, lazy and sun-speckled, as far as she could see.

"Good morning, Felicity," Ethan said. He wore a faded T-shirt that matched the blue in his eyes.

Jane looked up. "We don't have yeast."

Well, Felicity thought, that was odd. Why would Jane want yeast?

"Bacon?" Alison asked.

The smell was irresistible, plus she'd strayed way off the virtuous vegetarian path last night when she ate steak. "Please," Felicity said. She poured herself a mug of coffee, lightened its caffeine attack with milk and sugar, and settled at the table.

"Why do you need yeast?" she asked her sister.

Ethan said, "I went into town this morning and picked some up."

"Oh, good!" Jane looked at Felicity. "We're going to make bread!"

"We are?" Felicity asked. "Can't we just buy some?"

Jane and Ethan exchanged glances and laughed, and all at once Felicity was suspicious. How had her sister and Ethan become such a *pair*? They sat together beaming with secret knowledge, as if they were the popular kids at school.

"Ethan, you explain," Jane said.

Ethan rose and poured himself more coffee. "I was telling Jane last night that I like to bake. Bread, mostly, but cakes and muffins, that sort of stuff, too. I like working with yeast. It's organic. It's magic." Returning to his seat, he offered, "I'll teach you, too, if you'd like."

Felicity caught the laser-swift *Do it and die* message her older sister deployed with squinted eyes. "No, thanks. I've made bread before. I want to enjoy myself while I'm a free woman."

Alison set a plate of scrambled eggs and bacon before Felicity.

"Oh, Mom, thanks, this smells heavenly."

"You're welcome, sweetie. And I have a surprise for you."

Felicity, mouth full of bacon, could only raise a questioning eyebrow.

"Jane's going to spend the morning making bread with Ethan. And, I've booked a massage for you."

"A massage!" Felicity was breathless. "I haven't had a massage in forever!"

Alison smiled. "I thought you'd like that. And after lunch, I want to take you girls shopping."

"Shopping? Why?" Was that a conspiratorial look that flashed between her mother and Jane?

"Because I can," Alison said, laughing. "Because I love having my daughters here with me and I want to buy you both some cute summer dresses."

Felicity said, "Maybe we should get something for the children instead—"

Her mother cut her off. "I'm buying clothes for *my* children."

Felicity's heart sank a little. She would *love* having some brand-new, never-before-worn clothes from a classy Nantucket shop, but it wouldn't please Noah if she allowed herself to slide out of the clear clean sunlight of virtuousness into the evil, seductive consumer shade. Well, she decided, as she ate her insanely delicious eggs and bacon, she could just go along and pretend she didn't want anything.

Rising, she carried her dish and cup, rinsed them, and stacked them in the dishwasher. She hugged Alison. "That was divine, Mom, thank you."

"You're welcome, Filly." Alison kissed her daughter's cheek. "We should leave for your massage in about fifteen minutes."

Felicity cast one more suspicious glance at Jane and Ethan, who were happily scrolling down a list of recipes on a laptop on the kitchen table.

"Felicity?" Alison called from the front hall.

"Coming!" Felicity called. To Jane and Ethan, she said, "Bye for now."

"Bye, honey, have a great massage," Jane said, her eyes focused on the computer screen.

Jane was relieved when she heard her sister and mother leave the house. She'd sensed a flicker of jealousy from Felicity, and couldn't help but enjoy it. Just a little.

"I think basic white bread," Ethan said.

"Okay, good."

"Stand next to me. I'll give you directions. You do the work."

"Oh, thanks so much," Jane joked. As she moved, she became vividly aware of her body. She and Ethan both wore shorts, flip-flops, and T-shirts. Jane wasn't wearing a bra. She wasn't as voluptuous as Felicity and often went braless at home. When she did, Scott never noticed, so when Jane dressed this morning, she had, without thinking, gone without a bra.

Well, maybe she had thought about it for a fraction of a moment.

"Hey, it's the best way to learn. Okay, first, empty the yeast in the bowl and add two and a fourth cups of warm water."

Jane went to the sink and turned on the taps, fiddling with them both to get the right temperature. "How warm is warm?"

She had the back of her hand under the flow of water. Ethan came over and put his hand under the water. He didn't touch her hand, but his chest brushed against her shoulder and arm. It was almost as if he were holding her. Jane stood paralyzed, bombarded by sensations. He smelled of soap and shampoo—his hair was still damp—and gave off a warmth that made her body tingle. If she turned slightly, she could kiss him.

"This is good," Ethan said.

Jane almost said, "I know," but she caught hold of her senses and realized he wasn't talking about standing next to her. He was talking about the water temperature.

She filled the cup twice and poured two and a fourth cups of water over the yeast, which immediately began to bubble.

"Oh, look!" she said. "It's like an experiment in science class."

"I gather you enjoyed science class."

"Loved it." She glanced at him and was almost knocked off her feet by the wattage of his smile. "What next?"

"We add the sugar, salt, and oil." Ethan brought the staples from the cupboard and stood quietly while she measured them out. "Now add three cups of flour. Beat it all until it's smooth. No, don't just stir. Beat. Good. Now, add three more cups of flour, a half cup or so at a time, and keep beating."

Jane picked up the bowl and held it against her while she beat the dough. "Wonderful smell," she said.

"That's the yeast."

She added more flour. "Hey, this is getting difficult. Are you sure we need this much flour?"

"Absolutely sure." Ethan watched her and finally said, "Okay. Now we'll turn it on to the bread board and knead it. First, you have to sprinkle flour on the board."

Jane picked up the bag of flour and carefully shook out a dusting of flour.

"You'll need more than that. Like this." Ethan shook out a blizzard of flour.

"But that's so . . . messy," Jane said. She'd never known flour was so delicate and flyaway, landing on their clothes, the table, the floor.

"Being clean's no fun," Ethan said, looking right into her eyes as he spoke.

Her breath caught in her throat.

"Besides," Ethan continued, "some of this flour will become part of the bread. Now, turn the dough out on this bread board. Knead it for about ten minutes." He checked his watch. "I'll time you."

Jane dumped the dough out. Its yielding bulk seemed almost living. Ethan stood close to her, watching, and she could hardly think. She squeezed part of the dough and then another section, until Ethan corrected her.

"No, *knead*. Haven't you ever kneaded before?"

What she heard was *Haven't you ever needed before?* She was speechless.

"Here. Let me show you." Ethan stood behind her, placed his hands on top of her hands, and began to knead. "Like this."

His body touched hers now, as he pushed and pulled the dough so that it became more elastic. Jane could feel his breath against her hair, his chest against her shoulders.

"Okay," Ethan said. "Now you do it."

He moved away from her. She knew she should be glad and maybe in some faraway corner of her rational mind she was, but her body yearned for him to return. Forcing herself to pay attention to the bread, she kneaded and folded and kneaded and folded again.

"It's getting silky," she said.

"Good. I've greased this bowl. Put the dough in and turn it so that it's got grease on all sides. Then we'll cover it with a dish towel and let it rise."

She had to move next to him as she lifted the yielding dough into her hands and placed it inside the bowl. It was so quiet in the room she could hear her breathing, and his, and she realized his breath was coming fast, and hearing it was such an intimate thing that her entire body blazed.

"There," she said. Her voice was shaking. Her face was glowing. She found the courage to look at him and ask, "So, now what?"

His gaze was intense. "Now we wait."

"How long will that take?"

"About an hour or two. I'll turn it out and knead it one more time. When you all return from lunch, we can shape it into loaves and put it in the oven."

"Oh. Oh, okay. I'll . . ." Her voice was hoarse. Her mind, her brilliant legal mind, was a puddle of melted chocolate.

"How should we pass the time?" Ethan put his hand on her arm, pulling her closer to him.

"I'm afraid that what I would like to do and what I ought to do are different," she said, her voice trembling.

"Such a lawyer," Ethan teased, and he pulled her hard against him. He cupped her head in his hand and brought his mouth down to hers. His breath smelled like coffee and cinnamon.

He drew back, gazing into her eyes. "I want to take you to bed."

"I want that, too," Jane told him. "But I can't. This is crazy." Pushing away from him, she said, "I love my husband."

"And yet you'd like it if I kissed you again?" Ethan asked.

"Yes," she answered honestly.

But when he moved toward her she backed away, hitting her arm on the stove. "No. No, I can't. I'm going to go shower . . ."

She turned and hurried from the room.

In the privacy of her bedroom, she forced her body through her daily yoga routine. *This is good,* she thought as she stretched. This was what she needed. Her routine. Being away from home, away from the familiar, had unanchored her.

She loved Scott. Truly. That crazy moment with Ethan was simply displaced lust for something else. She had to talk to Scott again, to make him understand how a child would make their marriage even stronger. She didn't need to have sex with another man. She needed to have a baby, Scott's baby. She would make him realize this tomorrow evening, when she was home.

six

I t seemed absolutely perfect, even necessary, for the three women to drive to the Wauwinet in Jane's rented Mini Cooper convertible. Alison sat in the passenger seat, loving the sun on her face and the wind in her hair, as Jane drove along winding Polpis Road.

In the back, Felicity was pouting. When Alison had picked up Felicity after her massage, she'd pointed out that Felicity's skin was still oily and her dress was clinging to her. Alison suggested that she run the sundress through the wash while Felicity took a quick shower and put on one of Alison's floaty summer dresses.

Felicity was insulted. She said Alison didn't approve of Felicity's clothes, didn't think her clothes were *good enough* to wear to lunch at that posh place. Her mother had never understood Felicity's commitment to living a life centered around saving the environment! After her shower, however, she'd slipped on one of the sundresses, a loose crinkle cotton in azure which Felicity refused to admit looked lovely even though she couldn't help staring at herself in the mirror. It was difficult, Alison knew, to be pulled between parent and spouse, and Felicity, more than Jane, had always been the child who wanted peace and friendship among everyone she knew. Alison suspected Felicity was trying not to feel guilty about loving this dress.

On the other hand, behind the steering wheel, Jane was practically shining with delight. If Alison didn't know better, she'd think her older daughter was on some kind of drug. Jane wore an expression of bliss on her face, and Alison didn't think it was caused by the scenery.

"You're in a good mood today," Alison observed.

"Oh, I *know*," Jane replied, laughing, not saying why.

Alison suspected she knew the reason: Ethan had undoubtedly flirted with Jane while they made the bread. She remembered the days when she'd been Jane's age, an old married woman missing the chemical high that a simple smile from a handsome stranger could provide. Even a wolf whistle from construction workers would make her endorphins light up. Alison thought Scott was a wonderful husband, but probably not very romantic.

Well, Alison reminded herself, her daughters were adults, in charge of their own lives, and they had always been their own complete and particular selves, different from each other, different from Alison. She never had known all their secrets and she couldn't expect to know their secrets now. More than that, she didn't *want* to know their secrets.

Jane steered the Mini Cooper off Polpis Road onto the even narrower road to the Wauwinet. Sun flashed through the towering evergreens. They came to the Trustees of Reservations gatehouse, and Jane braked, but the season hadn't started yet, and no one came out to check for a sticker, so they proceeded slowly over the speed bump and beneath the arching trees and turned into the parking lot of the Wauwinet hotel.

"Look at the *flowers*," Jane gushed as they walked up the winding brick path.

They were greeted and led around to the harbor side of the hotel and settled at a table on the porch.

"We won't have champagne," Alison told her daughters. "We've got to keep our heads clear for shopping this afternoon."

The waiter came to take their orders. Alison leaned back in her chair and gazed out over the plush green lawn leading to the water. "Isn't this a gorgeous spot? Can you imagine how fabulous our wedding will be?"

"It's beautiful here, Mom," Jane agreed.

White sails skimmed the shining blue waters of the head of Nantucket harbor, where a long golden beach curved into the distance. An extravagant border of rugosa roses, the shrub that grew wild on the island, perfuming the air with its sweet attar, marked the edge of the beach.

"You could get all fantastic here," Jane mused. "Have David arrive by Viking ship with banners flying."

"Oh, yes!" Happily, Felicity came out of her gloom. "Or you could be like a princess, Mom, floating in on a boat covered with flowers."

Alison laughed. "I'm a little old to be a princess—"

"Cleopatra, then," Jane suggested.

"Right!" Felicity clapped her hands. "Jane and I could be your servants. We'd fan you with enormous peacock feathers."

"I think it's a good thing I didn't order champagne," Alison said. "Heaven knows what you'd dream up then."

For lunch, Alison and Jane both enjoyed delicious lobster rolls. Felicity had an enormous Wagyu burger.

"It's your fault," she told her mother. "You've awakened my taste for red meat."

"Isn't Wagyu beef the kind they breed in Japan and massage every day?" Jane asked.

"I've heard that's a myth," Alison said. "But it is especially delicious and tender—and expensive."

"Oh, I hope the cow was massaged every day," Felicity said. "This would have been a happy cow."

"You should know," Jane joked, adding to clarify, "I mean you just had a massage." She turned to Alison. "How many people are coming to your wedding, Mom?"

"Not too many. About eighty."

"Don't you feel strange, leaving all the decisions to what's-her-name, David's assistant?"

"Heather. And no, I don't. Heather does the research. She and her husband have a house here, so they know whom to contact. She's friends with Michael Molinar, who owns Flowers on Chestnut, so he can advise her about what will work. Then she shows us the possibilities for tents, menus, music, and so on. David and I discuss and decide and Heather implements our decisions. It's like throwing a party and having it catered."

"But it's your *wedding*," Felicity stressed.

"Yes, and it will be *here,* isolated from the world," Alison responded. "Nature will be our cathedral. The sky and sun and waves will be our witnesses. David and I have so much, all we need. David worked hard all his life. We've both lost our beloved spouses. It's a miracle that we've found each other. We want to share our great good fortune and our joy by giving our family and friends a wonderful fairy-tale weekend."

Alison's face glowed as she spoke. Felicity and Jane looked at each other, surprised by so much passion coming from their mother.

"I've never heard you talk that way before," Jane said softly.

"I've never felt this way before," Alison replied with a smile. "Now. Let's skip dessert and go into town, shall we? I'm in the mood to shop!"

Nantucket had many fabulous stores along the brick tic-tac-toe grid of the main town and also along the wharves in boutiques that had once been fishermen's shacks. They surrendered to a shopping mania, drunk on color and fabric and glitter and style. At Murray's

Toggery, Alison bought Felicity and Jane clever little tops and capri pants and some Jack Rogers sandals, which, Alison said, *everyone* wears. Felicity found tops at Vis-A-Vis that were loose and flowing, very romantic, with lace or embroidery, not at all the blue-and-white-striped things that screamed *I own a yacht*. Both girls found silk shirts and light jackets at Zero Main. Alison noted with satisfaction that Felicity didn't make any kind of a fuss about trying on such gorgeous clothes.

They drove home in the late afternoon. When they walked into the house, they stopped dead, as if in a trance.

"Bread!" Jane cried. "Ethan's baked the bread!"

They dropped their shopping bags and hurried into the kitchen. Ethan was there, huge and masculine in board shorts, a T-shirt, flip-flops—and an apron.

"This is every woman's dream." Jane sighed. "A handsome man in the kitchen."

"Good to know," Ethan joked, and he flashed a glance at Jane, who blushed.

Alison's radar pinged. What was happening to her serious, sensible daughter? She stepped between them. "It smells like it just came out of the oven."

"It did." Ethan dried his hands. "I took the butter out of the refrigerator a while ago to soften it. And I made fresh lemonade. With real lemons."

"Can we keep him, Mom?" Jane joked. "Maybe chained in the basement?"

"We'll let him out to cook for us," Felicity added, sliding around the table to gaze down at the crusty loaf.

They sat at the table eating the warm, crusty bread, almost incapable of conversation. Afterward, Felicity and Alison went upstairs to nap after their hard day of lunching and shopping.

"I'm going down for a swim," Ethan said.

Alison paused with her hand on the bannister, waiting to hear what Jane would say.

"Have fun," Jane said. "I think I'll read for a while."

"That's boring. You can read anytime. But a day like today is rare. Come on. Swim with me."

Jane hesitated. She'd told him this morning she was married and would not betray her vows. And after all, he was only inviting her to go for a swim. But the thought of them together in the silky water, buffeted against each other by the waves, their bodies bare except for the merest strips of clothing . . . she was appalled at how much she wanted to swim with him.

She stood up. "Actually, I think I'll take a nap. All this sun and good food is acting like a tranquilizer. Enjoy your swim." She left the room. She almost ran.

In the early evening, they all piled into Alison's Jeep and headed out to Madaket. Felicity rode in the passenger seat, with Jane and Ethan in the backseat. Alison kept checking on them in her rearview mirror. *Stop it*, Alison told herself. *They're adults.*

She focused on her younger daughter. "Felicity," Alison said, "I want to know all about my grandchildren. How are they? Details, please."

Felicity brightened. "Well, Alice is, as you know, finishing first grade. She's an excellent student and she has lots of friends, and at home she's intolerably bossy!"

Alison laughed. "First children often are."

"I can hear you!" Jane reminded them.

"And as for Luke! He likes running and yelling at the top of his voice." Felicity reached into her shoulder bag. "Here. I've got new photos on my phone. I took them before I came."

"I'll look at them when we're settled on the beach," Alison said. She steered the Jeep off the main road onto a narrow lane blocked by a railing and a gigantic sand dune. "Girls, Ethan, here we are!"

Alison parked the Jeep at the end of the road. "Everybody has to carry something," she said, clicking the hatch door open. "I'll take two beach chairs. Ethan, can you get the others?"

"Got them."

"I'll take the coolers," Jane said, reaching in for two blue and white plastic containers.

"Um, I'll take the picnic basket," Felicity said unhappily, because she was stuck with the most cumbersome object.

"It's too heavy for you to carry alone," Ethan told her. He tucked the beach chairs under his arm. "I'll take this end."

It was a real hike to get to the top, but once they were there, they looked down to see Madaket Beach spread out before them in butterscotch perfection, and waves coming all the way from Europe to spill lazily onto the sand.

"Gosh." Felicity sighed. "This is amazing."

"It is," Alison agreed. "Now you know why I wanted to bring you girls out here. Most people go to the Jetties Beach or Surfside, but I think this is my favorite."

Laughing, they half-walked, half-slid down the dune. They chose a spot and set up the beach chairs, one on each corner of the red-and-white-checked cloth Alison took from the hamper. The sun was already slanting down in the sky—it was late, almost seven-thirty.

They sat back in their chairs, their bare feet in the soft sand, watching the waves roll up and sink into the sand. For a few moments, no one spoke.

"It's hypnotic," Jane murmured.

"The quiet," Felicity said. "I love how quiet it is, only the sound of the waves, and no child crying."

At that moment, a gull flew overhead, screeching. Everyone laughed.

"Ready for wine?" Ethan asked.

"Absolutely," Jane said.

Alison turned to her daughter. "Felicity, let me see your phone. I want to look at the photos of your children."

Felicity happily handed it to her. Alison scrolled through the pictures, laughing and exclaiming at her grandchildren's sweet faces, silly postures.

"Let me see," Jane asked.

Ethan took the phone next. "You've got really adorable kids," he told Felicity.

Felicity beamed. "Thanks."

Alison set out a late evening snack. They were still full from the bread but needed something more. Deviled eggs. Carrots and broccoli. Cheddar cheese and grapes.

"Do you have children, Ethan?" Felicity asked.

Ethan smiled. "I do. A daughter. Canny—she's named after Cantuta, the Peruvian national flower. It's supposed to be magic, and we're experimenting with it on the farm—not in a magic mushroom way. Canny lives with me during the school year and spends the summer months and winter vacation with her mother in Peru."

"Your wife, ex-wife, her mother, lets her daughter live with you most of the time?" Felicity was stunned.

"It was Canny's choice. She skypes with her mother almost every evening." Ethan met Felicity's shocked gaze calmly. "My ex-wife, Esmeralda, is a lawyer. Her father is a judge in Lima. She's brilliant and ambitious. When we married, she gave living on my farm a good try, but it's isolated, in upstate Vermont. She's a city girl. She speaks five languages, and she's seriously involved with the politics of her country."

"How did you meet her?" Jane asked.

"I was traveling through South America. I had a friend in Lima, a guy I'd gone to boarding school with, and I stopped for a few days to see him, and I met Esmeralda at a party. We were married six months later."

"How romantic," Alison said. "What was your wedding like?"

"We had two of them. First, in Peru. Esmeralda is Catholic. Then, a second wedding on our farm." Ethan laughed ruefully. "We had two weddings, one child, and not much of a marriage."

"Very different weddings?" Jane asked.

"Absolutely. The first was in the Cathedral Basilica of St. John the Apostle and Evangelist. A magnificent cathedral in the heart of downtown Lima. We had several hundred guests, and Esmeralda"—Ethan smiled, remembering—"resembled a walking five-tiered wedding cake as she came down the aisle. Enough lace and glitter for five brides. Then, on the farm, it was the exact opposite. We had a tent in the yard in case of rain, but it didn't, so we held the ceremony in the orchard when the trees were blooming. We had about forty guests, including various dogs, cats, and ducks. The reception was in the barn."

"And what did Esmeralda wear then?" Felicity asked. "Sorry for a girly-girl question."

"No problem. She wore a kind of long white slip embroidered with daisies and stalks of wheat. She had it designed and made for her. And a wreath of flowers in her hair. And red cowboy boots with sparkles. We had a country-western band and a barbecue and we danced and partied until sunrise."

"Sounds fabulous!" Jane said.

"Why did you two divorce?" Felicity asked.

"*Felicity,*" Jane said.

"What?" Felicity smiled sweetly at her sister. "I'm just trying to get to know Ethan. After all, he's going to be our brother."

"*Step*brother," Jane corrected.

"We wanted two completely different lives," Ethan said. "It's as simple as that. I'm not sorry. I got Canny out of the deal."

Felicity telegraphed a look at Jane.

"Look." Alison pointed to the sky. "This is the part I love, when the sun's rays turn the edges of the clouds pink."

They were silent for a while, watching the spectacle of the slowly setting sun.

"Oh, Jane," Felicity said spontaneously, "isn't it wonderful here on Nantucket? Let's make plans to come back here as often as possible. I'll bring the children, so you can get to know them."

"I want some time with them, too!" Alison reminded Felicity.

"Sure, Mom. Then Jane and I can spend some—what is it called—*quality time* together."

"That's a good idea, Filly," Jane said. "Yes, let's come here as often as possible this summer."

Maybe it was the way the sun slanted in Felicity's eyes, but it seemed that Jane was looking at Ethan, not at Felicity, when she spoke.

seven

Sunday morning, Felicity stayed snug in her bed, luxuriating in the pleasure of this weekend: the incredibly blue ocean, the sea breeze, the sun on her shoulders, the delicious food, yesterday's massage, and, she had to admit, the blissful silence, the utter *luxury* of walking and talking without being pulled on or summoned by a child's cry.

Yet she missed her family. After she'd showered and dressed, she picked up her iPhone.

"Mommy Mommy Mommy!" Luke screamed into the phone, inadvertently pushing all the buttons so that beeps and rings interrupted his voice. And then the phone went dead.

Felicity waited a few seconds and tried again. "Hi, Mommy." Her older child, her competent daughter, Alice, had the phone now. In the background, Luke, deprived of the phone, was shouting.

"How are you all, darling?"

"Daddy's letting us watch cartoons!"

"Oh, how special," Felicity cooed, as a flick of resentment stung her. Noah didn't like *her* allowing the children to watch television.

"And Ingrid came over last night to bring us dinner and watch a movie!"

Felicity rocked backward, hit hard in her chest. "Ingrid came over?" she echoed.

Ingrid came over. Ingrid Black was Noah's assistant at work. Felicity had met her at the company party last Christmas. Fifty people, more or less, milled around the large function room at the Marriott hotel in Newton. It had a great view of the Charles River, or it did during daylight hours. In December, it was dark at five, although you could still see the sparkling lights of cars passing on Commonwealth Avenue.

Luke was five and Felicity joked that she still hadn't lost all her baby weight. Her breasts were plump in spite of all the nursing she'd done, so she'd worn her prettiest dress, cut low to show off her cleavage, falling in loose layers over her stomach and hips. She'd had her hair coiffed at a salon, a luxury for her, and she'd had the time to put on lipstick and blush and eyeliner because Crystal, their babysitter, was already there, reading to the children.

Noah wore a black cashmere turtleneck and black pants. "You look very Steve Jobs," Felicity had teased, and Noah had not laughed. In the car on the way to the hotel, they hadn't really talked, even though thirty minutes together without a child shrieking was a rare experience.

Felicity had tried. "I'm wondering if you could do some boy stuff with Luke," she'd said. "He's wildly energetic. I bet he'll be a natural at sports."

Noah sighed. "I'll try. But you know this is a critical time for Green Food."

Felicity felt her mouth tighten into the disapproving moue she kept making without thinking these days. It was *always* a critical time for Noah's business. *Lighten up,* she ordered herself. Frantically, she searched her brain for a topic she could discuss that wasn't about the children or why the downstairs toilet kept clogging. Something fun. But she didn't even know celebrity gossip these days, so she'd been silent for the rest of the ride.

Noah had his hand on Felicity's back when they entered the party, but he was so much the star that he was quickly surrounded by his staff. Felicity had gone off to the bar to get a glass of wine. She'd settled alone at a table, watching the crowd, smiling to see how the staff clustered around Noah. He would be in such a good mood for the next few days!

One woman gazed up at Noah with shining adoration. She was short and her face was—Felicity chided herself for even thinking this, she was a feminist after all!—ordinary. She always tried to be generous with her thoughts even if no one else could hear her thinking them. *Well*, Felicity had thought kindly, *the woman has blond hair. Blondes are always special.* She knew. She was blond.

"May I join you?" Another wife, married to one of the scientists experimenting with green food, sat at the table.

"Of course. I'm Felicity."

"I'm Cynthia Levine. Goodness, look over there, Ingrid Black is about to climb up her boss's arm."

Felicity had felt her mouth tighten as she looked. Ingrid had both hands on Noah's arm and was standing inappropriately close to his body. "That's my husband. Noah Wellington."

"Oops. Foot, meet mouth." Cynthia had laughed. "I wouldn't worry. Men like our husbands need to be worshipped." Her eyes had flicked over Felicity. "Besides, he's not going to sleep with *that* when he's got *you*."

Felicity had shifted uncomfortably in her chair. "That makes me feel . . . uncharitable."

"Well, honey, don't think for a moment that woman has any charity in her heart for *you*. Believe me. I know."

Another company wife had joined them, and the conversation had changed to Christmas talk.

During the drive home, Felicity had said lightly, because Noah was in a relaxed, post-party mood, "I think Ingrid Black was coming on to you."

"Oh, for God's sake," Noah had snapped. "Everyone comes on to me, I'm the boss."

"And you are," Felicity had said, softening her tone, "awfully handsome."

He hadn't replied.

Now her daughter's voice brought her back to the present.

"Daddy said he couldn't watch us and cook at the same time, so he invited Ingrid," Alice explained sensibly. "She's so nice, Mommy. She brought over *Frozen*! All right, Luke, jeez, don't grab!"

"Hi, Mommy. I am Luke."

"Yes, you are, sweetheart, and I love hearing your voice. What are you doing right now?"

Silence. Finally, "Mommy when are you coming home?"

"I'll be home today, Lukey."

"Mommy, Ingrid had food."

"What kind of food, sweetie?"

"FOOD!" Luke yelled, as if his mother had gone deaf.

"Macaroni and cheese," Alice prompted from the background. "And asparagus—"

"I hate aspagurus!" Luke screamed, before dropping the phone with a thud.

Felicity could envision it, their house phone usually cradled in the kitchen, now lying on the family room floor with the television blasting in the background.

"Luke?" she called. "Luke! Luke, I need to talk to your father!"

After a short wait, she heard rustling noises and Alice said, "Daddy says he can't come to the phone now."

"Can you ask Daddy to call me later? Can you remember that?"

Another thud. The line went dead.

Felicity put down her phone and sat very still, as if any movement would cause more chaos in her heart. Clearly the children didn't miss her. That was a good thing, even if they were watching the evil television instead of doing creative crafts.

But the problem was: Why was Ingrid over at the house last night? Noah could cook. He was an excellent cook, slow but thorough. He probably had been too overwhelmed with work . . . but had Ingrid dropped off the food and the video, or, what was it Luke said, *Ingrid came over last night to bring us dinner and watch a movie.*

And Alice had said, *She's so nice.*

Was Ingrid nice?

Noah hadn't come to the phone to speak to her now. He must have heard the children talking about Ingrid. Was he afraid Felicity would ask him about her?

What should she do now? Should she call him back and demand to speak to him? Was she making something out of nothing?

"Filly?" Alison came into the bedroom. "Are you ready to go?"

"Um, sure." Felicity forced herself to smile. "Totally." She carried her backpack—she couldn't wear it in a car—and hurried down the stairs.

"I thought we'd have a stroll around town, and then brunch at Cru. I bought you a plane ticket. You leave at one, Felicity."

"Thanks, Mom."

"And my plane's at two," Jane said.

"The kids will be glad to see you," Alison said to Felicity.

"I know," Felicity agreed, and she felt warm all over at the thought. Then she realized that she didn't know if Noah would be glad to see her. She wasn't sure she'd be glad to see him. She wanted to know why Ingrid had come over last night, but she hated confrontations.

As she listened to Alison chatter, Felicity wondered if her mother had ever had this kind of problem with her marriage. Felicity's father had been drop-dead handsome, and she wasn't thinking this because he was her father. It was a fact. Alison had been beautiful, still was beautiful, for an older woman, but had she worried as she grew older and her husband continued his work as a pediatrician? Maybe she should have. After all, Alison had met Mark at his office when she took Jane in for a consultation. Alison had still been married to Jane's father, Flint. Didn't Alison worry as the years passed that some new yummy mummy might attract Mark, at least for a fling? After all, Alison grew older, but the mothers bringing in little children must have seemed endlessly young. Did her father ever have an affair?

Did her mother?

Scott offered to pick Jane up at JFK, but she insisted on taking a cab. She didn't want to bother him when he was so busy, she said. What she didn't say was that she wanted one more hour to organize her thoughts. Plan her attack, more specifically.

She leaned her head back on the seat. The cab went over the Queensboro Bridge and entered Manhattan. Was she being impulsive, wanting a child? She'd certainly been impulsive when she'd kissed Ethan. This morning, she'd exchanged cellphone numbers with Ethan and agreed, quietly, standing in the upstairs hall of the Nantucket house, to let each other know when they were able to go to the island again. They hadn't touched, but the electric pull between them had seemed as powerful as the moon on the tides.

Later, as Jane, Felicity, and Alison left for brunch, Jane had given Ethan a quick hug, keeping her body slanted so that only her arms touched him. *Virtue triumphs!* Jane told herself. But at the airport, Alison had handed a small foil-wrapped parcel to Jane. "You forgot this, darling," Alison said. "I know you'll want to share some of this delicious bread with Scott."

Now, as the tall buildings and congested traffic blocked Jane's thoughts of the gorgeous island and dropped her back into her real life, she thought the bread in her bag was like a little lump of guilt. She wasn't one hundred percent certain that her mother hadn't noticed the intense attraction between Jane and Ethan.

And what did it all mean? She loved Scott, she *did*. She trusted his love for her. She knew he'd never be unfaithful to her.

And until this weekend she'd *known* she'd never be unfaithful to Scott.

Well, she hadn't *been* unfaithful! She had only wanted to be.

She needed to be brutally realistic. It had been only a moment's magic. In the grand scheme of things, looking down on a kind of calendar of the days and weeks and months of her life, the time she'd spent with Ethan was so minuscule, so insignificant, it was like trying to find a pebble on the steps of the Metropolitan Museum of Art from a satellite in outer space. In the vast expanse of her life, the yearning, the desire, was only a speck, something no one else could see.

And yet.

Maybe, she thought, her longing for a child was causing her to be more sexually, sensually awake.

The cab stopped in front of their building. She swiped her credit card and tipped the driver and gathered her purse and her briefcase (which she hadn't opened once this weekend) and her suitcase and stepped out onto the sunny street.

She paused for a moment. May in the city was such a great month. No bitter wind howling down the long avenues, no dirty slush to slip in on the sidewalks, instead trees and flowers blooming, the air mild and sweet . . . okay, not sweet exactly, she was getting carried away. But the summer heat hadn't yet arrived to intensify the smells of gasoline and millions of overheated people and their dogs.

She entered the building and leaned against the elevator wall as she rode up to the fifteenth floor. She felt like she was being transported from one life to another, and she knew the moment those elevator doors opened that Nantucket magic would evaporate like a bubble.

She found her keys in her bag and undid the locks. She stepped into their apartment. She set her suitcase on the floor and dumped her keys in the bowl on the foyer table and laid her bag next to it.

"Scott? I'm back!"

"You're early!" His voice came from the room they used as a joint office.

"I am. I missed you. But I had a wonderful time. David's beach house is stunning. You'll have to come with me to see it."

As she talked, she pulled her small roller suitcase behind her down the hall and into their bedroom.

And she waited for Scott to come out of their office and give her a welcome-home kiss.

Nothing.

She sat on the bed, kicked off her heels, and massaged her feet. Walking in warm sand on the beach versus walking in stilettos on hard sidewalk: no contest.

"Did you miss me?" she called. She wanted him to come to her.

"Of course!" he called back.

On bare feet, she padded down the hall and into the office. Scott was at the computer, squinting at a chart, moving the mouse.

"You're working hard for a Sunday." She moved behind him and put her hands on his shoulders and smooched the top of his head.

"I didn't think you'd be back until later. I've got to get this analysis done."

"Okay." She noticed, as if for the first time, how luxurious his hair was. "You've got beautiful hair, Scott, so dark and thick, like an animal's pelt."

He shook his head sharply, as if shooing away a fly. "That tickles."

She removed her hands. "I'll go unpack. And shower."

At the door he called, "Hey."

She stopped.

"I'm glad you're home. But you *are* early. And I need to finish this. It's important. Give me twenty more minutes, okay?"

"Okay." She had to be fair. This was the way they were. Both of them. *Finish the work first*; she could cross-stitch it on a wall hanging. She shouldn't, couldn't, judge Scott by the few foolish moments she'd spent with Ethan.

In their bedroom, she unpacked her clothes and sorted them: laundry, dry cleaner, shoe rack. She removed her flip-flops from the plastic bag she'd kept them in. They still had some sand on them. She took a long moment to hold them, remembering. Then she held them over the wastebasket and brushed the sand away.

She showered, pulled on yoga pants and a T-shirt, and carried her briefcase into their office.

"Almost done," Scott said.

She unpacked her laptop. She'd thought she'd have time on the island to read through at least one file, but somehow she hadn't worked all weekend. Like a drug, the need to work pulled at her mind. She could start—

"Done!" Scott rose from his desk chair, stretched, and yawned. "What shall we order in for dinner?"

She kept her back to him. "Whatever you want. And I've brought you the most delicious bread. I made it *myself*. It's unbelievable. I'll heat it up for you for an *amuse-bouche*."

"I'll tell you what I'd like to amuse my mouth." Scott put his arms around her waist and kissed her neck.

"Oh, good," Jane joked lightly. "I didn't think you'd missed me at all."

"God, I know, Jane. I'm sorry. But in my defense, I'm stressed."

"You sound like a lawyer."

"I am a lawyer."

"You're a husband, too." She turned in his arms and looked up at him.

He smiled. He had a wonderful smile. "I promise to perform my husbandly duties later on, or even before we eat, depending on which of your appetites is stronger. I set the DVR to tape the Sunday morning show, so we can watch it while we eat." He stepped back and checked his watch. "Time for a Scotch."

eight

Rain was falling as the ten-seater plane began its shuddering wobble down the Nantucket runway. Felicity had no real dread of flying, but as they lifted off the ground into the clouds, she felt itchy with anxiety. She knew the pilot had instruments, but the dense white vapor around the plane was unsettling.

She closed her eyes and forced herself to focus on something positive. It had been sunny this morning and gorgeous at lunch today at the restaurant on the wharf. And it had been a good time for the three of them, much laughter, delicious food, and a sense that the coming summer might bring them all closer. For the first time in years, Felicity had felt a real affinity with Jane, perhaps because her perfect older sister with the perfect accomplished life wanted something Felicity had. But Felicity had also noticed the sexual tension between Jane and Ethan. They were only flirting, she reassured herself. Absolutely just flirting. Felicity scolded herself for being jealous that for once a man hadn't chosen her over her sister.

And she was taut with worry about Ingrid being with Noah and her children last night . . . the fear of infidelity hummed around her mind like a bothersome bee.

It was cloudy in Boston when the plane landed. Her clothes weren't warm enough for the surprising early summer chill. Was she coming down with a cold? Why was she so dreary today?

Her spirits lifted when she came into the terminal.

Her children raced toward her. "Mommy Mommy Mommy!"

Alice hurtled herself toward Felicity, determined to get to her first. She wore a flowered shirt and plaid shorts and polka dot knee socks, because that was the way Alice liked to dress. Felicity noticed that no one, meaning Noah, had brushed Alice's long blond curls today.

Luke barreled toward Felicity, tackling her at the knees, almost knocking her down. Squatting on the floor, her arms around both children, Felicity looked up at her husband. "Hi, there."

"Hey." Noah's expression was stiff, fake happy.

She stood and kissed him. His kiss was cool, and he pulled away quickly. But then he had never been comfortable with public displays of affection.

In the Volvo station wagon on the ride home, the children talked and giggled so much Felicity and Noah couldn't have any kind of a conversation, and that was the way it always was. But anxiety made Felicity reckless, and as they left Route 2 for the winding roads of their suburb, she said easily, carelessly, "So, I hear Ingrid came over last night."

She was Noah's wife. She'd lived with him for eight years. She could read even his unspoken words. His hands tightened on the steering wheel and his jaw tensed.

Alice burst out, "She brought us a huge pan of macaroni and cheese—"

Luke yelled. "Mommy, we watched *Frozen*. She gave us the DVD. Can we watch it when we get home?"

"How nice of Ingrid," Felicity said, smiling over the back of her seat at her children. "And how unusual for Daddy to allow you to watch a DVD."

"I know, Mommy," Alice agreed.

Noah glared at the road without speaking.

"Did you bring us any presents, Mommy?"

"No, sweeties, I didn't have time."

Noah pulled into their driveway. The children exploded out of the car, racing to the backyard where they were allowed to play while Felicity kept an eye on them from the kitchen. Noah unlocked the front door and held it open for Felicity as she entered.

Felicity dropped her backpack on the low chest in the front hall. Noah headed to his den at the side of the house.

"Noah, wait. I'd like to know . . . Could we talk about Ingrid being here?"

He didn't turn to face her. "Let's talk about it after dinner." He went into his den and shut the door.

"Well," Felicity said to the closed door, "now I'm really worried."

Still, she managed to finish the day as if everything was normal. She'd left a tuna noodle casserole in the refrigerator for the weekend, and since that hadn't been touched, she heated it up for their dinner, noticing as she worked in the kitchen that there were no signs of the macaroni and cheese or the dreadful asparagus. She did find an unfinished quart of chocolate ice cream in the freezer. Ice cream was a special treat in this healthy household. Pulling back the lid, she checked and found that only a small iceberg of ice cream was left. So, a DVD and ice cream, too.

She poured herself a glass of wine.

Dinner was chaotic, as usual. Felicity bathed the children so she could reconnect with them after two nights and three days away. Alice didn't like it when Luke's toothbrush touched hers. Luke insisted it was his turn to choose the bedtime story. Their concerns were so trivial, she thought, in comparison to the black storm cloud brewing around her mind and heart, a storm that could roar their lives away.

Finally, after the children had been fed, bathed, read to, and tucked in, when they were absolutely asleep, Felicity made herself a cup of chamomile tea and went into the den where Noah was studying a spreadsheet.

"Noah? Could we talk?"

Noah looked up. He was a handsome man. Blond hair, blue eyes, much like Felicity's own, and replicated in their children. "What's up?"

She sat in a chair across from him. "Is something going on with you and Ingrid?"

Noah made a scoffing noise. "Yes. We had passionate sex on the living room rug while the kids watched *Frozen* in the den."

"You don't have to be that way about it. You've never had any employee over to the house before, except at group parties."

"Well, you haven't left me alone with the kids before," Noah shot back. "And I've been telling you it's a crucial time right now at work. I can only stretch myself so far."

"It's always a crucial time at work for you," Felicity said softly.

"Felicity. Don't do this."

She nodded. She knew what he meant. It was always Felicity complaining, never Noah. They had agreed that she would handle the children, the house, the daily necessities while Noah focused on establishing Green Food and financially supporting the family.

"I'm sorry," she said. "I just get . . ." She hated sounding pathetic. "But hey," she said, brightening. "Want to have some passionate sex on the living room rug?"

Noah smiled. "Can it wait? I've got to finish analyzing these figures."

Disappointment rippled through her. But she caught herself before she complained again. She smiled back. She rose and went to him, running her fingers lightly along his lips. "Of course it can wait. I'll be upstairs in bed, reading. And waiting."

Noah brushed his head against her hand. "Thanks, Filly. I'll be up soon."

But it was midnight when Felicity turned off her bedside lamp and fell asleep, and Noah had not come to bed.

After Ethan and the girls left, Alison walked through the large, empty house, checking to be sure windows were shut in case of rain, looking for anything left behind, stripping the beds and starting a load of laundry even though this was Alani's task, because the truth was, she enjoyed doing laundry, and she needed this period of transition from busy house to lonely house. No, not lonely. Quiet. There had been years in her life when she would have paid money for quiet.

Finally she poured herself a glass of iced tea and sat out on the deck, looking at the ocean. It was Sunday evening. She'd make herself a salad and finish off the last chunk of homemade bread and watch *Masterpiece Theatre*. For now, she relaxed and let her thoughts flow.

The weekend had gone well, better than she'd expected or hoped for. Her daughters had obviously enjoyed being with each other, which was a great pleasure—and a great relief. Ethan had been his usual charming self and both girls seemed to like him. But Alison had missed David.

Her phone buzzed. She wasn't surprised to see David's number on the caller ID. It often seemed as if they had ESP. She thought about him; he called.

"Hi, sweetheart," she answered. "Where are you?"

"At home. Lying on the bed."

"Mmm, I'll be right there."

"Sorry, but I've got the remote in my hand. The Red Sox game starts in ten minutes."

Alison laughed. "I wouldn't dream of interrupting that."

"How did the weekend go?"

"Actually, I think it went really well. The girls had a walk on the beach together and didn't pull each other's hair out, and we agreed on their bridesmaid dresses, and they loved the Wauwinet. Well, who wouldn't? Oh, and Ethan was here!"

"Yeah, I knew he was at loose ends this weekend. Canny flew home to Esmeralda on Tuesday. Her private school gets out earlier than the public schools, and she was eager to be with her mother."

"It's good that he was here. He helped a friend put his boat in the water, and he spent some time with us. He actually taught Jane how to bake bread."

"That doesn't sound like Jane."

"I know. But she enjoyed it. I think something about being on this island makes us all relax and do things we'd never think of doing in our normal lives. Felicity let me buy her some new clothes."

"She did? I thought she was completely immersed in her Mother Goddess Save the World Eat Beans role."

"She's different when Noah's not around. She ate *meat*. Steak for dinner and bacon for breakfast."

David laughed his low chuckling laugh. "What a temptress you are. Are you coming home tomorrow?"

"Absolutely. It's lonely here without you. I'll try to get down here when the children—yours or mine—want to come, but I want to be with you as much as I can."

"Good. That's what I want, too."

Alison heard a sudden roar, and she knew the game was starting. "Go watch your game," she said. "I'll call you before I go to sleep tonight."

During the work week, Jane forced herself to remain pleasant, calm, engaging. And so the evenings she spent with Scott passed without argument.

But when Thursday evening came, as she slipped into bed next to her husband, Jane said, "Scott, I wish you'd come to the island with me this weekend. I enjoyed being there so much, and I know you'd enjoy it, too. David Gladstone's house is like a contemporary castle. All modern and clean and full of light and air. And it's huge, so if Felicity and her brood are there, or David's son, Ethan"—she felt a zing through her body as she said Ethan's name—"we could still have our privacy."

"I'm glad you had a good time," Scott said. "And I agreed we'll go there for the wedding. And let's go after our hiking trip in August."

"I want to go *instead* of the Wales trip."

"You're kidding." Scott quirked an eyebrow. "We've been planning it all year. We've made all the flight and hotel reservations—"

"I know that. But we also bought the travel insurance so we won't lose any money if we cancel."

"You want to cancel the hiking trip? Jane, honestly, I don't understand this sudden love for sand and sunshine. You've never been a beach girl."

"Scott, you have to come with me to understand. We won't have to lie in the sun. We can bike, kayak, sail, play tennis, golf—"

"Yes, but we can't hike."

"Well, we don't *have* to hike. No one's holding a gun to your head saying: *You Must Hike*. Plus, we can certainly *walk*. I've read about all sorts of paths and trails." Reaching over, Jane put her hand on Scott's. "Why not come with me this weekend? I think once you're there, you'll see what I mean. David's daughter, Poppy, will be there. She's being groomed to take over the company, so the two of you can talk business all the time."

Scott reached for the remote control and clicked on the TV. "I want to catch the BBC news. I think Japan's moving some money."

In one supple move, Jane whipped around to sit on her husband's legs, blocking his view of the television. "We have money. Now I want something else. I want *family*. I need family. I'm sorry your parents are dead. I'm sorry you're an only child. But you know you've always enjoyed being around my mother, and isn't it fun talking about Felicity after we've seen her? My family is your family, too, Scott. All I'm asking for is one weekend."

Scott clicked the TV off. He leaned back against the headboard, his striped pajamas so crisp from the laundry it seemed he was still dressed for work.

"You've changed," he said.

"Yeah, I have," Jane agreed. "That's what happens in life. Things change. People change."

"I think you're trying to blackmail me."

"What?"

"Before we married, you and I agreed we wouldn't have children, and now you've decided you want a baby. Or even two."

"Scott—"

"You're going to work yourself up into a frenzy and accuse me of being aloof and strange because I don't want children and I don't want to hang out with your sister's children and your mother's fiancé's daughter's children. You think if I come see all those adorable kids, I'll want one of my own."

Sometimes, Jane thought, she believed Scott could read her mind.

"I have never *worked myself up into a frenzy*," she argued.

"No? When you first brought up the subject of children, and I said no way, didn't you burst into tears and spend all day—a beautiful sunny Sunday—crying?"

"That hardly qualifies as a frenzy."

"Look, Jane, first of all, move. You're crushing my legs."

She sat beside him on the bed, gathering her thoughts. She remembered the advice a law teacher had given her: don't try to win the enormous argument at first. Just try to get a *yes* about a small matter. *Isn't it a nice day? Didn't we meet at the ballet?* Give back a *yes* to show you're willing to negotiate.

"How about this. If you'll come to Nantucket for the weekend, I promise I won't bring up the matter of children for an entire week."

"I love you, but that bargain won't work. We made an agreement when we got married and I won't shift from my position. Anyway, I can't understand why it's so important to you. You've

always said your sister's family is noisy and undisciplined and chaotic. And now David's children and grandchildren will be there,
too? Sorry. I'm going to pass."

"Maybe you're *afraid* of change, Scott," Jane challenged.
"Maybe you're so stuck in your rut you can't notice what you're
missing."

Scott shrugged. "Maybe." Reaching over, he turned off his bedside lamp and lay down to sleep. On his side. With his back to Jane.

"Well, I'm changing, Scott," Jane said quietly. "I'm widening
my horizons."

Her husband didn't reply. He was very good at not replying.

Jane wanted to hit him with her pillow. She wanted to burst into
tears. She turned off her lamp and slid under the covers, and lay
there, unable to fall asleep.

nine

On a balmy Friday in the middle of June, Alison stood with her housekeeper, Alani, working on a chart. What had seemed like a delightful idea during Alison's phone calls with her children and with David's children now seemed like a complicated puzzle. *Everyone* was coming for the weekend. Oh, except Noah. And Scott still hadn't made up his mind. So, on David's side, that left Ethan, a lone male; and David's daughter, Poppy O'Reilly; and Poppy's husband, Patrick; and their two children, Daphne, eight, and Hunter, six. Plus Jane, probably alone, and Felicity and Felicity's children, Alice, seven, and Luke, five.

So, counting Alison and David, that made twelve people for five bedrooms.

"Mr. Ethan will use the foldout sofa," Alani told Alison. "He's very nice, no problem."

Alani was young, only about forty, but her voluptuous body and languid personality sometimes made Alison wish Alani were her grandmother. She also wished, when she had a free moment for such a frivolous thought, that Alani would do Alison's hair in one of the many fantastic arrangements Alani did her own. Today Alani had multiple braids curling in and out to make a kind of space-age crown.

"All right, then. Thanks, Alani. If you could bring some towels and sheets and a pillow down for Ethan, I'll put together the seafood casserole."

Felicity's children ate only Annie's organic mac and cheese, but for this weekend, she had agreed they could eat Alison's five-cheese mac and cheese, while the adults shared the seafood casserole. Tomorrow night, David was planning a cookout with hamburgers, hot dogs, and, for Felicity and her children, tofu hot dogs. Alison wondered if Felicity would choose a hamburger without Noah there to watch her. But no—Felicity's children would undoubtedly notice.

Now, as she set a pot of water on to boil for the rice—organic brown rice, to be exact—her thoughts were tangled. She hoped everyone would get along, but she worried that would be a problem. Alison had met David's daughter and son-in-law only once, at a dinner in Boston. Poppy had made it clear that David was *her* possession and Poppy considered Alison an interloper. Plus, Poppy had mentioned David's first wife, Poppy and Ethan's mother, constantly, and in terms that made Emma seem like a gorgeous saint.

Jane could take on Poppy, Alison decided. Jane was as bossy as Poppy and a lawyer in a prestigious firm. Ethan would be the easy one. He could hang out with Felicity.

"Noah, please." By early Saturday morning, Felicity had packed the children's suitcases and her own as well, and they absolutely had to leave in the next ten minutes in order to make the drive down to Hyannis and catch the ferry. "It's beautiful there. Mom wants to see you. The children need some time with all of us together."

"I don't know why you keep pushing me on this, Felicity." Noah forced himself from his computer, where he'd been since five in the morning, when he threw himself from bed, made a strong pot of coffee, and settled down to work. "I have to get this grant done. It's crucial to Green Food. It's not a matter of whether or not I *want* to go, it's simply that I *can't* go."

Felicity was standing by his desk, looming over him and she knew how he hated that. So she was surprised when Noah suddenly stood up and put his hands on her shoulders.

"Look," he said with soft intensity, "try to think of it this way. Remember when you were in labor with Alice? You were working hard, and you couldn't stop. That's where I am with this grant. I've gotten up a head of steam and I'm going to push right on through till I get it done. With you and the children gone, and with me here without any interruptions from my team, I'll be able to accomplish twice as much as I could on any normal work day."

Felicity studied her husband. Sometimes his concentrated drive to save the world made her crazy, made her want to run out and buy bags of Fritos and gallons of ice cream and serve it to her family for dinner. But most of the time she admired him for his ethics. And now as he stood before her, she saw the dark half moons beneath his eyes and the slight rash of acne that broke out along his neck when he was stressed.

"Mother." Alice stood in the door of the den with her hands on her hips. "According to my watch, if we don't leave in three minutes, we'll miss the ferry."

Noah pulled Felicity closer, whispering, "Are you sure that child is ours?"

Felicity smiled, amused that Noah couldn't see how Alice's anxious bossiness echoed his own.

"Come on, then," Noah said to his daughter. He took his car keys from the hall table. "Let's get this show on the road."

He was taking time out of his day to drive them from the suburb of Lexington to Hyannis, Felicity reminded herself. Added to the drive back, that was three hours out of his day. She tried to be grateful for that.

. . .

Once again, Jane flew in from New York and rented a car at the Nantucket airport. She preferred having her own transportation rather than relying on someone else, and she needed the psychological freedom she felt from knowing she could leave whenever she chose.

As she approached David's house on Surfside Beach, she told herself to shove the wasp hive of anger at Scott into the darkest corner of her mind. This weekend was not about her; it was about her mother and David. They were offering a luxurious place to stay on a gorgeous island—it would be churlish not to be happy.

But she wasn't happy. She was angry at Scott, and she was tied up in knots about this baby thing. She had seldom been jealous of Felicity, even if her younger sister was so much prettier and more endearing, but listening to Felicity talk about her children had been difficult, like being thirsty with no water near.

Okay, well, *Ethan* had made Jane forget her baby cravings, but that was another problem. *He* was another problem. She didn't want to be unfaithful to Scott, and yet she also really did. It wasn't simply a matter of sexual chemistry, it was also a completely irrational need to wound Scott, to perform an extremely childish act of "So there!"

She imagined snapping a shot of Ethan on her phone and sending it to Scott with the message: *If you don't agree to having a child, I'm going to sleep with this man.* It would be blackmail, it would be revenge, it would be like a thwarted child pounding a closed door, trying to get her own way.

All of that passion, all of that heat, had to be tamped down the moment she arrived at David's house. This was her mother's time. Alison had been an attentive, loving mother and she had been lonely and unhappy after Mark's death. Now Alison had found happiness again, and she was offering, and David was offering, the exceptional gift of long summer days on a sun-kissed island. Jane vowed to herself that this weekend, just for two days—surely she could manage two days—she would put all thoughts of babies out of her mind. She would hang out with her mother, she would be kind to Felicity, she would ignore Ethan and take long walks on the beach thinking of nothing but the sweetness of the breeze in her hair and the warm sand on the soles of her feet.

David's house had a circular drive. Three cars were already parked on the bricks. Jane pulled her car behind a Jeep SUV, turned off the engine, and stepped out into the sunshine. The forecast was for a warm, sunny weekend. She leaned against her rental car and closed her eyes, taking a moment to enjoy the sun on her face.

And everyone arrived, in a kaleidoscope of kisses, hugs, loud high-pitched voices, running feet, slammed doors, flushing toilets, and adults yelling, "Wash your hands!" David told the children, in his most serious voice, that they couldn't go down to the beach unless an adult was with them—that was THE RULE OF THE HOUSE. So while the adults went yammering away as they unloaded their luggage, eight-year-old Daphne, who possessed an uncanny ability for organizing children, led them into the garage to find the vacillating sprinkler for the hose, and soon the four children were on the back lawn running in and out of the water and whooping with glee.

Alison made a large pitcher of iced tea and another large pitcher of pink lemonade. If only, she thought, adults could become friendly with the good-natured ease of children. Patrick O'Reilly worked for an agency representing athletes, and Alison thought Patrick was perfectly suited for the job. He was tall, with the big shoulders and broad chest of a football linebacker, a thatch of unruly red hair, sparkling brown eyes, and an oft-broken nose. It amused Alison, how slender, elegant Poppy could make Patrick hop to it with a word or a look. Poppy was attractive, with the Gladstones' large blue eyes and glossy blond hair, but she seemed constantly exasperated, and she probably was, with two children at home and an important position at the Gladstone company offices. As Alison surreptitiously watched, she noticed that Ethan and his sister were cool toward each other. Poppy seemed to be the good child, serious and responsible, while Ethan was the irresistibly adorable rebel. Ethan obviously liked Poppy's husband; today they shook hands in greeting and settled into a discussion about the Red Sox.

Alison set the pitchers on the kitchen table with a stack of paper cups. She'd been at enough children's birthday parties to know not to use glasses.

"Ethan," she said, "I'm sorry you have to sleep on the pullout bed."

"Don't worry about it. It's perfect, actually, for what I plan to do." His grin was mischievous, lopsided.

"What do you plan to do?"

He said with false piety, "Get a good night's sleep down here away from the noise of dozens of children."

Ethan was far too young to sound so happy simply to get a good night's sleep, but Alison didn't question him.

The day spilled out like colored marbles, people going in all directions, laughing, running, and swimming. In a great mass, they went down to the beach and bravely tried to swim in the cold ocean water. The children shrieked and complained until Drill Sergeant Daphne took them under her wing and inspired them to build an enormous sand castle. By dinnertime, Alice was under her spell—Daphne was tall and self-confident as well as being the oldest—and the children would have eaten porridge without honey if Daphne had told them that was all they could have.

After dinner, everyone sat out on the deck, enjoying the cool evening air and the changing sky. Felicity kept saying that it was time to put the children to bed, but she was having her second slice of blueberry pie and couldn't rouse herself from her lounger. Jane sat near her at the round wooden table drinking sparkling water. Ethan and Patrick were cleaning the kitchen, a fairly massive job after so many people had eaten blueberry pie and ice cream. Alison protested that no, *she* should do the kitchen, they were here on a little holiday, but David took Alison's hand and led her outside, where he whispered, "Let them clean the kitchen. They're trying to impress you, to make you like them."

"But I *do* like them!" Alison whispered.

"Yeah, well, it won't hurt to make them sweat a little. You've already done so much, making this huge dinner." He touched Alison's knee with his own. "Besides, I need you to rest up so you've got some energy left for later."

Alison squeezed his hand.

Jane had her phone on the table, even though she knew her mother did not approve of having it out when there were real people to talk with. She needed her phone for defense—defense against her own rogue desires. Each time Ethan looked at her, Jane experienced his gaze as if it were a caress. How could Jane possibly do what her mother wanted and *make friends* with David's children when she wanted to have sex with one of them?

Damn Scott. He could at least call.

All right, Jane thought. She'd make an effort. "Poppy, I think you work with your father at English Garden Creams, right?"

Poppy yawned. "I do."

"What sorts of—" Jane began.

But Poppy interrupted. "—work do I do? I'm taking over the company from Dad. But not before maternity leave when I have this little one." She patted her belly smugly, as if too stunned with hormonal pleasure to make an effort to have a conversation.

Jane stopped breathing. Poppy was pregnant? She already had two children. How did Poppy get three children and Jane didn't get any? This was completely ridiculous thinking, Jane knew, but she was paralyzed with envy.

"How far along are you?" Felicity asked.

"Four months, more or less."

"So you're probably over the morning sickness bit," Felicity said. "I remember—"

"Oh, God, I don't know. It's so boring, talking about pregnancy." Poppy stood up. "I'm going to bed. I can't seem to get enough sleep. Good night, everyone."

Jane and Felicity exchanged glances as Poppy strolled into the house.

"I thought we'd sail out to Coatue tomorrow," David said. "Take a picnic, swim."

"Sounds good, Dad," Ethan said, coming out from the kitchen.

Patrick was right behind him, a tall, broad-shouldered, red-headed Viking of a man. "Kitchen's done," he announced.

Jane checked her phone—no messages. "Tomorrow's forecast is for clouds," Jane told the group, reading from the small screen. "High in the low eighties, wind at fifteen miles per hour, humidity fifty percent."

"Perfect," David said.

"No message from Scott?" Felicity asked.

"Not yet." Jane was on the verge of tears. Damn Scott! But she would drown herself before she cried in front of everyone. She stood up. "I'm going for a walk. Felicity?"

"I'll stay here. The children," she added in explanation.

The year had almost reached the summer solstice, and light remained in the sky past nine o'clock. Ethan had brought glow sticks for the children, who were now playing hide-and-seek around the house and in the bushes.

"It's past their bedtime and they've been wild," Felicity added. "Any minute now one of them will start crying and I'll have to wrestle them to bed."

Ethan rose. "I could use a walk after having two helpings of blueberry pie." He patted his perfectly flat belly.

Uh-oh! Jane thought, but with everyone watching, she said, "Sure. Join me."

Single file, Jane and Ethan walked through the wild rosebushes to the beach. The white curls of surf were almost fluorescent in the fading light, and they surged up and sank into the warm sand with soft sounds like whispers.

Jane ambled in and out of the waves, aware that Ethan was near her, near enough to touch. Not that she would touch even his hand, of course she wouldn't. It was enough to have him near. To know that he had chosen to join her.

"You said you enjoy hiking," Ethan said. "Where have you gone?"

Jane knew she was blushing with pleasure simply because Ethan remembered what she'd said at their first meeting. She bent over to hide her face, pretending to inspect a shell. "Mostly in the U.S. Colorado, Death Valley, Sedona, Mount Washington in New Hampshire. And Scotland, last year."

Ethan walked nearer to her, almost touching. "So you like adventure, a taste of danger."

Was that a challenge? Jane said lightly, "Nothing compared to you. Hang gliding? Skydiving?"

"Life is short," Ethan said. "I believe we should live large, follow our desires."

Jane sniffed. "Only someone who is independently wealthy can say that."

"I'm not so sure. For some adventures money is necessary. But some of our best adventures money can't buy."

Jane waved a hand at the ocean. "True."

"Or this." Ethan stopped her, taking her shoulders in his hands and turning her to face him.

Jane tried to pull away . . . but she didn't try hard. Still, she said, "I can't. We can't."

He pulled her closer. "If it were just you and me and the beach and the ocean, tell me you wouldn't want me to touch you and hold you and kiss you and make love to you."

Jane put her hands on his chest to push him away, but the contact sent desire racing through her. "We're not alone on a desert island."

"Well, we are on an island," Ethan pointed out. "And right now, we're alone."

He kissed her then, wrapping his arms around her, sliding his lips gently against hers so that she felt his breath and the silk of his skin. He was taller than she was, just the perfect height to meet her upturned mouth, and as he kissed her, he pulled her against him, so she felt his body all up and down, pressed against hers.

He drew her down to her knees. He was on his knees, kissing her, and the cool night surf swept up and swirled around them.

I can't do this, Jane thought, but she had never wanted anything more.

Abruptly, Ethan dropped his arms and stood up. "Damn."

Jane almost toppled into the water. Ethan caught her by the shoulders and helped her to her feet.

"Look," he whispered.

She turned. Bars of glowing green light were advancing toward them—Daphne, the tallest, in the lead, the other children behind her, and a grown-up, they couldn't quite make out just who, taking up the rear.

"The joys of a large family," Ethan said.

"Uncle Ethan! Uncle Ethan! Wait for us!" Daphne called.

The children raced up to them, waving their glow sticks and shouting. Felicity sauntered behind, keeping her eye on the little ones, but taking a moment to telegraph a message to Jane: *I saw you kissing him.*

ten

Sunday morning, Alison woke to the tapping of raindrops against the window.

"Oh, no," she moaned, turning over and burying her head beneath a pillow. David had planned to take them all sailing over to Coatue for a picnic, but it wouldn't be much fun in the rain. David had warned her that on Nantucket even June days could be too cool for the beach. "Does the weather forecaster ever get it right for this island?"

"Can't count on it." David lifted a corner of her pillow. "We'll take them to the Whaling Museum," he said, as if he read her mind.

"Oh, David, you're a genius!" She tossed the pillow aside so she could give him a long, enthusiastic smooch.

After she showered and dressed, Alison went downstairs. Ethan was in the kitchen, making pancakes.

"Good morning, Ethan! Oh, heaven, you've made coffee. Is anyone else up?"

"All the kids, of course. They're still in their pajamas, all watching cartoons in the den. I told them I'd call when breakfast is ready."

Alison poured herself a large mug of coffee, added milk, and took a fortifying sip. She leaned against the counter, watching Ethan work at the stove. "Felicity and Noah don't let their kids watch television."

"That's harsh," Ethan said.

"I agree. But I don't interfere when I visit them. And I think here on the island we all should abide by David's and my rules, and for heaven's sake, it's raining, so they can watch television all day if they want."

"I agree." Ethan lightly flipped some pancakes on to a pan and set them into the oven to keep warm. He poured more batter into the skillet.

"David said we can take everyone to the Whaling Museum today."

"Good idea. The kids will love it."

Alison opened the refrigerator door. "Have we got enough bacon . . . yes. I'll start microwaving it. I prefer doing it this way because the fat soaks into the paper towel . . ."

"Good morning." Jane came into the room, wearing a slightly frayed yacht club sweatshirt. "I hope you don't mind. I found this on a hook and I'm freezing. I didn't think to bring warm clothes."

"We've got plenty of sweaters and warm clothes here," Alison said. "Help yourself."

"Hi, Jane," Ethan said. "How did you sleep?"

"Beautifully, thanks," Jane told him as she poured herself a mug of coffee. "I love sleeping with the ocean breezes drifting through the windows. It's like sliding into a dream. How did *you* sleep, Ethan?"

"Okay, once I settled down." Ethan flipped the pancakes.

Alison kept her eyes on the bacon she was laying out on the paper towel–covered plate. Was she crazy to think there was some kind of undertone, some sort of playful almost *flirtation* in Ethan's and Jane's voices? Well, she couldn't blame Jane. Ethan was gorgeous, and funny and smart, too. And it was a pleasure to hear a kind of mischief in her older daughter's voice. Jane lived such a serious, grown-up life. It would do her a world of good to be flirted with by Ethan. Alison knew Jane was far too responsible to take it any further.

Soon the others drifted in, lured by the aroma of bacon.

The adults stood around the kitchen drinking coffee, or in Felicity's case, green tea, while the four children sat at the table eating pancakes.

"Poppy," Alison said, "did you get my email and the video of bridesmaid dresses?"

"Yeah, I got it," Poppy said bluntly. She bent to pull Daphne's hair back into a low ponytail.

Alison persisted. "What did you think?"

"We'll talk about it later." Poppy went to the sink and ran the water full force. She drank a glass of water, then returned to her children.

All righty, then, Alison thought. *Later.*

"So, kids," Felicity said, "since it's raining today, we're all going to go see the Whaling Museum."

"Does it have whales in it, Mommy?" Luke asked, eyes wide.

Daphne and Hunter laughed.

"Duh!" Hunter yelled. "It has a great big old whale *skeleton,*" he continued, bugging his eyes out.

"Patrick and I will take our kids somewhere else," Poppy said. "They've already seen the Whaling Museum."

"Oh," Felicity began. "I thought this would be a good way for the children . . ."

"I'm done, Mommy," Luke said, sliding off his chair.

"Felicity, you might want to wash his hands before he gets sticky syrup everywhere," Poppy said.

"Of course." Felicity bit back an irritated response.

"Here, Filly," Jane said, handing her a wet paper towel.

"We use only cloth towels," Felicity said weakly. But her younger child was squirming and all the kids were talking at once. She took the paper towel, grateful for her sister's support.

As the day went on, Felicity was happily surprised at how engaged Jane was with her niece and nephew. Children were noisy and messy, that was simply a fact, and Jane was usually so anal and starchy, but as soon as it was agreed they'd go to the Whaling Museum, Jane announced she'd take Felicity and her children in her rented car. And at the museum, Jane had taken Alice around with her, giving Felicity some precious one-on-one time with Luke. Maybe Jane was testing herself, to see if she truly enjoyed children.

By noon, the rain had stopped, but the sky was still cloudy. They met their mother and David and his clan at Barnaby's Place in the Bookworks and let the kids each choose a book to buy. While David paid at the counter, the others herded the children outdoors where Daphne, who had insisted on buying a jump rope instead of a book, drove the others into jealous squeals as she leapt up and down on the sidewalk.

"We're quite a mob, aren't we?" Felicity whispered to her mother.

Alison nodded. "Yes, but at least it's stopped raining so the children can be outdoors."

David came out of the shop. "We'll take everyone to lunch at Something Natural. They have picnic tables out on the lawn and trees to climb on."

"Oh, darling, you're a genius!" Alison cooed and kissed David on the mouth.

Felicity turned away. Why did she feel such a twinge in her belly when she saw her mother and David kissing? She was glad for her mother, and she honestly liked David. So it wasn't that kind of envy.

Maybe it was because she hadn't spontaneously kissed Noah like that for a long time. He was always so busy with work, and she was always so busy with the children . . . Maybe the twinge was a kind of worry. Even a kind of warning?

· · ·

After lunch, back at the house, as everyone spilled out of the cars, Daphne shouted, "Hide-and-seek time!"

"Outside? Not many places to hide," Alice remarked.

Felicity held her breath. Alice was seven, a year younger than Daphne, and until now had followed the older girl's lead. Both girls had strong personalities—Felicity hoped they wouldn't argue.

"You're right," Daphne agreed. "We'll play hide-and-seek in the house."

Poppy stood with her hands braced on her back. "I'm exhausted. I need a nap."

Alison yawned. "I could use a nap, too."

"Well, I'm taking charge of tonight's dinner," Ethan announced. "It's time everyone tasted my delectable eggplant parmesan."

"We don't have any eggplant," Alison told him.

"I'll go buy some," Ethan told her. "Want to come along, Felicity? You could help choose salad makings."

"Sure, I'll come." Felicity smiled, absurdly pleased to have been chosen instead of Jane. "But the children—"

Patrick spoke up. "Jane and I can watch the children. We'll give them some time in the house, and if the sun comes out we'll take them down to the beach."

"Is that okay with you, Jane?" Felicity asked.

Was Jane's smile a bit too bright? "Sure!"

Daphne gathered the children into a cluster and was seriously giving them the rules of hide-and-seek. "I'll hide first," she said, and raced into the house.

"How are you going to get any sleep?" Felicity asked Poppy.

"Are you kidding?" Poppy asked. "You could prop me against a post at a rock concert and I'd fall asleep. Hormones." She blew a kiss at her husband, called "Thanks!," and went into the house, followed by Alison.

"I'll just check on the Red Sox." David went inside, heading toward the den.

"Felicity?" Ethan swept an arm toward the open passenger door. "The front seat is yours."

Dear Lord, he is handsome, Felicity thought.

Ethan drove them back into town and down Polpis Road to Moors End Farm, where Felicity found an abundance of ripe tomatoes, eggplant, onions, lettuces, carrots, and red and green peppers. They stashed the bags in the back of the Jeep and headed into town to buy red wine. In the liquor store, Ethan held out various bottles, asking Felicity's opinion, as if she were sophisticated enough to have an opinion about red wines.

On the drive home, Ethan said, "I hope you'll help me prepare dinner, Felicity. That will give Alison a break, and besides, that way I'll get to know you better."

Felicity almost melted into the leather car seat with pleasure. Ethan wanted to get to know her. So he wasn't a flirt, after all. He was simply a good guy trying to make connections between his father's family and Alison's. It was only that he was so handsome that he seemed to be flirting.

Back at the house, they each took bags from the Jeep to carry inside.

The sun was slowly creeping out from behind the clouds and the air was humid. They carried their groceries down the hall and into the kitchen. They found the family gathered there, all of them with terrified faces.

"What's happened?" Felicity cried.

Poppy said, "It's okay, Felicity, we'll find him. While I was napping, the kids played hide-and-seek, and we seem to have misplaced Luke."

Felicity's heart lurched. " *'Misplaced'* him? What do you mean?"

Everyone talked at once. Ethan took Felicity's bags from her and went toward the refrigerator.

Patrick raised his voice. "Let's have some quiet. We only now found out. Daphne, you're the oldest, so can you tell us what happened?"

"That's not fair," Poppy snapped. "You can't blame it on her."

"I'm not blaming anything on anyone," Patrick told his wife. "I'm just asking Daphne, who has been so wonderful at entertaining all the kids, to tell us what has happened."

With everyone looking at her, Daphne seemed to shrink from a broad-shouldered, domineering miniature troop leader into a frightened child.

Patrick knelt next to his daughter and put his arm around her. "It's okay, Daphne. We just need to know what you know to help us find Luke. Remember, he's only five, not a big kid like you."

"We played hide-and-seek," Daphne said in a very small voice. "It took a long time because the house is so big . . ."

Alice spoke up. "We took turns. By age, to make it fair. First Daphne hid, then I did, then Hunter, then Luke was last."

Alison squatted down on her heels to face Daphne. "Honey, can you tell us where you hid? Luke is only five, so I'll bet he hid somewhere one of you hid."

"I hid in the closet upstairs where the blankets are!" Hunter yelled. "I climbed to the top shelf and no one could find me in forever!"

"It's true," Daphne said. "Hunter was the hardest to find. He had the best hiding place. I hid behind Granddad's clothes in the closet in their bedroom."

"I hid behind the sofa in the den," Alice said.

"So you all played inside the house, right?" Poppy asked.

The three children nodded.

Poppy said, "*And no one went outside,* right?"

"I don't think so," Daphne said in a small voice.

"Jane, where were *you*?" Poppy demanded. "You were here at the house, right?"

"Right. I sat outside on the deck with Patrick. We were just hanging out, but also we were keeping an eye on the path to the beach to be sure no one went down to the water."

Felicity's breath froze. "Down to the water."

"Are you sure, Jane?" Alison pushed herself up to a standing position. "You're absolutely one hundred percent sure you didn't see anyone go to the water?"

Jane glanced at Patrick. "We didn't see anyone, did we?"

"I'm sure we didn't," Patrick agreed.

Ethan said in a no-nonsense tone, "I'm going down to the beach anyway, just to check."

"All right, then." David took charge. "Let's search the house slowly and thoroughly. We'll look in every closet, beneath every sofa or bed, any place where a five-year-old could squeeze himself. Alison, you and I and Jane will do this floor. The rest of you do the second floor."

"What about the attic?" Jane asked.

"Nothing's up there. It can be accessed only by a pull-down door. Luke couldn't possibly reach it."

"Children, go into the den and watch television," Poppy ordered. "Now."

"Yay!" yelled Hunter.

"No. I want to help search," Daphne protested.

"Me, too," echoed Alice.

Poppy began, *"I said—"*

Ignoring them, Felicity raced up the stairs, calling her son's name. Jane came close behind her, with Patrick, Alison, and the little girls close behind.

"Luke? Luke!" Felicity called and the others echoed her.

They searched the bedrooms and the bathrooms, looking behind the shower curtain and inside the bathroom cupboards. Nothing. Felicity began to cry quietly. Jane put an arm around her.

"It will be all right. We'll find him. *Luke,*" Jane continued in a soft, gentle tone, "wherever you are, please come out. Your mommy is crying because she misses you."

Suddenly, soundlessly, the cushioned window seat at the end of the hall began to rise up. Luke's sweet little face appeared, flushed with heat and damp with sweat and tears.

"Oh, Luke!" Felicity ran to her son, pulled him out of the hollow space, and held him tight. For a moment she just examined her child from head to toe to be sure he was okay. Then, as the others looked on, relieved, Felicity asked, "Honey, why didn't you come out before, when we were all searching for you?"

Luke squirmed in his mother's arms. "Daphne said I couldn't."

"NO, I did not!" Daphne yelled.

Luke began to cry. "Daphne said to scare you."

"MOM!" Daphne protested. "I did NOT say that!"

"Daphne said I would get a prize if I didn't come out." Luke stared at Daphne, confused and frightened.

"You little liar!" Daphne cried, stamping her foot.

Poppy bent to soothe her daughter. "Luke's only five. He doesn't know what he's saying."

Alice put her hands on her hips, looking like an indignant schoolteacher. "Yes, Luke does too know what he's saying!"

"Alice," Poppy said in syrupy tones, "let's all be friendly, okay?"

Don't you dare tell my child what to do! Felicity thought, but clamped her lips together. Clearly this was a *moment*. Felicity had been here before, when children fought and the parents had to sort it out without hurting anyone's feelings. Felicity wanted to defuse the possible grenade of the situation, but she also wanted Luke to know she believed him.

Alice glared at her mother. Felicity stroked Luke's hair. The little boy was calming down, but Daphne stood with her fist clenched, nearly vibrating with anger. Patrick looked at Felicity, waiting for her to say something. In spite of her sweet words, Poppy was glaring at Felicity as if she wanted to set her on fire with her eyes.

"Yes," Felicity said calmly, "Poppy is right. We should all be friendly. No one got hurt, everyone's fine, and I'll bet we're all hungry for dinner. I'm going to take Luke into the bathroom and wash his face. Alice, want to come help? Poppy, maybe you can go downstairs and tell the others that Luke is okay."

Poppy's eyes narrowed. She was, after all, a vice president of a major company. She was used to giving the orders. She aimed a last dart at Felicity, unwilling to go away with the matter unsettled. "I guess we'll never know the truth—"

"Mommy!" Daphne cried.

"—but we're all so glad Luke is okay, right? That's the important thing."

In the bathroom, Jane held Luke while Alice, Daphne, and Hunter crowded in the doorway, watching. Felicity gently washed Luke's tears away with a cool cloth.

Or tried to. Luke's tears kept rolling down his cheeks and his entire small body shook with his effort to swallow his sobs.

"I want to go home, Mommy," Luke cried. "Please. I want Fuzzy. I want my bed. I want Daddy."

Oh, give me the wisdom of Solomon, Felicity prayed. She'd like to go home, too, right now, escape back to the house she knew and loved, back to Noah's consolation and warm embrace. But she knew she couldn't leave now. It would make the episode with Luke in the window seat into a more significant matter than it really was. She couldn't let this shadow her mother's wedding or the long relationship Felicity and her family would have with their future extended family. And no one had been hurt.

"We are going home, sweetie," Felicity said. "But first Ethan and I are going to cook a delicious dinner! After we eat, we're getting on the ferry to Hyannis. Daddy will be waiting for us, to drive us home."

"And we can watch a DVD during the drive," Alice added helpfully. "Maybe *Mary Poppins.*"

"Mary Poopins!" Luke yelled, laughing hysterically at his joke.

"Mary Poopins!" Hunter echoed, falling on the floor with laughter.

"Honestly." Daphne rolled her eyes.

Disaster averted, Felicity thought. But she kind of hated Poppy.

. . .

Felicity and Ethan prepared the aromatic eggplant parmesan for the adults and corkscrew pasta with tomato sauce for the children. With warm garlic bread and a salad, it would be a soothing meal to end a complicated day. The red wine would help, too.

Felicity was amused and a little bit smug about all the times Jane came into the kitchen, saying she needed to fill the ice bucket, and maybe she'd prepare a tray of nuts and olives to nibble on with their drinks on the deck. Ethan was focused on cooking, though, so Felicity didn't think Jane would be jealous, and anyway, what was she even thinking! Felicity was married and Jane was married and she and Jane were finally becoming good friends. It was absolutely adolescent to want Ethan to flirt with her in front of Jane!

In any case, no one flirted with anyone, and quickly the meal was over and Felicity had to round up her children and get them ready for the ferry ride back to Hyannis. Poppy and Patrick organized their family for the airport.

Before Felicity left, she found Jane in the kitchen and gave her a good long hug.

"See you soon, I hope."

"Soon," Jane answered.

David drove Felicity and her children to the ferry. Alison drove Poppy and her family to the airport in Jane's rental car and returned it so Jane wouldn't have to rush at the airport. David picked Alison up and brought her home.

Jane and Ethan were alone in the big house, clearing the table and cleaning the kitchen. For a while they worked in silence. Jane brought the dishes in and handed them to Ethan to rinse and put in the dishwasher. Such an ordinary, boring thing to do, but when their hands touched, her pulse skyrocketed. The atmosphere grew thick with unacknowledged lust. Jane slid open the door to the deck to let cool air into the room. She stood, looking out at the sea and sky, and after a moment, Ethan came to stand behind her. He didn't touch her, but she could feel his breath.

"It turned into a clear night," Ethan said.

"It did." She didn't turn around to face him.

"Jane." Ethan put his hand on her waist.

For one long moment, she allowed herself to soak in the sensual pleasure of his touch. The devil on one shoulder whispered: *Go ahead, no one else will ever know.* But the angel on her other shoulder stamped her foot. *You'll know. And it will only lead to trouble.*

"The laundry!" Jane said, relieved to think of it. "I want to get some laundry started, I don't want my mother to have to deal with all of it."

Ethan stepped back to let Jane pass. In the laundry room, bath and beach towels rose in a soggy heap on the floor. Jane put a few of the bath towels into the washing machine.

"Maybe," she said brightly to Ethan, "you could take those beach towels out and give them a good shake over the deck railing. Get rid of the sand before they go in the wash."

Ethan smiled. "At your service, madam."

Once he had gathered up the striped beach towels, Jane continued putting the softer, plusher bath towels in the wash. Had she ever felt such soft fabric? It was like hugging a stuffed animal. She buried her face in the thick white bath sheet and moaned very quietly. It wasn't the towel that was ringing her chimes. Obviously, she was going mad, acting like a repressed spinster.

Ethan came back into the room. "I think I got them all. Do you want to add them in with the bath towels or do a separate load?"

"Um, separate load, I think." She knew he'd seen her with her face in the towel and forced a laugh. "These bath towels are so heavenly. I need to get some."

Ethan grinned. "Jane, I think you're suffering from sensory deprivation."

"Of course not!" she argued. "How could I? I mean, I can see and hear the ocean, I can smell the wild roses, I've just eaten your delicious eggplant parmesan—'' She went silent. What was the fifth sense?

"Touch," Ethan said, as if he'd read her mind and he continued, with a smile and a joking lilt in his voice. "You're molesting that towel because you need to be touched."

"Oh, that's silly," Jane said. Turning away from him, she stuffed the towel into the machine.

"Maybe." Ethan handed her more towels. "Maybe not."

Jane busily put in the detergent and pushed all the buttons. And then there she was, alone in the room with Ethan and nothing else needing to be done.

He stepped closer to her and put his hand along her cheek. "You're so beautiful."

She couldn't move. She was melting.

Keeping his hand on her cheek, he bent down and kissed her neck, his warm breath stirring her hair. He moved so that only an inch existed between their bodies as he kissed the hollow of her throat and her cheek, his mouth hovering teasingly just above her mouth.

"We're back!" David strode in the front door and down the hall.

Jane tore herself away from Ethan. "We're in here starting the laundry."

"Thanks for doing that," David called. "I want to catch the end of the Red Sox game."

"I've got to finish packing and get to the airport," Jane said, not meeting Ethan's eyes.

She hurried up the stairs to her bedroom and quickly tossed her belongings into her suitcase.

When she came down, her mother and Ethan were in the front hall.

"Felicity and Poppy are off. I returned your rental car. I'll drive you and Ethan to the airport." Alison checked her watch. "If we go now, I can get back in time for *Masterpiece Theatre*." She beckoned to Jane and Ethan.

"Come along, children," she said teasingly.

If you only knew how R-rated we've been acting this evening, Jane thought. She was glad to let Ethan, with his long legs, sit in the front of the Jeep while she sat in the back, too far away for him to touch. At this point in her life, she wasn't sure she could resist him. She wasn't sure she wanted to.

eleven

By eight o'clock Sunday evening, they had all gone.

The house was peaceful.

"I'm beat," David confessed. "Why is running a company easier than spending time with one's family?"

"You can't fire your family," Alison joked. "You were wonderful today, David, and it was a three-ring circus. Watch *Masterpiece Theatre* with me."

They settled side by side on the sofa. Alison loved that she and David were so comfortable with each other that they could admit they needed the zombie-mind that television provided. They needed to discuss this first gathering of their individual tribes, but they needed some downtime before they talked.

After the show was over, Alison went up to shower while David watched the news. She was in her lavender nightgown when David came up. Usually she slept in a T-shirt, but David seemed to appreciate seeing her in lace and silk, and she enjoyed every moment of his appreciation.

She heard him brushing his teeth, stripping down to his boxers, tossing his clothes in the laundry basket, all familiar sounds that gave her a sense of contentment, of being at home. When he slipped under the covers next to her, she turned to him, putting her hand on his chest.

"Who won the Red Sox game today?" she asked.

"The Sox. Like they always do, they came from behind to pull it out with a couple of home runs in the ninth inning."

"Do you think they'll make it to the World Series this year?"

"Too soon to say."

Alison shifted positions, moving closer. To her surprise, David sat up, adjusting the pillows behind him.

"Ally, we need to talk about something."

"I know." She sat up, too, slanting to face him. "I think the weekend went well, don't you? I know there were some difficult moments, but you know how it is with children, they'll fight one minute and play with each other the next."

David took Alison's hand in hers and held it, tracing the lines of her palm. "The thing is, the video you sent Poppy of the bridesmaids' gowns. Or whatever your attendants are called. Poppy doesn't like them."

Alison drew back in surprise. "Go on."

"Well, you know, Poppy's baby is due in November. She'll be seven months pregnant in early September. She said this pregnancy, her third, is giving her terrible varicose veins. She's embarrassed by them and doesn't want to wear a short skirt like you and your girls want to wear. She wants to wear a long gown." David paused. "That means all of you have to wear long gowns."

"But, but—" Alison sputtered. She wanted to announce in no uncertain terms: *Your daughter can't dictate what kind of wedding dress I wear!* She took a deep breath. "But, David, I've already chosen my dress. It's been fitted and altered. And as soon as my girls agreed on their dresses, we emailed the links to Poppy. And Poppy has said nothing to me about this." Alison tried to sound unruffled, but her blood pressure was spiking.

"Okay. That's because only now, when she's finishing her fourth month, is she noticing how the veins are sticking out on her legs. Did you spot them when she was here?"

Alison took a deep breath. This was only a wedding, not a world peace summit. "No, I can't say I did. She looked lovely, and scarcely pregnant."

"Well, she said the veins aren't so bad now, but by the date of our wedding, they'll look like worms crawling up her legs—that's Poppy's image, not mine. So you can see why she would want a floor-length gown."

Alison sat very quietly. Thoughts crowded her mind, many of them not very complimentary. "I guess I assumed that you would talk with Ethan and Poppy about what to wear, since they're your attendants."

"Of course. But Ethan and I are wearing tuxes. I can't ask my daughter to wear a tux."

"Of course not. But I've looked at wedding magazines. I'm sure I've seen wedding photos with the attendants wearing various lengths of dresses. Why don't I talk to the consultant in New York. Then I'll call Poppy, or maybe we can Skype and talk it out."

David went silent. After a minute, he said, "I hope, and I know you hope, that our children can become, if not friends, at least friendly."

"Good grief, David, of course I do. I thought our families got along really well this weekend."

"So changing the gowns to long isn't a deal-breaker then."

"A *deal-breaker*? Do you mean you'll call off the wedding if I don't accede to your daughter's wishes about what I should wear to my wedding?" Alison couldn't prevent an emotional quiver from lacing her voice.

"No, no, of course not. I misspoke. I shouldn't have said deal-breaker. I just meant . . . well, Poppy suggested we put our wedding off until after her baby is born. If I'd known she was pregnant, I would have incorporated her due date into our larger schedule. It's not as if you and I are in a hurry, right?"

"True. But we have booked the hotel and sent out Save the Date cards. In September the weather will be perfect for our wedding and for guests coming to and going from the island. Your assistant has done a lot of work already, and we need to consider *all* the family. I'm sure we'll be able to find a solution to the gown problem."

"Right." David nodded. "You're right."

"And if we wait until after Poppy has her baby . . . well, the Wauwinet closes in the winter. We're looking at next spring."

"You've got a point," David admitted, and he didn't look happy when he said it.

"I'm exhausted," Alison said. *And I'd like to punch a hole in the wall,* she thought, but smothered her anger. "Let's talk to the girls this week. We'll get it settled."

"Sure." David turned off his bedside lamp and slid down onto his pillow.

Alison did the same. And she was the one to lean over and kiss David good night. And then they both turned on their sides, lying back-to-back, staring at the dark.

From: Alison
To: Jane and Felicity
Subject: Wedding frocks

David said Poppy's worried about wearing a knee-length dress at our wedding because she has terrible varicose veins from her pregnancy. Says that by September, the veins will look like worms crawling up her legs. She would like to wear a long gown and she wants us all to wear long gowns so she isn't the odd man (woman) out.

Advice? We all want this to be a happy family event.

Love, Mom

From: Felicity
To: Jane and Mom
Subject: Worms

I know how she feels. I don't get varicose veins, but toward the end of my pregnancies, my hair got thin and oily and I got blotches on my face that went away after the baby was born. Does she get blotches on her face?

I'm thinking about possible alternatives to short/long gowns.

xo Felicity

From: Jane
To: Mom and Felicity
Subject: Really?

Mom. This is *your* wedding. Poppy can't dictate what you or we wear. We have already chosen our dresses. She is David's attendant, not yours. I thought she was a smart executive for David's firm. She sounds like a little girl trying to get her own way.

xoJ

From: Alison
To: Jane and Felicity
Subject: Wedding

You both know I'm not as technologically advanced as you are, but I worry TERRIBLY about anyone else ever accidentally seeing these emails and I would be extremely grateful if we could discuss this issue without calling names or casting aspersions.

Love, Mom

• • •

Jane and Scott had agreed to meet at Amarela for dinner. Jane knew they weren't going for the excellent food and heady Brazilian drinks made with cachaça. They both wanted to talk and they knew they would behave more calmly out in public, but if they raised their voices, no one in the restaurant would notice, even if Jane stood up and socked Scott in the nose.

Not that she would.

But she kind of wanted to. Once again, when she returned from Nantucket, Scott had been obsessed with work, and grumpy because of it. She'd seen him through these intense work periods before, and he'd lived with her when she went through them, when sometimes a case got so sticky and complicated and huge and full of details that her head felt it would explode if she had to recall one more minor point. It was like cramming for exams. Afterward, Jane or Scott would collapse with relief, sleep for ten hours and eat the most delicious—and artery-clogging—food they could find. Their sense of humor would return. And their sensuality.

Scott was in one of those phases now, and she knew not to press him. On the other hand, she'd heard tales of woe from career-oriented friends who had trouble getting pregnant, and she worried about that. She was thirty-two and wanted as much time as possible to try.

She got to the restaurant before he did and was shown to a wonderful quiet table in the side room. She studied her phone—it was amusing, how all the people alone at the other tables were looking at their phones—and caught her mother's latest email about the great gown debate.

"Hi, babe." Scott came to their table and leaned to kiss her cheek before sitting down.

"Hi," Jane said, smiling. She was completely aware of how women's heads turned to watch him stride through the room, this tall, slender, dark-haired handsome man in a pinstripe suit.

Scott sat across from her. "Have you ordered our drinks?"

"Not yet. I was waiting for you."

Scott waved the waiter over and ordered their drinks. "You're looking really beautiful tonight, honey. I think those days on the island did you good."

Her breath caught with surprise. He was giving her an opening into the whole summer-event discussion.

"Thanks! I got a tan. And honestly, it's so relaxing, walking on the beach, listening to the waves crash, feeling the sun on my shoulders."

Scott leaned back in his chair and studied Jane. "How's work going?"

Jane shrugged. "It's good. It's fine. Same old, same old, reading codes and small print until my eyes cross."

"Are you bored with it all?"

Jane took a moment to enjoy her drink. Scott might be overwhelmed with legal matters, but he was here with her now, and as relaxed as he'd been in a long time.

"Not bored at all," she told him. "It's routine, and you know how I like routine."

Scott smiled, and she knew that particular smile well.

Well, there you go, Jane said to herself, *you've walked right into his trap.*

"I do know you like your routine, Jane. That's why I'm surprised at all the changes you're suggesting."

One of the things she loved most about Scott was his mind. He was brilliant and cunning. But so was Jane. They had enjoyed sparring matches before, but none had mattered to her as much as this one. First, she had to decide which change to discuss. Spending their vacation on Nantucket. Or having a child. The Nantucket matter was a kind of taster for the main course. She would gladly give up Nantucket and go hiking with him if he would agree to have children.

But after all, this was not a legal conflict concerning massive corporations. This was about her life. Their lives. Their lives together.

"So. I'm suggesting—*no.*" She folded her hands on the table.

"Scott, I *want* to have children. Maybe just one child. Probably just one child, because I will also want to keep working, at least part-time. I could find the name of a wonderful nanny from our friends or someone at the office. My mother might even come to stay and help. You wouldn't have to change your routine. And we would have a child of our own."

"You've given this a lot of thought."

"That's true. You know I love you. I love our life together. But I'm sure it could be enriched immeasurably if we had a child."

"And I'm just as certain that our lives together would be ruined."

They stared at each other, deadlocked.

The waiter appeared at that moment, took their orders, and diplomatically disappeared.

"Here's what I think, Jane, and hear me out." Scott leaned forward, speaking in a low but firm tone. "I think that when you spend time with your mother and your sister, you fall under some kind of *spell*. You forget who you are. You forget who *we* are. You want to stop being you and be more like them. You lose your edges and blur into them. You're not the Jane I know and love."

"Wow. I had no idea you thought that. You'll have to give me a moment to think about it." She sipped her drink while she reflected on his words. "Okay, so first, you need to remember that you're an only child. Your parents were both undemonstrative. They sent you to boarding school when you were twelve. So you don't have the experience of, as you put it, *blurring* into your family. You're one of the most self-contained people I know."

Scott nodded. "I would agree with that."

"Well, fine, but I don't see that as a good thing. People are *meant* to 'blur' into each other. That doesn't take anything away from you. It adds to you. It adds depth, dimension to your life, your spirit."

"You couldn't wait to get away from your sister. You told me she drove you crazy with all her little princess ways."

"Yes. Yes, I did say that, and I meant it. But I love her even so, and I loved her then, even when I hated her. That's what families

are like. Well, some families. Some families are terribly dysfunctional, but most families, even the dysfunctional ones, are part of
what helps us understand the world. Helps us feel at home in the
world.

"The thing is only *now* am I realizing how lucky I was with my
family. I know when I met you, I told you they drove me crazy, and
often they still do, but the older I get, the more I appreciate having
those two women as *my* women. My family."

"You've never talked this way before."

"I don't suppose I've ever understood this before." She smiled
at Scott and reached for his hand. "Honey, I feel like you've just
reached into my heart and opened a new door."

Scott smiled. "I think that's the cachaça's magic, not mine."

"I've grown up," Jane mused aloud. "Mother has grown older,
and Felicity has grown up, too. We used to be so competitive. Not
so much now. And it's true, being around Felicity's children has cast
a spell over me—"

Scott pulled his hand away.

Jane pretended not to notice. "—but I've been wanting a child
long before I went to Nantucket. Even though I know the time will
come when our child will be longing to escape from us as much as I
was when I was a teenager."

"*Our* child. You're speaking as if it's already decided."

Jane gave her husband her best winning smile. "Well?"

"It's not. Of course it's not already decided. Or, if you want to be
clear, it was decided before we got married, when we agreed with
each other that we didn't want children."

Her smile vanished. "So, I want a child, and you don't. What
shall we do?"

"Well, first of all, Jane, I want you to promise you won't sneak
us into parenthood."

"What do you mean?"

"I mean, don't stop taking the pill and just *'forget'* to tell me.
Don't trick me."

"Do you think I would do that? God, Scott, that's insulting! And

I've never been a sneak." Jane felt hot tears spring to her eyes. "I don't know how you can say such a thing to me."

"That's how I feel when *you* say you want a child. And please don't cry. That's unfair. And it won't change my mind."

"You've just moved my heart from open to shut at warp speed," Jane said, trying to calm herself. "First you opened me up, let me get all mushy, then you knocked me down. Good legal trick, Scott, but I don't think I've ever felt as distant from you as I do now. I don't think I've ever disliked you as much."

"Back at you," Scott said.

Jane's jaw dropped.

The waiter appeared with their appetizers. The food was beautifully prepared and displayed, but Jane wasn't hungry. She was stunned, she was horrified at Scott's words, which seemed much more insulting and bitter than hers. She'd never believed she could *hate* Scott, but that was how she felt. She hated him. If she were any other woman, she'd toss down her napkin and storm off. She'd never stormed off in her entire life.

Scott took up his knife and fork and ate. Jane sat with her hands in her lap, focusing on taking deep breaths. She knew he could do this, flip a switch and move from an argument to the next thing, eating or falling asleep, as if he were an automaton. But she also knew how she could touch him, how she could bring him to her, how they could be together. This was not a dispute over legal matters. This was deeply personal. Maybe she'd done it all backward. Maybe if he spent some time with her on the island . . . Maybe if he saw Felicity's children, and Poppy's, too, he'd be charmed. He'd fall under their spell, too.

"I don't want to feel distant from you, Scott." She spoke quietly, as if coaxing a lion to lie down. "You are *my person*. My life is with you. I don't think I was under my family's spell. I think it was more the magic of Nantucket. So much light and air and space, and the ocean is so vast and natural, well, of course it's natural, but it's natural in a way that gives me perspective on life. It's as if the ocean is a gift, a continual gift, making the ordinary into the miraculous."

"It certainly makes you eloquent," Scott said, giving her a small smile.

So she had brought them out of their deadlock. She hadn't succeeded in convincing him to have a child. But maybe she could convince him to come to the island. "I wish you'd come see it with me. I wish you'd come for just a couple of days. We could walk on the beach. We could kayak or sail . . ."

"All right, Jane, I'll go to Nantucket with you. For a weekend. On one condition. That you don't say even one word about us having a child."

"You drive a hard bargain," Jane told him.

"I've been told that before," he said. "Now eat your bolinhos. They're delicious."

twelve

Noah was at his office. Alice was at day camp. Luke was trailing around behind Felicity as she performed her normal Monday tasks. Sweeping the kitchen floor. Making the beds. Doing the laundry. She wished Luke would play with his Legos, heaven knew he had enough, but Luke was a sociable kid and some days he couldn't be happy without someone near. So she sang nonsense songs while she worked, children's songs she'd learned when she was a child that were still sung by children.

"The ants go marching one by one, hoorah, hooray . . ."

She'd put in a load of children's clothes—how many thousands of children's socks did she wash in a week? She went into the master bathroom and hauled her clothes and Noah's and their bedsheets and dumped them into her wicker laundry basket.

"The ants go marching two by two, hoorah, hooray . . ."

When her cell buzzed, she checked the caller ID. Noah! He almost never called her during the day.

Happily, she answered, "Hey, baby."

"Felicity? This is Ingrid Black. Noah asked me to tell you that he left a folder on his desk in his house. He'd like you to bring it here right away."

Felicity sank down onto the edge of the bathtub, breathless with shock. Why did *Ingrid* have Noah's private phone? And who was *she* to speak to Felicity in such autocratic tones?

"Felicity, are you there?"

"Yes. Yes, I'm here," Felicity answered faintly. All sorts of responses were swirling through her mind and she knew she'd better not say any of them. "I'll bring the folder in. Can you tell me what it says, or what color, so I'm sure to bring—"

"It's in his leather portfolio that he always carries. You don't need to read anything on it, just pick it up and bring it to us."

So now it was "bring it to *us*"?

"I'll be there as soon as I can." Felicity killed the call before Ingrid could say another word.

She found the leather folder in the middle of Noah's desk. Because Ingrid had told her not to read anything, she took the time to read through some of the papers, which were filled with numbers and graphs and charts and seemed deathly boring.

"Come on, Luke, we're going for a ride to Daddy's office!" She took him out to his car seat, dropped her enormous bag and Noah's folder on the passenger seat, and started the SUV.

Her phone buzzed again.

"Yes?" Felicity said warily.

Ingrid said, "Felicity, don't worry about bringing it in to the building. I'll be waiting at the door, watching for you. I'll come out and get it."

"Oh, don't worry about that," Felicity said sweetly. "I'll have Luke carry it in to Noah. Luke loves coming to his daddy's office." Once again she killed the connection.

Noah's office was on a ring road off Route 128, eight lanes of frustrated drivers going eighty miles an hour. Felicity hated it, but put a happy DVD in for Luke and drove carefully in the slow lane. The trip there and back would use up the entire morning, so she decided to change her plans and stop by Suze's house on the way home. Luke could play with Suze's little girl, and Suze would love hearing about what a bossy cow Ingrid was.

She could have taken the circle drive that led to the front door of the old brick building that Noah and his partners had bought from a failed stationery supply company.

But if she did that, she guessed Ingrid would rush out and snatch the folder before Felicity could get Luke undone from his car seat. So she drove around the building and parked in a free space in the employees' parking lot. She gave Luke the folder to carry as they went inside. Felicity knew the layout of the company because three years before—before Ingrid had even been hired—Noah and his partners, the twenty-year-old boy geniuses with prodigious chemistry skills and few hygienic abilities, had shown Felicity and his investors through the building, focusing on the labs, so spotlessly clean and sparkling with instruments that cost more than jewels.

Noah had been full of hope then. He had seemed *younger*. He had finished his Ph.D. at MIT, and with the help of friends, Go-FundMe, and his parents' money, had started his company Green Food. He was energetic and optimistic. These days he was simply exhausted, Felicity thought, dealing with reports and government-issued guidelines and the excruciatingly slow process of chemical trials.

Luke had been inside the building several times over the years, so when they arrived in the main hallway, Felicity squatted down at eye level with her son.

"Lukey, would you like to take this folder to your daddy's office?"

Luke nodded, his entire chubby body jumping up and down with excitement.

"Off you go, then. Be careful. Don't drop it. Do you remember where Daddy's office is? Okay, sweetie—wait, no running!"

But Luke was already hurtling himself through the hall, carrying the folder in both hands. Felicity followed behind him. They rounded a corner and saw, a short distance away, Noah's office. Its walls were glass, so Felicity could see Noah's desk and computer and chairs, and no Noah. In front of his office, standing beside her desk like a guard to the inner sanctum, stood Ingrid.

Ingrid wore black. She always wore black, probably because she thought it made her look chic or professional. Or because she thought it hid her extra weight, Felicity thought uncharitably.

"Hi, Ingrid," Felicity said. "We've brought Noah's folder."

Ingrid ignored Felicity and bent over to face Luke. She held out her hand for him to put the folder in. "Hi, Luke. Thank you for bringing the folder. Would you like a sugar doughnut?"

Luke froze. Felicity knew her son was weighing the pleasure of presenting the folder to his father against the pleasure of having a sugar doughnut—a treat not allowed at home.

"I have to give this to Daddy." Luke clutched the folder to his chest.

"I'm sorry, sweetie," Ingrid cooed, "but Daddy's in a meeting. I'll take it to him." She reached out for it.

Luke took a few steps back. "It's for Daddy."

Go Luke! Felicity thought. "Hi, Ingrid," Felicity said, "it's so nice to see you again. Could you tell us what room my husband is in? I'm sure he'd be pleased to have his son bring him his folder. And I'll tell Luke to be fast like the wind."

Ingrid stood to face Felicity. "This is an important meeting. I really don't think Noah would want to be interrupted."

"It can't be *that* important," Felicity said. "Noah didn't mention it this morning, and he had no trouble falling asleep last night. He always has to take an Ambien the night before an important meeting." *Subtext: I sleep with the man.*

"Oh, dear," Ingrid said, pretending to soften, but with a steely glint in her eyes giving her away, "all I can say is that he asked me expressly not to be disturbed."

Felicity almost laughed, from nervous tension and from the absurdity of the situation. She felt like she and Ingrid were two stags clashing antlers, although wasn't it the males who did that?

"Daddy!" Luke yelled and took off running down the hall.

Felicity turned to see Noah walking toward them.

"Luke! You brought me my folder! Thank you!" Noah lifted his son up in his arms and carried him toward Felicity and Ingrid. He stopped next to Felicity and kissed her cheek. "Thanks for driving out here, hon. I know it interrupts your day."

"We're glad to do it, aren't we, Luke?" Felicity said, smiling.

"Ingrid's going to give me a sugar doughnut!"

"What?" Noah asked.

"Ingrid kindly offered to give Luke a sugar doughnut," Felicity said.

"I don't think we have any doughnuts," Noah told his son. "But we have bananas and apples. Want a banana?"

"I have a sugar doughnut in my bag," Ingrid said.

"Well, then, I suppose . . . but you know how I feel about sugar, Ingrid." Noah set his son on the floor. "I've got to get back to the meeting." He walked off, carrying his folder.

"Here's the doughnut, Luke," Ingrid said, reaching into her bag and handing it toward the little boy.

Felicity intercepted it. "We'll wait until he's strapped into his car seat. Otherwise, you'll have crumbs all over the floor. Luke, what do you say to Ingrid?"

"Thank you," Luke said, not entirely convincingly because he didn't have his hands on the doughnut yet.

Felicity did a one-arm pickup of Luke, tucked him onto her hip, and with the doughnut in the other hand, she headed back to the parking lot, smiling all the way.

. . .

Alison had never spent much time with Poppy before, and in all honesty, she never wanted to. She understood that David's daughter's arrogance and hard edge came from being the vice president of a large company. Jane was like that herself, often. But Alison needed to talk this over with someone before she called Poppy and discussed wedding gowns. Her daughters were busy with their own lives, plus it seemed unfair to Poppy to keep talking to Jane and Felicity about Poppy, and David would think they were ganging up against Poppy, which maybe they kind of were . . . so she asked her best friend, Margo, to meet her at Boston's Legal Sea Foods for lunch.

Over white wine and wild-caught salmon, she explained the situation. She knew Margo would laugh. During the thirty years of their friendship, they'd seen each other through divorces, deaths, and rebelling—Margo had called them *revolting*—teenagers. This, a disagreement about gowns for Alison's third wedding, seemed trivial in comparison.

"But it's not trivial," Alison insisted. "I don't need Poppy to *love* me, but I'd like to think we could like each other. She's a grown woman, she has children and a high-powered career. I can't understand why she's making such fuss about the length of her gown."

"You know what people say," Margo told her. "It's never about the gown."

"Well, what does *that* mean?"

"Think about it. Maybe Poppy will never be friendly. You're taking her mother's place."

"Her mother died—"

"*Still.* Before you, Poppy was the number one female in her father's life. Now she's pushed back to number two. And not only does she have to share her father with you, you're bringing along two pretty daughters."

Alison shook her head. "I thought when David said he'd have Heather take care of everything that I could handle an exciting wedding. But I'm doing things all out of order. Now I've got to deal with Poppy about the gown, and we haven't even approached the subject of flower girls and their dresses."

"Well, there you are," Margo said, lifting her hands. "Ask her about her daughter, if she'd like to be head flower girl and what the flower girls should wear. That will give her some control over the wedding, and she might be more reasonable about the gown."

"Hm. But what will Felicity think about that?"

"Who's the older of the two?"

"Daphne, Poppy's daughter. She's eight."

"So there's your reason—"

"But shouldn't the bride get to choose the flower girls? Aren't flower girls the *bride's* attendants?"

"Well, right. But why not choose Daphne? That will make a kind of bridge between your family and David's."

"That's an optimistic way to see it," Alison said. "I'll think about it."

Poppy told Alison she was too busy for lunch, but if she could come to the Belmont park playground at five, Poppy would meet her there and they could talk while her children played.

Alison brought graham crackers and cartons of juice for everyone, and when Poppy said, "I'll take those and give them to the kids later," Alison smiled and let Poppy take them. She felt like a dog rolling over on her back, showing her vulnerable tummy.

They settled on a bench in the shade. For a few moments, they watched Daphne and Hunter run for the slides and monkey bars.

"Your children are adorable," Alison said.

"Thanks."

Alison dove right in. "I wanted to ask you, Poppy, whether you'd like to have Daphne be head flower girl for the wedding."

Poppy didn't gush or even smile. "Is that appropriate?"

"Appropriate?"

"Aren't the flower girls part of the bride's side?"

"Well, yes, I suppose, although I haven't read a rule book. But you know, my wedding to David is more about a wonderful celebration. We can kind of throw the rule book away." When Poppy didn't respond, Alison continued, "And I'm hoping my grandchildren and David's will become friends."

Still watching her children, Poppy said, "That depends on how my father changes his will."

Alison straightened her back. "I don't understand."

"Dad's told us he's changing his will. He wants to be certain that you're *taken care of* in case he dies before you." Poppy snapped her head around to glare at Alison. "And of course he will die before you, it's a statistical reality that men die before women."

"Poppy, believe me, I hope I die before David. I can't imagine being happy without him. But also, David and I have never discussed his will."

"I know. He said you're all airy-fairy about money."

"Your father said I'm *'airy-fairy about money'*?"

Poppy sighed loudly. "He might not have used those exact words, but he doesn't think you care about money."

"Well, I don't! I mean, of course I do, but I'm perfectly fine financially and my needs are modest. Please don't think I'm marrying your father for his money. I've never cared that much about wealth, and at my age, I've learned what's important and it's not money. I never imagined I'd meet such a wonderful man and fall so deeply in love. It's almost miraculous that he feels the same way about me. Money simply doesn't come into it."

Poppy rolled her eyes. "So my father's becoming as fiscally irresponsible as you. I think you should talk to him about all this."

"I think you and Ethan and I should talk to David together."

Poppy relaxed. "All right. We'll do that."

Alison played with her engagement ring and tried to gather her thoughts.

"Poppy, I really wanted to talk to you about your gown for the wedding."

"Good. Dad told you why you need to wear a long gown?"

"No," Alison responded calmly, "he told me why *you want* to wear a long gown. I've already chosen my gown and had it altered to fit. I'm sorry I didn't speak with you about this before, but it was only a few weeks ago that I talked to my own daughters about their dresses. Everything's happened so fast."

"It sure has," Poppy agreed sourly.

Not to be derailed, Alison continued, "So I've gone through some bridal magazines, and checked on some websites, and you know these days, anything goes."

Alison reached into her bag and took out several bright pages torn from magazines. She tried to hand them to Poppy. Poppy didn't take them.

"So . . . you see, on this page, the attendants are wearing four different lengths of dresses. And here, an attendant is wearing gorgeous palazzo pants. You could wear those with an expandable waistband so you'd be comfortable. And a beautiful tunic over them."

Poppy actually turned her head and looked at the page. She took it in her hand. "You're right. Something like this might work."

Alison was so relieved to hear those words she nearly fell off the bench.

"But there's another problem," Poppy said.

Dear Lord, what now? Alison thought.

"I don't want to wear pink. It doesn't look good on me, not with my strawberry-blond hair."

Alison was prepared for this. "Then don't wear pink, Poppy. I mean, your father and your brother are wearing tuxes. You're really an attendant for your father, so you could wear black."

Poppy met Alison's eyes, squinting as if to read her motives for this suggestion. "Hm," Poppy said finally. "Yes. I think I'd like to wear black to your wedding."

thirteen

Later that day, Alison made vodka tonics with slices of lime and glaciers of ice, and carried them into David's study. The humid heat was unusual for the middle of June, making people cranky. The north side of their Boston apartment was shaded by an enormous maple tree, and with the curtains drawn and the air conditioner on, it was the coolest room in the house. They sat in club chairs on either side of the fireplace now decorated with a large vase of silk flowers.

"Thanks. This is exactly what I need," David said.

"I know," Alison agreed. "I'm not a fan of hot weather, no pun intended."

"How was your meeting with Poppy?"

"We had a good conversation. She's going to wear a pantsuit, in black, in keeping with you and Ethan."

"Black on a woman? That sounds odd."

"That's only because we're so old," Alison teased. "Black is the chic new color in wedding attire these days."

"As long as Poppy and you are happy, I'm good with it." David took a long drink and relaxed into the cushions.

"Poppy did raise an issue with me," Alison continued, shifting to get comfortable in her chair as she brought up an uncomfortable topic. "She's concerned about how you're going to change your will."

David looked surprised. "She told you that?"

"Yes. In fact, when I said I hoped our families would be friends, she said that depended on how you change your will. She said that you think I'm fiscally irresponsible and that I'm causing you to be fiscally irresponsible, too." To her surprise, Alison began to cry. "Oh, David, I hate saying all this, I feel like a grade-school tattle-tale. And you know I don't care about money, I have money, not like *your* money, for sure, but I don't want you to feel you have to leave me any money, because I don't want to even think about you leaving me!"

David leaned over to take her hand. "Hey. It's all right. I should have spoken with you before about this. I apologize. Poppy can be pigheaded, I know that, and that's exactly why I told her I was going to change my will. I haven't done it yet, but I told her I was going to, partly because it's true and partly as a kind of kick in the butt. She's got to learn to delegate, especially now that she's going to have another baby. She takes too much on herself. She tends to think she's the only one who can do anything right. I think that's one reason Ethan has little to do with the company."

"I understand what you're saying, David, but this somehow leaves me caught in the middle. As long as Poppy thinks you're leaving me more money than she thinks I should have, she's going to dislike me for it, and my girls, too."

To her shock, David put down his drink and paced the floor. "I should have seen this coming. Poppy is brilliant and ambitious, which makes her perfect for leading the company, but she's con-

flated my will and our wedding. And I don't like this. Not at all.
She's a clever girl, but not so clever she can manipulate me."

Alarmed by his tone, Alison stood up. "David, calm down. And
really, I have no idea what you're talking about."

"Poppy told you that whether or not her family and yours could
be friends depends on how I write my will. Is that correct?" Sparks
seemed to shoot from his eyes as he spoke.

"That's correct," she replied, keeping her voice soft.

"I'm going to have a talk with her about this."

Alison reached out her hand. "David, please. I'll feel terrible if
this causes a quarrel between you and your daughter. Really, don't
change your will, it's not necessary."

"It's absolutely necessary. You're going to be my wife. I hope I
live to a hale and hearty one hundred, but you are eight years
younger than I am. You are only fifty-five, and I want to provide for
you. It's also important that Poppy understands she cannot now or
ever tell me what to do."

Alison started to argue, then thought better of it. "Sweetheart,
please. Come to the breakfast room. I've made wonderful cold sal-
ads and garlic bread. We'll feel better when we've eaten."

That caught David's attention. *"A cold salad?"*

Alison laughed when she saw his expression. David was not a
salad kind of guy.

"It's mostly chicken and olives and potatoes," she told him. "It's
on a bed of lettuce, which you don't have to eat if you don't want to,
and there are some marinated green beans. I know you like those."
She kissed his cheek and led him out of the study, relieved to move
him away from his anger.

It was a challenging day. The children didn't want to play outside,
but if they stayed in the air-conditioned house, they didn't use up
all their energy. They became crazy and silly, running through the
house, accidentally knocking lamps over, spilling jigsaw puzzle

pieces. When Felicity finally got them in their rooms and on their beds, if not asleep, it was almost ten o'clock. Noah still had not come home. Impatient, Felicity called Noah's cell.

"I'm almost home," he said. "Pulling in the driveway now."

Felicity tried to shake off her irritation.

"Hi, hon," she greeted Noah when he came in. "Long day?"

"Long, but good. Really good. I think I've lined up another investor. A big one."

"Great! Have you had dinner?"

Noah stood at the hall table, flipping through the mail. Preoccupied, he said, "Yeah. Ingrid and I went out to Giaconda's."

"You went out to dinner with Ingrid?"

Noah caught the tension in Felicity's tone. "Yes, and I often go out to dinner with Ingrid. She's my personal assistant. She knows about everything that's going on. More, in some cases. We both have to eat sometime, so it only makes sense that we eat while we talk. Don't look that way, Felicity. You know Ingrid's an important part of the team. A crucial part, actually."

Felicity struggled to restrain her anger. Forcing a smile, she said, "Could you use a nice cold drink? It's been such a hot day."

"I'll take a beer, but I need a shower first." Noah headed up the stairs.

"You need a shower?"

Noah stopped dead, glaring down at Felicity. "Because it's hot—oh, come on, Felicity! You think I slept with Ingrid? For God's sake, why can't you get it, how hard I'm working? Ingrid is my *colleague*. Some things are more important than sex!" He stormed up the stairs.

While he showered, Felicity finished tidying the kitchen, a chore she usually enjoyed. No one bothered her there; she could be alone with her thoughts. She hadn't known that Noah often ate dinner with Ingrid, and it upset her, even though she knew what Noah had said was true. Ingrid *was* a crucial part of the team. She had both the scientific laboratory knowledge and the skill to use this knowledge for writing grants.

Still, a thread of worry wove through her thoughts. Felicity knew she had to keep her jealousy hidden.

By the time Noah came down, clean and relaxed, wearing only his boxer shorts, Felicity was smiling. Without speaking, they both headed to the den, the coolest room in the house.

"How were the kids today?" Noah asked.

"Insane," Felicity told him. "Well, Alice was okay. She played house and dress-up. But poor Luke. He's a ball of energy. It's too hot for him to spend much time outside, although I did set up the sprinkler and the water play table in the backyard."

"The forecast is for more of the same," Noah said.

"I know," Felicity said, moaning a little.

The next morning when her cell buzzed, Felicity was still in bed. Noah had gone to work and Felicity was letting the children watch cartoons on her computer.

"Hi, Filly," Jane said. "Listen, are you going to the island this weekend?"

"I hadn't planned on it."

"The Nantucket weekend forecast calls for sunshine, high seventies. You should come. Bring Noah."

"I don't know if Noah can get away."

"Tell him Scott's coming. The guys get along fairly well, don't you think?"

"I don't know, to be honest. They've never spent much time together. But if Scott's coming, then I think Noah will be more likely to come . . . let me talk to Noah tonight and get back to you."

"Come anyway with the children," Jane said. "Please?"

Felicity couldn't help feeling a rush of pleasure that her sister wanted to see her children. "I will."

Felicity threw back the covers and jumped out of bed. Suddenly the day seemed brighter. She was foolishly pleased that Jane wanted to see her and the children this weekend, and even more complimented that Jane thought Scott would like to see Noah. Scott and

Noah were as alike as A and Z, Scott so stiff and judgmental, Noah so earthy-crunchy, but maybe the island could work some magic. Certainly Jane had been warmer to Felicity when they were on the island than she had been in a long time.

As Felicity showered, she decided she'd take the kids to the Children's Museum today. It would be crowded, but the kids loved the exhibits and they could work off some of their energy.

She sang in the shower.

Noah didn't like her to phone him at work, so she waited until he came home to talk to him about Nantucket. As usual, he didn't get home until the children were in bed, but she had kept his dinner warm. She sat at the table with him, sipping a mug of green tea, when she brought up the idea.

"This weekend?" Noah said. "Sorry. Can't."

"Oh, sweetie, you work so hard. It would do you good to have a little fun in the sun."

Noah took another bite of his macaroni and cheese with lobster—one of his favorite meals. He sipped some wine. "I thought I'd put it on the calendar. I guess I forgot. Ingrid's birthday is Saturday, and we're taking her out to dinner."

Felicity bit her tongue. After a moment, she said, "Oh, well, then I should stay home, too. I'll get a babysitter."

"No need. Spouses aren't invited."

"Spouses aren't invited," Felicity echoed. "Why not?"

"Because you all would be miserable and bored while we make inside jokes and talk about work. You and the other wives shouldn't come. You don't *get* what we do. You don't understand how important it is."

"But I *do*—"

"And I'm aware that you don't like Ingrid, so why would you even want to attend her birthday party?"

"I've never been unpleasant to Ingrid!"

"No, but it's clear that you don't like her." Noah leaned forward. "Be honest. *Do* you like her?"

Felicity toyed with her mug. "All right, fine. I don't. Because she's a woman who gets to spend so much time with you. More time than I get most weeks." She looked up at Noah. "I guess I'm jealous."

"That's ridiculous."

Felicity waited for her husband to elaborate, to tell her there was no kind of competition at all, but Noah simply finished his meal, tossed back the last drop of his wine, and set his napkin on the table.

"Noah, stop." Felicity seldom spoke this way to her husband. "Don't dismiss what I'm saying. I don't mean I'm worried about you doing anything . . . *romantic* . . . with her. I mean that the children hardly ever get to spend time with you. *I* hardly get to spend time with you."

"You shouldn't be jealous, Filly," Noah said, and his voice was softer. "Ingrid is a workhorse, and that's all. She's also a stockholder, so she has a lot to gain if we can get this off the ground and go public. The time I spend with her is all about work. You know, *I've told you*, these first few years will be crucial. Nothing less than saving the planet is at stake here."

Felicity bit her lip so she wouldn't smile. She loved Noah, she admired and adored him for his idealistic goals. At the same time, she found him slightly, maybe even embarrassingly, naïve. Noah took several science-oriented magazines, and from time to time Felicity read an article. She learned that he was not the only scientist working on "green food," and certainly not the most highly esteemed. She learned that the problems facing the future needed more than green food for the planet to be saved.

But after all, what did she really know? Noah attended a great many scientific conferences. He had to be as aware of his competition as she was. She knew she should prop him up, not bother him with minor issues.

"You're right, Noah. I do understand. But I wonder—couldn't

you come to the island some weekend? I've read that a vacation is helpful, even necessary. It allows the mind to rest and reboot. You haven't had a vacation for months."

Noah sighed. "Yes, I've read about that, too. You're right. Look, I'll try to clear off a weekend later this summer."

"Oh, Noah, thank you!" Felicity moved around the table to embrace Noah.

"Look," he said, pushing her away, "calm down. It's not definite yet. And I need a shower and bed. I'm beat."

"Of course," she said. And she removed her arms from around his shoulders, and began to take his dishes to the sink.

fourteen

Saturday morning, as Alison boarded the ten-seater plane from Boston to Nantucket, she gave the other passengers a quick glance, wondering if she knew any of them. And wondering if any one of them flying to the daydream island was as cranky about it as she was.

It wasn't that she didn't like people; she did. She loved her daughters, in spite of their occasional tendency to squabble. She adored her grandchildren. She felt real affection for Ethan, who wasn't coming this time, and she enjoyed Poppy's husband, Patrick, who was coming. She was fond of Poppy's two children, but she was nervous about any interaction with Poppy herself, because David hadn't yet found the time to discuss his will with Poppy. Felicity's husband wasn't coming, and Alison knew Felicity was sad about that, especially because Jane's husband was coming. But Alison was glad she'd have some time with Scott, who'd always seemed a bit aloof. Maybe she'd get to know him better this weekend.

Really, she was just a bit angry with David for making her face this weekend alone. He claimed the necessities of work, and when Alison had asked, reasonably and pleasantly, why *Poppy* wasn't doing the work, David had simply replied, "Exactly."

Alison felt like her life had become a chessboard with the pieces all tossed up into the air, landing in incomprehensible patterns.

Then she saw the island, an emerald jewel set in the sapphire sea. Each time she flew in, she was mesmerized by the sight of the shoals extending out from the island, and the three lighthouses, and the harbor where sailboats clustered. A ferry was slowly pulling away from the island and into the deeper waters on its way to the mainland.

She was being foolish. Negative. It was a glorious summer day, she was engaged to a man she adored, and their families were becoming friends. Of course there would be a certain amount of discord—they were all human beings, after all. What Alison needed to do was to focus on being a good hostess. She'd already spoken with the housekeeper about fresh sheets on the beds and fresh towels in the bathrooms. Alani had also stocked the cupboards and refrigerator with the basic necessities. Later, Alison would go off to Sayle's to see what fish was fresh and to buy fresh vegetables at Moors End. Once she was back on the island, she knew she'd feel more optimistic.

And with the children came the bliss. Alice, Luke, Daphne, and Hunter thundered into the house with whoops of joy at being back on the island. Felicity's two threw themselves at Alison, hugging her so hard she almost fell over, while Daphne, child dictator, waited impatiently behind them, reminding them that they had to change into their swimming suits *now.*

"You can't go to the water yet," Poppy said. "I'm exhausted from the trip."

"I'll go down with them," Felicity volunteered.

"And I'll go," Jane said.

"I'll go, too," Scott said. "Just let me change my clothes. Unless you need help with something, Alison."

"No, I'm fine. Please, go, swim."

"Thanks." Jane kissed her mother. She was bubblier, brighter than usual, perhaps because Scott was with her.

"There are beach towels on the table on the deck," Alison called. To Poppy, she said, "Now that you're all here, I'm going off to buy fresh veggies. Is there anything you need?"

"Just a nap."

"Yes, of course, Poppy. Have a nice long rest."

Alison had spent some time researching recipes and planning to be ready to feed the family three times a day. She decided she'd cook what she enjoyed cooking and buy the rest. She couldn't expect everyone to like the same things, so she made sure there was a variety. She bought fresh tuna to marinate in olive oil, ginger, and garlic for grilling, and crimson vine-ripened tomatoes, and Bartlett's potato salad and macaroni salad, and newly picked carrots, which she'd cook with butter and a touch of brown sugar to tempt the children, and an enormous bag of peas in the pod. The children loved popping open the pods and eating the fresh sweet peas. A fruit torte from the Nantucket Bake Shop. She bought ice cream bars for the children, and she stopped at the liquor store to stock up for the adults. At the last moment, she tossed in several bags of chips.

When she returned to the house, she was surprised to see Scott waiting to help her unload.

"Oh, you don't have to do this, Scott, I can manage," she protested.

"I think I really have to do this," Scott said with a twinkle in his eye. "You've bought so much food, and you're so terribly old, I'd feel guilty if I allowed you to carry all these bags without my help."

Alison cocked her head and studied her son-in-law. "You're not a beach person," she concluded.

Scott grinned. "I guess not. I did try. I watched the children so they wouldn't drown. Everyone else is down there now, tossing the beach ball around. They're like an amoeba, everyone in one big blob."

Grinning, Alison nodded toward the hatch. "Those bags are the heaviest. Since I'm so terribly old, I'll go on in and be ready to unpack."

While Scott brought in the groceries, Alison went out on the deck to look down at the beach. Sure enough, everyone was engaged in some kind of spontaneous game that seemed like a combination of volleyball and football. She could hear the squeals and laughter, and she smiled, wanting to snap a memory of this, her family and David's, playing on the beach. Maybe the weekend wouldn't be so bad, after all.

Late in the afternoon, the "Beach People," as Alison and Scott nicknamed the others, came trudging up to the house, sunburned and hungry and tired. They all took turns getting the sand off in the outdoor shower before running into the house for a proper wash and scrub, and soon the scent of strawberry-kiwi shampoo drifted through the house. Alison sent the children down to the lawn to shell and eat the peas, while the adults relaxed on the deck with cool drinks.

Scott offered to grill the tuna, Jane and Felicity took over preparing everything else, and finally all ten people were at the table, with Luke sitting on pillows, squeezed between Felicity and Alison.

"Too bad David and Ethan couldn't come this time," Felicity said.

"And too bad Noah couldn't come," Alison answered. "Someday we'll get everyone here at the same time."

Jane laughed. "I can't even imagine how much fun that will be."

Or not, Alison thought.

Patrick spoke up. "So, Scott, Poppy tells me you're a lawyer."

"That's right," Scott began. "I work for—"

"Eeeek!" Luke screamed, giggling, and slid sideways off the pile of pillows, landing on the floor.

The other children giggled like hyenas.

"We need books," Alison said, and went off to gather a pile while Felicity removed the pillows and lifted her son onto the pile of books Alison had substituted.

Scott opened his mouth to speak again, but Felicity's daughter, Alice, announced in her clear, high, confident voice, "I'm going to set up a website called *Now, Please*. It will be a list of things that need to be invented."

"Really?" Jane asked. "For example?"

"Well, our teacher keeps telling us we need to save the world, and that even though we're only in first grade, we should try to help. So far I have two ideas. The first is that we shouldn't use plastic straws because we need to stop using so much plastic, but *everyone* uses plastic straws, so someone should invent a permanent accordion straw that we'd use over and over again. It could be made from something like aluminum. It would be our own personal straw. It could live folded small in a little aluminum egg that would fit in our pockets. At the end of the day, we'd stick it in the dishwasher and it would be good to go for the next day."

"Alice," Patrick said, "that's a brilliant idea. You've given it a lot of thought, haven't you?"

Daphne, miffed at the sight of her own father praising Alice, quickly spoke up. "We *all* had to think of inventions like that on Earth Day, *back in the first grade*."

"What was your idea?" Jane inquired.

"I suggested we use leaves instead of toilet paper. That's what people did for thousands of years. That would save our forests—"

"Wipe my bum with leaves?" Daphne's brother, Hunter, shrieked.

"Bum!" Luke echoed. "Leaves!"

The two boys exploded with laughter, yelling, "Wipe my bum

with seaweed!" and other hilarious variations, rocking and tilting in their chairs until, no surprise, Luke fell off the chair again. This time, he snatched the tablecloth in an attempt to keep from falling. He pulled his own plate and glass onto the floor before Alison, seated next to Luke, managed to secure the cloth.

Poppy and Felicity removed both boys from the dining room table and set them in the kitchen with paper plates of food.

"I'm standing right here while you two bad little children eat," Poppy said. "Then you can play outside, but not before."

Felicity started to speak, then took a deep breath. It was always awkward, watching another mother discipline her own child. It seemed presumptive now. A small voice in Felicity's mind whined, *But your daughter, Daphne, started it by talking about leaves and toilet paper!* But she wanted her relationship with Poppy to be cordial, so she simply added, "Luke, you heard what Poppy said."

"Bum leaf," Luke whispered with a sly smile.

"That's enough," Felicity said sternly.

Later, Patrick and Scott watched the Red Sox in the den while Alison, Felicity, and Poppy put the children to bed. Jane stacked the dishwasher and wiped down the counters, taking her time. She hoped Scott was bonding with Poppy's husband. Patrick seemed like a good guy, and Jane appreciated that Patrick had taken the initiative and asked Scott about his work. Maybe they'd talk in the den. Maybe Patrick would tell Scott that children weren't always as frenzied as they'd been at the dining room table.

"Hey, sis." Felicity entered the room, carrying glasses from other parts of the house. She put them in the dishwasher. "Want to take a walk on the beach?"

"Honestly, I was hoping to take a walk on the beach with Scott."

"It looks like Scott is settled in for the night with the Red Sox and Patrick."

"Yeah. That's good, right? For the guys to get to know each other. Okay, yeah, let's take a walk," Jane agreed.

"Good. I have something I want to talk to you about."

"Should we tell the others we're going?"

"No. Let's just slip out the door now."

They padded, barefoot, down the steps from the deck and through the low shrubs to the expanse of beach. The sand was cool beneath their feet. For a while as they strolled in and out of the lazy waves, they chatted casually. They laughed about the boys and their silliness. They agreed that Alice's idea about a permanent accordion straw was brilliant, except it wouldn't really work. People, especially children, would lose their straws down the backs of chairs and between seats in cars.

They were silent for a few moments, and then Jane inhaled deeply. "I talked to Scott about children and he's being a real shit. We got into a terrible fight—in a restaurant, so I didn't shout or throw things. It's true, when we married we agreed we wouldn't have children. But I've changed my mind. And Scott won't even think about it. Honestly, he is so anal, so meticulous, so set in routine—"

"Pot, kettle," Felicity said.

"All right, I am, too. I admit it. But you can't do the kind of work we do without being fussy and exacting."

"Okay, let's think about this. Would you stop working if you had a baby?"

"Of course, for a while. Then maybe I'd work part-time. It means we won't have as much money, but truthfully? We're not paupers."

"Not to get into details, and please don't tell me how much money you make or I'm afraid I'd either kill you or drown myself right now, but could you live on only Scott's salary?"

"Not in New York. Not the way we want to live. Believe me, I've thought about this. Plus, I'm not sure I want to work only part-time. I *am* sure I don't want to stop working. I love what I do and I'm good at it. But when I see you holding little Luke after his bath, he smells so sweet, he's just lovely, and Alice, well, she's a pistol! Clever and beautiful. And I think, *I want one of those.*"

As they turned back toward the house, Felicity wrapped one arm around Jane and hugged her. She was almost ready to burst into tears at the thought of her brilliant, super-smart, hard-shelled sister expressing such sweet emotions about Felicity's children. Swallowing hard, she said, "But you know, Jane, it isn't always like that. It's never getting a good night's sleep and worrying constantly and dealing with more vomit than you saw even at college frat parties."

Jane burst out laughing. "Thanks for that image, Felicity! And please don't say all this to Scott, not that he'll ever talk to you or anyone about it. Okay, that's what's going on with me. It's not going to be solved soon, if ever, but it helps to talk about it. Now, what's your problem?"

"It's Ingrid," Felicity confided gloomily. "Noah's secretary, assistant, whatever she's called. Noah didn't come here this weekend because the office was giving Ingrid a birthday party. I know she's important for keeping his work on schedule, but she's so *possessive* of Noah. Half the time, when I phone Noah, Ingrid answers and tells me he's too busy to talk, she'll take a message. I want to say, *I'll give you a message, bitch.*"

"How old is she?"

"I'm not sure. Somewhere in her twenties, I guess."

"So, young. Is she pretty?"

Felicity shrugged. "I'm way prettier. But yeah, I guess she's okay-looking." She abruptly halted in the sand. "Do you think Noah's having an affair with her?"

"How could I know? You should talk to him about it. But also, you should google 'office wife.' That's become a real phenomenon. Actually, it probably has always been a problem. I've heard about it for years. The office wife knows all the daily details and trials and successes the man goes through with work. She shares all the in-jokes the wife doesn't even know about. She makes life easier for the man at work. Think about it. When he comes in for the day, she hands him his coffee, notices his new haircut, and says she'll deal with the call to the unhappy lawyer. Or whatever. She protects him. She makes a sweet, comfy nest for her boss. That's her job."

They began walking again. Felicity said, "I see. And when Noah comes home to me, he's got two noisy children, a leaking bathroom pipe, and a pile of household bills. But how can I change that? Noah wanted children as much as I did. He even wants more."

"I don't know. Maybe you should get a sitter and go on a date at least once a week."

"Yeah, we used to do that . . . good idea, Jane."

"And maybe you should hire cleaning help, once a week, so you're not so overwhelmed with housework. Maybe you could get out and treat yourself to a massage once a week, or a mani-pedi."

Felicity laughed. "I like the idea about cleaning help, but trust me, I'm not going to be in the market for a mani-pedi for a few more years. I'm lucky to find time to wash my hair." Spontaneously, she took her sister's hand. "I feel so much better after talking to you, Jane. I feel less gloomy about it all."

"Me, too. And all this helps, too." She gestured toward the ocean, the waves catching flashes of light from the setting sun.

fifteen

Sunday morning Patrick and Scott drove to the Downyflake and Cumberland Farms, returning with bags of doughnuts and cinnamon rolls and newspapers and magazines. Felicity and Poppy settled their children at the table with orange juice and pastries, then allowed them to play outside in the sprinkler while the adults sat on the deck, sipping coffee and reading. Poppy and Felicity were showing one another the newest styles in fashion and snorting with laughter, while Alison sipped her coffee and smiled at the sight of her daughter and David's becoming friends.

And then, bloodcurdling shrieks came from the yard.

"MOMMY!" Luke screamed.

All the adults rushed down the steps to find the four children in a tug-of-war over a large, deflated ride-on rubber whale.

"It's *mine*!" Luke screamed.

"No, it's *mine*!" Hunter yelled.

"*Our* daddy got it for *us* last year when we came here," Daphne bellowed.

"But you never even noticed it," Alice shrieked. "It was stuck under the steps and if Luke hadn't crawled under to get it, you wouldn't even know it was there."

"*I* saw it!" Luke cried. "*I* did! *I* crawled under the steps! *I* got it out!"

"Children, children!" Alison tried to get between the two boys. "Calm down. We can sort this out, we can make this fair for everyone."

"How are you going to do that?" Poppy snapped, hands on her hips.

"They could share," Alison suggested. "They could take turns."

"NO! It's *my* whale!" Hunter yelled, and with one final tug, he wrenched the long black rubber mass from Luke's hands.

Luke tried to get hold of it again. Hunter raised his arms and slammed Luke in the face with the whale.

"Ow!" Luke screamed, falling to the ground.

"Oh, my God," Felicity cried. "Luke's bleeding!" She knelt over her son. "Sweetie, let Mommy look at your forehead."

"No way can he be bleeding," Poppy said officiously. "That thing is only a piece of rubber."

"But it has two hard plastic tubes for blowing in the air," Patrick told her quietly. "I think one of the tubes made the wound."

Poppy shot daggers at her husband. "It's hardly a *wound*."

Jane took a moment to check out her husband's reaction to the quarrel. Scott had backed away from the group and stood watching with amazement, as if he'd never seen children fight before.

Alison took charge. "Felicity, take Luke and wash his cut. We've got ointment and Band-Aids in the downstairs bathroom. Patrick, would you please take the whale and fold it up again and return it to its home under the porch?"

"But it's *mine*," Hunter protested, bursting into tears.

"Hunter should apologize to Luke for hitting him," Jane said.

"He didn't mean to," Poppy argued. "He pulled it away and it was simply physics that caused the object to fly back. Hunter wasn't *aiming* at Luke."

"No one gets the whale right now," Alison pronounced sternly. "It's time the children went down to the beach for a swim."

Poppy glared at Alison.

Alison glared right back at her future daughter-in-law. "We should have one last swim. In a few hours we have to shower and pack and catch planes back to the real world."

Patrick agreed. "She's right. Come on, Daphne, Hunter. I'll race you to the water."

Poppy stood frowning.

Hunter dropped the whale and ran off, whooping. Luke gave the whale a long, covetous look. He saw his mother's face, and his grandmother's face, and his little shoulders sagged and he stayed away from the whale.

Felicity was proud of her son. "Come on," she said, taking his hand. "We'll look at your cut and then I'll swim with you. You, too, Alice."

Jane started to head for the water. She stopped, turning to her husband. "Aren't you coming in? For one last swim?"

"No, thanks," Scott said. "I'm going to shower and start packing."

"I'll go down with you, Jane," Alison said. "I could use a nice cooling dip right now."

As they flew back to New York, Jane and Scott didn't talk. Scott wore his earphones whenever he flew, with his phone set to the latest news or a podcast. He wore his earphones in the taxi to their apartment, too.

That was fine with Jane. She knew Scott's habits well. She had plenty of habits of her own and was uncomfortable breaking them. So she unpacked both their suitcases, started a load of laundry, and set her laptop on the kitchen table so she could check her email. She ordered in Thai from their favorite place and put together a small salad. She opened a bottle of pinot grigio. They would eat at six o'clock tonight, because Scott always watched *60 Minutes,* which came on at seven.

When the food delivery arrived, Scott said, "Smells wonderful."

So that was promising. Scott was in a good mood and eating would make him feel more relaxed. She kept his wineglass topped up.

As they ate, they idly discussed the latest news. When they were finished, she took a deep breath, said a little prayer, and approached the *children* topic with her husband.

"Did you enjoy Nantucket?" she asked.

Scott shrugged. "Lying on the beach is not my idea of fun. You know that. But it was great to see your mother again, and Patrick seems likes a good guy. I don't know how he can stand being married to Poppy. She's such a ballbuster."

"What? No! She's just hormonal." She started to add: *Because she's pregnant.* She bit her tongue.

"And Patrick's naturally laid-back. He's all about sports. He can name the stats on any of the Patriots or Red Sox for the past five years. I like him."

Encouraged by this, Jane said, "I know. And Daphne and Hunter are darling, aren't they?"

"*Darling?* God, no. They're little monsters."

Jane blinked. "Oh, I wouldn't say—"

"Well, I would. I saw Hunter aim that whale at Luke. That's bratty and mean. And neither one of his parents disciplined him."

Jane tried to explain. "It's hard when so many family members are around. They probably didn't want to embarrass Hunter by chastising him in front of everyone. Plus, Luke likes to tussle with Hunter. It makes him feel like a big boy."

"Well, I hope it put the idea of children for us out of your head. I don't have the patience for that kind of thing. And neither do you."

"Oh, but, Scott, didn't you love watching them when they were sweet and not fighting? And that was most of the time. Daphne and

Alice were so cute playing together down on the beach, making sand houses and people out of rocks."

Scott stared at Jane. "Sometimes I feel like I don't know who you are."

In defeat, Jane said, "I'm going to take a shower and go to bed."

Noah had said he didn't have time to drive down to Hyannis to pick up Felicity and the kids at the ferry. Alison had shown Felicity how she and her children could get home without the expense of flying to Boston—and it was quite an expense. Alice and Luke were up for an adventure, so they took the fast ferry to Hyannis, the bus to Boston, the T to Belmont, and a taxi to their house. Luke was goggle-eyed every moment of the trip, loving all the different vehicles and their sounds and vibrations. Alice read a book.

Felicity relaxed, replaying the weekend. The walk on the beach with Jane had been the high point of this trip. It had been a long time since she'd felt so close to her sister. Really, had she ever been so close to Jane? Growing up, they had never confided in each other. Jane had been almost unapproachable, busy with her own friends and her ambitions. Felicity had been thrilled to be drum majorette and queen of the senior prom, and yet all the time she'd been aware that Jane had been almost amused by such glories. And Felicity had been guilty, too, consumed with being the prettiest, the most popu-lar, the little queen bee of her own school hive. Jane's academic achievements were boring.

When Felicity married Noah and the children came along, Jane had been super generous, sending engraved sterling silver tooth-brush cups to celebrate their births and wonderful, expensive birth-day and Christmas gifts. Felicity had dutifully sent pictures of the kids, assuming they'd be of little interest to Jane, but now Felicity began to think that those photographs and the informal photos she emailed Jane might have inspired Jane to want children of her own. This weekend, Jane, perfect elegant Jane, seemed to enjoy Felicity's imperfect (but adorable) children. In turn, Felicity had provided a good sounding board for Jane and her desire to have babies of her own.

They were closer than they had ever been before. Could it be that in growing up they had cast off some of their own jealousies and small-mindedness? It was as if the years had worn away their defenses, insecurities, and differences, and now they were softer, open to the possibilities of a true friendship. Felicity smiled to herself. Sometimes the workings of the world astonished her.

The taxi stopped in front of their house. She paid the driver, who lifted out the luggage, and followed her children as they ran to the house. A car she didn't recognize, a red convertible, was parked across the street, and Felicity idly wondered who in the world was visiting her neighbor, an older, and rather eccentric, woman.

She opened her door. The children flew inside, screaming, "Daddy Daddy Daddy!" They always greeted their father with amazed adulation, as if he'd just beamed down from Mars.

Felicity set her duffel on the hall floor and stepped into her living room.

Noah was on the sofa. Ingrid was seated next to him.

Felicity's heart thumped so hard her entire body jerked.

In the five seconds it took her children to throw themselves at their father, Felicity noted first, that Noah and Ingrid were not touching. They weren't quite close enough to touch. Second, piles of paper towered on the coffee table, and they each had a Sharpie in hand. Third, Noah was wearing his reading glasses, which indicated that he was working.

"You're home early," Noah remarked from behind the tangle of his children's enthusiastic embraces.

"We had an adventure!" Luke told his father. "We went on the bus! We went on the T!"

In his excitement, Luke kicked Ingrid on the leg. Ingrid flinched but said nothing. Also, she didn't move away. She sat there, smiling at Felicity.

"Children, settle down," Felicity ordered. "Poor Daddy can't breathe." As Alice and Luke climbed off Noah, Felicity approached him and leaned down to kiss his mouth. "Hello, darling."

Noah was surprised enough to smile. Luke and Alice made gagging noises. While Noah was recovering, Felicity smoothly said, "Luke, Alice, let's have some manners, please. Say hello to Daddy's assistant, Ingrid. You've met Ingrid before."

"Hello, Ingrid," Alice and Luke chimed together.

"Hello, Luke, Alice," Ingrid responded. "Did you have fun on the island?"

Luke screamed a long "Yes!" while Alice reported, "It was excellent." Picking up her father's hand, she said, "We missed you, Daddy. Promise you'll come next time!"

"Promise promise promise!" Luke echoed, jumping up and down.

"We'll see."

Felicity picked up her wriggling son. "So sorry, Ingrid, about the interruption. I can tell you and Noah are working. Kids, come on, we've got to unpack your bags and put stuff in the laundry." *No one is as cool as I am,* Felicity told herself, leading her children from the room.

Of course she was shocked, jealous, *furious* to find Ingrid sitting on the sofa with Noah on a Sunday afternoon! Angry energy boiled up inside her and she wanted to strangle them both. She wanted to scream and hit something. But she was going to control herself. The best thing she could do was to act as if it didn't matter a bit to her that Ingrid had come to the house on a weekend when she, Felicity, Noah's wife, was away.

But oh, it mattered.

David was in Terminal C, waiting for Alison when her plane arrived from Nantucket.

"How was it?" he asked, after he kissed her thoroughly.

"Like *Masterpiece Theatre* occasionally interrupted by *Shrek*," Alison told him, laughing.

They walked to the short-term parking garage, found David's Lexus, and for a few moments they embraced and kissed like a pair of teenagers. Then they settled in for the drive.

Alison put her hand on David's thigh. "I missed you."

"I missed you. Tell me everything."

Alison paused, gathering her thoughts. "Scott was a pleasant surprise. He helped with the shopping and the cooking. The children had fun together, most of the time, though we did have a couple of meltdowns. I'll tell you about those later. How was your weekend? Did you accomplish what you were planning?"

"I did. I caught up on work. And I saw my lawyer and changed my will."

Alison blinked. "Oh? Want to talk about it?"

"Why not." David deftly steered through the lane changes. "It's simple. As it was before, the company and its assets will be divided between Poppy and Ethan. My own personal money, including whatever proceeds come from the sale of my Boston apartment, goes solely to you. The Nantucket house is divided among Poppy, Ethan, and you."

Alison gasped. "David, that's generous of you, but it's too generous. It's lovely of you to will me the proceeds from your Boston home, but to give me a third of the Nantucket house, well, that's *too much*. It's not fair."

"Look, it's *my* house that I bought and paid for with *my* money, and you are going to be my wife. We will be spending a considerable amount of time there. More than Poppy and Ethan ever will. And your children and grandchildren enjoy the place. I'd like to see my grandchildren and your grandchildren vacationing there as adults."

Alison laughed. "So you plan to live to one hundred."

"Damn right I do! I know I'm not going to live forever. I'm very fond of the Nantucket house and I know it's a rare and marvelous gift to leave to my children and to you and your children. Maybe their children will talk about their eccentric old man who bought the place."

Alison reached out and gently stroked the side of David's face. "Dear one. What generous thoughts."

But as David wound his way through the congested streets, Alison worried. What would Poppy think? What about Ethan?

"I want to be with you when you tell your children about the will," Alison said at last. "I think they will have some issues about it, and I want to be clear about what you say and what they say. And as grateful as I am for your generosity, I don't think Poppy is going to like it. You should be prepared for a fight, I think."

David smiled. "I've fought lots of battles over money in my life, Alison. And I know my children well. I think I can handle this."

I'm not sure I can, Alison thought. But she kept her peace until they were home. They were quiet as they went through the small foyer and took the ornate brass elevator up to David's apartment.

"Hungry?" Alison asked.

"Not really." Clearly, he was preoccupied.

"I could scramble some eggs . . ."

"Give me about thirty minutes. I've been going over accounts and I want to finish."

"Fine. I'll unpack and have a shower."

Alison stood under the hot running water for a long time, not thinking, but relaxing, catching her breath. She always seemed to be trying to think ahead, about ferry and plane schedules, whether she had enough food, enough beer, and where the grandchildren were . . . It was luxurious to be alone as she rubbed lotion into her arms and brushed out her wet hair. She slid into a light silk kimono and went downstairs and into David's study. While David slowly put his computer to sleep and organized his desk, Alison poured them each a drink and handed one to David. He sank into a chair, sighing as if he had the weight of the world on his shoulders.

"What's wrong?" Alison asked.

"It's Poppy," he said. He leaned back in his chair and ran his hands through his hair.

"Poppy? What's Poppy?"

"She's screwing up at work. I've found a load of errors, and I'm fixing them and now I have to go through everything. This isn't like her at all. I don't know what's gotten into her."

Alison laughed. "I know exactly what's gotten into her. She's pregnant, David! She's building you a new grandchild. Cut her some slack."

"I wouldn't cut any other employee some slack, especially not the women. I've been lectured too often about equality in the workplace. Anyway, it can't be the pregnancy. She wasn't this scattered with the first two children."

"Every pregnancy's different."

"Emma's were the same. And she never got so absentminded."

"Poppy and Emma are two different women. And from what you've said, Emma was never involved in your business."

"But she was. Emma gave elaborate parties and dinners."

"Now, David," Alison said, keeping her voice light, "you're just being perverse. Do you mean to say that hosting parties and dinners is equal to what you're expecting Poppy to do?"

"Humph." David did not lose any argument easily. He sipped his brandy and rubbed his forehead. "Okay, yes, of course you're right. I suppose I do need to give Poppy a break." He hesitated before admitting, "You know, I hate to say it, but I'm finding it difficult, handing the reins over to Poppy—not because she's a girl—"

"—woman," Alison softly corrected.

"—but because I'd find it hard giving over control to anyone. I know I don't have the energy or quick wits I used to have, but I've spent my life building the company and it's wrenching to give it away."

For a long moment, Alison was quiet, thinking. "Okay, then, how about this? Why not wait until Poppy's had her baby, and had a few months to enjoy her new child—babies are so delicious when they're small. Plus, Poppy won't get a good night's sleep for a year. You must remember that from when you and Emma had your babies. Give yourself another year or two before handing the company over."

"But we're going to travel, you and I, after our wedding. We've booked a cruise through the Baltic and up to Saint Petersburg."

Alison smiled. "I think Saint Petersburg will still be there in another year or two."

David stared. "You're unbelievable. Any other woman would be furious to have to wait another year for a honeymoon."

Alison cocked her head and looked stern. "Well, there is one condition."

"Really? What is it?"

"You have to come to the island more often. I don't mean just this summer, I mean all through the year. They've got so many fabulous events there, the Daffodil Festival, the Cranberry Festival, the Christmas Stroll. We should definitely come for those. Celebrations of each season. We should enjoy each day, every day. You know that saying about putting things you want to do on your bucket list and doing them before you die? I saw someone wearing a T-shirt that said, 'I'M LIVING MY BUCKET LIST.' Isn't that clever? We don't have to go on a cruise to enjoy life. You just need to ease up on work, come to the island more."

David said, "Alison, your cheeks have gone red. Are you having a hot flash?"

"No, idiot, I'm *excited*! Excited about having you with me on that fabulous island. I enjoy my girls and grandchildren, and your family, too, but it's *you* I want to be with." Suddenly, she had a thought. "And, David! You could make Poppy co-CEO of your company. You could *share* the work. That would be good for both of you. She'd have time for her baby, and then she'd take over the tiller and you'd have time with me."

"Okay, I see what you're getting at. You really believe I should continue working for a year?"

"Actually, David, I think you should continue working for *years*.

I don't know why we didn't think of this before, but the man I fell in love with is a lion, a tiger. You've built that company from a small enterprise into a towering success. You're working with young techies on ways to increase your sales through the Internet, and I know you like to be hands-on. Gosh, why didn't I see this before? You love your work! You shouldn't retire."

David ran his hands through his hair again, thinking. "You're right. If I'm honest, I don't want to retire. I don't want to hand over the reins to Poppy. But Poppy wants to be head of the company."

"But remember, Poppy is young. She knows stuff you don't know. She has ideas you don't have. You need to share the work—and the glory. And you need to start taking a couple of days a week away from work. We can go to the island. We can go to museums and concerts in Boston. You can lead a more balanced life."

"What about you?" David asked. "No honeymoon?"

Alison ran her hand down his beloved face. "Whenever we're together, that's all the honeymoon I need."

sixteen

Felicity understood that she possessed an unrealistic view of marriage. Her parents had been happy together, and Felicity had assumed her marriage would be happy, too.

Or, wait, she thought. She didn't mean happy or even easy. She'd thought marriage between two people would be a joint effort. Fifty-fifty. Maybe sixty-forty.

Now she knew she'd been naïve.

Her situation was compounded by the fact that in the group of mothers Felicity saw on a regular basis, usually at someplace like the park or the school with the kids, no other mother seemed as conflicted about her own marriage as Felicity was about hers. She knew, of course, they couldn't all be floating on rosy clouds of matrimonial bliss, but while they all complained—with laughter—about their husbands, no one expressed the doubts and the downright anger Felicity felt.

She spent three days muttering to herself, and finally, in the middle of the week, she called Jane.

"I was just going to phone you!" Jane said.

"You were?" Felicity couldn't help smiling.

"What's going on?" Jane asked.

"Do you have a moment?"

"Of course. Where are you?"

"I'm in the attic."

Jane laughed. "Isn't it hot up there?"

"Sweltering. But this way the kids can't hear me."

"Wow. Tell me everything."

"You first," Felicity said.

"No, you first," Jane said. "Please. I need to get out of my Slough of Despond."

"Your what?"

"It's from *The Pilgrim's Progress* . . . never mind. Tell me."

"All right, well, the coming weekend is the Fourth of July. Fireworks, cookouts, the All-American day, right? Mom has invited us all down for the long weekend and it's going to be wicked hot those days. Plus, I've been to the island twice and Noah hasn't deigned to come even once."

"And he doesn't want to come for the Fourth?" Jane asked.

"He doesn't! He won't! And do you know why? Because Ingrid, his 'office wife,' is having a huge cookout for everyone who works for Green Food."

"But the Fourth is a family holiday, isn't it?"

"Exactly! That's what I told Noah and he said children are invited, too, and get this, the astonishing Ingrid has a *swimming pool*!"

"Um, Mom's got the ocean . . ."

"Noah says the salt in the ocean bothers his eyes."

"And the chorine in a pool doesn't?"

"Noah says he *has* to be at Ingrid's cookout. He says it will be a perfect time to network with his employees on a personal basis."

"What are you going to do?"

"I don't know. That's why I called you."

Jane laughed. "Yes, because I'm such a wizard in the marriage department."

"Wait, tell me more about you."

"Well, guess what. Scott won't go to Nantucket for the Fourth, either. We've always gone to the summer home of one of the partners of his firm, and he's insisting he'll go there even if he has to go without me. We had a major fight. I'm really angry, Felicity. I'm angry enough to end this."

"Oh, Jane, no. You and Scott are so perfect for each other. *With* each other."

"I thought we were," Jane said sadly. "I'm not so sure anymore."

The sisters were quiet for a long moment, deep in thought.

"Well, Filly, this ought to put your Independence Day picnic in perspective," Jane said with a wry laugh.

"Actually, it does. You'll be going to Nantucket, won't you?"

"You bet I am. And I hope that yummy Ethan is there, too."

"What? Why? Oh, Jane, don't be a fool."

"Why not? Ethan's handsome and sexy and willing."

"Don't even. You know Ethan's just a serial flirt. What you have with Scott is profound. You don't want to muddy your marriage with some stupid flirtation."

"Don't worry, Felicity, if I muddy my marriage, as you say, I'll be sure it's more than flirtation."

"Jane!" Felicity burst into tears. "Infidelity is nothing to joke about!"

"Oh, silly Filly, don't cry. I'm not going to sleep with him. I'm just hoping Scott isn't drowning his sorrows with one of the female lawyers in his firm."

"Scott wouldn't do that."

"No, I don't think he would. He might want to, but he takes all his vows seriously."

"So do I," Felicity said, her voice thoughtful, forlorn.

"You're thinking Noah doesn't?"

"I don't know. I don't think he's having a . . . *sexual* . . . affair with Ingrid, but I hate that he chooses her cookout over our family's." Felicity took a deep breath. "But I'm glad we talked. I'm going to give in and go to Ingrid's party. With the kids. That will show Noah that I'm committed to helping him in his work. And it will remind Ingrid that Noah has a family."

"Well, damn it, *I'm* going to Nantucket!"

"Jane, please. Be good."

Jane snorted. "When have I ever been anything else?"

Alison was disappointed to learn that Felicity and her family weren't coming for the holiday weekend. The fireworks, set off at Jetties Beach, were always spectacular.

Jane was coming for the full four days, without Scott. Ethan was coming, and Poppy and Patrick and their children. And most wonderfully, David would be there, and he promised not to talk about work. Alison did everything she could to get ready—stocking up on groceries and making breakfast casseroles and dinner stews she could freeze to go with the succulent veggies she'd buy fresh every day. The weather had skyrocketed into the eighties, with humidity swamping the air. The fireworks were to be held on Monday the third, if the island didn't get the thick fog that often blew in. Alison's resolution for this particular weekend was to be especially nice to Poppy, to get to know her better, to become, possibly, her friend.

But when Poppy and her family arrived on Saturday afternoon, Poppy huffed out a hostile-sounding hello before walking away from her. True, Poppy and Patrick were loaded down with suitcases and backpacks, and they were both trying to herd Daphne and Hunter upstairs to their rooms to unpack and change into bathing suits. David and Ethan didn't see Poppy's snub because they were outside, blowing up the rubber whale and hosing off some beach chairs.

"Have you all had lunch?" Alison asked Patrick as he headed up the stairs.

"We have, thanks. We're good. The kids are eager to get down to the beach."

"Great!" Alison went back to the kitchen to, as her mother had often said, have a little think. A bowl of fresh fruit sat on the kitchen table. Iced tea and pink lemonade were in plastic (unbreakable) pitchers in the refrigerator. Several kinds of beer waited in the refrigerator door. The sheets were fresh on the beds, bath towels and beach towels towered in the bathrooms, the kitchen was bursting with food to feed a mob, and yet Alison was troubled by a chill of foreboding, as if her very bones were warning of an approaching storm.

She wore shorts, a loose T-shirt, and flip-flops. This morning she'd had a lovely long swim to cool off after she'd finished cooking and baking. Jane hadn't arrived yet. She would come in the late afternoon, and as she had before, she'd rent her own car. Jane liked to be self-sufficient. So Alison was free, really, to relax. She could read a novel or take a nap or sit out on the deck watching the others and being available—that was what her inner self was cautioning her to do: to be available.

She was in the downstairs bathroom applying another coat of sunblock when Daphne and Hunter thundered down the stairs in their bathing suits. Their father followed, yelling, "Wait for me, kids!" The back door slammed. Alison heard Patrick and his kids greeting David and Ethan.

"Alison."

Alison turned. Poppy stood in the bathroom door, her face like a storm cloud.

"Poppy! I didn't hear you come down. Would you like some sunblock? I like this kind especially, it doesn't sting your eyes . . ."

"We need to talk," Poppy said bluntly.

Alison flinched at the other woman's tone. "What?"

"In the den." Poppy turned and walked away.

After a moment, Alison followed.

Poppy was pacing in front of the fireplace.

"Poppy, what—"

"What gives you the right to delay my taking control of the company?"

"Poppy, I don't understand. Let's sit down and—"

"Do you think, because I'm pregnant, I have to sit down?"

"For heaven's sake, Poppy. No. I think because I'm older than you are, *I* need to sit down." Alison sank onto a chair. "Okay. Now. Please. Tell me what you're so upset about."

"Don't pretend not to know. You told my father he shouldn't make me CEO of the company because I'm pregnant."

"I see." Alison tapped her lip. What a mess. David had mentioned in passing, in their flurried hours of packing for this weekend, that he had spoken with Poppy about waiting to take over the company, but he hadn't given Alison any details. Had David told Poppy *why* he wanted to wait? Had he pointed out to his beloved daughter that she was making all kinds of mistakes and not getting necessary reports and directives done in a timely fashion? Alison needed to speak with David before she could talk truthfully. This wasn't information Alison should give.

Alison equivocated. "That's not what I said."

"Are you calling my father a liar?"

"Of course not, Poppy." Alison took a few yoga breaths. She thought she knew a way through this mess, for now. "I think your father has so much to deal with, professionally and personally. Taking control of the company—which I *never* said you shouldn't do—and our forthcoming wedding and your pregnancy, will take a toll on your life for at least a year—"

"So cancel the wedding. Or postpone it."

"No, Poppy. That's not going to happen." Alison was angry now, working hard to remain cordial. She presented her offering. "Well, the *wedding* is going to happen, but David and I could postpone our honeymoon. That way he could be here while you have your baby, and he could hand over the control to you more gradually."

Poppy stared. "You would do that? You would postpone your honeymoon cruise?"

"Of course I would, Poppy. If that's what David wants, of course. It does seem like a good idea, doesn't it?"

Poppy bit her lip. She stared at the floor. In that moment, Alison saw the young woman in Poppy, the daughter of a mother who had died four years ago and was not there to share this new pregnancy with Poppy, to counsel Poppy, to intercede in all matters with Poppy's father on Poppy's behalf. Poppy was a woman alone, surrounded by males, her father, her brother, her husband. It really was too bad that Ethan refused to take any part in the management of the company. He could share the burden with Poppy; he could lighten her load. Poppy was brilliant and assertive and capable, but she was also a mother and a pregnant woman and a wife and a daughter. And now she was about to see her beloved father joined to another woman, the archetypal wicked stepmother.

Alison wanted very much for Poppy to consider her a friend, not an enemy. And at this moment, she experienced an unexpected surge of love and sympathy for the young woman who had so much on her hands—and in her body. Yet she was certain that if she attempted to make a conciliatory move—to embrace her, make a joke—if she tried to do that, Poppy would snap like a trap and take off Alison's hand.

So she waited quietly.

At last Poppy spoke. "That might work. I'll think about it."

"And, Poppy, one more thing."

Poppy squinted suspiciously. "What?"

"I'd love to have your advice about the wedding present I want to give David. You're the only one I can ask, really, because I need it to be kept a secret, something my daughters find impossible to do. Plus, you know your father best of all of us." She was flat-out flattering Poppy, and the younger woman seemed receptive.

"I can keep a secret," Poppy said. "Ethan, not so much."

"That's what I thought. So. I've spent time walking around town. I've noticed that many houses have quarterboards, like those on ships, with clever names, like PLEASANT DREAMS on Pleasant Street or LOVE OF FAIR on Fair Street. This house doesn't have a quarterboard, so I thought I'd have one made to give to David as a wedding gift."

"Hm. What would it say?" Poppy still looked suspicious.

"I was thinking GLAD TO BE HERE. Because your father's last name is Gladstone. And we're all glad to be here, right?"

"That's kind of corny."

Alison bit her tongue. "Too corny? What do you think of the idea in general?"

"I like the idea, but . . ."

"Okay, well, what about this one? GLAD TIDINGS. Because the house faces the ocean and the tides—"

"I get it. Yes, that's kind of clever. I like that one."

"All right then! I'll get right on it! *Glad* to have your input!"

"Don't tell Heather," Poppy said. "She'd be sure to tell Dad."

"Okay, good idea. I won't tell anyone else. It will be our secret."

Poppy almost smiled before she left the room. Fine, Alison thought, now Poppy believed she was making the decisions not only about the company and about her father's honeymoon plans but also about Alison's wedding present to David. So she and Poppy weren't friends yet, but they were collaborators in a major secret. That was a good start.

Jane flew in later that afternoon and made her way to the house in a rental car. David spent a great deal of time with his grand-children, and Alison saw how that made Poppy ease into a happy state that Alison hadn't seen her in before. Everyone was in a good mood, so for a day or two, Alison relaxed.

seventeen

Ingrid lived in a house, a real house, not a rented apartment like many of the young people who worked for Green Food. It was large, airy, and uncluttered, a house that could have been photographed for a magazine, everything crisp and dove gray and cream, open plan, the living room segueing easily into the dining room and kitchen. Glass doors slid open to the patio and swimming pool.

It was nicer than the house Noah and Felicity owned. As Felicity sat on a lawn chair, smearing sunblock on her children and putting water wings on Luke, she listened to the talk around her as other employees came out to the pool. "Wow," they said, or "Awesome," but no one asked how it was that Ingrid had such a house. So they must all know, and Noah must know, and there was another important matter that Noah shared with Ingrid but not with Felicity.

The other wives and significant others and female employees all wore bathing suits, mostly bikinis that showed off their already tanned bodies. When did they have time to tan? Felicity wore a bathing suit, too, and it was also a bikini, but she was self-conscious about the weight she carried on her hips and her sagging-from-nursing breasts. The worst thing was that there were no other children at the party. No other mothers. Not even one. Felicity knew she was not the oldest person there, but she wasn't young and carefree and cool and hip, or whatever they called themselves these days. She didn't even know what they called themselves, which made her feel at least another decade older. But when Alice took Luke's hand and tenderly helped him down the steps into the water, Felicity forgot about everything and sat smiling, lost in the beauty of her children.

A woman swept up. "Hello again! Remember me? I'm Cynthia Levine, we met at the Christmas party. I'll sit here, okay? We'll be the old married section."

Felicity smiled as Cynthia, bravely displaying dimpled thighs and a bulging belly in her black one piece, joined her.

"Your children are darling. I hope this little guy is as cute as yours." Cynthia settled herself on a lounger, setting a beach bag spilling over with towels, crackers, water, sunblock, and a chiffon cover-up next to her.

"You're pregnant! Congratulations!" Felicity's pleasure was real. At last, another mother on the Green Food wives' team.

"Yes, and I love it. I never have to hold my stomach in. And the Horny Bachelors have stopped flirting with me. They avoid me like the plague."

"The Horny Bachelors?"

"Don't tell me they haven't hit on you. They're young and obsessed with work and awkward in social situations and desperate to get laid without consequences. They especially like married women. See the guy with the man bun? And the guy with the tattoo? And the guy in the Hawaiian shirt?"

"Those guys have hit on you? Why don't they hit on the women on the staff?"

"Okay, well, first, there aren't enough women to go around, and second, the women want a *relationship*, the scariest word in the Green Food guy world."

"Well, I'm insulted," Felicity joked. "No guy's even talked to me and I'm married."

"You have children, another scary thing. Plus, you're married to the Big Guy and no one wants to get on his bad side."

"I wish someone would hit on her," Felicity whispered, nodding her head toward Ingrid, who was deep in conversation with Noah. "Actually, I wish someone would just hit her." Immediately, she said, "Oh, I don't mean that. I'm just jealous of the time she gets to spend with Noah. And how close they are because of work."

Cynthia gave Felicity a long look. "So you don't know?"

A frozen shiver of fear slid through Felicity's heart. "Know what?"

"Well, honey . . . I think your husband and Ingrid are close *outside* work. Okay, maybe not technically outside the *building*, but—"

Felicity clasped Cynthia's arm. "*Cynthia*. What are you saying?"

Cynthia patted Felicity's hand gently. "I'm sorry. I shouldn't have told you like this, here at a party, but we never see each other any other time so—"

"Is Noah sleeping with Ingrid?"

"I wouldn't say *sleeping*, exactly."

"Oh, for heaven's sake, I'm going to explode if you don't just say it!"

"Well, you have to understand, I wasn't there, Terry, my husband, told me, and he got it secondhand. Topaz, the redheaded girl over there? She went to the supply closet for some more toner, and it was locked, but she wriggled the handle and the door opened and Ingrid and Noah were in there all over each other. Kissing. And Noah had pulled Ingrid's skirt up and had his hands on her bum. So that's not actually having sex and it's certainly not *sleeping*—I've never understood why we use that term, sleeping, it's not exactly descriptive of what is actually happening."

Felicity couldn't breathe. Sounds around her dimmed, and her sight went wonky. She pressed her hands against her stomach and bent forward.

"Felicity? Are you okay? Oh, damn, I'm sorry I told you."

"I'm okay. Just shocked. Give me a minute." Felicity breathed through her nose. She stared at her feet for a few long moments. Sitting erect again, she asked, "Is Topaz a reliable source?" Immediately she burst out laughing, rather hysterically. "Listen to me, I sound like a journalist."

"Felicity, I'm so sorry. And they were only making out. And yes, Topaz is a truthful person. She's nice. She's kind of odd, all about computer stuff, but she wouldn't make this up. And my husband, well, he's a straight arrow, drives me crazy sometimes, and he didn't snicker about what Topaz said. In fact, he was, well, uncomfortable about it. He wondered how this would affect the company."

"The company," Felicity snorted. "I'm beginning to hate the company."

"Mommy! Look!" Alice was waving to her from the pool. She was walking backward in the shallow end, towing Luke with her hands.

"Oh, good girl, Alice!" Felicity called. "Lukey, are you learning to swim?"

"I'm a tanker, Mommy. Alice is a tugboat!"

"Awesome!" Felicity yelled. Looking at Cynthia, she said, "I need to go play with my children. You'll find, once you have your little one, that you become an ace at being schizophrenic. I'd like to stab Noah and Ingrid or at least throw rocks at them, but instead I'm going to be happy mommy."

"Is it okay that I told you?" Cynthia asked.

"Yes. It was exactly the right thing to do." She rose and walked down the steps into the pool. "Oooh," she said to her children, who came swimming to her as if they'd been born with fins. "It's cold."

"Do what I do, Mommy," Alice advised. "Just get wet all the way to your shoulders. Get it over with in one big shock."

"Excellent idea, Alice," Felicity said. She slipped beneath the water, swam down to touch the bottom, and came up dripping wet.

"Are you okay, Mommy?" Alice asked.

"Absolutely," Felicity responded and dove down again to tickle her son's foot.

Her children were sleeping. Alice had been so tired she'd closed her eyes and drifted off at once, but Luke was overexcited by the day of swimming and had trouble relaxing. Felicity sat on the side of his bed and lightly ran her fingers over his back, singing lullabies very softly. She was in no hurry to leave her children's room. Because when she did, she had to confront Noah.

Finally, Luke slept, lying on his belly, face turned to the side, long lashes brushing his sunburned cheeks. Such innocence, Felicity thought, with a pang in her heart. This child adored his father. Luke was only five years old. How confusing it would be if his father left this home to live with another woman. Felicity felt as if her heart was being ripped open.

She rose from the bed, pulling the monster truck sheet up over his shoulders. She left the room and walked into the bathroom, where she locked the door and stood staring at her face in the mirror. She had showered with the children, and her hair was still damp, but the same rosy glow that brightened her son's cheeks brightened hers. She wore a light cotton caftan she'd got at a thrift shop. She seldom wore it because it fell to her ankles and tripped her going up the stairs. But tonight she wanted the extra material coverage, as if she was going into battle.

And she was going into battle.

Noah was in the kitchen, standing at the sink, drinking down a glass of ice water.

"I think I'm dehydrated," he said, facing the window.

"Noah. We need to talk. Now. Please." Felicity put her hands on the back of a kitchen chair for support.

Her husband gave her a weary glance. "Babe, it'll have to wait until tomorrow. I'm beat. All that sun—"

"I know about you and Ingrid. Cynthia Levine told me what Topaz saw."

Noah's mouth twitched in an oddly childish guilty smile. "And what did Topaz see?"

"She saw you with Ingrid. Kissing Ingrid, and—" Felicity gagged. She put her hand over her mouth.

"For Christ's sake!" Noah swore. "You have no idea how my company works, do you?"

"Maybe not. Would you sit down and talk to me about it?"

Angrily, Noah yanked out a chair and sat. He still had not met Felicity's eyes.

Felicity waited.

"Look." Noah sighed, running his hands through his hair. "I really don't need this right now. I've got a company to run and a product to test and an ad plan to create."

"And I've got a family to protect," Felicity replied.

"Your *family*. That's all you care about."

"That's not true, Noah. I do everything I can to take care of you. I cook you healthy meals and keep your clothes clean and ironed. The children adore you. If I spend more time with the children than with you, it's because you're never here. *I* would spend more time with you if you were ever here."

"That's because I'm working my ass off! Day and night! These are the crucial days and weeks and hours, Felicity, I've told you again and again!"

"And making out with Ingrid in the storage closet is crucial to your work?"

"Come on, Felicity, let's not get into this now."

Her heart froze. "What is *this*?"

Noah crossed his arms over his chest and clenched his teeth.

"Are you having sex with her?"

Noah raised his eyes to the ceiling, exasperated.

Felicity's voice was quiet, steady, although her hands, clasped on her lap, were trembling. "Please, Noah. I deserve to know."

Grumpily, like a cornered child, Noah said, "No, I'm not having sex with her."

"But you want to."

"It's complicated."

"Tell me how."

Noah let out a sigh. "I can't expect you to understand. It's like doctors and nurses, Felicity. They're under so much constant pressure, they have sex whenever and wherever they can to release the pressure, to stop thinking for a moment."

"So . . ." Felicity took a moment to gather her thoughts. "So you could have sex with any of your female employees? Have you been in the supply closet with other women?"

"For God's sake, Felicity. You're getting irrational."

"So, it's only Ingrid you've been with. Do you love her?"

Noah dropped his head. Muttered something.

"I didn't hear you, Noah."

He lifted his head and looked Felicity right in the eyes. "I don't know. I don't think so. But I know *she* loves *me* more than you do."

Stung, Felicity almost cried: *Oh, don't be such a* baby, *Noah!* But she held her tongue. "Oh," she said. "Wow. What a terribly sad thing to think, Noah. It's not true, you know, I love you more than the world. But romance often gets lost in marriage."

"That's for sure."

Felicity spoke slowly, finding her way, watching Noah's reactions. "I know you're tired and terribly stressed. I do know that. I know you're working toward something enormous and world-changing. I know you can't find time for a vacation, but really, I think it would help your work if you took just a weekend off. A weekend to come to the island with me and the kids. Alison would spoil you with wonderful food, and you could swim in the ocean— and you know, Noah, the ocean *is* magical. I mean, scientifically magical. I've read articles about this. Being near the ocean, looking out at the ocean, that soothes your thoughts. And you could lie on the beach with the sun on your back and not think of anything at all. And that's good for your brain, too, I've read about that."

She watched carefully. Noah's shoulders dropped, the muscles in his neck and jaw relaxed, his breathing deepened.

"So the ocean will give you new energy. And I can take you behind a sand dune and remind you of some of the things we did when we were first married."

"I've got so much to do, Felicity."

"You can leave it for two days."

"I don't know, Felicity."

"Let's find out."

Monday night the Nantucket fireworks were magical, a true extravaganza, made even more exciting by the boats in the harbor that blew their horns whenever an especially fabulous pinwheel dazzled through the air. By the time the grand finale had finished, the children were hoarse from yelling and Alison's hands stung from applauding. Because of the crowd, the family had to park their cars blocks away. As the Gladstones and Jane hiked back among the throng of other people, everyone, even the children, was too tired to talk. Once they arrived back at the house, Daphne and Hunter went to bed without begging to stay up later.

"Let's play bridge," Ethan suggested. "Jane's agreed to be my partner. Dad, want to play? Poppy?"

"I'm exhausted," Poppy told her brother. "Patrick has to rub my feet. After all, they've been carrying his baby all day."

"Good night, all." Patrick waved as his wife pulled him up the stairs.

"We're going up, too," David said. "I'm going to curl up with my laptop and catch up on the news."

"Isn't he romantic?" Alison complained, but her eyes twinkled. "I've got a book to finish. Can't wait to see how it all turns out."

"I guess I'll go up, too," Jane said.

"What?" Ethan protested. "You old fogies are going to leave me down here all alone? It's too early." He caught Jane's hand and tugged gently. "Stay and keep me company."

There was that damned sexual electric spark again! Jane knew her mother could see how she was blushing.

"Scrabble," Ethan specified. "Let's play Scrabble."

"I don't know. I'm tired." In truth, Jane felt anything but tired with Ethan standing so near, holding her hand.

"Just one game," Ethan implored.

Jane hesitated. It would be one thing to agree to be his partner in bridge, with two other people at the table with them. But spending any time alone with Ethan could be dangerous. Yet she was so angry with Scott for not coming with her for this long weekend . . . "One game," she said. "In the kitchen." That room had the brightest lights.

"Be good, children," Alison called as she and David went up the stairs to bed.

Ethan brought the game out of a cupboard and set it on the kitchen table. He sat down, and Jane sat across from him. Ethan's blue T-shirt fit smoothly over his muscled torso and tanned biceps. The sun had bleached his hair to a shining gold, and he hadn't had it cut recently, so it fell down over his forehead and shaggily around his face. He looked younger than he was, like a carefree surfer dude. An appropriate look for him, Jane thought. He may not surf, but he certainly seemed carefree. Did he not care at all that he was trying to seduce a married woman?

And how could she blame him, when she knew she was, at the least, approachable.

Ethan spilled the tiles out onto the table, and Jane helped him turn the letters facedown, being careful not to let her hand touch his.

After they chose their seven tiles and were arranging them on the tray, Ethan asked, "Want some coffee?"

"No, thanks. I'm going to have trouble sleeping without adding caffeine to the mix." As soon as Jane spoke, she wanted to call the words back. Hurriedly, she added, "Because of work. I'm tasked with a complicated project, and I guess I feel guilty being here instead of being at home. At the office, I mean. I should be at the office."

"Hey, Jane, it's summer. It's the Fourth of July weekend. Your boss wouldn't expect you to be working on a holiday."

"Maybe not. But I certainly have worked on weekends and holidays before. I guess I don't feel comfortable being here."

"I think you're too hard on yourself," Ethan said. He stopped talking and set his tiles on the board, forming the word *cheese*.

"Hey, thanks for all the *E*'s," Jane said, and quickly made the word *greater*.

She loved words. She usually won at Scrabble. It was a relief, the way her mind latched onto the game, overriding her other concerns as she focused on winning points. She snickered smugly when she got an *X*. "Ha!" she exclaimed as she made the word *example,* with Ethan's *E* at the end of the word.

"Well done," Ethan said, writing down the points on the scorecard.

He built his word from her *E: desire*.

Jane's body flashed with heat. Ethan's hand was on the table, close, male, with long, clean nails and hair on his knuckles. His shoulders were broad, his arms thick with muscle, and the palms of his hands were calloused from working on the farm. All she had to do, and all she wanted to do at this moment in her life, was to touch her hand to his, to allow herself to accept the current of pleasure that rushed through her whenever they touched. Here he was, this beautiful man, and no quarrel lay between them, their relationship was new and fresh and, because of their families, fraught with a kind of playful wickedness. She imagined what Scott was doing now, probably already home from his Fourth of July party, in his office, diligently working away. Had Jane become just as assiduous? Had her work routine fallen around the hours of her life like a cage? Could she never be spontaneous? Were her wild, hedonistic days over? Had she become a living blueprint with all her next moves blocked out, never to be changed? If she stayed with Scott, she would never know how it felt to be pregnant, to hold a baby in her arms. If she stayed with Scott, her life was laid out in a pattern as gridlocked as a jail cell.

But she loved Scott. She did love him. She had vowed to be faithful to him.

What she had with Ethan, whatever foolish relationship she was building with him, was only a game, with no more meaning than the Scrabble letters on the board.

Jane stood up. "I'm sorry, Ethan, but suddenly I'm exhausted. I've got to get some sleep."

"Jane . . ." Ethan stood up, too. "I didn't mean to insult you—"

"No, I know that, it's not that. I'm just terribly tired. I'll see you tomorrow."

She went out of the room and up the stairs, leaving Ethan behind to put away the Scrabble game.

Tuesday, after a lazy morning, they all sailed to Coatue on David's boat. The sky was a high sapphire blue and the long curved beach at the fourth point was quiet and unpopulated except for the usual shrieking gulls. They ate sandwiches and potato chips and cookies, and swam in the cool turquoise water, and lay back on their beach towels, surrendering to the warmth of the sun. To Alison's surprise, both Ethan and Jane spent time with Daphne and Hunter, playing with them in the water, walking along the shore, searching for treasures, and Poppy was able to put her straw sun hat over her face and fall asleep. Patrick took the opportunity to go for a long, challenging swim farther away from shore than usual, and he came back grinning from ear to ear.

"You went far out, Daddy!" Daphne said.

"I know," Patrick said. "Just giving my muscles a workout." He picked his daughter up and swung her around while she squealed with glee.

In the late afternoon, they sailed back to the island and moored the boat and drove back to the house. Even the children were quiet, partly from the sunny day, partly from the ice cream cones they were enjoying. At home, Poppy took the children off to shower and David fell flat on the bed and was instantly asleep. Alison took a brisk shower and dressed, loving her tanned limbs and the glow of the sun on her face. She pulled on a loose cotton shift, slid her feet into sandals, and went down to the kitchen to unpack the picnic baskets. But Jane and Ethan had already done that.

"We've ordered pizza," Ethan said. "Patrick's gone off to pick it up. We want to eat in front of the television and watch a movie."

"It will have to be PG because of the kids," Alison reminded them.

"My brain's so melted, PG is about all I can handle," Jane joked.

The family crowded into the den with drinks and pizzas and lots of napkins to watch *Descendants 2*. David came down with bedhead hair and joined them, and for a while Alison was content, not worried about anyone.

Except, maybe . . . Ethan and Jane were becoming awfully chummy. They sat side by side on the floor, leaning against a chair, their arms and thighs not quite, but almost, touching. It looked as if they were a couple. What did that mean?

Nothing, Alison told herself. David had often teased Alison, saying that if she didn't have anything to worry about, she'd worry because she wasn't worrying.

She smiled to herself and took another piece of pizza.

eighteen

During the middle of July, Felicity's children, and Poppy's, too, were signed up for camps, and Jane and Scott were crushed with work. David needed to work, too, so Alison invited her best friend, Margo, down for a few days. They walked and talked and shopped and dined, and in the humid evenings they sequestered themselves in front of the television and watched very romantic and completely unrealistic movies. It was better than seeing a therapist.

Still, even after Margo's visit, Alison continued to worry about David's family and hers. The whole idea of coming to the Nantucket house as often as possible in the summer was to gradually knit her family with David's. Alison had romantically envisioned herself as the wise and gracious matriarch, providing this newly formed and energetic family with a stable and generous center.

That wasn't why she was marrying David, of course. She really didn't need any more family. At this time in her life, she should be relaxing, exploring her own desires and dreams, her "bucket list." She certainly should be enjoying the unexpected and almost miraculous love she'd found with David.

But she wondered what was up with Jane and Ethan. Right from that first morning with the bread, they seemed to be entering into some sort of relationship. The very way they *looked* at each other all the time made Alison uncomfortable. But what could Alison do? What should she do? Their children were not adolescents! She felt a heaviness in her belly that seemed very much like fear.

She had not raised her daughters to be cheaters. She had tried to teach them that marriage meant fidelity. But of course, hadn't Alison set the pattern when she'd left Jane's father to marry Mark? She'd explained her reasoning to her daughters, as clearly as anyone could explain the complicated muddle of life. She'd been so young when she'd married Flint. He'd been the first boy she'd had sex with and they'd married because she was pregnant. Had she loved Flint? Had he loved her? It was necessity and the need to do the right thing that caused them to marry. And she would have stayed with Flint, really, she would have. When their beautiful daughter was born, Alison and Flint made a home together and worked hard to create a life. But how hard they had both had to work to make their little family seem like a happy one. Alison knew Flint harbored a festering anger toward her for trapping him—how old-fashioned, that thought, that she had trapped him, as if her entire goal in life had been to obtain a husband. As the months went by, they had not grown to love each other. Alison had tolerated Flint, and Flint had resented her. But he was a good man, and his parents were religious and strict and judgmental. Flint would never have left Alison.

She did not regret for one second that she'd been the one to leave Flint. She hadn't cared if Flint hated her. Alison had been drowning, and Mark was air and sunshine and moon glow and joy.

Maybe her daughters couldn't understand all this when they were little, and Alison had never told Jane how unhappy she'd been with Flint, how he had married her but then disliked her, rejected her. After the divorce, Flint had cut himself off completely from Alison and, more important, from his own daughter. He had moved across the country and never been in touch with Jane at all, never sent child support, never sent a birthday card or Christmas present. Alison didn't even know where Flint was now. She supposed she could google him, but she didn't care enough to bother. Flint's parents had chosen not to be part of Jane's life, either, although Alison could sense that there was regret in their anger.

But Alison and Jane and then Felicity had had Mark as the man in their lives, and he had been wonderful.

Now Alison had David. But that did not mean that David had replaced Mark in any way as a father to Jane and Felicity. Alison knew full well she would never be considered a stepmother to Ethan and Poppy, and she didn't want to be. The "children" were all adults now.

But she *had* hoped they would simply *like* each other.

And now Jane seemed to like Ethan too much.

And what could Alison do about that?

On the last Friday in July, Jane sat in a small armchair in their bedroom and watched Scott pack his suitcase. He wore a checked button-down shirt, jeans, and his hiking boots, because they took up too much space in his luggage.

"I can't believe you're really doing this," Jane said.

"I can't believe you're not doing this," Scott retorted. He folded his socks and tucked them around the edge of the case to cushion his other clothes.

Jane rubbed her face with her hands. They had been up long past midnight, talking and arguing. Jane had cried. Whenever she cried, Scott ignored her. He said her tears were unfair. He loved her, he said, and he didn't want to make her sad, but they had agreed on this trip, just as they had agreed on not having children. Around three in the morning, Scott simply left the room. Jane waited. The apartment was quiet. Jane found him asleep on the living room sofa.

She returned to their bedroom and fell asleep, exhausted, on their bed.

They slept late—and they both felt weird and guilty and slightly nervous because of this. They always felt off-kilter on their first days of vacation, when they didn't follow their routine. They drank coffee and showered, moving around each other without speaking.

Today Scott was leaving for Wales.

He really was going on the hiking trip. Without Jane.

Jane said, "I'm going to make some eggs and toast. We both need food. You've got time to eat."

Scott checked his watch. Of course he checked his watch. Jane wasn't hungry; she was sick at heart, sick in her belly, too. But she knew they would both feel better after eating some warm food.

"We're both so tired," Jane said. "Your plane doesn't leave until this evening."

"But I have to get to the airport two hours early for security check-in."

"I know. But we both need to eat."

She padded barefoot to the kitchen. Summer heat oozed over the city, and although she had turned on the central air-conditioning, it was still warm in the apartment. She went around the rooms, closing the blinds and the curtains against the light. In the kitchen, she set out a bowl and several eggs and butter and cheese. While the eggs were cooking and the bread was toasting, she halved oranges and made fresh juice.

"Breakfast is ready," she called and laughed wryly to herself. It was one o'clock in the afternoon.

Scott sat at the kitchen table across from Jane. "Thanks."

"You're welcome."

Oh, Lord, Jane thought, when had they become so formal with each other? Wait, she knew exactly when, sometime during last night after they had yelled at each other. Their silence as they ate was a kind of truce.

"I'll clean the kitchen," Scott said when they'd finished eating.

"That's not necessary. You've got to finish packing."

"I'm almost done. You did the cooking. It's only fair for me to wash up."

Jane laughed, jaggedly, almost hysterically. "Scott, Scott, this is *crazy*. We're acting like two strangers who will be, I don't know—*murdered*—if we don't do everything absolutely equally."

"Fine," Scott replied. He stood up. "You wash up. I've got some emails to answer."

When he turned to leave the room, Jane had a savage urge to throw something at him. Not a knife, but maybe the saltshaker. Aiming not for his head, but for his back. Instead, she buried her face in her hands as her laughter turned into tears.

She blew her nose on a paper towel and set about rinsing the dishes and loading the dishwasher. She returned to their bedroom and leaned against the door, looking in. "Three weeks," she said. "We haven't been apart for three weeks since we were married."

Scott was folding shirts carefully, exactly. He didn't turn from his task. "True."

"I'll miss you."

He kept his back to Jane and said in a neutral tone, "I'll miss you."

Scott's back was long and muscular, and his hands were beautiful. She'd always loved his hands. She approached him and held him against her, wrapping her arms around him, stopping him. She felt his heart beat—steadily, how else would Scott's heart beat?—and felt the rise and fall of his breathing.

"You might have an affair in Wales," she said calmly.

"I doubt it. I'm sure I'll be exhausted from hiking."

"I might have an affair," she said, just as calmly, thinking of Ethan.

"Well, if you get pregnant from your affair, we'll get divorced. I'm not raising another man's child."

"Whoa." Jane dropped her arms and stepped away from her husband. It was the first time the word *divorce* had been used. "So you're thinking of *divorce*?"

"Aren't you?" Scott turned to look at her. He folded his arms over his chest. "Be realistic, Jane. If you want children so fiercely, you'll have to divorce me and marry another man."

"You would let that happen," she said, heart pounding.

"If you make it happen," Scott answered.

Jane took a deep breath. "I had hoped that this time away from each other, this break, might make you reconsider the whole having-children thing."

"Jane, I'm doing what you and I have always done. I'm going hiking. I'm seeing a new world, a different land. I'll be testing my own strength and stamina. Eating unusual food. All that. All that you and I have done together for years. Why would I want to spoil an exciting experience by rerunning our argument through my mind? I'm the same person I've always been, doing the same things I've always done, and I've said all that I have to say about your sudden bizarre need to have a child. When I go out the door, I won't be considering the 'whole having-children thing.' And when I come back in the door, trust me, my thinking won't have changed."

"Scott, it's as if you've become a stranger to me. I don't *know* you. Has our love, our marriage, been nothing but an elaborate pretense?"

Scott sighed heavily. He walked away from her, around the bed, to stand next to the window facing out. Facing away from Jane.

"Maybe it has. On both our parts. How do I know that you haven't been lying all along when you said you didn't want children? How do I know that you weren't only saying what you thought I wanted to hear?"

"Scott!"

"Wait. Hear me out. I told you I didn't want children because I want to travel. That's true. It's also true that my family was nothing like yours." He paused. He stood very still, keeping his back to Jane, clenching and unclenching his hands.

Jane waited.

"My mother was an alcoholic. My father was strict and unemotional. I suppose they cared for each other, in their own way. All my life, they repeated the same pattern. Mother would drink more and more, and become incapable of even tossing my clothes into the washing machine or cooking dinner—I'm talking about when I was six years old—so I had to scrounge around and make my own peanut butter and jelly sandwiches for dinner. I often wore the same clothes to school for a week. My father would come home later and later until finally he couldn't bear my mother's drunkenness one more moment, and then . . . They would fight. Really fight. For hours. They would throw things. Sometimes they hit each other."

Jane's hand flew to her throat. "That's terrible. Poor little boy. You must have been so frightened."

"Yes. I was frightened." Scott turned. He met Jane's eyes. Tears glimmered in his own. "My father never hit *me*. Nor did my mother. They did their best to care for me, but they were joined in some kind of sick pattern that they couldn't help repeating. After their fight, after someone hit someone, the quiet would come, like after a storm. Then, for a while, Mother didn't drink and Dad came home for dinner, and we were like a normal family. Except I was always on guard, always anxious, waiting for the pattern to start over again. Mother drinking. Dad not noticing. Mother drinking too much. Dad getting angry. The fight."

Jane's heart twisted with pity. "I'm so sorry, Scott. I wish you had told me this before." Her words made anger flare inside her. "And why didn't you? How could you have kept this from me all these years?"

Scott hung his head. "Would you have married me if I'd told you?"

"Of course I would have!" Jane crossed the room, wanting to embrace her husband, wanting to heal his sadness.

"Don't, Jane." Scott stepped back. "I never wanted you to know this about me. I've seen a therapist. I've learned to cope. But it's part of who I am. I can't make the memories disappear. And I *won't* have a child. Because I don't know what kind of father I would be. Frankly, it terrifies me to think of being a father. Just the thought gives me nightmares."

"But, Scott, you and I are different from your parents!"

"Yes, because we keep ourselves in control. I thought you were in complete agreement with me on this. Isn't our life full and rich enough for you?"

"We do have a wonderful life. But I want children and I know in my heart that you and I would be good parents. Please, let's go to a therapist together."

Scott sniffed. "You mean, go to a therapist who will help me change my mind?"

"I didn't mean—"

"Be honest. Of course that's what you meant. You want to change me. Why don't *you* change yourself?"

"Scott—"

"What am I saying?" Scott said sadly. "You already have changed. You want children, and you're not going to stop pushing me for them. You wanted to go to Wales, and now you don't. I knew I shouldn't tell you. I knew it would change us, what we have together."

"But it hasn't." Jane swallowed her tears. "I am heartbroken about your childhood, Scott. But that doesn't change how I feel about you. About us. I love you. Oh, Scott, I'm so so sad about your parents. But I'm glad you told me. It makes me feel even closer to you. I want to hold you, I want to kiss you, I want to tell you that nothing you say will make me stop loving you."

"And when I say I refuse to have children, you will still love me?" Before she could answer, Scott threw down the gauntlet. "Now that I've told you all this, now that you understand me more, will you give up this crazy idea of having children?"

Her breath caught in her throat. "I still want children. With *you*. I know *you*, Scott. You are an amazing man, a wonderful, loving husband. You'll be a wonderful, loving father."

Scott shook his head sorrowfully. "No, Jane. I mean it. I will not have children with you or anyone." Abruptly, he pulled his suitcase toward him and zipped it shut. "I'm going now. I'll be in touch."

"Scott, wait! At least kiss me goodbye!"

But he walked away, down the hall, and out the door, which he closed very gently. She was alone in the apartment. She knew Scott was shaken by his confession. She understood him enough to comprehend how difficult it had been for him to tell her about his childhood. She understood him so much more clearly now, why he defended himself against intimacy, why he needed to travel. As if he were afraid to stay in any kind of home.

She felt shattered. She sank onto the bed and stared at the wall, this wall that had heard their most wrenching confessions. This weekend she wasn't going to Nantucket, and good thing, because she was a completely confused, maudlin mess. She stayed in the apartment with the air-conditioning set to high while she huddled in her favorite sweater and a blanket, watching old black-and-white movies and crying. She was not the bright, decisive, professional Jane. She was the miserable, confused, soggy Jane. But she knew what she had to do. She had to choose what she would give up. What she wanted most.

nineteen

On Thursday, Jane received one terse text from Scott. *It's amazing here.*

No *Wish you were here.* No *Miss you.* No *I love you.*

Miffed, she'd texted back: *It's amazing here.*

And that was so not true. It was hot. It was humid. She had slogged through the heat from their apartment to her office and home again. She hadn't enjoyed her privacy as much as she'd thought she would. After eating too much popcorn and ice cream while watching old movies Wednesday night, she called friends and met them for dinner. Liz had just had an ectopic pregnancy and had been in the hospital and now had only one ovary. Belinda was getting divorced. Jane told them she was mad at Scott, but their problems were momentous and she was too confused about what she wanted to tell them any more than that.

She packed Thursday night and took her luggage to the office with her on Friday. During lunch, she went to Zabar's and bought caviar, bagels, imported olives, mustard, chocolates, dried apricots, cinnamon rugelach, cheese sticks, and gourmet nuts. She left work one hour early and headed for the flight to Nantucket.

To her great disappointment, her sister and family weren't coming to Nantucket until next weekend, but Poppy and her family were there, one happy family. Jane felt unmoored. Unwanted. The outsider.

This weekend Alison was uninterested in Jane or the fact that Scott had gone to Wales alone. Jane's mother was focusing all her charm and time on Poppy and her kids. Jane could understand this. Poppy was a difficult person to please, and in the service of happy families, Alison was showing Poppy and David how much Alison enjoyed Poppy, how she was including her in everything they did.

So why didn't David spend time with Jane? Of course, Jane knew, David was beyond enthralled by his grandchildren. He played games with them, swam with them, built sand castles with them, tickled and hugged them, and truly, Hunter and Daphne were beautiful, adorable children. Who wouldn't be in love with them?

Poppy and Patrick were certainly all about their children. Poppy hardly spoke to Jane. It was as if Poppy didn't even *see* her. Poppy was so busy with her father and husband and children, and being pregnant with her third child, she didn't have time for anyone outside the family. Poppy was also a princess, doted on by her father. Jane wished her stepfather were still alive, to dote on her. But of course, if Mark were still alive, Jane's mother wouldn't be engaged to David, and none of this Nantucket world would have existed. And of course, Jane's own birth father was somewhere in the world, not that he ever contacted Jane, and usually she didn't mind, but now as she sat like an orphan outcast by a happy family, she missed him. Missed what she'd never had.

Really, Jane knew, it was the silence from Scott that hurt. When they had to travel for work, they phoned each other at least every two days just to check in. It had been a week, and Scott had texted only once. No phone call, no email. She could be the one to contact him, but their last argument the day he'd left had been brutal. She could understand his reluctance to have children because of his own childhood, and she was sad for him, it pierced her heart. But hadn't their marriage shown him how life could be? They had been happy together! Of course they'd squabbled and conflicted, the way any two people would do over years of living together. But they had always known their love was steadfast. They had always trusted one another.

And now they didn't. She didn't even know if they would stay married.

So there she was, as ripe as Eve's apple, hanging by a thread to the bough of her life, ready for trouble, for romance, for someone to choose her.

Ethan.

During the past two weeks, while Jane was plugging away at work and Ethan was running his farm, they hadn't communicated, and really, why should they? But today, as they played with Daphne and Hunter, a kind of bond wove its way around them, invisible but powerful. Ethan was a champion at playing, Jane realized that. During water Frisbee with Daphne and Hunter, Ethan was a goofball, jumping backward to make a catch and falling deep down into the waves, disappearing for what seemed like hours, and suddenly popping up with a grin, water streaming down his face. When they walked along the shore with the kids, and they all stopped to bend down and study a shell or rock, Ethan's arm had brushed hers, and something unseen but completely real zapped a streak of lust through Jane's body. Later, they played an underwater game of passing a carrot from mouth to mouth, no hands allowed, and somehow Jane had taken the carrot from Hunter's mouth without bumping into his face, but when she'd given it to Ethan, their lips met in a brief, clandestine kiss.

In the early evening, Jane was still in her bikini as she moved around the kitchen, helping her mother make a cold pasta salad to go with the roast chicken they were having for dinner, when Ethan stomped in from the deck, a towel over his shoulders, his hair slick with water and standing up in cowlicks.

"Jane!" On the deck behind him, Hunter was chasing his sister with a dead horseshoe crab. "Whadda ya say we blow this joint? Let's get cleaned up and go into town and have some adult time."

Jane paused. His suggestion was provoking so many different responses, she couldn't speak. She glanced over at Alison.

"Go, Jane." Alison was preoccupied, washing broccoli. "It will be fun for you to see the town at night."

"Well . . . okay, all right, yeah," Jane said. "I'll take a shower and change."

"Me, too," Ethan replied. "See you back down here in twenty."

They took Jane's car because it was a convertible and because it was a beautiful night.

"The stars are so bright on this island," Jane said as she slid behind the steering wheel.

Ethan laughed. "I agree, and thank you very much, but that's all the nature I can tolerate right now. Please let's go barhopping."

Surprised, Jane said, "I don't know where the bars are."

"I do. Just head into town and take the first parking place you can find."

As she turned out of the drive, she clicked on the radio to a good rock station. She didn't want to talk. She wanted to change, to shed her good daughter identity for something new, because she certainly wasn't going to be the good wife. Or even, for that matter, the good lawyer, concerned with what was wrong and what was right. She was wearing a low-cut violet halter dress that made her tan glow. She was going to let the night take her where it wanted.

She found a spot to park on Federal Street, by a jewelry store.

"I've always wondered why this street isn't called Centre Street instead of the street one block over," Jane said as they strolled down to Main Street. "I mean, this street is more accurately at the center of town."

"I'm sure there's some significant historical reason," Ethan said, and reaching out, he took her hand.

Her breath caught in her throat, but she kept her hand in his.

The vitality of the town was different at this time of night. Children were in bed, and many of the adults were out of their sporty beach clothes, wearing chic dress clothes instead. The scent of expensive perfumes drifted by.

"Hungry?" Ethan asked.

"Kind of. Maybe we could have tapas with our drinks."

They were given a table on the terrace at the Boarding House, where they sat in the fresh evening air, and for a while they amused themselves watching all the fabulous people stroll by. They ordered specialty drinks, the Sunburned Peach, a concoction of vodka, coconut water, and white peach for Jane, and Summer Fog, made of gin, muddled cucumber, and mint for Ethan.

"Oh, wow," Jane said after taking a sip of her drink. "I'd forgotten how cocktails are much more potent than wine. We'd better order some food."

So they ordered spicy grilled octopus, and crab dip with sea salt chips, and angel hair pasta with Romano parmesan and pepper. At first they ate hungrily, savoring each bite, but by the time they'd finished the king oyster mushrooms, they were sated. They leaned back in their chairs and licked the salt and olive oil from their lips.

Jane was aware that she was slightly intoxicated—by the drinks and the food and the anything-is-possible atmosphere of the fresh, warm Nantucket night air. She decided to go with it.

"Tell me about your daughter," she told Ethan.

He smiled. "My favorite subject. Canny is nine years old and precociously clever. She's a beauty, like her mother, but more than that, she's got a kind of self-possession, a *poise,* that amazes me. She speaks three languages—English, Spanish, and Portuguese, because Peru borders Brazil. And more than anything else in the world, she wants a baby brother or sister."

"Will she get one?"

"Not from her mother. Esmeralda is obsessed with her country, working to create some reason and stability in the chaos of politics. From me, I don't know. I take being a father and a husband seriously, but I also feel committed to my summer children's program. I suppose it all depends on whether or not I meet a woman who wants children and could tolerate me."

"Are you so terribly bad?" Jane asked.

"Not bad. Just eccentric."

"I want children," Jane said, then stopped. She had shocked herself by saying those words to this relative stranger. "Relative stranger," she said, amused. "That's what we are, relative strangers. See? Because of our parents, we're going to be relatives, but really, we're strangers."

Ethan smiled. "I think I'll order coffee for both of us."

"Good idea." Oh, Lord, Jane thought, Ethan thought she was drunk. And she was, a little bit. "But it's true, I do want children. At least a child. I didn't think I ever would, but over this past year I've started longing for one and Scott won't hear about it. We agreed when we married we'd have no children, and he's furious at me for changing my mind. My heart. Whatever, and I didn't change it. *It* changed *me*."

"So that's why he's in Wales and you're here."

"Yes." Jane put one elbow on the table and propped her chin on her hand. "I don't know how we're going to resolve this. We're both stubborn. And now we're both angry."

"Why doesn't Scott want children?" Ethan asked.

"Because they're a hindrance to the life we had thought we wanted. We both love to travel, and we work hard and like our work and we're becoming kind of rich, which means a lot to both of us. Neither of us grew up wealthy. We weren't *poor*, but there were times when I could sense that money was a problem for my parents, and for heaven's sake, my stepfather was a doctor! I think it was a drain on them, sending both of us to college. And Scott wasn't . . . close . . . to his parents." She wouldn't say more than that about Scott's childhood. She felt guilty enough just telling Ethan this much about her husband. "He had to pay his own way through school. He got some scholarships, but mostly he had to take out student loans, and I know he felt like he'd never, ever, be out of debt. But we are out of debt now, we're very nicely in the black. Our circumstances have changed but Scott won't see it."

"That's too bad," Ethan said. "You would have beautiful children. And I'll bet if you got him in bed and propositioned him just the right way, he'd do anything you want."

Jane met Ethan's eyes. "That's the sexiest thing anyone has ever said to me."

Ethan said softly, "I want to kiss you."

Whoa, Jane thought. *Whiplash.* One moment she was whining about Scott and Ethan was a sympathetic friend, and suddenly he was sweet-talking her and it was working. She wanted to crawl over the table and into his lap.

"I want to take you someplace," Ethan said.

"You mean now?"

"Right now. It's someplace private, where I can kiss you the way I want to."

"Oh." Jane sat back in her chair and hugged herself. "Are we drunk?"

"Maybe a little bit. Jane, you had only two cocktails. I don't think your faculties are affected."

"I don't know," Jane said thoughtfully. "I feel . . . different. You know, I've always been good. A good girl, a good sister, a good student, a good wife."

"Let's go find out what else you're good at," Ethan suggested, and signed the bill and took Jane's hand and led her to her car.

He drove, which was a relief to Jane, because she felt, not drunk exactly, but not herself. In all the years of her marriage, she'd never so much as lightheartedly flirted with another man. But had she ever met a man like Ethan? He was gorgeous, and smart, and funny, and *unpredictable*. That was the pull, that he was unpredictable, and she felt, when she was with him, that she could be that way, too.

She leaned back in her seat and looked up at the stars. At some point, she reached over and put her hand on Ethan's thigh. His quick intake of breath surprised her, and she felt a sense of power, a sense of herself as a sexually attractive woman, and that was delicious. She scarcely paid attention to the road as Ethan drove out of town and around the rotary and down the winding Polpis Road. They passed the Shipwreck & Lifesaving Museum, and several mega-mansions, and then Ethan turned right. He slowed down. They were on a rutted dirt road, with shrubs and bushes scratching at the sides of the car. No lights shone.

"Where are we?" she asked.

"On the moors. No one's ever here, and I know a really private spot."

In the moonlight, the landscape was slightly rolling and open and vast.

"It's conservation land," Ethan said, as if reading her thoughts. "No buildings allowed here. Only deer, birds, and mice inhabit this area. Maybe a few feral cats. Over there"—he pointed—"is a spot where we pick wild blueberries. The purest taste in the world." He turned again, driving off the road and onto a small grassy area tucked beneath overhanging trees.

He cut the engine. For a moment, they sat in silence, letting the night air, the night sky, the few small night noises, encompass them.

"Jane." Ethan pulled her face to his and bent to kiss her.

Oh, his mouth was sweet. The night air was slightly cool, and his arms were warm as he embraced her. He took a moment to slide his seat and hers back as far as they would go, and then she reclined and he moved over her, still kissing, still warm and sweet. He was in no hurry. He smelled like sunshine and gin, and his body was strong and muscular. When he put his hand on her breast, Jane gasped. A honeyed longing surged through her body, and when he put his knee between her legs, she almost bit Ethan's mouth from the sheer rush of desire.

Ethan put his hand under her dress and slid it up to her waist. Jane twisted beneath him. At the same time, in the back of her mind, which mostly was molten with need, a small, clear voice said: *Are you really going to do this?*

"Ethan," she said, her voice husky and low. Gently she pushed him away.

Flash. A blinding white light illuminated Ethan's face, the dashboard of the car, Jane's hands, and the greenery around them.

"I don't believe this," Ethan muttered.

Quickly he returned to his own seat, but he couldn't get the back fully raised before a man in a brown uniform with a badge saying RANGER on the pocket appeared at the driver's side. As Jane struggled to raise her own seat, she looked back at the source of the blinding light and saw a large four-wheel-drive parked behind them, a spotlight on the dashboard.

"Good evening," the ranger said politely. "How are you folks doing?"

"We're okay, thanks." Ethan glanced at Jane, his expression unreadable.

"I guess you're not aware that this area is closed at night."

"Ah. No. Was not aware." Ethan nodded, staring straight ahead.

"So I'll have to ask you all to move along."

"Okay. We'll do that."

Ethan's voice was strange, Jane thought. Was he mumbling? She was completely alert, mortified, and also oddly proud of herself. The good Jane who never caused a problem in high school had been caught making out in a secretive off-limits-after-dark spot and ordered to move along by an official in a uniform. She kind of wanted to take her phone out and snap a shot of the ranger.

The ranger returned to his truck. The spotlight went out, and the truck backed up and around a corner. And then it stayed there. Waiting.

Ethan started the car and pulled out onto the dirt road, slowly retracing their path to the main paved road. He didn't speak, but after they were headed toward town and the ranger's truck was no longer behind them, Ethan burst out laughing.

"I'm sorry, Jane," he said. "I'm sorry. Are you okay?"

"I'm fine. Hey, it was a thrill! A completely new experience."

"I know, right? I wanted to ask the ranger not to tell my parents, but he might not have thought that was as funny as I did." Reaching over, he took Jane's hand. "I'm sorry. I had no idea the moors were closed after dark. Man, what a shock that spotlight was! Worked better than a cold shower."

Jane laughed. "*Are* we going to tell our parents? Or anyone?"

"Not my father, for sure, and not Poppy. She's out of sorts these days. Not your mother, I hope, although that's your decision. But I'm sure she'd tell my father."

"I might tell Felicity," Jane said. "She can keep a secret and I know she'd see the humor in it." Jane's voice trailed off. What, exactly, was *it*? They didn't make love, but Jane and Ethan most obviously had been on the brink. What was she thinking?

When they reached David's house, Jane hurried straight up the stairs to her room, afraid her lipstick was smeared all over her face.

And afraid of what she had almost done.

twenty

From: Jane

To: Felicity

Subject: You won't even

Please come to the island next weekend. Pleeeeeeeeese! So much to tell you & don't want to do it on phone.

To: Jane

From: Felicity

Subject: WHAT?!

Anyway, we're all coming, even Noah.

As Felicity and her family—including Noah—waited in line to board the small plane to fly them from Boston to Nantucket, Felicity sent prayers of gratitude for her mother and David's kindness. To be absolutely accurate, it was David who had offered to pay the exorbitant cost of airline tickets so that Noah wouldn't have to spend his precious working time driving to the Cape and taking the ferry over. Felicity knew her mother sensed the difficulty Felicity was having simply getting her husband to the island, and it was Alison, Felicity also knew, who had suggested to David that he supply the expensive tickets.

The airline agent called the flight and led them down a series of stairs and out to the tarmac where they walked over to the ten-seater Cessna 402, stowed their laptops and purses in the plane's wings, and climbed the few steps into the cabin. As the engines began to rumble, the pilot informed them the flight would take around forty-five minutes and that the wind was moderate.

So, more to be thankful for. The kids loved it when the plane bounced around—they thought it was fun. It made Felicity want to throw up and she'd worried that it would anger Noah, who was uncomfortable when he wasn't in charge of anything—a vehicle, a trip, a company. It was too noisy in the cabin to talk, so Alice bent her head and read her book. Luke stared out the window, enchanted, yelling at his parents to look at the tiny boats in the water. Noah sat scrolling on his phone, his jaw clenched. But it was a beginning.

To Felicity's surprise, they found David waiting for them at the airport. He shook hands with Noah and kissed Felicity and the children.

"The Jeep has seatbelts for five people, so Alison and I duked it out to see who got to meet you here. She wanted to come, but I won." David lifted a duffel bag and took Alice's hand. "We're parked out this way."

Noah had met David before, once, at Christmas. Felicity and Alison had chatted happily about the children and clothes, but they'd both kept a watchful eye on the men. Noah had dominated the conversation, but David had actually seemed interested. He'd asked questions that Felicity would never have thought of, questions that made Noah puff up a little, glad to be taken seriously by an older, time-tested businessman.

In the airport parking lot, Felicity told Noah to take the front passenger seat. It had more room for his long legs, she said, and she happily buckled herself in the backseat, between the two children, who were bouncing with eagerness to get to the beach. At the house, after receiving warm hugs from Alison, the kids thundered up to the bedroom to put on bathing suits.

"Are Poppy and the kids here?" Felicity asked.

"Not yet. They'll arrive this afternoon."

"Great. I'll go up and help the kids get their suits on." She turned to Noah.

"Want to come down for a swim?"

"Not now. Maybe later," Noah said.

Oh, Lord, Felicity inwardly moaned.

"I'm going to sit on the deck and talk with David awhile," Noah continued.

Felicity perked up. Good. This was good. David was without doubt the alpha male; it was a compliment to Noah that David was spending so much time with him.

"Hey, sis." Jane strolled into the bathroom where Felicity was struggling to get Luke into his swim trunks. Alice stood on a short stool, admiring her braided hair.

"Hey, Auntie Jane, I've got sharks!" Luke pointed to his trunks.

"Cool," Jane told him, and kissed his forehead.

"I've got mermaids," Alice told Jane.

"You *look* like a mermaid," Jane told her.

Felicity stood up to hug Jane. "I'm so glad you're here!"

"Me, too, and you have no idea," Jane said.

"Give me a hint," Felicity said over her shoulder as she rubbed sunblock into her children's faces and limbs.

"Ethan," Jane said, and she winked.

"Wait till we get to the beach," Felicity said. "We can talk without, um, *little pitchers.*"

"I *know* what that means, Mom," Alice said disdainfully. "You and Auntie Jane want to tell each other secrets."

"Aren't you a clever girl," Jane said. She knelt down to the children's level. "Well, guess what. I have secrets for you." She gathered her niece and nephew close and whispered to them.

"YAY!" Luke shouted.

"You are the coolest adult in the world!" Alice added.

The two children raced down the steps, across the deck, and down the sandy path to the beach, where two giant inflatable water toys waited: a white unicorn with a pink mane and a dragon. In minutes they were bobbing in the shallows, screaming with joy.

"Jane, what wonderful presents!"

Jane grinned. "Method in my madness, kid. I brought a couple for Poppy's kids, too. Now we can talk." She unfolded her beach chair and set it next to Felicity's.

"All right, spill."

"Last weekend? When you all weren't here? Ethan was here. And so was I. So he invited me out to dinner and . . ." Jane spoke with mischievous slowness, drawing out each word.

"And?"

"And we ate at the Boarding House. The food was excellent, and the drinks—"

Felicity slapped her sister's shoulder. "Stop that. I don't need to hear about the food. What happened? Did he kiss you?"

Jane laughed. "Um, yeah. He kissed me. A *lot*. In fact, he drove me out to a secret spot on the moors, off on a dirt road where nobody ever goes at night. I had the top down on the convertible, and the air was warm, and Ethan and I had a good old make-out session. Better than anything I ever had in high school. We reclined our seats, and Ethan moved over on top of me, and—"

Felicity's heart clutched. "Oh, please, Jane, no. Don't tell me you had sex with him."

Jane drew back. "Why not?"

"Why not? Because you're *married.* It's one thing to flirt with a guy, even kiss him, and it's such a boost to the ego to have him pursue you. But it's wrong to have sex with him. If you're married, you're supposed to be faithful."

Felicity burst into tears.

"Oh, honey." Jane put a consoling hand on her sister's arm but Felicity shook it off. "Is Noah sleeping with Ingrid?"

Angrily, Felicity brushed the tears off her cheeks. "Maybe, I don't know, but the point is, Jane, you shouldn't be having sex with Ethan when you're married to Scott! No matter what Scott's doing, you should be faithful to your husband!"

Jane sat back in her beach chair and took a moment. She waved at the kids, who were gleefully butting into each other with their inflatable creatures. When Felicity had stopped crying, Jane said quietly, "No, we didn't have sex. A park ranger came along and told us to leave. That spoiled the mood, and I thought it would make a funny story. I told you how it is with Scott and me. We may be headed for divorce. I can't imagine how we'll resolve our differences. Right now we are diametrically opposed. And it was delicious to have such a sexy man wanting me."

"I hope you and Scott don't get divorced." Felicity reached out and took Jane's hand. "I think you're a really great couple."

Jane squeezed her sister's hand. "I get how you feel about marriage, but I honestly can't promise anything."

Felicity sighed. "I know I was laughing about Ethan flirting with you, but having sex is taking it to a whole different level, Jane, and I know what I'm talking about. Noah says he hasn't had sex with Ingrid yet, and for some odd reason, I believe him. If he does have sex with her . . . how can I stay married to him? And what about the children?"

"At least Noah is here now," Jane reminded her sister. "He's here and it's going to be a gorgeous weekend, so he can relax and enjoy his family. He'll remember how important his home life is. Try not to worry, at least for this weekend."

"Okay, then, you stay away from Ethan so I won't have to worry about you."

Jane shook her head ruefully and held out her hand. "Deal. Shake on it."

They shook and Felicity hugged Jane. "I love you."

"I love you, too. Now let's go for a swim."

Lunch was late, and afterward the children, sun-stunned from the water, collapsed on the sofa in the den, watching television. The adults lingered at the table, idly chatting, picking red grapes and cherries from the fruit bowl.

"Will you be able to come here for a weekend or two in August?" Alison asked Noah.

Felicity froze. She'd never asked her mother to inquire about Noah's plans, and why was she asking, anyway, what did it matter to Alison? Noah hated to be put on the spot.

"I'm not sure," Noah answered. "My work is in a crucial stage right now."

"I'm asking because I'd love for you to see the hotel where our wedding and the reception will be," Alison explained with a smile.

"It's sublime," Jane chimed in. "Heavenly."

Noah frowned. "I'd like to see it, but I don't know when I'll find time to get back here."

David spoke up. "Look, why don't I drive you out to the hotel today, Noah? In fact, the manager is a friend of mine. He might let us use a couple of kayaks. We can explore the head of the harbor and get a beer after."

Noah looked uncomfortable. "I've never been in a kayak."

"It's as easy as sitting in a chair," David said. "And they insist we wear life jackets, so you don't have to worry about drowning."

"I wasn't worried about that," Noah grumbled.

Felicity held her breath. Was her husband going to be rude to his future stepfather-in-law?

"Let's go, then." David pushed back his chair and rose. "We'll be home around five," he told Alison, and gave her a quick kiss.

Noah followed David from the kitchen, not bothering to speak to Felicity.

The front door shut. Two car doors slammed. David's Jeep roared off.

"Well, girls, what shall we do now?" Alison asked with a smile.

Jane looked at her mother. "Felicity thinks Noah's having an affair."

Felicity said, "And Jane wants to go to bed with Ethan."

Later in the afternoon, Alison told her daughters she was tired and needed a nap.

"Are you okay, Mom?" Jane asked, slightly alarmed.

"I'm fine, sweetie. Just old."

"You're not old, Mom!" Felicity protested.

"If you want to take the kids into town, my car keys are on that hook," Alison said. She kissed the top of both daughters' heads and left the room. She climbed the stairs and entered the master bedroom and locked the door behind her. She didn't want to rest on the chaise longue by the window—the day was too bright, and she was not in the mood to enjoy the scene.

She curled up on her bed, facing the wall, pulling an old soft quilt made by her grandmother up over her. The room was air-conditioned, and she needed the sense of comfort the quilt gave her.

She was deeply disturbed by what her daughters had shared with her. She'd sat in the kitchen, listening as Felicity talked about Noah's relationship with his personal assistant and Jane spoke of her desire for children and Scott's adamant refusal to consider it. The old instinctive need to protect her daughters rose within her, a tide as natural and unavoidable as the surf swelling up on the ocean. These men! These ridiculous, blockheaded men, who had vowed to love her daughters and were now making them miserable. But what could Alison do? They were grown men; they couldn't be scolded or cajoled or even bribed into changing. Oh, why in the world did people get married?

She rolled over to her other side, and as if her thoughts were small wooden blocks, another thought clicked into place. *Of course* she couldn't do anything about all this. Her daughters were grown, too. They were healthy, intelligent, capable women, and really, weren't they being a bit . . . *insensitive?* . . . to dump all this on Alison just a few weeks before her wedding? They were, after all, relatively young. Alison was fifty-five. She had done her duty to the girls. She had kept them well fed and safe and loved for the first twenty years of their lives, and she had worked part-time to make special trips and clothes possible. Would this never end? Would they stand at Alison's deathbed as she gasped for her last breath, tattling on each other and complaining about their problems?

Okay, Alison told herself, she was overwrought. After all, Felicity and Jane hadn't asked for advice from Alison, they had simply shared their lives with her. How many women did Alison know who didn't have that close connection with their children, who saw their children only at Christmas and had no clue what problems and joys they had?

But, to put the cherry on top of the dysfunctional sundae, Poppy was making a mess of her work for David's company.

How foolish she'd been, thinking that David's assistant would take care of *all* the arrangements for their wedding party. Alison wished she could send Heather a memo telling her to deal with Noah and Scott.

At some point, Alison must have fallen into a light doze, because it was after four when she opened her eyes. Yawning, she stretched, feeling wonderfully rested. She refreshed herself in the bathroom, brushing her hair, adding a touch of lipstick, and then she opened the bedroom door and stepped out into the hall.

"Well, I think you're disgusting!" It was Poppy, hissing.

A man laughed. Alison's mind sorted quickly and informed her: Ethan. Poppy and Ethan were downstairs in the front hall, arguing.

"Poppy, come on. Don't be such a puritan. I've always flirted with women. You know that. It's one of my hobbies."

"I'm a puritan? You're a *slut*."

Ethan sighed and his voice was exasperated. "Give me a break. You're just hormonal these days. You're not seeing things clearly."

"I'm seeing that you're not divorced like you're telling Jane and Felicity you are."

"So? I'm separated. Moving toward divorce."

"Yes, and how many years have you been *separated*?"

"We live in different countries. We're both working," Ethan said.

"Well, I'm going to tell Dad," Poppy informed Ethan.

"That's ridiculous. What are you, five years old? What's Dad going to do, ground me? Besides, he's got enough on his plate now, with you taking over the company."

"What do you mean by that?" Poppy snapped.

"Calm down. I only mean it's a big deal, stepping away from the family company. It's a life passage. He's stepping out of a lifetime as the chairman of a huge organization into being a retired old man."

"Daddy will *never* be just another retired old man!" Poppy cried.

"I didn't mean it that way. Come on, Poppy, let's get a drink and chill. We're getting way too dramatic about all this."

"I can't drink. I'm pregnant, remember?"

Their voices faded as they left the hall for the kitchen. Alison realized she'd been holding her breath. She absolutely did not want David's children to know she'd overheard them. She wondered whether she should tell Jane that Ethan wasn't actually divorced. But after all, Jane was still married to Scott.

The front door opened and her grandchildren thundered in, followed by Felicity and Jane.

"Swimming, yay!" Luke yelled, tossing his paper bag of new toys on the floor.

"Luke, no." Felicity bent over to pick up the bag. "I told you and Alice if you kept on fussing you wouldn't be able to swim anymore today."

Aha, Alison thought, as both children went into fits of screaming. *Here's something I can help with.*

Alison walked down the stairs and put an arm around Felicity. "Hello, darling." She lowered her voice to a whisper. "I've always thought that one should never give a punishment to children that makes it even more unpleasant for the mother."

Felicity gawked. "What?"

"If they can't swim, what will they do with all their energy?"

"Oh," Felicity said. "Right. Clever." She knelt down and brought her children close to her. "I've changed my mind. You can go swimming now, as soon as Jane and I get our bathing suits on. Because you were fussing in the car, you can't have dessert tonight."

Luke and Alice exchanged glances, agreeing without words: This was a compromise they could accept.

"Fine," Alice said. "I'll put on my bathing suit."

"You, too, Luke. And don't leave your clothes in the hall," Felicity told them.

twenty-one

That night, Jane insisted she'd prepare dinner. She settled her mother and David in chairs on the deck with a pitcher of sangria and glasses rattling with ice. When Felicity offered to help, Jane said, "Absolutely not. This is my treat. Go have a drink with your husband."

The four children had showered and shampooed and were outside playing an unorthodox game of badminton. Their shouts of laughter, their helpless giggles, drifted in on the light breeze. Jane smiled. The laughter was contagious.

She was making two different dishes: a comforting, familiar, tuna noodle casserole for the four kids and pasta with fresh tuna, red onions, olives, and shaved parmesan for the adults. She found several bottles of red wine to pair with the pasta dish and she'd poured herself a glass to enjoy while she was cooking.

She set the dining room table for the adults and the kitchen table for the four children. She set out a green salad and the wineglasses and was back in the kitchen, grating the parmesan, when she sensed someone entering the kitchen.

"Hey," Ethan said.

Jane looked at him. His tan was more golden, his blond hair more sun-streaked, and his blue eyes flashed whenever he met Jane's. After their adventure on the moors, they'd returned to the sleeping house and crept quietly to their own beds. The next day, as scheduled, they'd both flown home. Since then, he'd texted her once, and she had not replied. She was trying to be thoughtful about this. She was trying to be good.

"Hey," Jane replied.

"Whatever you're making smells delicious."

Jane nodded toward the open bottle. "Pour yourself a glass of wine."

Ethan did, moving slowly, deliberately, doing that thing he'd done the day they made the bread, coming just near enough to Jane that he almost touched her, then turning away. Her body responded. She wanted to reach out and pull him to her. She wanted to press her body against his.

"I texted you this week," Ethan said, leaning against the counter next to the stove. "You didn't answer."

Her pulse was throbbing in every part of her body. She'd become a human engine of desire.

"Okay," she said aloud to herself, "I've sautéed the tuna and the pasta's bubbling. Salad's on the table. I've got five minutes before I call everyone in for dinner."

Ethan gently rested his hand on her wrist, turning her toward him. "Can we take a ride after dinner?"

This is how people need air, Jane thought. *They might want to drown and hold their breath and sink into the ocean, but the body wants to live and bursts to the surface.* The irony tonight was that Ethan was the air, and Jane had to force herself not to take it.

"Ethan, no. Wait, let me say this. I want to have sex with you, but I'm married, and so I won't have sex with you."

"Your husband is in Wales, right?"

"He is. And we, Scott and I, are farther apart than we've ever been, and I don't mean geographically. I'm angry at him, and I'm disappointed by him, and I don't really know whether we'll stay married or not—"

Ethan slid his hand up her arm so that he was touching the side of her breast. "I don't see—"

"I can't. I won't. I mean it, I can't betray my marriage vows."

"Scott will never know," Ethan said softly.

Jane shrugged. "Yeah, he will. Because I'll tell him. Because that's the way I am. I don't know what I thought I was doing, Ethan, going to the moors with you. I'm crazy attracted to you, and I acted like a teenager. I'm sorry, and I'm not pleased with myself. But whatever you and I have going on, it has to end. I'm ending it."

Ethan leaned forward, as if he were going to kiss her mouth, but he put his lips to her ear and whispered, "We'll see about that."

His whisper sent a shiver through her.

The buzzer sounded.

"Pasta's ready," Jane said. "Would you tell everyone to come in for dinner?"

By nine o'clock that night, all four children were zonked out asleep, the kitchen had been cleaned, the dishwasher was pleasantly churning, and the adults were gathered around the kitchen table playing poker.

Jane held five pathetically low cards, but she was good at keeping a poker face, so she matched the ante without a pause. After all, they were playing for kitchen matches.

The families were finally in a good space, she thought, studying those around her. Her mother and David were relaxed, shooting each other fond glances and making jokes.

Noah was low-key, drinking a beer and laughing at jokes, acting like a normal human being. Felicity was trying just a bit too hard to be sparklingly appreciative of every word that fell from Noah's mouth.

Poppy was eating nuts and chips and anything within reach. "I'm a hog. I know. I'm eating for two."

"For two hogs," Patrick quipped, and instead of getting mad, Poppy replied, "Yes, honey, and we're both yours." And she snorted twice, loudly. So that was a side of Poppy Jane hadn't seen before!

And Ethan. He sat on the other side of the table, between his father and Felicity.

When her eyes met Ethan's, she felt a shock of desire so strong, she was surprised it didn't set the air on fire around them.

She hadn't heard from Scott since his first text. This silence angered Jane, made her afraid that Scott had decided the marriage was over, and a wriggling little wish for some kind of revenge made her think she would damn well disregard Felicity's advice and take whatever Ethan was offering.

"Jane," Alison said, "where do you think Scott is right now?"

Jane stared at her mother. How many times in her childhood and adolescence had Alison done this very thing, zeroing in on exactly what was in Jane's mind at that very moment?

"Um, well, he's in Wales," Jane said, gathering her thoughts. "He wants to hike to the top of Mount Snowdon, which is only about thirty-five hundred feet but it's a difficult and dangerous climb. The weather changes as you go up. It gets colder and the fog can be so thick you can't see your hand in front of you. And he's taking the Watkin trail. Miss a step and you plunge down either side . . ."

"Stop it," Felicity said. "You're scaring yourself. Don't be so dramatic."

"No, no, she's right." David spoke up. "I had friends who hiked there one summer. They had sweatshirts on, and halfway up they decided to snack on the Snickers in their pockets, and the candy bars were frozen hard. That path you mentioned is highly exposed and slippery, even when it's sunny down below."

"So that's why you've seemed preoccupied," Alison said. "I've been wondering. You're not like your normal self."

Jane didn't dare look at Ethan, but she sensed that he was suddenly fascinated with his poker hand.

"Call him," Felicity said.

"It's the middle of the night there," Jane said. "I'm being foolish. Scott's an experienced hiker."

"He is," Jane's mother agreed. "I've been amazed at the places you and he have gone together. I drool over your videos." Alison looked around the table. "Have any of you ever been to Zermatt, Switzerland? It's at the foot of the Matterhorn. I'm still reeling from the beauty of the photos you took there, Jane. You and Scott are a fascinating couple, traveling to such astonishing places. Those photos of you both climbing with ropes attached to you and your guide! My goodness, the trust you must have in each other. And yet, when you're in the city, you both flourish in a completely different environment. You're so urban and professional, and when you two took me to the fundraiser for the opera, you both looked like movie stars. Scott in a tux? A Ralph Lauren ad."

Jane laughed. "Mom, I think you're getting carried away."

Felicity spoke up. "No, Mom's right. Scott in a tux is a romance novel fantasy."

David interrupted, "All right, enough adoration of Scott. You've got real men here and we want to play poker."

Jane glanced down at her cards, but any concentration she'd had on the game had vanished. She couldn't stop thinking about Scott and what her mother said about the trust Jane and Scott must share. It was true, they had been in places when they had physically relied on each other to ascend, to keep from falling, and whenever they reached their goal at the top of a ridge or open land after a narrow ledge, they'd shared such elation, they'd shouted and kissed and Jane had loved Scott so deeply and she had felt his love in return.

They had each other's backs in their professions, as well. Staying up late into the night discussing problems at work, giving each other good advice and pointing out the blind spots. They'd flattered and charmed each other's bosses at parties, they'd shared the effort of giving dinners at home for colleagues. They'd provided excellent sounding boards for each other's creative thoughts, they'd cheered and drank champagne at celebrations and consoled one another with long talks deep into the night.

They were such good friends.

Never before had they come up against such a bump, a barrier, in the fluid river of their marriage. Their marriage was like a reliable, watertight craft that she had slammed into a rock, and she didn't know if this vessel would split in two or somehow remain sound.

But she didn't want to lose Scott. She saw that now; she *felt* it. She loved him and believed in his love for her.

"I'm out," Jane said, tossing down her cards. "I've got to make a phone call."

She left the table, not caring if Ethan watched her go.

In the privacy of her room, Jane tried Scott's number.

No answer. She didn't leave a message.

Sunday dawned hot and humid. After packing picnic lunches and coolers of cold drinks, the group headed to Coatue, the sandy peninsula of land with five points making five small coves. David sailed his catboat, which wasn't big enough to take the entire group, so Patrick, who had handled David's motorboat before, powered them through the harbor. Felicity worried that Noah would feel insulted because he hadn't been asked to steer the motorboat and she sighed with relief when she saw Ethan hand Noah a lemonade and sit down next to him to talk.

It was, Felicity thought, a perfect summer day. They swam and

ate and dozed in the sun. Jane led Alice and Luke on a beachcomb-
ing trek through the dunes, so both Felicity and Noah took a nap in
the shade of the beach umbrellas.

They were all drowsy with heat and sunshine as they sailed back
to the harbor, moored the boats, and drove through town to David's
house. Jane drove herself back to the airport to catch her plane back
to New York, while Felicity ushered her children through showers
and shampoos and into clean clothes. David drove the Wellingtons
to their plane. Noah shook hands manfully with David and promised to come back soon, but once they were in line for boarding,
Noah whipped out his phone and ignored his wife and children.
That was all right, Felicity thought. At least he'd come to the island.
And he'd enjoyed his time with David and Patrick and Ethan. It
was possible Noah had been charmed by the island and Felicity's
blended family. It was possible that the golden glow of Nantucket
would make Noah forget whatever pleasures Ingrid was offering.

Everyone was glad to be home. Felicity tucked her children into
their own beds. She started to pull on one of the old T-shirts she
slept in, but a thought occurred to her. Noah had been silent on the
drive home, but she was certain he'd had a good time. He had
seemed to get along very well with David. So Felicity put on a nightgown, a real nightgown instead of a T-shirt, short and lacy and al-
luring. She went down to the den to seduce her husband.

Noah was sitting on the sofa, not isolated in a chair. A good sign.
Felicity curled up in the arm of the sofa, facing him.

"So, did you have a good weekend?" she asked.

"Anyone could have a good time staying at a multimillion-dollar
rich boy's summer castle." Noah's words spilled out in a bitter
surge.

Felicity was stunned. "But, uh, didn't you think that David was
nice?"

Noah turned to face Felicity and he was angry. "David *should* be
nice with all that money."

"Well, Noah, I don't think there's a correlation between wealth and niceness. Look at Bernie Madoff. Look at—"

"My point exactly! These guys who own the world are nothing more than conspicuously consuming crooks!"

"David isn't a croo—"

Noah interrupted her. "Of course he is! He's raping the island, despoiling the natural beaches, sucking up fuel for his damned powerboat, not to mention the house, the damned *beach* house, has air-conditioning! And heat!"

"The family has always spent a lot of time on the island in the off-season," Felicity explained. "They come for the Cranberry Festival, Thanksgiving, the Stroll, Christmas, Daffodil weekend—"

"All unnatural reasons to come to the island!" Noah rose from the sofa and paced the floor, slamming his fist into the palm of his hand.

"Well, *Thanksgiving*—"

"A man like that makes me want to vomit. Such a show-off, an egomaniac who doesn't give a shit about nature unless it's got a sticker he can put on his four-wheel drive vehicle! Felicity, I used to admire your mother. I thought she was a good woman, a smart woman, but now I think she's just another pretty face who's gotten her claws into a rich man!"

"How dare you!" Angered, Felicity stood up and blocked her husband's pacing. "How dare you say that about my mother. She's not a gold digger!"

"You're blind if you can't see it."

"Noah, come on, you're being irrational."

"You think? I might be, because that whole setup makes me so damned mad. Have you seen the Wauwinet? David is taking that expensive hotel over for an entire weekend? He can throw away money that should be spent on charities, on wildlife conservation groups, on helping this poor world instead of throwing parties for his group of miserable moneygrubbers! I tell you, Felicity, there is no way in hell I'm going to that wedding."

Felicity's hands flew up to her heart, as if afraid it would stop.

"Oh, Noah. Don't say that. Please. You have to go. Your children will be in the wedding. I'll be in the wedding. My mother would be heartbroken if you didn't come."

"That's her choice," Noah said. "She's chosen the dark side. I'm not going over there."

Felicity stared. Who was this man? She opened her mouth to plead—and instead, she found herself saying, " 'The dark side'? How do you define the dark side? I would say that a husband having an affair with his personal assistant is about as dark as it gets."

Noah recoiled. "Don't drag Ingrid into this."

"Ingrid. You want to protect *Ingrid*? Noah, I am your wife. The mother of your children. If you think David's evil because he has money, what about you? What would your adoring employees think if you got divorced so you can fuck Ingrid?"

"I never mentioned divorce."

"Well, *I* did. Just now." Felicity was standing almost toe-to-toe with her husband, as close as she'd been physically in weeks. Energy was zapping between them, and she knew her face was as red as his, and both of them were breathing heavily, but this was the dynamics of battle, not love.

"You're being absurd," Noah said.

"Oh, I can get crazier," Felicity warned, and she had no idea where these words and the strength to power them was coming from, but she was filled full of a righteousness that she'd been denying for weeks. "I think Ingrid is a danger to our marriage. Either you fire Ingrid, or I'm leaving you."

Noah's face turned from crimson to an unhealthy burgundy, and as angry as she was, Felicity's heart tripped with worry—had she just given her husband a stroke?

"You would do that," he said.

"I would."

"Fine, then. Let's make a deal. I'll fire Ingrid if *you* cut off connections with your family."

"Oh, Noah!" Felicity burst into tears. Her power popped like a bubble. "You know I would never do that! I can't do that!"

She folded into a lump on the sofa, elbows on knees, face in her hand, sobbing.

"I'm not going to let you blackmail me with tears," Noah said.

He left the room.

Felicity continued weeping until she was all cried out. She sat on the sofa, straining to hear where Noah was in the house. Would he come back in? Surely they couldn't leave the argument at this bleak, unresolved spot. She was confused and mad and sad. Had she been strong or had she been foolish?

Rising, she swept her cheeks dry with her hands. She walked into the kitchen for a glass of water to soothe her aching throat. As she stood there drinking, she heard a door shut, and she knew from experience it was the door to their guest room.

At least it wasn't the front door, she thought.

"Well!" Alison said to David once their children had gone and David had watched the Red Sox beat the Yankees, "I think this was a good weekend for everyone."

They were sitting in the den, in separate chairs. Alison was knitting a blanket for Poppy's new baby, and the regular movement of the soft yarn through her fingers worked like a meditation.

David cast a longing eye at the desk where his laptop sat.

"I know you want to read the Sunday newspapers, but you can give me a minute or two. Tell me what you think about the weekend."

David laughed. "Sweetheart, not everything needs to be assessed and inspected. It was a fine weekend, a normal weekend."

"Humor me," Alison said. "Tell me, for example, what you think of Noah."

David considered his thoughts before answering. "I like the man. I think he's wound tight, but that's no surprise given the fact that he's trying to start up a new product, a new company. We had a good talk out at the Wauwinet. His company, Green Food, seems like a viable nutrition option to me, even an important one. It cheers me up a great deal to see our young people taking on the challenges we oldies have given them with such a complicated world."

"I'm so glad you liked him!" Alison held up her knitting. "For Poppy's new baby."

David glanced at it. "Nice," he replied dutifully. "I'm thinking I might invest in Green Food. They could use an influx of capital, and I'd like to help them out."

"David, how wonderful!"

"Don't say anything yet, please. I've got to go over some figures before I say anything to him. I'm not sure how much I can free up."

"I won't say a word," Alison promised.

"Seriously, Alison. I don't want to get his hopes up only to disappoint him."

"I don't want to do that, either. But I'm pleased you're considering this."

"How do you feel about the weekend?" David asked.

Alison smiled. She loved it when David would do what she called "feeling talk" with her. "I thought it went well. I'm worried that Jane hasn't heard from Scott. I hope he's okay."

"Scott's a seasoned traveler," David reminded her.

"True." Alison stopped knitting. "I think whatever little flame of passion ignited between your son and my daughter has died down."

"Oh, Ethan's always been a flirt." David waved his hand as if dismissing a fly.

"And how's Poppy?"

"Now that her morning sickness has passed, she's got her head on straight. I think it was an enormous gift to her, postponing our honeymoon. It will ease the transition of control. It's probably better for the employees, too."

"Is it better for you?" Alison asked. "You don't seem upset that you're still working instead of playing golf."

David said, "You might be right. But what about you? If I work, even part-time, what will you do?"

Alison laughed. In a soft Southern voice, she cooed, "Why, darlin', I'll lie around watchin' TV and eatin' chocolates, jus' like I always do."

"All right, point made." David sent another look at his laptop. "And by the way, I don't want to check on work. I want to check on our wedding weekend. Not everyone has responded. And I need an update from Heather about the flowers and the welcome baskets and the band. Heather wanted a group from Boston, but I've heard the island band Coq Au Vin is good. I've listened to a CD and I'm glad we booked them."

Alison moved over to sit on David's lap. "I think you're more excited about this occasion than I am."

"Maybe I am. I've spent too many months looking at the past. I like facing forward again. Why don't I get my laptop and we can run through the plans? I can email Heather—it's only eight-thirty—"

Heather, Alison thought grouchily. Heather was so infinitely capable. Did she make Alison seem incompetent by comparison? But Alison knew she was a star at organization when it came to life. All her life she'd managed children, husband, and even her parents and Mark's parents as they'd aged and toddled off into retirement homes. Alison had managed to get Jane to soccer matches and Felicity to ballet practice and picked up Mark's dry cleaning and baked dozens of brownies for fundraisers. She'd worked as a receptionist for a busy dental practice. Of course she could deal with flowers, music, invitations, and all the complicated arrangements of their wedding. The truth was, Alison was glad to have Heather doing all this work. It freed Alison up for being with her family.

But she was here, now, Alison reminded herself. And there was one thing she could do that would make David happy . . .

"It's Sunday. You shouldn't bother her on Sunday. Anyway, why don't we *not* think about the future?" Alison suggested. "Why don't we think of something we can do right now?"

She wrapped her arms around David and kissed him softly, all over his face, down his neck, behind his ear.

David groaned and ran his hands over Alison. "I know what we can do right now. And right here."

"Yes," Alison agreed. "Everyone's gone. We're alone in the house." Rising, she took David's hand and pulled him to the sofa.

"This feels . . . decadent," David said.

"Yes, it feels as if we're teenagers again, doesn't it? Not waiting to go to a bed, making love where we are because that's what feels—*necessary.*"

As she and David arranged themselves on the sofa, Alison experienced a flush of great affection for the man who was struggling to undo his belt with some kind of grace. At that moment, David seemed to her the perfect man, capable of exerting power, acting creatively and decisively, and still able to transform himself from business executive to gentle lover. His chest hair was silver, and his face was becoming jowly. But Alison silently shrieked to think what her face looked like now, as her jaw lay pressed into her wrinkled neck. They were no longer young. Lovemaking was no longer desperate. It was tender, and sweet, a spring rain rather than a thunderstorm and—

—and David kicked his trousers onto the floor and Alison slipped her pants off. David lowered himself onto her, and suddenly she was young again, overwhelmed, *taken.* Surprised by what her body—her body and David's—could still do.

twenty-two

When Felicity awoke, it was late, after eight, but it was summer and she could hear her children playing in their rooms, so she rose leisurely, taking time for a full body stretch from her fingers to her toes.

She wasn't surprised that Noah wasn't in their bed. Last night he'd slept in the guest bedroom, his phone and laptop with him. Oh, how she wished she could hack into his email! She'd had trouble falling asleep, wondering if Noah was texting Ingrid.

Sexting Ingrid.

She pulled on shorts and a T-shirt. A quick peek at the guest room proved Noah was already up and out of the house. Felicity rounded up Alice and Luke and shepherded them to the kitchen where they ate cereal while she drank a lifesaving cup of coffee and packed their lunches. This week both kids were in day camp from

ten in the morning until four in the afternoon. They had friends
who would be there, as well, and Felicity knew some of the
counselors—healthy, cheery young women with ponytails and colorful braided bracelets that they taught the children to make on
rainy days at camp.

"Backpacks!" Felicity reminded her children.

It amused her, and comforted her, to see how readily Alice and
Luke did what she told them. They couldn't wait to get to camp.
They flew to the car and snapped on their seatbelts and jabbered
with each other during the ride to the small farm with its barn and
pond and tree houses. Four teenage girls and boys were waiting at
the gated driveway to collect the children. Alice and Luke yelled,
"Bye, Mom!" and exploded out of the SUV and into the camp-
ground.

Felicity drove away slowly, her mind stirring with thoughts like
a sleeping animal waking. The counselors had been so genuinely
happy to see the children. True, the counselors were young and energetic and it was fun to be outdoors on a great summer day. But it
was more than that. The teens' faces had brightened when they saw
the children, they reached out to hug them, to hear Alice and Luke
jabber away. They liked working with children.

When Felicity saw the sign for Walden Pond, she turned and
drove down the forested two-lane road. She parked in the lot,
pleased to see that it was still half empty, crossed the street, and
walked down to the pond. On the beach, several families were
swimming, and two women marched along the trail on the far side
of the pond.

Felicity found the trailhead and began walking. She'd been here
before, with her children or with friends, but today she was alone,
and she was glad. Somehow all this natural space around her gave
her thoughts space to roam free.

She'd cried herself to sleep last night, and her heart was heavy
today. Noah had thrown down a powerful ultimatum—he would
fire Ingrid if Felicity would break with her family. It made sense to

her, she thought it would make sense to *anyone*, that Noah should fire Ingrid because Ingrid was a risk to his marriage. But how in the world could Felicity's family be a risk to her marriage to Noah?

Well, she thought, as she brushed a willow branch away from her face, Noah had been furious last night about the kind of money David had. Maybe that was it.

Okay, Felicity said to herself, following her thoughts as they led her along an unknown path. Noah was worried about money. Always. His first and most continuous stressor was the future of his company. He was working hard, she knew that, and he wanted to make his business a success not only for financial reasons, but of course money was part of it.

His second largest stressor was personal money. Money for the house, for clothes for the children, vacations for the children, never mind vacations for him. Did it hurt his pride that David Gladstone could provide such a luxurious vacation for Felicity and Noah and their children when Noah couldn't possibly afford a night for his family on that island?

Keep thinking, she told herself. *You're getting somewhere.*

She stepped over a fallen log. Noah was so proud of their house because from the outside it looked elegant, pricey. But only Felicity knew how they had to cut corners with their money when it came to eating out, repairing the air-conditioning, taking the children to water parks like the Great Wolf Lodge.

Their money.

Could she help financially? In September both children would be in school all day, Alice in second grade, Luke in first. She would have enough time freed up for at least a part-time job . . . but what could she do? She'd majored in education and psychology in college, but after she met Noah, she cared about nothing in the world besides being with him. When she got pregnant just before graduation, Noah had been as delighted as Felicity. She was certain of that. Noah had been full of ambition and hope for his business, and having a wife to take care of the routine matters of life—buying groceries, cooking, doing laundry—that had seemed absolutely right to him.

But now? Now, seven years after graduation, Felicity had her degree in education, but no state preschool teaching certificate.

But she knew how to get one. She knew where to find the information she needed to bone up on to take the examination. She had friends who would help her.

She had friends who would hire her. Preschools always needed teachers.

Did she want to work in a preschool? Felicity tried to return to her mindset in the early days of her college career, when she was still young and free and could choose whatever route her heart desired. Her father had paid for her education, she'd lived in a dorm or at home, she had no pressing debts and all the world was before her. She could have majored in English because she loved reading, or in social work because she loved people, but she had instinctively gone for education, because she loved children, the younger, the better. She'd made money during the summer as an aide in a local preschool, and she'd loved every minute of it. Sitting in a circle with the children, teaching them songs, or marshaling them into lines to go out for a field trip, seeing their faces when they were allowed to hold a frog in their hands . . .

Felicity realized she was walking faster and faster, almost running, and when she tripped over another log, she forced herself to slow down.

Be honest, she told herself. *Any money you make teaching preschool is hardly going to help Noah with the cost of running the house and our lives.*

But, she argued with herself, it would be *some* money. And it would show Noah she was on his side, trying to help.

When he came home tonight, she would ask him about her idea. In the meantime, she couldn't wait to get home to her laptop. She was sure there was a preschool near the children's elementary school. How cool would that be?

. . .

Jane was in her office at the law firm, but she couldn't concentrate on her work because she was so angry at Scott. Why wouldn't he answer his phone? How childish! In the back of her mind, a small worry fluttered its wings like a trapped moth, but she refused to give in to any fear that something might have happened to him. He was a careful climber. And a very stubborn man.

Just before noon, her cellphone buzzed. The number displayed had a 44 followed by too many digits. Was that the prefix for Wales? She reached for her phone.

"May I please speak with Mrs. Jane Hudson, please?" The voice was unfamiliar.

"This is she," Jane said, a chill of dread racing through her.

"This is Derfel Aberfa. I'm the liaison officer for the Llanberis Mountain Rescue League."

"Mountain rescue? What's happened? Is Scott all right?"

"A hiker on Mount Snowdon found Scott Hudson's cellphone near the Crib Goch path. Another hiker reported talking with him earlier today on the path. Mr. Hudson told him he was headed for the summit. Where the phone was found, and the fact that it was shattered, indicates that Mr. Hudson might have fallen. We could access some information from the phone but it won't send or receive calls."

"Maybe he went back to the hotel, or to buy a new phone?"

"Your husband told Mr. Davies, the hiker who spoke with him, that he was staying at the resort Portmeirion. We've called, and he has a room, but he was not there. Someone went to check. We have left him a message on his room phone. The Llanberis Mountain Rescue League has begun a search. On Portmeirion's records, you are listed as his emergency contact. Would you have any idea what color shirt or jumper Mr. Hudson might be wearing?"

Jane's mind froze. Oh, Lord, what kind of wife was she? Then, in a rush, she knew. "Scott is a fairly experienced hiker. We've read about Mount Snowdon and how cold it can be toward the summit. I'm sure he would be wearing a navy blue fleece jacket, and a blue wool cap with the New York Yankees logo. I think he would have a backpack with him with water and trail mix."

"Good. Thank you, Mrs. Hudson." Mr. Aberfa paused. "Will you be able to come to Wales?"

"Yes, yes, I'll get the first plane I can."

"Your best bet is to fly into Manchester rather than London. You can take the train to Bangor. That's faster and safer than renting a car, especially if you aren't accustomed to driving on the left side of the road."

"Yes, I'll do that. Thank you for the information."

"Is this the number where you can be contacted?"

"Yes."

"We'll have further communications," Derfel Aberfa said.

"Thank you."

They disconnected. Jane sent emails to her coworkers, grabbed her purse, and took a cab home. She hurried to the closet, reaching to the top shelf for her rolling suitcase. She set it on the bed, unzipped it, and opened her dresser drawer, taking a handful of panties and tossing them in the small suitcase.

"No, stupid," she told herself, and ignoring the bag, she took her laptop from the top of the dresser onto her bed. Sitting crosslegged in front of it, she searched for the earliest flight she could get to Manchester from New York. It would take an hour to get to Kennedy, and an hour, more or less, to get through security. She booked a flight on British Airways. She raced into the bathroom and brushed her teeth and found the travel kit she always had waiting. She tossed that in the suitcase with socks and a shirt and a sweater, and then she thought that Scott would need clean clothes, too, although of course he had some still at his hotel. She organized her purse, remembered to get her passport from her home office desk, and pulled on a light cashmere sweater. It was still too hot to need the warmth, but she needed the sense of comfort. She hurried out to the street and flagged down a cab.

• • •

David had asked Alison to come into his office to go over all the wedding details with Heather, so Monday morning Alison chose her most elegant summer dress, a simple dark blue linen sheath with cap sleeves and a high mandarin collar. While she liked Heather, she was always slightly overwhelmed by her reserved and formal manner. Heather was in her fifties, charming, with the kind of short blond hairstyle made popular by Princess Diana. When they'd first met, she'd worried that David's assistant might harbor romantic designs on him. David assured her this was not the case. Heather was happily married to Cecil Willet, a surgeon at Mass General.

David had gone into the office early, so Alison drove her own car along the crowded eight-lane racetrack that was Route 128. The English Garden Creams general management offices were housed in a handsome brick and glass high-rise near Natick. The products were made in the larger, lower brick building situated on a winding road behind the main offices. Alison found a parking space beneath a shady tree and walked along the brick pathway surrounded by blooming shrubbery to the main door. She gave her name to the receptionist at the tall desk in the large and gorgeous lobby, and took the elevator to the top floor.

She stepped off the elevator, walked down the hall, and stepped into another receptionist's office. Immediately Heather came from her glassed-in office, two large and beautiful dogs by her side. Today she wore a simple lavender linen dress and a string of pearls. Alison had never seen a linen dress so free of wrinkles. She made a mental note to ask the all-capable Heather how she did it.

"Alison! Hello. Don't be afraid. I had to bring the boys to work today because they've got their annual vet exams at two and I didn't want to have to drive all the way home when the vet's place is so near here. Go on, pet them, they love it."

"Hello, gorgeous," Alison said, petting the black Lab while the yellow Lab pushed at her hand for equal attention. "Noble heads."

Heather absolutely beamed. "Yes. They're English Labs. Charlie is the black and Henry the yellow. They're littermates, but they have completely different personalities —Henry is dominant, serious, and protective. Charlie is the mischievous and outgoing one." Heather squatted on her very high heels and nuzzled the dogs.

"They're wonderful," Alison said, trying not to look too amused. This was as effusive and friendly as Heather had ever been.

"Yes, they are, aren't they? They were named after the whale ship *Charles and Henry* on which Herman Melville sailed in 1842. They love to run and they're great swimmers."

"Perfect for Nantucket."

"True. Cecil and I have been taking them down every weekend. Of course, that's made it easier for me to coordinate the wedding with Brie at the Wauwinet. Which reminds me, that's why you're here." Effortlessly, Heather rose.

She must do yoga, Alison thought.

"Let's go in to David's office."

Alison followed Heather as they went through her office with its three walls of windows and one wall of mahogany. They stepped inside David's office, which was large, thickly carpeted, and beautifully furnished. Charlie and Henry came along, quietly settling in a far corner.

"Hello, Alison." David rose from behind his desk.

"Oops! I forgot to bring the folder," Heather said and left the room.

This allowed David a moment to give Alison a kiss. The dogs thumped their tails approvingly.

"She forgot the folder on purpose, didn't she?" Alison whispered, smiling.

"I'm sure she did. She is the perfect assistant." With his hand on her shoulder, David led Alison to the leather sofa.

Heather returned with the folders, one for each of them. "Before we begin, does anyone want coffee? Sparkling water?" She indicated a table in the corner with a coffee maker, handsome china cups and saucers, a cut glass pitcher of ice water, and glasses.

David and Alison both asked for coffee. Heather brought them their cups and finally settled, perching on the edge of a chair, as if ready to take off any moment.

"Very well, here we go," Heather said. "Your wedding is Saturday, September ninth, three weeks away. I mailed out the invitations a week ago and already we've had some replies. I have the guest list here and I'm checking people on or off accordingly." Heather glanced up, smiling. "So far, no regrets. I'm sure people can't wait to attend this wedding!"

Alison quickly scanned the pages in the folder. Heather had locked in Katie Kaizer for photographer and videographer. She'd ordered and arranged forty welcome baskets, made to look like woven Nantucket lightship baskets, filled with notepads and matching pens in ocean blues, sterling silver "white whale" wine-bottle stoppers, miniature wooden sailboats filled with chocolate-covered cranberries, silver compasses with lids, and picture frames embossed with silver shells.

"The guests' gifts are marvelous, Heather," Alison said.

Heather beamed. "I thought you'd like them. Now. Offshore Tents will arrive on Friday to set up the tents. Because they will be set on grass, they'll use pole tents, which can provide a more romantic look, swooping up to peaks with flying banners. Very King Arthur. They helped me figure out how much square footage we'll need based on the number of guests, how many guests we think will dance, the number of persons in the band, and so on." She leaned forward to show David the charts.

Alison took a moment to close her eyes. She knew David wanted a great party, but if she had had to work with such numbers and graphs, she'd lose her mind. She took out her phone and tapped in a note to herself to buy something very special for Heather.

"Brie has typed up a mock program for your wedding. You both were going to decide on the processional music you'd like played, and also, I need you to go over the ceremony with me. You can take this home and make your decisions and email me. I'll want to have it finalized within a week so I can have a program printed. Now, I need to be absolutely sure about this. You want the ceremony inside the tent, right?"

"Yes," Alison answered. "That way, I won't be fretting constantly about whether or not it's going to rain, or worse, blow the way it did last September when hurricanes down south made the Nantucket winds powerful." Also, Alison thought with a smile, she wanted to marry in the tent because it would have a floor, and she could wear her high heels and show off her great legs and not worry about sinking into the grass or sand.

"Great. Got it. Okay, if the weather's good, everyone can go outside after the ceremony where tables of canapés will be set up on the lawn and waiters will have trays of champagne. If the weather's bad, the after party could be held in the hotel's library while round tables and chairs are set up in the tent for the dinner."

"What about live music for the reception?" David asked.

"You asked for Coq Au Vin and they've signed on. And that's it!" Heather said, clapping her hands on her lap.

Both dogs immediately sat at attention.

"Oh, sorry, sorry. Lie down, Charlie, Henry, false alarm." Heather smiled. "They are so well trained—too well trained. David, Alison, do you have any questions?"

"I don't," Alison replied. "I might later, after I've studied all this. Heather, you are doing so much work. I'm so grateful."

"Yes," David said. "This is impressive. Thank you."

Heather cleared her throat, and now she looked uncomfortable, troubled. "David, would it be possible for me to have a few moments to talk with you about . . . another matter?"

"Of course."

"Would you like me to leave the room?" Alison asked, assuming Heather wanted to talk business.

"Yes," Heather said, "well, no. I don't know. It's a personal matter . . ."

David touched Alison's arm. "Stay."

"It's about Poppy," Heather said reluctantly.

"Ah. Why am I not surprised," David said. "Go on."

"Please don't think I'm telling tales or trying to cause problems. But I need some clear direction from you. Poppy does not want me to continue with the wedding organization. She said that it's personal, not company, business. She told me to turn all this"—Heather gestured to the folders—"over to Alison. She said it is Alison's task. That if Alison doesn't want to do it, or can't do it, she should hire a wedding planner to do it, to coordinate with Brie at the Wauwinet."

Alison took a deep breath and looked down at her hands. Next to her, David's body had tensed.

"I see," David said at last. "Heather, I'm sorry you got caught in the middle like this. I'm still the head of the company, and I am continuing to task you with the responsibilities for planning the wedding. I'll talk to Poppy about this as soon as possible."

He hadn't shouted, but iron had entered his voice. Alison thought he must sound like this during business negotiations.

"Good. Fine. Thank you, David."

"Thank *you*, Heather."

Felicity was so engrossed in scanning preschool sites and organizing dinner that she didn't check her cell until late afternoon, when a friend dropped the kids home from camp and they rushed into the backyard to play. When she saw that Jane had left several messages, her pulse quickened. Something was wrong. She called her sister.

"Jane?"

"Felicity, something's happened to Scott. I'm at the airport. I'm going to Wales," Jane blurted. "Well, Manchester first. Then a train to Bangor. A rescue group called me. The head of the group, I mean. They've found Scott's cellphone somewhere on Mount Snowdon, but no sign of Scott. They've checked with his hotel and he's not there. Derfel Aberfa told me—"

"Derfel Aberfa?"

"It's a Welsh name. He's the man who phoned me. He told me

he'd call if he had any other information, if they found Scott. He hasn't called. It's been over six hours and he hasn't called. Felicity, I'm so frightened."

Felicity could hear the fear in her sister's voice. "Oh, Jane, this is so scary. But I'm sure Scott is okay. I'm sure he is. He's an expert climber, you know that."

"I do. I know. We were going to climb Mount Snowdon to prepare for climbing Mount Everest. Snowdon sounds like an easy climb, and it can be, but it's also very tricky, fog can sweep in and block out all signs of trails, the wind can blow a person practically off a trail . . ."

"Jane. Jane! Listen. Do you want me to fly over and go with you?"

"Oh, Felicity, thank you." Jane began to weep. "You're so kind. No. No, not yet, maybe later, or maybe not. I just have to wait and see, don't I? I mean, he *is* a good climber. We don't know where he is, maybe he gave up and hiked back down and now he's sitting in a pub having a beer and eating a sandwich."

"But his cellphone . . ."

"Maybe he dropped it without noticing. That's possible. Isn't it? Isn't it possible?"

"Yes, of course it's possible. Jane, take some deep breaths for me now, okay?"

"Okay."

"Tell me, have you eaten anything today?"

"Coffee. I'm running on coffee."

"Eat something. Eat a doughnut. Carbs will calm you down."

"You sound like Mother."

"Well, I am a mother."

Jane sobbed. "*I'm* not. Scott said he would divorce me so I could go have someone else's baby."

"Oh, Jane, no. He didn't mean it. In the heat of the moment people say all sorts of stupid things."

"Scott's not like that. He's not impulsive. He meant what he said, and that's when I left him. But, Felicity, I love him more than

I want children. I didn't know it then, but I know it now. I wish I could make a bargain with God. If Scott is safe, I won't ever talk about having children again." Jane began to sob again.

It broke Felicity's heart to hear Jane crying. "Oh, Jane. Oh, honey. Those bargains with God don't always work, you know. I mean—I don't know what I mean. Just go slowly, right? One step at a time. Don't confuse everything. Scott didn't fall because you want children. Maybe Scott didn't even fall. Just take that train to Bangor—isn't there a Bangor, Maine?"

"There is. It must have been settled by the Welsh."

"Okay, well, go to Bangor, Wales, and talk to that nice mountain rescue man—golly, Jane, just think! If they sent a *helicopter* to rescue Scott, you might meet Prince William!"

Jane's cries changed into a kind of choking laughter. "Felicity, only you would transform a possibility of death into an opportunity to meet Prince William."

Felicity smiled to herself. Her silliness had broken the flow of Jane's fear. Only for a moment, maybe, but that was better than nothing.

"I wish we lived closer," Felicity said.

"Well, so do I. But first, I need Scott to be alive."

"Do you want me to call Mom?"

"I'll call her now."

"Okay. Please, let me know—day or night. I'll come if you need me."

"I love you, Felicity!"

"I love you, Jane!"

"Thanks, Felicity. I'll call."

Felicity sat on the sofa with her phone in her hand and stared at the coffee table. Yesterday she'd picked some dahlias from her garden and put them in a vase on the table. They were so colorful, red, orange, yellow. Closing her eyes, she said a prayer for Scott's safety. *You never know what will happen next,* she thought, and the thought propelled her out of the living room and into the kitchen. She looked out the window and saw both children playing in the sprinkler. Felicity didn't have a swimming pool like Ingrid's, but she did have two beautiful children who were running and shrieking with glee through the curtain of rainbowed drops.

She checked the time on the clock on the stove. Crystal, the favorite babysitter, would be here any moment. Felicity wouldn't be gone more than an hour. She had talked with Kat, the head of the Small Steps Preschool, and was going for an interview with her at five-fifteen. The beginning wage was fifteen dollars an hour. If Felicity worked forty hours a week, she would make six hundred dollars a week or twenty-four hundred dollars a month. She would be working when her children were in school, and best of all, Small Steps was on the same block as the elementary school. Kat had said it would be a plus in Felicity's favor that she didn't need benefits or health care coverage. Noah's business took care of that.

Felicity wore a light summer dress and sturdy sandals. She'd put her long blond hair in a braid—somehow it seemed that a woman who worked with little children would have a braid. She wore only Burt's Bees Lip Balm for makeup. She knew from taking care of Alice and Luke when they were small that she seldom had a free moment to even consider what she looked like.

She didn't have to take the job. She may not even get the job. But this was a summer of changes, and soon she'd have a new element to add to the mix of her frazzled marriage.

twenty-three

David had asked Poppy to meet him and Alison for lunch at the Taj, an elegant, posh hotel across the street from the Boston Public Garden.

"Well, that's depressing," Poppy had replied to his invitation. "Are you planning to fire me and you know I won't make a scene there?"

David had held back a sigh. "I'm not planning to fire you, Poppy. I only want to talk in pleasant surroundings while I have a good meal."

Alison wore a severely cut blue silk dress, high heels, and pearls. David wore his blazer, which he often did, and which always made Alison want to fling herself at him and have sex. There was something about that blazer . . . But she restrained herself that day as they were shown to a table. While they were being seated, Poppy arrived, six months pregnant and looking it. David rose to kiss his daughter's cheek. Alison said hello. They made civil conversation while they ordered their meals and a bottle of wine.

When the waiter left, Poppy folded her hands on the table. "All right. I'm here."

"Poppy," David said, "I spoke with Heather. She told me you don't want Heather doing the wedding arrangements—"

"Ha!" Poppy's laugh was an angry bark. "I knew you would do this. I knew that's why you wanted this meeting. Dad, you are such a total control freak! Of *course* Heather shouldn't be making the arrangements! Alison should! Heather has work to do for the company, the company I could run quite well without your interference."

Alison held back a gasp. Glancing from father to daughter, she saw so many physical similarities. The pale skin, thick blond hair—going gray in David's case—the wide shoulders and long torsos. They radiated the same tension, clearly holding back strong emotions.

"You've conflated several issues just now, Poppy." David paused to sip his wine. "Shall we discuss the wedding arrangements first, or who's in charge of the company, or how you intend to cope with being a chief executive officer when you have a new baby?"

Poppy's eyes blazed. She opened her mouth to speak.

David spoke before she could. "Or we could discuss my will. I know you're concerned about that."

Red spots as round as roses appeared on Poppy's cheeks while the rest of her face went white. "Dad. Come on. That's harsh."

David shrugged. "I've always had a will. You and Ethan have always been apprised of its contents. I've made some changes. Only recently. I don't have copies for you and Ethan and Alison yet."

"Dad, I didn't mention your will. I was talking about the wedding, and the company, and for months you said you wanted to retire!"

"Well, let me finish about the will before we go on to other matters. Poppy, I'm leaving you and Ethan the company and all its assets. The split is seventy-thirty. You will receive seventy percent and have the controlling vote. Ethan, who I realize is not helpful at the moment, could grow up. He could change. Or his experiments with exotic flowers could actually be helpful."

"That's fine, Dad," Poppy muttered.

"As for the rest . . . I am dividing my personal assets three ways, among you, your brother, and Alison. I'm leaving the Boston apartment to Alison and the Nantucket house to you and Ethan and Alison. You know I've established trusts for Daphne and Hunter and Canny's college tuitions. I'm going to do the same for your new child, and also for Alice and Luke."

"Dad! Alice and Luke are not your grandchildren."

"No, but once Alison and I marry, they will be my step-grandchildren."

"And leaving a trust for Canny!" Poppy's lips tightened. "Her mother can pay tuition—she can practically buy Canny a college!" Her eyes widened. "Is Canny coming for your wedding? Is Esmeralda?"

"They've been invited, of course. They haven't replied. I doubt that they'll appear. Esmeralda is so busy with government work."

Poppy twisted her hands together, worried. "If you establish college trusts for Alison's grandchildren, that will take a bite out of your personal assets."

"Yes. That's true."

"So that's less for Ethan and me and Alison when . . ." Poppy could not say the words.

"When I die," David finished for her. "That's true. But still, you and your family will be well provided for. As for English Garden Creams, you will be the engineer of its future success or failure."

"*If*," Poppy said, "you ever allow me to take the reins for the company."

"Ah. A new topic of conversation."

At that moment, the waiter appeared, setting their plates down in front of them, smoothly introducing each dish. For Alison, Bay of Fundy salmon. For Poppy, a spring green omelet with vegetables and goat cheese. For David, steak frites.

David raised his wine glass. "Bon appétit."

Poppy ignored her food. "Dad, you said when you got married, you'd turn the company over to me. To my management. I have some really good ideas for change that I'd like to implement, and I don't want to have to spend time explaining them to you or arguing about them. You're either the CEO or I am."

David cut a bite of steak and took a moment to enjoy it. "Excellent," he announced. "Poppy, Alison, have some frites. I won't be able to eat them all."

"You're stalling," Poppy said.

David put down his knife and fork. "My darling and beloved daughter, do you really think it's wise to take over the operation of our company by yourself? Now? Heather has informed me that you've missed a tax deadline, and botched a few contracts, and unfortunately lost an account."

"Oh, *Heather!*" Poppy huffed. "And it wasn't an important account."

"All our accounts are important. The point is, Poppy, I'm still here, still capable, and still willing to continue to head our company while you take the time to enjoy your baby. And we can gradually make the transition from me to you with less stress on both of us. We can work together."

With much of the fight gone from her voice, Poppy grumbled, "You *said* you wanted to step down."

"I did. I know. And I meant it. But as you know, Alison doesn't mind waiting a year or so for our honeymoon travels, and that year will give you and me time to make this very significant adjustment to our lives. Not to mention to the company."

Poppy bit her lip. For just a flash of a moment, Alison thought Poppy might put her thumb in her mouth. She looked like a little girl who'd been caught making a few minor mistakes, and Alison could only imagine how Poppy's chagrin was wringing David's heart. *How in the world could an important company be run by a family?* Alison wondered.

The same way a family was run, she decided, by a world of

schedules and teamwork, laughter and anger, misunderstandings and kindnesses, by hard work and hurt feelings and forgiveness, all held together by love.

"I could do that," Poppy at last conceded. "I'd like to do that, really. It *is* hard with a new baby."

"So, we'll give ourselves a year?"

"Agreed." Poppy extended her hand and David shook it.

For a while they all paid attention to their food, which was delicious. The wine was soothing. Alison felt the atmosphere around their table changing, as if storm clouds were rolling away, as if the sun was shining again.

"But," Poppy said.

Alison wanted to roll her eyes, but kept staring down at her plate.

"I still don't think it's right for Heather to be doing the wedding arrangements."

"That's not up for negotiation," David said calmly. "It's underway. It's done."

"*Fine.*" Poppy sulked for one last time, and then heartily dug into her omelet.

Throughout lunch, Alison's phone had been vibrating almost constantly.

"I've got to check my phone," she told David and Poppy, and took up her purse and went down the hall and into the ladies' room.

Jane had called and left messages several times. Alison clicked on the most recent message.

Jane sounded rattled; she was talking fast. "Mom? Mom, I've been trying to reach you. I'm about to board a British Airways flight to Manchester and then I'll take a train to Wales. A mountain rescue group has called to tell me Scott's missing. They think he might have fallen. Listen, I talked to Felicity, she knows everything I know. I'll phone you both when I have anything new to report. Love you."

Alison's heart jumped in her chest. *No*, she thought. Not Scott. He was reserved and quiet, but Alison thought Jane and Scott had a satisfying marriage. Adrenaline kicked into her bloodstream. Fight or flight. But what could she do? Nothing. She couldn't dismiss this problem and pretend everything would be fine, and she could do nothing to solve the problem, she couldn't fly over to Wales and search an entire mountain.

She did the only thing she could do. She closed her eyes and bowed her head and prayed.

When she returned to the dining room, David rose and helped settle her chair.

"Jane phoned. Scott's missing. She had a call from a mountain rescue team. She's flying to Manchester now."

David put his hand on Alison's. "How can we help?"

"I don't know," Alison told him. "I can't think."

"Whenever something frightening happens to me," Poppy said, "like when my friend had a lump in her breast, or when Hunter fell out of a tree and broke his arm, I scrub the bathrooms. Seriously. It's like a bargain with fate. I do something I really hate doing like cleaning the toilet, and I feel like I'm tilting the balance of destiny back toward what's good."

Alison managed a smile. "What an unusual way to cope, and oddly, I can understand your logic."

"Let me tell you, it's worked every time. Plus, my toilets are spotless."

"Maybe I'll try it," Alison said weakly.

"You should. I hope it works for you."

Such a strange superstition, Alison thought, and she was grateful that Poppy had offered this advice to her. Poppy had opened up a bit, had showed that she wanted, in her own way, to help. Someday, Alison hoped, she and Poppy would laugh about it.

Until then . . . "Well," Alison said, "I think I'll go home and scrub some toilets."

Felicity had considered feeding the children early and bundling them off to the den to watch a movie so she could have some time alone with Noah. But often the children were unintentional buffers for the adults. Noah didn't swear as much with the children around. Felicity didn't cry.

So she served the vegetable lasagna and the green salad and whole-wheat rolls to her entire family, and she was glad, because Noah was in a dark mood and the children, in their silly ways, made him smile.

She'd prepared cups of fresh fruit for dessert.

"Alice. Luke. You may take your fruit into the den, and you may watch *The Lego Movie,* but you must use your fork for the fruit, and you must absolutely use napkins. No wiping fruit juice on your shirt, okay?"

The children would have promised anything for a movie, Felicity was well aware of that. This meant she'd have time to talk seriously with Noah; she supposed she should be thankful to Ingrid for bringing the first DVD into the house.

"Let's go into the living room," Felicity suggested. "I have some good news and some bad news."

Reluctantly, Noah rose from the table. "I'm not in the mood for this."

"The bad news is that Jane had a call from a mountain rescue group in Wales. Scott's gone missing. They're searching the mountain for him, and Jane has flown to the UK."

"Huh." Noah shook his head. "That's too bad. I kind of liked the guy."

"No past tense yet, Noah! Mom and I are keeping in touch with Jane, as much as we can while she's traveling and not always in an area with a cell tower."

"I hope they find him," Noah said. "I always thought he took too many risks. Maybe he'll learn he's not a superman."

Felicity took a deep breath. "Okay, now for the good news." She took her husband's hand and pulled him into the living room. They sat at opposite ends of the sofa. Felicity cocked her head and smiled at Noah. Noah stared at the wall.

"Noah, drumroll please—I've got a job!"

Her words surprised him so much he actually turned and looked at her. "What?"

"I've got a job, Noah! At the Small Steps Preschool. I'll work forty hours a week, so I'll be home with the children after their school. I'll make fifteen dollars an hour, so that's six hundred dollars a week, which means twenty-four hundred dollars a month!"

Noah frowned. "Why would you do that?"

"Why would I take a job?" Felicity was so proud of herself, so happy, she nearly bounced. "Because that way I can help you, Noah! That means you won't have to worry about almost two thousand dollars a month—that's twenty-four thousand dollars a year you can invest in your company!"

"Oh, Felicity," Noah said. Rising, he went to the window and looked out, keeping his back to her.

She waited quietly. She waited for him to thank her.

Finally, her husband turned to face her. "Felicity," Noah said, "twenty-four thousand dollars a year is *nothing*."

It was like being hit in the chest. "What?" Felicity stood up. "It most certainly is something! It means groceries and the mortgage paid and clothes for the children and—"

"Oh, Felicity." Noah crossed the room and took his wife in his arms. "I'm so sorry. I didn't mean to insult you, of course it's something, and I'm amazed that you would do this, that you would try to help me . . ." His voice broke.

Felicity pulled herself away from his embrace. She needed to see his face. And yes, Noah had tears in his eyes. Her heart dropped. Had he already slept with Ingrid? Something had changed.

"Felicity, for what I'm trying to do, for Green Food, that amount of money is a pittance. I need money in the *hundreds* of thousands. I need *millions*."

"Oh." She felt like a fool. The truth was, she'd never paid attention to anything he'd said about the cost of building his company. She'd been overwhelmed with trying to get Alice to relinquish her pacifier and toilet-training Luke. She'd been paying close attention to the household allowance Noah gave her, and checking out online recipes for one more thing to make with chickpeas and tofu. "I didn't realize," she said finally. "I'm sorry."

Noah dropped his arms and turned away. "No, I'm the one who should be sorry. I was so certain of my idea—and I still am, I believe it will happen—but it's taking longer, it's more complicated, than I expected. I was thinking months. Now I'm thinking *years* for development and testing."

"I see." Felicity did see—Noah's shoulders were shaking. Was he crying?

Gently, she put her hand on his back. "Well, you've got years. *We've* got years."

Noah shook his head. Reaching into his pocket, he pulled out a handkerchief and nosily blew his nose. "I'm so afraid, Felicity. I'm terrified of failing. Every day I live with the fear of failure, and I know I'll never be able to give you and the kids a really nice house, I'll never be able to take you all on a vacation to Disneyland. I'm sorry Mark is dead, but I'm glad he'll never see what a failure I am. I don't have a secure job like Scott, and Jane makes as much money as he does and they don't have to spend it on child care."

"Noah, you told me it will be a long process, getting Green Food—"

"I didn't get the NIH grants."

"Ah. I see. Well, I'm sorry, Noah. But you'll get other grants."

"Will I?"

"Of course! If you didn't get those grants from NIH, that wasn't because you don't have a brilliant idea—you do!—it was because so many other scientists have applied for a bunch of other things. Science is competitive. Everyone wants to invent cheap fuel and cures for diseases. You *know* that, *you* told me that."

Noah pinched the bridge of his nose and took a long breath. "I could use a drink."

"Wine?"

"Scotch."

Felicity saw how red Noah's face had gotten, and how shiny it was with tears. She went through to the dining room and reached to the top cupboard in their cabinet, the one too high for Luke to reach even if he stood on a chair. Taking down the Glenfiddich, she poured the golden liquid into a cut glass tumbler—a wedding present, part of a set they seldom used. After a moment's thought, she poured herself a bit as well. She returned to the living room and handed the drink to Noah.

"Thanks." Noah had regained his composure. His voice was under control. Almost cold. He tossed back the drink. "Look. I don't want to worry you. We're not in danger of folding yet. But we're not ready to move on to the next step, either."

"I see." Felicity sank into a chair across from him. "I get it."

"Then you get why I hate being around David Gladstone and his crew, with their summer house and their boats and their preposterously ostentatious wedding. It makes me feel small and hopeless in comparison."

"Noah . . ."

"That's why I like being with Ingrid. She understands the problems, and still she idolizes me. She has the scientific background to understand what I'm doing. When Ingrid tells me we're going to succeed, it means something. Can't you understand? I can't give up Ingrid and still be around your super-achieving family. I'll feel like a loser."

A chill ran through Felicity's veins.

"That's why I'm not coming to the wedding," Noah said, and he stared at her as if daring her to object.

Felicity was stunned. Only moments ago she'd felt so close to her husband, she'd pitied him, wanted to soothe him, and only an hour ago she'd been so proud of herself, so optimistic because she'd gotten a job that according to Noah would be of no help at all.

She opened her mouth to argue, then stopped. She didn't want to argue anymore. She had done all she could to help Noah. But Noah wanted Ingrid and he didn't want Felicity's family.

So now she was going to help herself. She was going to take a job, and she was going back for certification as a teacher, because she knew she could be an excellent teacher, and the world needed good teachers as much as it needed green food.

"I'm sorry to hear that," Felicity said. "We'll all miss you."

She stood up, set her empty glass on the coffee table, and left the room.

twenty-four

As the British Airways plane began its descent, dread gripped Jane. She was almost there. She had dozed, off and on, as they crossed the Atlantic, and now it was only one-thirty at home, but here it was seven-thirty, and the sky was full of light. It disoriented her. It made her head hurt.

Looking out the window, she saw nothing but clouds. She could not see land or sky, she couldn't even see the plane's wing. So this was what Scott saw before he fell. Only white. No way to tell where to put his foot, no way to guess at direction. No wonder he fell. How frightening for him! She was so sorry, she felt *anguished,* not just that Scott had gone off alone to hike an unpredictable path over a craggy, complicated mountain, but that he might have gotten lost in the fog on the mountain and taken the wrong way, and she had not been with him.

What kind of wife was she?

She wanted to wail with anger, but she didn't want to frighten the man next to her, so she went to the tiny restroom and combed her hair and said to her reflection in the mirror, "You're a terrible wife."

When she returned to her seat, the landing process had begun, and before she knew it, the plane touched down with a reassuring thud. Then, the endless wait as the plane taxied toward the terminal. Keeping calm while passengers ahead of her filed off. The tortoise-slow line through Customs. She claimed her suitcase at the baggage terminal, got cash from the ATM, read signs, inquired at Visitor Services, and found the connection to the train to Bangor.

She boarded the train and found a seat with a table and room to stretch her legs.

Jane had placed her cellphone faceup on the table in front of her. For an hour or so, she gazed at the scenery the train passed through: farmlands giving way to evergreens, rolling hills becoming mountains with glimpses of streams running far below. Gradually, the train was enclosed in thick evergreens so that light flickered down through the trees. Even though she was tired and jittery with nerves, she tried to rest. She leaned against the seat and closed her eyes.

And saw Scott's face.

She'd first seen him during a class on torts at Harvard Law. He was handsome, but that wasn't why she kept looking at him. Something about him was so steady, so calm. He was a big guy, tall and broad-shouldered with big hands and feet. She thought he must have played football in high school or college, but later she discovered he'd been a rower. His movements were deliberate, economical. He didn't doodle on the edge of his notebook, although if ever there were a course that inspired doodling, this was it. He didn't shift in his seat, didn't squirm or jiggle his foot. He kept his eyes on the lecturing professor and seemed unaware of anything else in the room.

When class ended and everyone stood up, gathering their books and laptop computers and backpacks, Scott's first movement was to turn his head and meet Jane's eyes. His look was so intense, and he had a crooked smile on his face, as if all during that hour he'd been aware of her scrutiny. Jane had blushed.

She'd been twenty-four then, no giggling girl, and she'd known from the moment she first saw him that she wanted to connect with him somehow. So she waited, pretending to organize her papers, while the classroom emptied and only she and Scott were left. He came across the room and said, "Hey. I'm Scott."

"I'm Jane," she said, and for some reason she laughed. "I sound like I'm in a Tarzan movie."

"Tarzan. I always loved those movies. I always wanted to *be* Tarzan, swinging from vine to vine, free of social constraints."

"Free of taxation," she said.

"Free of clothes. Most of my clothes."

"I don't know." Jane cocked her head thoughtfully. "If you actually were in a jungle swinging from vine to vine, wouldn't you want some clothes? Especially some briefs? I mean, think of the bugs in the jungle, the snakes, the poisonous plants."

"You sound like someone who's traveled," Scott said.

"Um, yeah, to Paris and Quebec. No poisonous plants there."

"So you speak French." His eyes were hazel, streaked with green and gold, with a strong edge of dark blue around the circumference.

"Not really. I can get by when I have to, but I wouldn't say I'm fluent."

"I can get by in Spanish and some Mandarin," Scott told her. "So together, we could take on the world."

"Mandarin? Wow. Have you been to China?"

"No, but I want to go there. I want to travel everywhere," Scott said.

If that very moment he'd asked her to go with him to China or Rio or Russia, Jane would have gone. As it happened, he'd asked her to go with him for coffee. Coffee turned into a lazy dinner at an Italian restaurant, and then to bed at his apartment.

As a lover, Scott was unhurried and gentle, responsive to Jane's body, tender and sweet. They were very good together, and as they spent the next day talking and walking and reading, it seemed as if they'd always been together. Were meant to be together. They spent every possible moment with each other after that first meeting, and Jane knew they were going to marry, even though Scott, deliberate and responsible as always, waited a full year to propose. And then Jane did follow him everywhere—to Death Valley for their honeymoon. She was the only person she knew who had ever been to Death Valley.

Scott thought Jane was beautiful. She had never told him how jealous she was of her younger sister, Felicity, who was always surrounded by guys. She'd even been anxious about Scott meeting Felicity—he'd see that he'd chosen the least lovely sister. But Scott had been unaffected by Felicity's charms. He thought she was good-looking, but maybe—he didn't want to make Jane mad, he'd said—maybe she wore too much makeup, maybe she was just a bit silly, and obviously Felicity was jealous of Jane's good looks. Jane had laughed until she had a stitch in her side, and Scott had been puzzled by her reaction.

They were both ambitious, both hard workers who felt most in the zone when they were struggling with some legal document. Jane was hired by Mercer and Klein, and Scott was quickly snapped up by an equally prestigious firm, in the tax code law department. Their titles and salaries were commensurate, and they could schedule their vacation days together. Most years they didn't go to Boston to share Christmas with Alison and Felicity and Noah and their children. They did go the year Alice was a newborn, because Jane knew her sister would take offense if Jane didn't come to adore the baby and wait hand and foot on Felicity. That year Alison had put on the full Christmas extravaganza, with a tree so high it bent over at the ceiling, and so many presents they spilled out into the hallway. Carols on the CD player, gingerbread cookies and eggnog, pumpkin and apple pies. Roast goose—geese, three of them—because Alison knew how little meat was on a goose. Jane and Scott had gone to the Christmas Eve midnight church service with Alison and Mark, mostly, as they agreed later in the privacy of the bedroom, to get away from the baby, whose cries were ear-piercing. After that year, they'd felt free of family obligations, for a while.

Scott and Jane's stepfather, Mark, had gotten along famously. Of course, Mark got along famously with everyone. Scott and Noah were more like oil and water. Noah's hair fell to his shoulders, and for a few years he had a beard. Noah was very tall and thin; he looked and sometimes sounded like the leader of a cult. The first time they met, Scott had extended his hand for a conventional male hand-shake. Noah had instead clasped both hands around Scott's and in-toned, "Hello, Brother." Jane, standing behind Noah, had put her finger in her mouth, simulating gagging.

As the years passed and Noah's ideas gelled into an actual busi-ness with wealthy investors, he became less self-righteous and smug. He got his hair cut—because his children kept pulling and tugging it, he said—and he bought one good suit. He asked for Mark's advice. He asked for Scott's advice.

Still, always, after a holiday or a quick dinner when Jane and Scott were in New York, they returned to their own small household with relief. The pattern of their days was repetitive and soothing and sensual, too. It was luxurious to read the Sunday papers to-gether, propped on pillows, on their iPads or e-readers, drinking coffee Scott made and brought back to the bed. At some point, they'd make love. Afterward, they'd go out for a long, leisurely Sun-day brunch, and if it was raining, they'd visit a museum. If not, they took a stroll through Central Park. They met friends for dinner. They saw first-run plays. Sometimes, for a while, they went to their home office and worked. On vacations, they chose places that would take them away from the rush of the city. They hiked in Colorado and Utah. In Mexico, they ate *caldo tlalpeno* and drank tequila. In Death Valley, they ate rattlesnake and drank more tequila. They didn't want to go to China and the Far East until Scott had polished up his Mandarin. Jane tried to learn a little of the language. She re-membered sitting on the sofa with Scott, trying to say hello, and laughing until she almost fell onto the floor.

Scott was such a good man. Honest, reliable. He would never try to have sex with a married woman. Jane wanted to shake herself. She'd been so foolish, like a resentful child!

And then, her cellphone, lying in a blank rectangle on the table, vibrated. The caller ID number was odd—it was Welsh! Jane snatched up the phone.

"Mrs. Hudson? This is Derfel Aberfa. I am happy to report that your husband has been found and rescued."

"Oh! Thank you!" Jane burst into tears.

"He was not far from the Crib Goch path. He slipped on the damp rocks and fell into a gap between boulders. He has broken his arm and sustained some hypothermia, but otherwise he is doing well."

"Oh, I'm so glad, oh, thank you so much. May I speak to him?"

"He's being treated at the Ysbyty Gwynedd. The hospital in Bangor. Are you in Wales yet?"

"Yes, I think so. I'm on a train from Manchester. We're rocketing along tracks on the very edge of a mountain."

"Yes, you are in Wales. So when you arrive in Bangor, take a cab to the hospital. Your husband is there, now."

"How can I thank you? Is there a charge for your services?"

"Donations are always gratefully received. To rescue your husband took five team members, one S-92 rescue helicopter, and a team of Land Rovers over a period of five hours."

"Oh, I had no idea—a helicopter!" For one hysterical moment, Jane wanted to ask if Prince William had flown it. Felicity would be thrilled! "Will I meet you at the hospital?"

"No. A rescue team liaison will be there."

"Oh, good, but I wish I could meet you. You have been so helpful."

"It was a group effort."

"Yes, of course. Thank you. Thank everyone."

When the connection to Derfel Aberfa was cut, Jane put the phone down and sobbed into her hands. Jane was aware that others in the train were staring at her as if she were an exhibit in a museum, and once she had herself more or less in control, she stood up and looked around the cabin. "My husband had a fall on Mount Snowdon. That was a liaison from the Llanberis Mountain Rescue Team. They found him and he's waiting for me in the hospital with only a broken arm."

Some of the other passengers applauded. Everyone smiled. Jane sat back down and began texting Felicity and her mother.

Alison found an empty slot in the short-term parking lot at Logan airport and neatly pulled in between two SUVs. She pulled down the visor, checked her hair, and sighed. Her dark hair always went hopelessly limp in the humidity. She dabbed on a gloss of pale pink lipstick, double-checked that she had her car keys in her purse. With this new car, she didn't need to insert a key but simply put a foot on the brake and push a button. She kept trying to put the key in where there was no keyhole and every time she got in the car she felt as if she'd gone a little bit mad. She had to rearrange the habit of a lifetime, taking the key from the ignition, clasping it in her hand, getting out of the car, and locking it. Now she needed only to have the keys near her to start the car, but she had to have the keys in her hand to lock the car. A different pattern, different rhythm. It irritated her, and she was even more irritated at herself for minding so much. It made her feel old.

Well, she told herself, *there's a first-world problem if there ever was one*. She stepped out of the car, smoothed the front of her dress, and headed for the terminal. Anya, the brilliant seamstress at Flore Bridal Gowns, was flying in today to fit Alison's wedding dress. Anya was bringing Felicity's and Jane's as well, but Jane was over in Wales with Scott so the girls could try on theirs when they got to the island.

What an enormous relief it was that Scott was found with only a broken arm! Would Scott learn anything from his fall? Scott was so sure of himself, so unyielding, so doubt-free. Alison liked Scott, and she could see how Jane would love being with Scott. He was like a male Jane. But too much self-confidence was unpleasant; plus, it blinded people to the possibilities of other options.

Long ago, once she'd started playing around on the Internet, Alison had taken a test to see what personality type she was. Big surprise: she was a Nurturer. Nurturers were warm, loving, giving, forgiving, maternal, helpful, blah blah blah, but Nurturers were never Leaders. Leaders were strong, powerful, assured, capable of having visions and making those visions come true. Leaders didn't care if they were liked or if they hurt someone in their steady advance toward their goals.

David was a Leader. Obviously. He had inherited a company and made it a financial success. He was powerful and assured. But he hadn't had to step on anyone else's fingers as he climbed the ladder to success. He'd worked very hard for years. David was, Alison decided, a Kind Leader. He was the one who wanted their wedding to be a great celebration for his family and friends. Alison thought Scott was a Leader, and so was Jane. Could two Leaders stay happily married through the years? They would all have to wait and see.

Today everyone was safe. She needed to stop her brooding and focus on this day. After all, it was going to be exciting, and it was almost her *duty* to enjoy herself! Anya would arrive any moment, bringing with her Alison's wedding dress.

The plane was on time. Alison waited, as agreed, by the baggage claim. And there she was, coming down the stairs from the gate. Alison smiled and waved. Anya was a serious woman who seldom talked about anything other than the gown she was fitting. Alison thought Anya was originally from Russia, but there was a sternness about her that kept Alison from inquiring. It would seem intrusive.

"Hello, Anya," Alison said. "How was the flight?"

"Very nice," Anya replied. "The gowns are in boxes. They will be here."

They waited, and soon two large boxes and one small suitcase came trundling around on the conveyor belt. Anya and Alison wrestled them off. They weren't heavy, but they were large and cumbersome.

"Let's get them outside and you can wait with them while I get the car. I'll come around and pick you up."

"Yes. Very well." Anya was short and wide, with graying hair and dark eyes. Alison had seen Anya smile only a few times, all when Alison put on her gown and stood in front of a mirror in the marvelous dress.

It was a failing of Alison that she couldn't sit quietly in the presence of another person. During the thirty-minute drive to the apartment on Marlborough Street, Alison worked hard to get Anya to talk, but finally gave up and babbled on about her wedding, the gowns, and Poppy's decision to wear a floor-length pantsuit.

"Yes, Mrs. O'Reilly has contacted me. I will fit her outfit tomorrow," Anya said. "Pregnant women's bodies can change radically from day to day."

Aha! Alison thought. A topic in common. "Do you have children, Anya?"

"No."

Alison put on music. A light classical piece danced around the air for the rest of the drive.

In the apartment, Alison offered tea or coffee, but Anya was clearly eager to fit the dress. They went up to the guest bedroom, and together they lifted one large cardboard box onto the bed. Anya took Alison's dress from its stiff plastic garment bag and held it out for Alison to step into it.

The beautiful dress transformed her. Anya zipped the back and fussed around, making adjustments to the skirt, the bodice. But Alison simply gazed at her reflection in the mirror. She'd never been one to wear a *gown*. And maybe this wasn't even a gown, because it wasn't floor length.

Whatever it was, it was the most beautiful thing Alison had ever worn. The fitted ivory satin top was elegant in its simplicity. The skirt belled out from the waist in a fall of ivory silk panels, ending just at her knee.

"Oh, Anya," Alison said. "This is perfect."

"Actually, no, because the bodice pulls slightly at the back. I will need to let it out an inch here by the waistline. You have been eating too much."

Alison laughed out loud at Anya's blunt declaration. She stared at herself in the mirror, turning this way and that, while Anya bustled around with a tape measure. In the wedding boutique, Alison had been scattered, but here in her own home in her own bedroom, she took a deep breath and gave herself over to the pleasure of being cared for and even bossed around by someone else. She remembered her mother making clothes for her when she was a child, making Alison stand on a stool while her mother pinned up the hem.

"I brought this," Anya said, lifting something small and ivory from another box. "You might like, you might not like. But I think is good."

Alison bent her knees so Anya could place the short, round satin hat, like something Jacqueline Kennedy might have worn, on Alison's hair. A chin-length veil of ivory net sprinkled with a few sparkling crystals surrounded Alison's face, and the back of the hat was embellished with a small ivory satin rose and more crystals.

Alison burst into tears.

"You like, eh?" Anya crossed her arms over her chest and smiled triumphantly.

"Oh, Anya, I could kiss you!" Alison cried.

"Okay, not necessary." Anya took a few steps back. "You have shoes?"

"Yes. Yes, I have the shoes. I had them dyed to match the fabric sample you gave me. They're in a box in the closet. I'll get them."

"No, no. I can get them. You need to see yourself in the mirror."

Anya pulled the box from the closet. She took off the lid and set the ivory satin high-heeled shoes in front of Alison. Alison put a hand, for balance, on Anya's shoulder and stepped into the shoes.

"Oh, my," Alison said. "Look at me. And I'm not even wearing jewelry or makeup."

"Yes. Is nice dress."

It's more than nice! Alison wanted to protest, but she understood that by keeping aloof, Anya was giving Alison the great gift of freedom. Freedom for this brief moment to indulge, to be thrilled, to admire herself and fill with eagerness for her wedding day, when the man she loved would see her looking like this, as splendidly dressed as a queen. This was why people had ceremonies to renew their vows, Alison thought, so they could celebrate the triumph of their lasting love, yes, but also to celebrate the beauty of being alive.

"Anya, I'm going to call my friend Margo and have her come over now to see this dress. Then we'll have coffee and cake."

"Very good idea," Anya said.

twenty-five

Welsh showed no relation to any language Jane had ever learned or even seen. Wales in Welsh was *Cymru*; Hospital was *Ysbyty*. Fortunately, all street signs were in both English and Welsh, and the taxi driver who parked in front of the airport spoke English.

When she arrived in Bangor, it was after two in the afternoon in Wales, but early morning in New York City. The time difference confused her poor brain, already tired from the rush to the airport and the plane ride and then the train journey. Even so, Jane was shot through with adrenaline. Finally, she was here! And Scott was alive! As the driver steered them through the unknown streets, Jane couldn't keep from babbling, telling the driver about Scott's fall, and her fear, and Derfel's call, and her utter relief.

"You've come a long way," the driver said.

"Yes," Jane responded thoughtfully. "Yes. You've no idea."

"Oh, I've been across the pond a few times myself."

"I didn't mean—Where did you go? New York City?"

"Ha! I might as well go to London. No, I like that place you have over there called Las Vegas. I enjoy playing cards and my wife takes in a few shows. One day we drive out into the desert and scare ourselves half to death looking at all that sand, then we come home happy."

"I've never been to Las Vegas," Jane admitted.

"No? You should go. Now here we are. I'll be taking you to the emergency entrance of the hospital," the driver told her.

"Of course." Jane bit her lip. "I hope they'll let me see him."

"Oh, they're very nice at the hospital," the driver assured her.

Jane paid the driver with her colorful new pounds and stepped out of the taxi. In front of her was a long, low building, with ambulances parked in bays nearby and a brightly lit room showing through wide glass double doors. The sign overhead said, MYNEDFA BRYS. Helpfully, it also said, EMERGENCY ENTRANCE.

Inside, she found an enclosed cubicle with two women chatting away in what sounded like Martian. As soon as she approached them, they became professional.

"Hello. How may we help you?"

Jane almost asked them why they assumed she wasn't Welsh, but then she realized she was dragging a rolling suitcase behind her.

"My husband is here, I think. He had a fall on Mount Snowdon earlier today. Or maybe it was yesterday. I mean, the time changes are making my brain fuzzy—" Now that she was here, actually in the Bangor, Wales, hospital, her body was acting crazy, shaking and trembling, and her mind wouldn't work.

"What is his name, please, dear?" The nurse was young, with bright brown eyes and creamy skin.

"Scott Hudson."

"Ah, yes. He has a broken arm."

"Can I see him?"

"Surely. Come along." The nurse stepped out of the small windowed office, gave Jane a smile—didn't that mean he was all right?—

and led Jane down a hallway, into an elevator, off at another floor, and down a hallway until she came to a room with an open door and a beeping machine and a figure lying very still on a hospital bed.

"Should I wake him?"

"Go on, dear. He'll be a bit groggy, you know, he's got a small morphine drip for the pain."

"The pain!"

"It's all right. He'll be glad to see you."

Jane leaned her suitcase against the wall and quietly approached the bed. There Scott was. Lying so still beneath the snow white sheet and blanket. His eyes were closed. Already he had a dark shadow of beard along his jaw. An IV stand stood next to him, and a liquid dripped slowly into a vein in his arm. Her strong, powerful, sturdy Scott, lying in a hospital bed, with his left arm encased in a plaster cast and a needle in his right arm!

"Look at his fingers, Mrs. Hudson." The nurse read a chart from the end of the bed, then moved close to Jane, as if to share her strength. "His fingers are pink. That means his circulation is fine. He'll probably be released tomorrow."

Jane swallowed her tears and came close to the bed. She took his good hand in hers, bent close to him, and said softly, "Scott? Scott. It's Jane. I'm here."

Scott's eyes opened. His utterly gorgeous hazel eyes. For a moment, he seemed to be orienting himself. After a minute, he said, "Jane."

Jane burst into tears.

"Hey," Scott said and tugged on her hand.

She leaned over and kissed him. She ran her hands over his face. "Oh, Scott, you're alive, you're here, you're okay."

"I know. I'm luckier than I deserve to be. I was an idiot . . ."

"No, anyone can fall. I read the comments on the Internet on the way over. No one can judge when the mist will come in. Tell me about your arm. Does it hurt?"

A weak smile. "Not now. I'm pumped full of drugs. It hurt like the devil when I fell."

"How did it happen? Tell me. Wait, can I sit on the bed or should I get a chair?"

She looked around. The nurse had quietly disappeared.

"Sit on the bed. This side."

Jane hitched herself up on the bed, and Scott kept hold of her hand.

"Tell me."

"It's not dramatic. It's ridiculously simple. I'd hiked up the Crib Goch path and I was beginning along the ridge. They call it a scramble there, because you need your hands. I was exhilarated, energized, I was so close, the air was sweet and pure—I thought I could run the rest of the way. It's magic up there, Jane. I want to climb Mount Snowdon with you sometime, not now, and not the path I took."

"How did you fall?"

Scott's eyes were bright. "Suddenly this thick white mist rolled in from nowhere and the temperature dropped. I took my sweatshirt out of my backpack and pulled it on over my head and that movement unbalanced me. My foot slipped. Down I went."

"Were you terrified?"

"I didn't have time to be scared. It happened so fast. It happened like *this*"—Scott snapped his fingers—"unimaginably quickly. I was sliding, almost rolling, and I reached out my arm to stop myself, and I knocked into a sharp edge of slate—it's slate everywhere up there. I hit the slate, and my body came down on top of my arm at the same time. I heard the bone crack. It hurt, but not as much as it did when I found myself lodged between two boulders."

"Scott, how frightening!"

"The fall was frightening. I felt better, safer, when I was stopped by the boulders. I could have fallen to my death from up there. People have. I was thankful to be stopped. I caught my breath. I went for my cellphone, but it had fallen out of the backpack when I got out my sweatshirt. The mist was still all around. I took off my backpack—that's when I knew for sure I'd broken my arm. The pain was red hot. I couldn't use it. I cursed and somehow wrestled

my backpack off with one hand. I got out my wool hat and put it on.
I drank some water. I had trail mix if I got hungry, but I wasn't hungry. I huddled tight, trying to keep warm, but my arm hurt like shit
and was kind of dangling, flopping. I had a flannel shirt in my backpack, I was wearing my T-shirt and had been warm enough in that
because I was moving. I made a kind of sling, tying the sleeves together in front—I had to use my left hand, the hand attached to the
broken arm, and that was a pain, I can tell you. But I got my arm
more or less immobilized against my chest."

"Smart," Jane said.

"It helped keep me from panicking, doing all that stuff. I drank
some water. Every so often, I'd yell out for help. I didn't hear anyone. I had no idea how far I'd fallen or if I was stuck near some kind
of trail. I was there ten hours."

"Ten hours! By yourself, and with a broken arm? Oh, Scott."
Careful not to jiggle his arm, Jane leaned forward to kiss his face.
"Scott, you're alive, you're here, that's all that matters."

"No. Wait, Jane." Awkwardly, he pushed Jane away.

Her heart stopped. He had pushed her away. He was trying to sit
up, and he pushed up with his good right arm until he was slightly
tilted toward her. She reached out to help him balance, and they
both laughed at how awkward this was, and then he flinched, and
she knew he was in pain even with the medication.

She asked, "Did you break anything else?"

"No, but I earned several Technicolor bruises. And my hands
are scraped." He held one hand up to show the reddened palm and
fingers. "But that's nothing. Jane, listen. I need to tell you something."

"It's all right, Scott," Jane said. She wanted to put her hand over
his lips to keep him from saying they should divorce. Because she
knew that was what he was going to say, that while he'd been curled
up in pain and cold alone and lost on a dangerous mountain, he had
realized how short life is, and how wrong it was for him, for them, to
live with each other when they both knew they wanted different
things from life.

"Jane, listen to me." Scott clasped her wrist with his good hand. "Look at me. Jane, it was terrifying up there, but it was also extraordinary. As if I'd been lifted away from everyday life and I could think about things with clarity, without interruption. I thought about our last conversation, and how angry I was when I left and how sorry I was that I'd gone off that way, so pompous and self-righteous and inflexible."

"Scott. Please—"

"And I remembered how you still loved me, after what I told you about my parents. You still wanted to be with me, to have children with me. You were so brave. You *are* so brave. On the mountain, I knew that when I was rescued I'd tell you I want to have children with you."

Jane blinked. She was fatigued from traveling, and fuzzy-headed, so had she misheard? "What?"

"Jane, I want to have children with you. I don't know, call it an epiphany, that's what people call it, a real come-to-Jesus moment, I thought how much I love you and how if I'd died—no, come on, don't cry, I didn't die—but if I had died, I would want to leave something real and unique behind on the earth and that would be a child. Children. Made from you and me. Jane—"

Tears rolled down her cheeks silently, for Jane couldn't find breath to make a sound. She gulped, trying to stop the tears, trying to control herself. This was so much, this was *too* much. "Am I dreaming?" she asked. "Is this real? Did you just say you want to have children with me?"

"I did say that. And it's not the pain medication speaking. All I wanted to do when they found me was call you and tell you, but I was in rough shape when they finally found me. At least I managed to ask the rescue team leader to let you know I'm okay. I can't begin to pronounce his name. But they got me here and gave me some shots while they yanked my arm back together and put it in a cast. Thank God for them. Thank God for you."

"Scott," Jane said, and now she'd found her breath and she was sobbing. "Scott, I don't have to have children. I want *you*. I need *you*. I didn't realize it, but I did, even before you fell, I missed you so much and I love you so much, so let's think about it. Let's get you out of the hospital and home, and then we can talk about it, okay?"

"Jane. I want children with you. Our children. And talking is not what I want to do to get them." Scott smiled.

A shiver of surprise laced with lust dazzled its way through Jane's body. "Oh, my darling, my love, my sweet Scott," she cried, and she knew she'd never said these sorts of romantic endearments to him before, because that had never been her way, their way. Yet now she could not stop calling him her darling, her dearest, her love. But her tears got her face all wet, so she had to control herself and dig tissue out of her purse and blow her nose. Then, embarrassed by her display of emotion, she smiled sheepishly. "I should let you get some sleep."

"Yes. You should get some, too." Scott's eyelids drooped.

"I—I don't know what time it is here. I need to find a hotel, an inn for tonight. I'll be back soon."

"I'll be waiting," Scott told her with a wry smile.

Jane watched her husband sink back into a healing sleep.

In the late afternoon, Felicity was sorting her clothes, seeing what would be best for working with little kids, when her cell buzzed.

"Sweetie," her mother said, sounding almost giddy, "the gowns are here! Anya brought them. I'm wearing mine and I'm totally fabulous!"

In the background, Anya muttered, "No, I need to let out the waist."

Alison was euphoric. "What a day this is! Scott's alive, and Jane's over in Wales, and my gown is gorgeous!"

"I can't wait to see it, Mom—"

Alison interrupted. "I'll take the gowns down to the island. You and your family are coming this weekend, aren't you?"

Felicity hesitated. It was the first week in September and Noah was still stonewalling her, adamant about not coming to the wedding. But her mother was so happy! Alison wanted so much for her daughters to have a wonderful summer, and they were having a wonderful summer! Well, everyone except Noah. Maybe she should simply ignore Noah and Ingrid. Maybe he'd get over her, or possibly, if he remained in the hateful mood he was in, he'd show Ingrid just a speck of his dark side and Ingrid would run away like the clever girl she seemed to be. But Felicity wasn't going to rain on her mother's parade.

"Of course, Mom," Felicity said brightly. "We'll be down this weekend."

Felicity sighed as she ended the call. She had to shake off this sadness before she went to Nantucket. Alison and David wanted to give their families and friends a sensational party. Felicity would not allow herself to mope and moan in front of Alison.

The front door slammed. Felicity startled. It was only a little after five. Could that be Noah? More likely, a serial rapist breaking into the house.

"Felicity!"

It was Noah, and weirdly, he sounded *happy*.

"In the kitchen," she called.

Noah came into the room like a tornado. He put both hands on Felicity's waist and picked her up and whirled her around as if they had suddenly been beamed onto *Dancing with the Stars*.

"It's a miracle!" Noah shouted. He kissed Felicity hard on the mouth and set her on the kitchen counter so her face was at his level.

"Are you okay?" Felicity asked.

"Okay? I'm *amazing*! It's going to happen, Felicity! It's really going to happen!"

"Did you have a breakthrough?"

"David Gladstone is investing in Green Food!"

"He is?"

"He is! Felicity, he *believes* in the idea! He's investing a million this year, with more money for the next five years."

"Wait, how do you know? When—"

"He phoned me yesterday and made an appointment for today.

Actually, I didn't know about the appointment because Ingrid forgot to tell me, but I was in the office when he came in, and he asked
to see my statistics and my business plan and we talked for two
hours, and he told me he likes my idea. He thinks it will work. He
believes in helping young people attain their goals. A million dollars, Felicity! A fantastic, amazing, enormous fat injection of cash
into the company. We can fit out another lab, hire more personnel,
move things along faster. This will make all the difference in the
world!"

Felicity slid off the counter and stepped away from Noah. He
was blazingly handsome now with his cheeks flushed and his eyes
brilliant. And she was glad that David was helping Noah. But . . .

"So I guess you won't want me to cut connections with my
mother and the wedding and David's family."

"Oh, Felicity, don't do this," Noah begged. "Come on, don't be
such a downer. We should celebrate! I think we've got some
champagne—have the kids eaten? Let's get a sitter and go out to eat.
This is one of the most important moments in my life!"

"I'm glad for you. So now you're coming to the wedding, right?
Or will you be busy with Ingrid?"

"Felicity. I'm going to reassign Ingrid."

"What?"

"After David left, I had a talk with Ingrid. I told her we
weren't . . ." Noah dropped his eyes as he struggled to find the
words. "What I mean is, I won't be seeing her again, not even in a
professional capacity. I'm moving her to HR."

Felicity stared at Noah, her husband, the father of her children,
this *maniac*. "I don't know what to say."

"I know!" Noah cried. "*I know!* Everything's new now, isn't it!
It's a new world, a new day, a new product, a new you and me!"
Noah frantically went through the cupboards and refrigerator.
"Champagne, we should have some champagne. White wine. No,
that's not the same at all. But the kids should be part of this. Let's
take the kids to Ben & Jerry's and we'll all have huge sundaes with
marshmallow and cherries!"

"Noah, are you all right? This isn't only about David investing with you, is it?"

Noah laughed. "Yes! No! I don't know. I can't separate it out, and why should I try, Felicity? Everything's different now!"

Felicity scrutinized her husband. Yes, he was crazy happy, but she'd seen him this way before, when the first and most important experiment they did with seaweed worked out the way they'd expected. She wanted to help him celebrate, this husband whom she had loved and still loved. But he was a man she didn't entirely trust. And maybe she never would again. Her heart felt like a helium balloon wanting to lift off into the sky, but with a lead weight inside, a small block of heaviness holding it down. At their wedding, she'd vowed for better and for worse, and here they both were in front of her at the same time. Noah's ebullience, his wild idealistic hope, and, true, his masculine handsomeness, shone before her like the sun. And he said he was going to transfer Ingrid to another department. Maybe he really was done with Ingrid.

But she could not forget the conversation when he'd said he wanted Felicity to cut connections with her family. With David. Ha. The irony. His relationship with Ingrid, whatever it was, and this bizarre swing from criticizing David to joyfully accepting his money, those matters were not so easily absorbed. She understood how significant David's money would be to Green Food, but she could not understand Noah's complete moral turnaround. Who *was* this man she was married to? What did he really want, other than to succeed at his work? How could he tell Felicity that only Ingrid could understand him, and then get rid of Ingrid, simply bat her away as if she were a flea?

And yet, was Felicity being a killjoy? Why couldn't she, why shouldn't she, help her husband rejoice in this miracle of David's generosity? She didn't hate Noah.

But she no longer loved him in the same way. It was not only Ingrid. It was not only his lack of any moral code.

It was that *Felicity* had changed. For so long, too long, she'd considered herself lacking in importance, in talent, especially when compared with her brilliant lawyer sister. Especially when her husband found another woman necessary to his life. It wasn't *Felicity* whom Noah had chosen. It was David and his money. She had undervalued her own worth, and it was only when she interviewed for the job with the preschool that she realized what *she* could do, what *she* could offer, had enormous value.

And maybe, with meaningful work, she could continue to stay married to Noah. For a while, at least, for the sake of the children.

Or maybe she would leave Noah. The thought shot through her like a beacon of light, illuminating possibilities she'd never seen before.

"Okay," she said, standing up. "Let's take the kids out for some ice cream."

In two steps, Noah was across the room, folding Felicity in his arms. "And after they've gone to bed, you and I can have our own private celebration."

Jane woke in a strange room. It took her a moment to realize she was in Wales. Scott was alive, and he wanted to have children with her! She was light-headed with jet lag and happiness. Hurriedly, she showered and dressed and checked out of the hotel and took a cab to the hospital. She laughed out loud when she realized she didn't have to pass through the emergency entrance but could stroll through the main door. The sun was shining, but if it had been raining, Jane would still have thought: *What a beautiful day!*

She found Scott in his room, his arm in a sling, dressed and ready to go. She hugged him enthusiastically but carefully, not wanting to press any bruises.

"How do you feel?" she asked.

"Lucky," Scott said.

A white-coated doctor came into the room, a handsome man with a startling amount of curly gray hair.

"We've set your bones and enclosed them safely in your big

white cast," the doctor said in his thick Welsh accent. "You're good to go, but you'll experience some soreness from your arm and other bruises. Take paracetamol or aspirin. You should check in with your physician when you get home. You'll need the cast for at least six weeks. I wouldn't advise any mountain climbing for a few months."

"Thank you, Doctor," Scott said.

They wanted to thank the doctor by name, but even though the name was on a tag, it was so very Welsh it was unpronounceable. Jane had found the Welsh for "Thank you" on her phone, and she and Scott both said, "*Diolch. Diolch* for everything." The way the nurse grinned told her she didn't have the correct pronunciation.

They took a cab to Scott's hotel in Portmeirion because his rental car was parked at the base of the Watkin Path. The A487 meandered past sunny coastlines and through shady forests. Jane held Scott's good hand as they rode along, looking out the windows at the lush mountainous landscape. Finally the driver turned onto a long private road and suddenly they were driving under an elaborate arch, entering the dreamlike seaside village created by the eccentric architect Sir Clough Williams-Ellis. They'd discovered this place online together when they researched hotels near Mount Snowdon. They'd agreed it would be fun to spend their days climbing a mountain and their nights in such a charming resort. But Jane had seen only pictures on a screen. The real thing was strange and wonderful.

"Wow!" Jane pressed her face against the window like a child at a candy shop. "How beautiful!"

The cab dropped them at the bottom of a hill, in front of the hotel.

"Do you like it here?" Jane asked as she helped Scott from the cab.

"I do. Very much, and I'll admit I'm surprised. It's outrageous, such a mixture of architectural styles, yet it's beautiful. Magical."

"It's magical that you're alive and safe," Jane told him.

Scott's suite was on the first floor of the hotel, the Peacock Suite.

"I remember reading about it on the website," Jane said. "King

Edward the Eighth stayed here in 1934, right?" She set her suitcase down in the bedroom and walked around, taking in the views. "Would you like to lie down? Rest?"

"I've spent too much time lying down. Let's walk around the grounds. They're spectacular."

She had never seen any place quite like this resort. It was a mixture of architectural styles and lush gardens. Here, a Greek temple with columns, there a great gold Buddha, statues and steps and everywhere an arch or a porthole showing a glimpse of yet another strange and beckoning landscape. There was a long, turquoise reflecting pool surrounded by pots of red geraniums, and farther down, a swimming pool not far from the estuary. They strolled along the paths, stopping in the temple, the grotto, the stone boat set in the estuary. The woodlands were as extravagantly ornate as the village with towering rhododendron, monkey puzzle trees, palm trees next to evergreens. They passed through the ghost garden and sat for a while at the overlook, watching the shining water of the Irish Sea slowly flow into the estuary.

Later, they showered and changed and had dinner at the elegant restaurant, overlooking the water. The late summer sky blazed with stars. They drank champagne and ate pheasant and fish, lingering over their desserts of fresh berries in cream.

"I'd like to return here someday," Jane said.

"So would I. Right now I'm ready to go home and collapse."

"Are you sore?"

"Sure, some. Mostly I'm just tired, really tired. Huddling on a mountainside seems to have used up my energy." He reached for her hand. "But I'd like to come back here, too."

"And maybe, if we find an easier trail, we can try Mount Snowdon again," Jane said, smiling.

"Or maybe we'll be so busy raising children, we won't get back here for years," Scott replied.

Jane squeezed Scott's hand. "You mean that, don't you? You've truly had a change of heart."

"Yes. Although I reserve the right to grumble and complain about sleepless nights and smelly diapers."

Jane quickly took a sip of wine to hide her smile. Wales *was* magical. Scott had gone from no children to more than one in a space of twenty-four hours.

The next day they reentered reality. They took a cab to the car park at the base of the Watkin trail, picked up Scott's rental car, and drove the long, winding road back to the Manchester airport. Jane did all the driving, of course, and for a while she was nervous about driving on the left side, but by the time they reached the highway to Manchester, she was comfortable. Scott slept beside her, his head against the window. They found business-class space on a flight to New York. They settled in, ate and slept and watched movies, and at last the huge plane landed at Kennedy airport. Their luggage arrived safely. They were sixth in line for a cab. Finally they were being driven from Kennedy to their apartment on the right side of the road.

twenty-six

Alison stood in the middle of her kitchen with a notepad in one hand and a pen in the other, and all she was doing with the pen was tapping it against her lip. All summer she'd prided herself on being the kind of mother/mother-in-law/fiancée who could, at a moment's notice, provide a delicious meal for fifteen when only ten had said they'd absolutely be there. This meal she had intended to be especially nice, because David's assistant, Heather, and her surgeon husband, Cecil, were coming and also because it would be the first time that Scott with his broken arm was on the island after his exciting adventure in Wales. Felicity and Noah and the children were out playing volleyball on the beach, one happy family. Ethan was here, and so were Poppy and Patrick and their children, so that made fifteen people.

To complicate matters, the weather had turned cool, windy, and cloudy. This often happened, Alison knew, but she wished it hadn't happened this weekend. David's beach house, and the beach itself, were at its best on the sunny hot days when they could all gather on the deck and watch the sun sparkle on the ocean. Today the ocean reflected the gloomy gray of the sky. It wasn't quite cold enough in the house to ask David to build a fire in the living room, but it was cool and dismal enough that Alison was changing her menu on the spur of the moment, from cold pasta dishes to hot.

She had enough striped bass for all the adults. Daphne and Hunter could have hot dogs. Or if they preferred, they could have sandwiches and chips and take trays into the den to watch television while they ate. Poppy's children were easy about food, they'd eat anything. She'd intended making a cold salad of brown rice with cooked broccoli florets and corn and chopped red peppers tossed in olive oil and balsamic vinegar, but now she decided to serve the rice and vegetables separately, and hot, so the children could pick and choose.

She sighed. Then she laughed at herself for sighing. Oh, what a difficult time she was having, what a terrible burden, to have to change her dinner plans! Here they were, two days before the wedding, and all she had to worry about was how to feed her family and friends! It had been a worry this summer, sensing that Jane and Scott were at odds, and knowing that Felicity's marriage was rocky, too. And Poppy had been such a brat, and Ethan had tried to seduce Jane, although maybe Alison should give him a break and believe that Ethan had fallen for Jane. He had acted that way. Alison had often wanted to warn Jane or reprimand Ethan, but they were adults. They wouldn't have listened to her.

But finally here they all were at the end of the summer, and Jane and Scott were, to hear Jane tell it, madly in love again after Scott's accident in Wales. And David had been so incredibly generous, investing in Green Food, which had seemed to transform Noah from an anxious, frowning, bad-tempered bag of nerves into the charming family man Alison had known him to be when Felicity first married him.

Life was never simple and not all days were happy, but over the years, Alison had come to believe, a normal life had its ups and downs, its sadnesses and its joys. And marriage certainly had its seasons. Often, you had to make the sunshine yourself. Today she determined not to allow one neuron in her brain to worry or fret. Today she would be grateful for all she had!

And now, her daughters were going to try on their bridesmaids dresses!

Jane and Felicity entered their mother's large walk-in closet and ran their hands over her row of dresses as they headed for their own gowns hanging in the back.

"Wow. Mom has some nice clothes," Felicity said. "Nicer than she had when she was married to Dad."

"Mom was too busy to care about clothes when she was married to Dad," Jane answered. "She was usually in jeans and a turtleneck."

"Here's yours," Felicity said, lifting a heavy plastic garment bag from the wooden rod. "And mine."

They unzipped the garment bags, stripped down to their undies, and stepped into the gowns. The satin rustled as they pulled the gowns on.

"Zip me and I'll zip you," Jane said.

When they were finished, they checked themselves out in the three-way mirror. The pale pink complemented Felicity's porcelain complexion, and the deep rose accentuated the drama of Jane's dark hair and eyes.

"You look like a princess," Jane told her sister.

"So do you," Felicity replied. "No, wait. No more princess. Let's go with queen."

"Mom's queen."

"Okay, duchess then. Or countess."

Jane stepped next to Felicity. She put her hand on her sister's waist. "Look at us. We both look so—*splendid*. Even after this crazy summer. And now I've got Scott safely home and Noah's dissed Ingrid and you've got a job you can't wait to start. Our lives are wonderful."

Felicity walked away from Jane. She sat on the end of the bed, smoothing the satin of her skirt. "Yes, we are fortunate. I understand that. But, Jane—I'm not sure I want to stay married to Noah."

"Oh, Filly." Jane sat on the bed next to her sister, searching Felicity's face. "Tell me why."

"Because I don't think we love each other anymore. I might even, well, *hate* is too strong a word, but I feel a kind of contempt for him. I told you what he did, how he said I had to break all my connections with my family. Then David said he was going to invest money in Green Food, and in an instant"—Felicity flashed her hands through the air—"Noah *adores* David and all of us. That is so . . . slimy."

"What does he think about your job at Small Steps?"

"Ha. He asked why I want to waste my time on something any half-wit can do. That's what he said. *Half-wit*. At first, I tried to argue with him, I emailed him articles about the importance of early childhood care, I quoted statistics to him, but really, I knew I wasn't going to change his mind. Because he's a narcissist, really." Felicity allowed herself a sad smile. "I researched that term, too. A narcissist has an exaggerated idea of how important they are. And they lack empathy for others. But it's more than that, Jane. It's me. A switch has been flicked in my heart. I don't love him anymore." Felicity took Jane's hands in hers. "I don't know what to do!"

"Okay," Jane said calmly. "Okay, first thing, don't cry. No crying now. We've got to go downstairs for dinner. Second, take a breath. You've had a lot to deal with this summer and you're starting a new job, and your schedule will throw everything into a new time frame, and your first duty is to your children, right?"

Felicity nodded.

Jane continued, "And take it day by day for a while. Give yourself time to get adjusted to your work. Let your thoughts settle. Remember how close I was to leaving Scott. I mean, life is long, marriage is for the long haul. We go through so many changes in our lives. But divorce is huge. For you and for your children." Jane grinned and shrugged. "Listen to me, you'd think I know what I'm talking about."

"No, Jane, really, everything you say helps me a lot. I wish you lived closer. I wish I could talk to you every day."

"Well, silly Filly, we don't have to live in the same state to do that. We've got our phones, and we can text. Hey, if I get pregnant, if I actually manage to have a child, you know I'll be calling you constantly." Jane stood up. "Now come on, let's take off these gorgeous gowns and go down to the kitchen before Mom ends up doing all the work herself."

The house absolutely bulged. Daphne and Hunter and Alice and Luke had spent the afternoon on the beach, and now they were all showering and putting on clean clothes. Pipes clanked, water ran, footsteps thumped back and forth on the second floor, mothers called out to their children, and occasionally a father would bellow a loud, low order, like a bassoon. It was a family symphony.

Tonight, for a few hours, Alison could relax with her family all around her, knowing that everyone was safe and happy. Tonight, nothing could go wrong.

Ethan was behaving like a perfect stepson, prepping vegetables, unloading the dishwasher, preparing a sumptuous platter of cheese and crackers and olives and bluefish pâté, opening the wines.

Jane had settled Scott in the den where he was playing chess with Daphne, who of course had showered and dressed first of all the children. Jane had brought a duffel bag of goodies from the city, and had taken the chopped ham and olives and orange slices and mixed them together and spread them on torn bits of baguettes. Felicity was setting the table.

Alison checked her watch. Heather and Cecil would be here any minute.

"I'll set these on the coffee table," Jane said. "And I'll lay out some napkins."

"Lovely." Alison was wrapping strips of bacon around scallops; it would take only minutes to broil them. Her radar, the proverbial eyes at the back of her head, had not picked up on anything flirtatious or awkward between Jane and Ethan.

Felicity entered the kitchen. "Mom, shall I fill the ice bucket and set it in the living room? Some of you will have wine, but I know David likes Scotch on the rocks."

"Good idea," Alison said and as she focused on securing a piece of bacon on a scallop with a toothpick, she heard Felicity at the freezer, trying to wrestle out a big plastic of ice cubes.

"Here, Felicity, let me help," Ethan said and Alison saw her darling, irresistible almost stepson angle his body against Felicity's, not quite touching, as he helped her lift out the heavy bag.

"Um, oh, thanks." Felicity's cheeks had gone bright pink.

"The ice bucket's up there," Alison announced, pointing toward a cupboard at the back of the kitchen.

Felicity reached up to take it off the high shelf, but couldn't quite reach. And there was Ethan, right behind her, stretching up to grasp the bucket and bring it down to the counter, and if the man could have done it any slower, Alison didn't know how.

Oh, Ethan, she wanted to say, *just stop.*

"Here, you hold the bag," Ethan told Felicity, "and I'll dig out the ice. The cubes are frozen together."

Even that sounded flirtatious to Alison.

"You look especially nice tonight, Felicity," Ethan said as he dug out the ice.

"Thank you."

"Ethan!" Alison called, startling herself as well as the others. "When you're through with the ice, could you please put this sheet into the broiler for me? The oven's so hot, it almost makes me faint." That wasn't true, and if Ethan thought about all the times Alison had used the broiler this summer, he would know it wasn't, but with a smile, Ethan answered, "Of course."

"The ice bucket's full. I'll just take it into the living room," Felicity said.

David was outside, in front of the house, waiting to greet Heather and Cecil.

"They're here!" David called.

"I'll watch the scallops," Ethan told Alison.

"Thanks," Alison said, and now she thought she'd been irrational, thinking that Ethan was flirting with Felicity. Ethan was simply a terribly nice and helpful man. It wasn't his fault that he was so handsome.

She went through into the hall, checking her hair in the mirror. She noticed she was still wearing her apron, the one that said, in bright red, KISS THE COOK. It was the only apron in the kitchen and she had no idea who had given it to whom, but she made a mental note to buy some other aprons, soon. She took off the apron, smoothed her shirt, and went out to greet her guests.

David was on the lawn at the front of the house, shaking hands with Cecil and being thoroughly sniffed around the ankles by Charlie and Henry, the two elegant British Labs, one black, one yellow.

"I hope you don't mind that we brought them," Heather said. "They're very good with children, and they'll be quiet in the house. Actually, they have better manners than some people we know." She laughed nervously.

Alison sank to her knees to greet the dogs. She held out her hand to pet them. In turn, they licked her hand and arm, but they didn't attempt to lick her face.

"Beautiful dogs. I'm so glad you brought them," she said to Heather.

Heather squatted down next to Alison. In a whisper, she said, "I don't tell everyone, but they're kind of emotional support animals. They were my 'emotional support animals' before it became a *thing*. Now lots of people have emotional support animals, and not to help with any physical disability but to provide, well, emotional support. I feel safer when they are with me. I'm calmer."

"But, Heather, you're always calm," Alison said.

"That's because I always have the dogs with me."

Alison thought of asking Heather what had happened to cause her to need the support, but decided this was not the time.

"Well, they're handsome animals, and I'm glad you brought them," Alison said. "Let's all go into the house and have a drink. I'll put some bowls of water down for the dogs, and maybe they'd like a bit of fish when it's ready?"

"Oh," Heather said, "I've brought the dogs' bowls. I'll fetch them from the car. They prefer drinking out of their own bowls. I've also brought food for them. They don't do well when they eat unusual foods. They need very specific diets."

They're dogs, Alison thought, and then in a rush of comprehension, she realized that the organized Heather was as eccentric as everyone else. "How nice!" She held the door open while Heather and the two dogs filed into the house.

A buoyant, irrational joy filled her as she walked with Heather, Cecil, and the dogs into the living room.

Dinner was over. The table was cleared and the dishes were done. Heather and Cecil and the dogs had gone home. The family was more or less collapsed in the den, which, Alison decided, might need more furniture so that everyone could gather comfortably. As it was, the adults were all seated on sofas and fat, comfortable chairs, but the four children were sprawled on the floor. Oh, well, Alison thought, children liked to sprawl on the floor.

Since everyone was here, David suggested they discuss the rehearsal dinner and other details of the wedding. But they were all relaxed after the enormous meal and the conversation and laughter.

Alison made an effort. "All right, everyone. Let's go over a few things. Heather and Cecil are giving us the rehearsal dinner at their house. Reverend Murray Kenny is flying down from Boston to officiate at the wedding. When everyone is seated, Reverend Kenny will accompany the groom—that's David—from a side door to the right of the altar."

Poppy interrupted, "I think we know the drill."

"Well, uh, good. Okay," Alison continued, "the rehearsal dinner."

"Mom," Jane interrupted. "I heard a car in the driveway."

"Yeah," Felicity agreed. "I think someone's knocking on the front door."

"I'll go," Poppy said, rising awkwardly, and carrying her belly before her like a ship in full sail, she left the room.

Alison heard voices. A child's voice. A woman's voice. Then, light running footsteps, and a little girl with straight black hair and huge brown eyes flew into the room. "Granddad!" she cried, throwing herself on David.

A moment later, Sofia Vergara stood in the doorway. Wait, Alison thought, no, that wasn't Sofia Vergara, this woman was younger than the actress. Her dress was light brown, almost exactly the color of her skin, which made her look nude, maybe the woman's intention. Her black hair was swooped up into a formal chignon. Her eyes were as black as night, her face exquisite, her figure voluptuous, her earrings emerald.

She was a goddess.

"Esmeralda," Ethan said, rising to his feet, his face pale with surprise. "What are you doing here?"

When Esmeralda spoke, her voice was deep and husky. "Darling, we flew in and I rented a car at the airport."

Her rental is probably a chariot drawn by four white horses, Alison thought giddily.

"But *why?*" Ethan persisted.

"I'm here for the wedding, of course. David did invite me."

"But I thought you weren't coming!" Poppy said, scowling.

Jane and Felicity flashed each other an unspoken message: *Looks like Poppy is not Esmeralda's biggest fan.*

Esmeralda smirked. "I wasn't going to come, but Canny begged me. How could I resist?"

Felicity leaned over to Noah and whispered, "Close your mouth. You're about to drool on your shirt."

Shocked, Ethan said, "But you told me you absolutely couldn't come."

Esmeralda smiled sweetly. "Canny's longing to take part in the ceremony. She wants to be the flower girl. We've even brought her dress."

From the floor, Daphne spoke up. "Alice and I are the flower girls. But I guess we can always have one more."

Alison stood up. Jane glanced at Felicity, wondering if her sister noticed their mother's bare feet and white shorts and the old white cotton shirt that had once belonged to David and now was silky soft from wearing. Alison wore no makeup; she seldom did when she was on the island, and the tan she'd acquired over the summer complemented her. Jane thought they were all aware of the contrast between Alison and the exotic Esmeralda. Esmeralda glittered. Alison *glowed*. Maybe that was what the passing years and all the challenges caused, a deepening of the light you could shine for others.

"Esmeralda, hello! I'm Alison, David's fiancée. I'm so pleased to meet you. I've heard so much about you." She held out her hand.

Esmeralda's handshake was brief. "So *you* are Alison. How very interesting." She didn't smile. Her long thick eyelashes accentuated her gleaming black eyes.

"Well," Alison sputtered, "I hope it's interesting in a good way."

David smoothly slid Canny into Ethan's arms and joined Alison.

"Hello, Esmeralda. This is a surprise."

"It was a spur of the moment decision." Esmeralda leaned forward and air kissed both sides of David's face. "I'm sure that if anyone can understand, you can, David. You and I, we are both extremely busy people."

Alison rolled her eyes at her daughters and quietly retreated to her chair.

David put an arm around Esmeralda's shoulders and introduced her to the group. Scott and Noah both stood, trying to hide schoolboy grins.

Jane stood too, and met Esmeralda's eyes. *You don't scare me, lady,* Jane messaged with her eyes. She shook Esmeralda's cool, smooth hand.

Both Luke and Alice had climbed into Felicity's lap, acting as if some kind of ogre had entered the room, so Felicity only waved hello. "Hi, Esmeralda. So nice to meet you. These are our children, Alice and Luke."

Alice piped up. "I'm going to be a flower girl!"

Esmeralda said, "Really."

David pulled her attention away from the little girl. "Sit down, Esmeralda. Join us. Would you like a drink?"

Esmeralda slithered across the room and descended gracefully onto the sofa in the empty space between Noah and Scott. Again Felicity's and Jane's eyes met as they held back laughs at the sight of their husbands' faces. The men looked thrilled, but also slightly terrified.

"I'd love a drink," Esmeralda said.

"What can I get you?" Alison asked.

"Oh, David knows. He always makes it exquisitely delicious."

Everyone in the room seemed to be in some kind of state that rendered them incapable of speech. *Honestly,* Alison thought. *She's only human!* As David left the room to prepare Esmeralda's exquisite drink, Alison focused on Canny, who was sitting on Ethan's lap.

"Hello, Canny. You and I have spoken on the phone several times when you were in school this past year, staying with your father in Vermont. Is it fun to be back in Lima?"

Canny was turning a ring around and around on her finger, and she kept her eyes on the ring. "I don't know," she said quietly.

"Of course you know, *querido,*" Esmeralda said. "You love it there with Mommy. And you have so many friends."

"I miss my horse," Canny mumbled.

Esmeralda laughed. "Ahh, horses!" With a wave of her hand, she dismissed that subject. She smiled at her sister-in-law. "Poppy, you are going to have *another* baby! Are you excited about this?"

Poppy put both hands on her belly protectively, as if warding off evil beams from Esmeralda. "Very."

Esmeralda lifted her gaze to Ethan's face. "And, my darling, how are you?"

"Doing well," Ethan answered, giving her a private smile.

Esmeralda stretched voluptuously. "Oh, I'm so tied up in knots from traveling. I wish I could have a nice long massage. Ethan, you were always so good at relaxing my muscles. Will you take me to your room and relax me, after I have my drink?" She aimed her gorgeous face at Alison. "Don't be shocked, dear Alison. Ethan and I are still technically married. We simply haven't gotten around to signing the divorce documents. So we can sleep together without offending anyone's beliefs."

Ethan winced. "Um, I'm sleeping on the foldout sofa. I mean the sofa you're sitting on becomes a double bed."

"How uncomfortable! It makes my poor back ache to even think of trying to sleep on such a thing." Esmeralda looked around the room, her eyes like a hawk's scanning for the weakest creature in the room.

Alison spoke up. "Esmeralda, you and Ethan can have our room. David and I will take the foldout bed."

"No, that's not right," Jane cried. "Scott and I will move. Esmeralda can have our bed."

"Don't be silly," Felicity says. "Scott has his arm in a cast. He shouldn't have to sleep on a foldout bed."

Everyone talked at once. Esmeralda sipped her drink and watched, like a cat licking her chops. After everyone in the room was babbling in confusion, Esmeralda said, "Please don't trouble yourselves. I have a reservation at the White Elephant for me and Canny. I'll need to conduct some business by email and text from my room. Maybe Canny can spend the day out here."

The three little girls glanced at each other. They were stepping stones: Canny, nine, Daphne, eight, and Alice, seven. Alison's stomach churned with nervousness for her granddaughter, who sat wide-eyed and tongue-tied. Daphne, of course, had met Canny before and played with her, and Felicity feared that the two older girls would bond into a smug little clique and leave Alice out.

Daphne piped up. "I've got an idea. If Canny's going to spend the day out here, why doesn't she sleep with me and Alice in our room? Alice and I can squinch up together in one bed and Canny can have the other."

Canny smiled. She had an adorable smile.

"Cool!" Alice said.

"Right!" Daphne clapped her hands and took charge. "Come on, Alice, let's show Canny our room!"

Daphne reached out to take Alice's hand and tug her, and with her other hand she grasped Canny's wrist. The three girls, hand in hand, flew out of the room and into the hall and up the stairs, and all the way Daphne and Alice and Canny were giggling. Hunter and Luke, realizing they could escape from the adults, too, raced out of the room and up the stairs.

"How sweet," Esmeralda cooed. She set her sights on Ethan. "That means you can come to my hotel with me, Ethan. That way you won't have to sleep on a terrible foldout bed."

Ethan stalled. "Oh, well, I don't mind the foldout sofa, and . . ."

"You know you won't get to spend any time with Canny tonight now that she's with her two darling friends," Esmeralda said.

It was like watching a tennis match, Alison thought, every head in the room flashing from Esmeralda to Ethan.

"Yes, well, that's probably true . . ."

Alison interrupted. "Esmeralda, are you hungry? Would you like a sandwich? Some fruit?"

Esmeralda kept her eyes on Ethan. "No, thank you, Alison."

"Tell me, Esmeralda," David said, and his voice was pleasant but weighted with authority. "What are you working on now?"

The bronze beauty finally broke eye contact with Ethan. She smiled at David. "Ah, it is so exciting. Lima will host the 2019 Pan American games. Forty-one nations will compete. New buildings are underway, and this means jobs for many people. I'm coordinating efforts for the publicity of the games."

"An enormous undertaking," David said.

"Yes, that is true." Esmeralda yawned and stretched slowly and sinuously, like a cat. "Please forgive me, but I've been traveling for hours. I need to go to bed." She lifted one eyebrow at Ethan. "Coming?"

"I'll just get my toothbrush." Ethan sprinted up the stairs.

As if entranced, all the men rose and followed Esmeralda to the front door. Alison went with them, leaving Jane, Felicity, and Poppy behind.

Jane said, "Wow."

"She's a Venus flytrap," Poppy muttered. "She eats men for breakfast."

"She thinks Canny's going to be the flower girl." Felicity chewed a fingernail.

"Don't worry. The three of us can handle her," Poppy assured the sisters.

They heard Ethan thudding down the stairs. The front door shut. The men and Alison returned to the den.

Alison looked slightly shell-shocked. "It's late. I think I'll go to bed, too. Last person up, turn off all the lights, okay?"

"We've got to get the kids to bed," Felicity said.

Jane and Scott lingered in the den, channel surfing, so that the others could get settled upstairs. Jane heard the laughter of the five children and the light thumps of their feet as they ran from bathroom to bed. Then, low adult voices murmured. Then, silence. The children had been really good all day, she thought—she hoped Scott had noticed. They hadn't discussed getting pregnant since they'd been back on the island. They were so busy, getting Scott to his doctor's appointment to check on his arm, unpacking from Wales and packing for the island, and then they'd arrived on Nantucket and were immediately caught up in the family activities. It was difficult, Jane thought, not to wince when children fought or screamed. But it was difficult, too, not to smile when the children came down for breakfast with their hair all bedheaded like a chicken's feathers, and their faces bright and glowing with life. The children laughed so easily, and slipped onto any adult's lap and cuddled up.

"It seems quiet up there," Jane said. "Shall we go to bed? We've got a busy day tomorrow."

"Yes," Scott said. "Let's head up. Although I'm not sure you'll be able to be quiet."

Jane cocked her head. "What? Why not?"

"Because," Scott said, looking pleased with himself, "I think it's time we had some unprotected sex."

Jane smiled. "But what about your arm?"

"I'll manage. Don't worry about that."

"I'll be quiet," Jane promised. And she leaned forward to kiss him, taking care not to hit his cast, and she thought this was the best kiss she'd had since she'd first met him, and she couldn't stop kissing him, and he couldn't stop kissing her, and awkwardly, grinning at themselves, they slid down onto the sofa together, and while the television continued to drone on about politics, they still kissed, not like man and wife, but like lovers. They didn't make it up to their room for an hour.

twenty-seven

It was the day before the wedding. After breakfast, Alison, Poppy, Felicity, and Jane gathered together in Alison's bedroom, to see the girls in their wedding finery. The little girls had shut the door to dress, giggling in Alison's walk-in closet. Then they threw open the door and filed out.

The matching flower girl dresses that Felicity and Poppy had agreed on for their daughters were simple and elegant. Both dresses had pink satin bodices with pale pink tulle tea-length skirts and a rose satin sash with a fat bow in back. Their shoes were pale pink ballet slippers.

Canny's dress was also pale pink, but it was crusted with faux pearls and thick loops of embroidery. Sequins sparkled, metallic lace crinkled, miniature rubies and emeralds gleamed as Canny slowly twirled so everyone could admire her dress.

"Your dress has more sparkly bits than ours," Alice remarked.

Canny said sweetly, "That's because I'm the head flower girl."

Daphne looked at her mother. "You and Alice's mom have bling on your waist. Why can't we have some sparkly stuff, even if we aren't the head flower girl?"

Poppy, aggravated by her sister-in-law's bold fashion statement, snapped, "Because for some reason Canny has more sparkles on her than the bride. And that many sparkles are not appropriate for—"

Abruptly, Alison stood up, clapping her hands. Esmeralda was still at the hotel with Ethan. Even though Canny was a confident child, she was still a child, needing an adult on her side.

"Daphne, you are absolutely right! You and Alice should have some bling, too. I've got a jewelry box just filled with rhinestones, which are like diamonds, that I've inherited from my mother and grandmother. I've been meaning to give them to you girls to let you play dress-up, but I'm going to get the box now. And you can choose what you'd like to wear in the wedding."

"Yay!" Daphne and Alice jumped up and down as Alison left the room.

Alison quickly returned with a deep blue velvet box. She put it on the bed and opened it. The little girls gasped. They pulled out rhinestone necklaces, rhinestone hair clips, rhinestone rings and bracelets.

Poppy rose to supervise. "Two apiece, girls. Just two. More than that, and you'll look tacky."

Alison noted Canny's frown.

"I think three apiece," Alison said. "Each girl should wear a sparkle in her hair. You, too, Canny. Come, let's find a sparkle for your hair."

Later that day, when the girls were swimming and the men were on the beach, the sisters summoned their mother to her room. They shut the door so they wouldn't be overheard.

"Mom," Jane said. "About Canny's dress . . ."

"What about it?" Alison asked sweetly.

"Oh, come on, Mom," Felicity whispered angrily. "What are you *doing*? This is your wedding, not a carnival!"

Alison faced both daughters and softly replied, "Yes. It is a wedding. *My* wedding, and a celebration of my union with David. And he is accepting, with love and"—she glanced meaningfully at Felicity—"generosity, my family, my two daughters, their husbands and children. In return, I'm accepting with love and with generosity of spirit, David's family. That includes Poppy, who is cranky and difficult, and is probably hoping I'll drop dead before the wedding. And Ethan, who is, I've noticed, a, well, the best word I can think of is *playboy*. He certainly seemed to be playing with *you*, Jane. And he acted as if he was divorced, and he wasn't. So frankly, Esmeralda, who is unusual and in your face and outrageously beautiful, is not that difficult to accept. And she has come here, and she's brought Canny, who is David's much-loved granddaughter, and who, I might add, has been accepted by your daughters with great pleasure. So if Canny wants to wear that sparkling dress, she should wear it. That's definitely the most celebratory dress I've ever seen."

"But, Mom," Jane protested. "*You're* the bride. You should be the most sparkling!"

Alison laughed. "Darlings, when you get to be my age, you know how to let go of the unimportant things so you have more space in your heart for what matters. My wedding is going to be beautiful, because so many people that David and I love will be here, and really, who cares what they wear."

"Jane's right," Felicity said. "It's a *wedding*, not just any day. It should be special."

"Girls, it will be wonderful!" Alison promised. "Now go away. I need to take a nap. We've got the rehearsal dinner tonight."

"Let's take a walk on the beach," Jane suggested.

Felicity nodded. "Good idea."

They took a moment in the kitchen to blot sunblock on their noses. Out on the deck, Poppy lay as limp as a fish on the lounger, her sunhat over her face. Esmeralda was still at the hotel.

Jane and Felicity tiptoed past Poppy, not wanting to wake her as they went across the deck and down the wooden steps and through the brush to the beach. When they were near the water's edge, they turned to each other, wide-eyed.

"Esmeralda!" Jane shrieked.

"I know!" Felicity agreed.

"And *Ethan*! What a tool! He told me he was divorced and the truth is, he's only separated!"

"Given the way he trotted right along after Esmeralda to go to her hotel last night, I wouldn't say they're all that separated!" Felicity kicked a pebble into the surf. "He was such a flirt!"

"I know. I totally fell for his act."

"Are you talking about my brother?"

Jane and Felicity exchanged guilty looks. Poppy was waddling through the brush, coming toward them.

"Busted," Jane admitted.

"Could you hear us?" Felicity asked.

Poppy grinned. "I didn't need to hear you. Whenever I see a couple of women huddled and pissed off, I know they're talking about Ethan."

"Well, he did try to seduce Jane," Felicity said defensively.

"I'm not surprised. Remember, I grew up with the guy. I've seen him go through women like I whip through a bag of chips." Poppy slanted her eyes at Jane. "Did he succeed?"

"No, thank heavens. But it was close," Jane admitted. "It wasn't only that he's so handsome and sexy. It was also that I was having some . . . *issues* with Scott."

"God, *marriage*," Poppy sympathized. "Could we walk? I need some exercise. My blood pressure's shooting up with the pregnancy."

Jane and Felicity fell into step with Poppy.

"*My* issues have been resolved," Jane said.

"For now," Poppy said. Quickly she added, "I mean, it seems to me that marriage is one long train ride of issues. Occasionally we get to sit down and eat in the dining car, but most of the time we're stumbling from car to car, trying to keep our balance."

Felicity burst out laughing. "Nice metaphor."

"That's why I enjoy working," Poppy admitted. "Dealing with twelve department heads arguing at full volume is easy-peasy after spending a day at home."

"I hear you," Felicity agreed.

The sun was warm on their shoulders, the sand hot on their feet. They stepped into the lazy waves to cool off.

"So what do you think of Esmeralda?" Poppy asked.

Jane and Felicity hesitated.

"She's beautiful," Jane said. "And so—*energetic*."

Poppy laughed. "That's one word for it. I've known her—kind of—for years, ever since Ethan married her. She and Ethan are well matched, both so gorgeous and so unable to settle down. We almost became friends after Daphne was born. We got the cousins together to play with each other, so we spent time together, too. But not for long. Esmeralda would invite me and the kids to her house, and then somehow she always got an absolutely essential phone call, state secrets and all that, so she'd disappear with her phone and I got stuck playing preschool with three children. She's a user."

"And Canny?" Felicity asked.

"Canny's a sweet little girl. My kids love her. Good thing, since she's their cousin."

"How does it work, this cousin thing?" Felicity mused aloud. "When our mother marries your father, does that make our children cousins?"

Jane said, "Step-cousins."

Poppy moaned, "Related somehow. This is far enough for me." Catching their looks, she clarified, "I mean I can't walk anymore. But you go on."

"No," Felicity said. "I'll go back to the house with you."

"So will I," Jane said.

The three strolled along in silence for a few minutes.

"Tomorrow's the wedding," Jane said.

"I'm going to look like a fat old crow in my black pantsuit," Poppy complained.

OMG, Jane thought, *Poppy has an insecurity!* She didn't dare meet Felicity's eyes, she knew her sister was as shocked as she was.

"No, you'll look elegant," Felicity said. "Elegant and lush and beautiful."

"Thanks," Poppy said, staring straight ahead.

Jane, walking next to Felicity, squeezed her sister's hand.

Heather, now known as She Who Knows Everything, had convinced Alison and David that it would be cruel, not to mention irrational, to expect five children, including two boys, to be quiet and well-mannered through a rehearsal dinner at a restaurant, so the evening before the wedding, the adults rounded up the children, and in a convoy of Jeeps and Range Rovers, they drove to the Willets' house in town. Their backyard was large, with several old maples for climbing and bushes for hiding behind. Also, of course, Henry and Charlie, the English Labs, were there, wagging their tails and hoping someone wanted to throw them a stick to fetch.

"Oh, how beautiful!" Alison cried, as the wedding party walked through the house and came to the French windows open to the backyard.

There on the patio, a long table had been set up, with a white tablecloth and a tapestry runner and vases of summer flowers in the middle of the table. Beautiful Portmeirion pottery plates had been laid, and Jane nudged Scott, whispering, "It's a *sign.*"

"It's a *coincidence,*" Scott told her, adding softly in her ear, "We don't need a sign."

The adults wandered around the yard, admiring the perennials, while the children climbed trees and played with the dogs. Then Heather and Cecil brought out large bowls of pasta, and a wooden bowl of fresh greens dressed in aromatic basil vinaigrette, and bread boards holding hot loaves of bread. The children were seated at the kitchen table, partly because the long table didn't have room for such a large group, and also because Heather gave the children paper plates.

"If you behave nicely and eat your dinner, you can play as soon as you've cleaned your plate," Poppy announced, eyeing each child separately.

After consulting with David and Ethan, Alison had invited Esmeralda to the rehearsal dinner.

Esmeralda had answered sweetly but firmly, "Thank you, Alison, but I plan to have dinner in my room at the hotel. I have a lot of work to do. I will attend the wedding, of course, because Canny will be the head flower girl, but I'm skipping the rehearsal dinner."

"My instincts tell me not to expect a reconciliation between Ethan and Esmeralda," Alison had told David afterward.

"That's fine with me," David murmured.

So eleven people seated themselves at the long table on the patio. Tall glasses of ice water sat at each place, and a pitcher of red wine sat at each end of the table. The sun was sinking toward the treetops, and the weather was dry and cool. The dogs, exhausted from running with the children, lay themselves quietly, and hopefully, beneath the children's table, waiting for food to drop. There were no waiters, no strangers, no noises except the singing of birds as they began to nestle in for the evening. Almost as if orchestrated on cue, everyone took a deep breath and settled back in their chairs, relaxing. Tomorrow would be formal and social and whirlwind. Tonight, they were at ease among family and friends.

Heather started the bowl of pasta around the table. Cecil poured wine for those who wanted it.

"How did the rehearsal go?" Heather asked.

Alison laughed and reached over to take David's hand. "We held it at home. Our friends will be checking into the hotel, and swimming and boating and sunbathing and so on, and they're starting to erect the tent. So we moved all the furniture around, and progressed from the bottom of the stairs, down the hall, and into the living room, where the hat rack stood in for the minister in front of the fireplace."

David added, "We had Mendelssohn on someone's phone, and the boys used sofa cushions for bearing the rings, and the little girls carried the napkin basket and the fruit bowls and pretended to toss the petals. The boys fidgeted all through the pretend ceremony, but Ethan and Poppy separated them and made them stand still. And the moment I kissed the bride—a quick peck—the boys made vomiting noises and ran outside to the deck."

"They've been warned," Poppy said. "Perfect behavior tomorrow or no TV for a week." She glanced down the table at Felicity. "Does that work for you?"

"It does," Felicity called back. "Good idea."

"I'm sure they'll be good tomorrow," Alison said. "I think they might find the congregation and the minister in his robes so overwhelming they'll be quiet from sheer terror."

"I know I will be," Ethan joked.

"No, you won't," his sister snapped. "You'll be trolling the room for some good-looking single woman to flirt with."

Ethan laughed and put his hand to his heart. "You wound me to the core."

"I've never seen a summer go by so fast," Jane said. "Has time sped up?"

"I think it's because you were on the island so much," Heather told her.

"And in the ocean and on the beach," Ethan said, giving Jane an obvious once-over gaze. "You've acquired quite a tan."

Jane stared across the table at her husband. "I've convinced Scott to spend some time with me this week. He's such a workhorse, he hasn't gotten any sun at all. Not to mention how he was stuck in the fog on a mountainside for day and a night."

"Really? Do tell us more!" Cecil said.

Jane watched Scott recounting his adventure. Everyone had questions, and as Scott answered, he became more and more relaxed and talkative. So maybe, Jane thought, with the help of a little red wine and the magic of Wales, Scott was finally becoming part of the family.

At some point, the children put their paper plates in the trash as they were directed, and politely but rapidly refused the offer of fruit for dessert, and raced out into the garden to play. No one at the long table wanted dessert, and they all lingered in their chairs, slowly finishing their very good wine, talking about their own adventures, and enjoying an unusual spirit of fellowship. The sun sank, and the sky became pale blue, and then black, as the stars came out, one by one.

David rose. "We all need to go home and get our beauty sleep. But first, I'd like to make a toast to Heather and Cecil for this delicious meal and elegant rehearsal dinner."

"Hear, hear!" the others cried, and raised their glasses, and drank.

"And now," David continued, "I'd like to make a brief speech. All summer I've thought about this wedding, this ceremony joining Alison and me. And this is what I've concluded: A marriage is a private bond between two people. But a *wedding* is a party for everyone, a celebration of life and love, a gathering of friends and relatives to rejoice in life's good food, champagne, dancing, laughter, and a golden moment in the passage of life. A marriage lasts years, through the good times and bad, and all the banal, boring everyday goings-on of living. A wedding is a brief flash, a unique, exceptional festivity with singing and flowers and good will among men—and women. A marriage is real life. A wedding is a fairy tale. But a wedding is also a promise that we will hold dear the joys of the fairy tale close to our hearts as we go through the years of our marriage."

After he spoke, the table was quiet, and Felicity and Jane wiped their eyes, and Cecil took Heather's hand, and the children and even the dogs stopped playing. For a brief moment, it was as if they were caught in a spell.

Then Scott chimed in, "Hear, hear!"

And all the others added their cries, and David leaned down to kiss Alison, who rose to meet his lips.

David took his seat. Alison stood.

"But wait!" she said in a joking tone. "There's more!"

Now that the moment had come, she was nervous. Her hands trembled and she clasped them together at waist level. "David has already given me his wedding present. You'll see it tomorrow when I walk down the aisle. Well, I have a wedding present for him, but it's so large and heavy I can't lift it myself. I want to thank Poppy for helping me decide on the perfect words." Alison caught the puzzled glance between her daughters. She could read their minds: *What?* they were thinking. *Mom had Poppy help her instead of us?* In a moment, they would understand.

Alison continued. "Heather and Cecil have helped me transport my gift to their house, because it's too big to hide out at Surfside."

An excited stirring passed over the table. Her new family and especially David leaned toward her, captivated.

"Cecil? Heather? Would you help me bring it out?"

Alison hurried into the Willets' house. Cecil and Heather followed. They had hidden the quarterboard behind a sofa in the family room. It was a narrow mahogany plank, six feet long, one foot wide, painted a navy blue almost dark enough to be black, all edges outlined with gold leaf. The words *Glad Tidings* were carved into the mahogany and painted with five layers of gold leaf, as were the pineapples, a whaling-day emblem of hospitality, which adorned each end.

Alison and the Willets had practiced carrying the heavy sign and now Cecil and Heather each hoisted an end while Alison supported the middle. They carefully carried it out to the patio.

The group's reaction was all that Alison had hoped it would be. Poppy stood up, looking terribly pleased with herself, and the others rose, too, cheering and applauding.

David said, "Alison, what a spectacular gift." He ran his hands over the painted and gilded and engraved words.

For a moment he couldn't speak, and tears welled in Alison's eyes. She was so thrilled that he liked the wedding present, so gladdened to see that it had moved the heart of the man she loved.

"*Glad Tidings.*" David turned to the group at the table. "Glad tidings, indeed. I'll call a carpenter tomorrow and have the quarterboard hung over the front door."

"Actually," Alison said, "you might have to wait a day or two to call the carpenter. Tomorrow we're getting married."

"A toast!" Scott lifted his glass. "A toast to *Glad Tidings!*"

They raised their glasses and called out their toasts. A sea breeze swept through the yard, so that the trees rustled and the women's skirts fluttered and for a moment all their hearts swelled like a sail on a boat heading for home.

twenty-eight

On the morning of her wedding day, Alison woke early. David slept next to her, but she was a bundle of nerves and she probably would be until today was over. Not that she wanted to rush through this day, no, she wanted to breathe and take it all in.

She quietly slipped from the bed and padded across the thick silky carpet to the huge window facing the Atlantic. The pleated alabaster Japanese shades were lowered at night to cover the window and block early morning light. They were raised by a remote control. It was over on David's bedside table, and she didn't want to wake him. She didn't need to see the entire view; she needed only a peek.

She lifted the side of a shade and peeked.

Blue sky. Sunshine.

Ahhhh.

She tiptoed back to bed and relaxed, closing her eyes, hoping to fall back asleep.

Next to her, on this, their wedding day, David, was snoring like a chainsaw. The wedding ceremony was at five o'clock that evening, but guests were invited to check into the hotel yesterday afternoon or any time today so they could unpack and spend the day enjoying the delights of the island. They could swim, sail, kayak, hike, or drive one of the BMWs into town. A buffet lunch was set up at the hotel from noon until two. After the ceremony, the champagne would flow, dinner would be served in the huge white tent with banners flying, and later, there would be dancing.

So really, Alison could stay in bed all day if she wanted.

She heard the front door being opened and softly closed. Alani had been hired for the day to run the kitchen, so that the children and grandchildren sleeping in other rooms of this house could eat whenever they wanted. Today, Alison didn't have to butter toast or wash a dish. And she didn't have to solve any problems or settle any family quarrels. All the details had been sorted. She snuggled back into her pillow, closing her eyes, savoring the luxury.

Felicity quietly made her way from the bedroom and down the stairs and through the sleeping house to the kitchen. She said hello to Alani, gratefully accepted the freshly brewed cup of coffee, and took it outside to drink on the deck.

She'd never been here, alone, with the whole world around her, so bright and wide with morning sunshine, lightly stirred by a sea breeze. She stretched her legs out on the lounger and sipped her coffee. No one walked on the beach, no one was swimming. Everyone else in the house was asleep. For a few moments, Felicity had time to reflect on all that had happened this summer.

First. She truly had a sister. Felicity and Jane had gone along through their adult lives without each other, but during this summer, they had bonded. They knew now that they had each other to lean on, to share miseries and joys with, to plot against their families with, to laugh with. That she loved her sister who loved her back was Felicity's happiest discovery.

The state of her marriage was the next revelation. Felicity was glad that Noah had done his best to join Felicity's family, even if his behavior had been inspired by David's generous financial assistance. She was relieved that Noah had reassigned Ingrid, and pleased that his new assistant was a hyperactive young man with ears like Prince Charles.

During every spare moment when she was riding the ferry to or from Nantucket, and her children were playing Nintendo DS or reading books, Felicity had been on her phone, searching out and reading articles about marriage. Specifically, about living with a scientist.

Noah was not the clichéd geek of television and movies. He was handsome and charismatic. But he was also driven, ambitious, self-absorbed, manic, and really, truly, neurotic. Felicity had taken tests. She'd checked all the boxes. Her husband was obsessive-compulsive about his scientific brainchild, he was terrified of other scientists getting there before him, and everything else—wife, children, home—everything else took second place. Actually more like tenth place.

Felicity thought that his relationship with Ingrid, whatever it had been, was the result of needing a lieutenant, an assistant, a Watson to his Holmes. Noah would always need a person like that, and Felicity could never be that person.

The bad news, the heartbreaking matter, was that Felicity and her children would never come first with Noah.

The good news was that Felicity was free to change. She could leave Noah, but she didn't want to. He was a good enough father to her children, and when he stepped out of his scientific fog, he could be a pleasant companion. They were a family. Not a perfect family, to be sure. But they were all right, would be all right.

And Felicity was going to take the job at the preschool, simply because she wanted to. So what if it didn't help Noah with his

financial worries. For a while, for a few years perhaps, David's infu-
sion of cash would weaken the fire of Noah's financial anxieties. The
job in the preschool would be for Felicity. She adored little children,
and she knew that preschool was a crucial stage in their understanding of the world. Alice and Luke were in school now. Their worlds
were getting wider.

And now Felicity would open up her world, too. She could not
save the world as Noah was trying to do with his green food. But she
could make one little child smile, she could give comfort to one
small child, and that would fill her heart. That would be sufficient
treasure for her.

Today was her mother's wedding, the beginning of a new life for
Alison.

Tomorrow would be the beginning of a new life for Felicity. And
honestly? She was ready to leave the lazy lounging on the beach, the
long, slow afternoons of falling asleep while reading, and the careless disorders of the day. But she was not going to return to the rigid
organization of the past few years. She was not going to base all her
happiness on Noah's relentless problems. She was going to take
good care of her family, but she would also open a door into another
world, a noisy, chaotic, giggling, wobbling world of small children,
and she couldn't wait to get started.

And she was going to eat bacon and let the children have some,
too.

"Mom gets married today," Jane whispered.

She was snuggled up as close as she could get to her husband.
His good arm was around her as they lay in bed beneath the light
covers.

"Mmm," Scott said, kissing the top of her head.

"I've been thinking," Jane continued softly. "I've been thinking
we could leave New York. Move to Boston."

Scott raised up a bit and looked down at her face. "Are you kidding?"

"Not kidding. Just think of the house we could buy in Boston. Real estate is so much cheaper than New York. *Everything's* so much cheaper than New York."

Scott flopped down on the bed, keeping an arm across Jane. "Where are all these ideas coming from? Your mother? Your sister?"

"No, they're my own ideas. But I wouldn't mind being closer to my family. Especially if . . ."

"I like your mother and David. I like your sister. Noah? Not so much. I'm not sure I'd want to be closer to him."

"I agree! We wouldn't move into the house next door." Jane laughed.

"And what about work? Our firms don't have an office in Boston."

"So we interview at other firms. We've got spectacular resumes."

"I don't know . . ."

"I've been thinking, how we are always spending money on traveling to faraway places. And yes, of course, our trips have been fantastic, but we have to work so hard to afford them that we never have time for ourselves at home. We don't have downtime together."

"We go to plays. We go to the symphony. Art openings."

"Yes, and we go to those places with friends. Although most of them aren't really *friends*. They're business associates. People we see only in our best clothes. We've never shared the rough and tumble of real life."

"But we never wanted to be like that."

"But maybe I do, now. And if we have children, wouldn't it be nice to be near Felicity and her kids? And my mother would be over the moon."

"It's kind of unsettling, thinking of such enormous changes, leaving New York for Boston."

"I know," she said. "And I'm not saying we have to do it right away, or do it at all. But isn't it nice to dream?"

Scott pulled her close and nuzzled his chin into Jane's hair. "Jane, life with you is full of surprises."

Jane smiled. "When we married, we agreed we wanted adventures. I think some of them can take place right in our own home."

Alison showered and creamed her skin, using English Garden Creams, of course. She sat very still, not talking or smiling, while Felicity bent over her, applying the perfect amount of foundation, eyeliner, mascara, and blush to her face. She accepted the new tube of red lipstick that was supposed to last all day, even if she ate—or kissed—and carefully applied it. She brushed her hair until it gleamed. She asked the others to leave the room to put on their own dresses while she donned her brand-new silk and lace underwear. Now she stepped into her ivory wedding gown.

"*Wow,*" she said. "You're looking pretty good for an old girl."

"Mom? We can hear you talking to yourself in there. Are you ready?"

It was Felicity, standing in the hall.

Alison opened the bedroom door, and her wedding attendants flooded in, babbling, exclaiming, laughing.

"You all look so beautiful!" Alison said, and burst into tears.

"Stop it, Mom. Stop it right now. You'll ruin your makeup." Felicity held Alison's shoulders and gave her the same *look* she often gave her children.

Alison sniffed back her tears.

"I'm going to zip you up," Jane told her. "Hold still."

Then came the friendly, familiar zing as the zipper interlocked the two sides, and Alison could actually hear it because everyone in the room had gone quiet, waiting for the moment when the dress was completely on Alison.

Then, everyone went: *Ahhhh.*

Anya had fit the dress to perfection. The ivory silk accentuated the tan Alison had achieved over the summer, and she absolutely glowed.

"And now, my wedding gift from David." Alison lifted a black velvet jewelry box off the dresser and opened it, bringing out the diamond jewelry.

The necklace sparkled against her skin like tiny rainbows of light.

"I'll fasten it," Felicity said.

Alison added the earrings, three-carat studs. "I'm ready!" she announced.

"Mom," Jane said. "You need to wear shoes."

This set the three little girls into hysterical laughter, and they bounced up and down on the bed, giggling, until they realized they could see themselves in the large mirror over the dresser. Then they settled down and smoothed their skirts and turned this way and that, eyeing themselves in their wedding finery.

Alison stepped into her ivory satin heels. "Now. Time for photos."

Everyone had a phone, and everyone was suddenly clicking and rearranging the groupings, and they were laughing like kids, all of them, when they heard a noise at the door.

Felicity ran downstairs.

"Mom!" Felicity cried. "The limousine's here."

"My heart is beating really fast," Alison said, pressing her hand against her chest. "I think I'm having a heart attack."

"I think you're having wedding-day flutters," Jane said sensibly, taking her mother's arm. "Let's go. We can drink champagne in the limo."

"We can?" Daphne asked.

"It's ginger ale for you three," Felicity said. "And not too much of it. You don't want to have to pee in the middle of the ceremony."

This idea sent the three little girls into more explosions of giggling, and Felicity and Jane had to separate them to get them downstairs and into the car.

Alison was left alone. For a few moments. To look at herself in the mirror.

She looked beautiful.

She couldn't stop smiling.

. . .

The limo driver had made a mash-up of wedding songs, and all the way from Surfside to Wauwinet, the group sang along to The Dixie Cups' "Chapel of Love" and the B-52s' "Love Shack" and "Celebration" with Kool & the Gang. By the time they arrived at the hotel, they were all breathless. Alison saw roses in the others' cheeks and knew her cheeks were pink, too.

The limo arrived at the Wauwinet at exactly four forty-five.

"Don't open the door yet!" Alison begged the driver. To her daughters, she said, "Is my lipstick smeared? How do I look?"

"No, your lipstick is perfect, and you look amazing," Jane said.

"And you girls all look like princesses," Felicity told Daphne and Alice and Canny.

"I don't want to be a princess," Canny said sternly. "I want to be president of the United States."

"Me, too!" Daphne cried.

"You can be my vice president," Canny said.

"NO. You can be president of Peru and I'll be president of the United States."

"Girls," Felicity said. "Here's your opportunity to show your future voters how elegant and stately you can be."

The girls nodded, agreeing, and with chins high, stepped out of the limo.

"Daphne," Alice whispered, "can I be your vice president?"

"Sure," Daphne said graciously.

And then suddenly they were out of the limo, gathered in all their glory on the sidewalk leading to the hotel entrance.

"Is it time?" Alison asked.

"It's time," Jane said.

They went into the hotel and through the wide hallway. By the door to the outside was a table with a florist waiting to hand the women their bouquets and the little girls their baskets of rose petals.

They stepped out onto the long, wide porch. In front of them the lawn spread like green velvet down to the beach and the brilliant blue water of the harbor. At the side of the hotel a glorious white tent with banners flying waited, and a boardwalk had been laid to the tent's entrance, where the main aisle was covered with white cloth. They could hear Mendelssohn filling the tent.

Hunter and Luke, clad in blue blazers, their hair slicked down, raced up.

"Come on!" Hunter ordered. "*Everyone's* waiting!"

"Boys," Alison said. "You both look so handsome. Can I kiss you?"

"Ugh, no!" Hunter said. He tugged his cousin's arm. "Come on. Get your pillow and the ring."

The florist lifted two red velvet pillows and two golden rings and placed them in the little boys' hands.

"I'm doing this," Hunter said, and took off, walking rapidly, Luke following.

When they got to the white aisle inside the tent, they stopped for a moment, giggling and nudging each other. They settled down inside the tent, walking down the aisle a lot faster than they'd been taught in rehearsal.

Then it was time for the women.

"You first," Felicity told her sister.

Jane looked alarmed. "I'm going to throw up."

"You're a lawyer," Felicity chided. "Get it together."

"But it's *Mom*!" Jane whispered.

"Go." Felicity gave her sister a nudge.

Bouquet in hand, Jane hurried down the boardwalk. At the tent's entrance, she stopped, and gathering her dignity, she went slowly down the aisle to the altar.

Felicity followed, biting her lip so she wouldn't dissolve into tears.

"Okay," Alison said to her flower girls. "You know what to do."

Off the little girls went, Canny first, then Daphne, and finally, Alice.

Alison took a deep breath, and followed.

Mendelssohn's "Wedding March" sounded as Alison stepped

into the tent. On either side of the aisle, people rose, their finery fluttering. Her best friend, Margo, wore a fabulous fascinator and a huge grin. Dr. Abbott and his wife, and all three of the dental hygienists Alison had worked with were together in one row. Heather and Cecil were there, at the end of an aisle. Charlie and Henry sat next to them, not a muscle twitching, elegant in their black bow ties. Other friends of David's were there, and two of the girls who had been friends of Jane and Felicity since childhood. A bolt of nerves struck Alison, and for a moment she paused. Then she saw them waiting for her, her family, all of them, and her beloved David, so handsome in his tux. Alison broke out into a great huge smile that lasted as she went down the aisle to stand by his side.

They had wanted the ceremony to be brief, and it was. It passed in a blur. The minister's words. The vows, when she and David gazed into each other's eyes as if gazing into the future. The exchanging of rings. And finally, the kiss.

"I now pronounce you husband and wife," the minister proclaimed. The congregation cheered and applauded. David and Alison proceeded down the aisle, and Alison smiled and wept tears of happiness.

They stepped out of the tent and onto the green velvet lawn. In front of them, the harbor waters glittered in the sunlight.

"Look, Grandma," Alice cried excitedly. "The water is covered with diamonds!"

The attendees filed out of the tent onto the grass. Near the outdoor patio stood a long table centered with an enormous arrangement of flowers and piled high with delicious finger foods. As people gathered on the lawn, waiters appeared with trays of champagne and sparkling water. People congratulated the newlyweds, and everyone told everyone else how gorgeous they were, and as friends met friends, cries of delight flew up in the air like small birds. Patrick helped Poppy to a chair on the patio where she sat in her expansive black pantsuit, hundreds of sequins and her mother's diamonds flashing in the sunlight, her belly proudly bulging. Ethan introduced Esmeralda to the guests. Esmeralda, wearing an impressively tight and low-cut emerald gown, languidly extended her hand, allowing people to shake it.

And then the family went to the boardwalk in front of the harbor and gathered together for the photographer to snap some formal shots. The little boys mugged and twitched and couldn't hold still. The little girls giggled and preened. Scott stood with his good arm around Jane. Felicity and Noah stood side by side, not touching. Esmeralda insinuated herself into the family, standing with one possessive hand on Ethan and one on Canny. Poppy pulled Patrick's arm and led him to the opposite side of the group. Everyone in the party gathered on the lawn to watch the photographer.

"Throw the bouquet!" Felicity ordered her mother. She called out, "Heads-up, everyone. The bride is tossing the bouquet!"

The party gathered expectantly on the lawn, laughing, the few unmarried women coaxing each other forward.

"Right!" Alison yelled back. "Here goes!"

She turned her back to the crowd and tossed the bouquet.

Charlie, the Lab, seeing something fly his way, performed a spectacular leap and caught the flowers in midair. The crowd cheered.

Alison slipped off her heels. The grass beneath her feet was warm and soft. In front of her the crowd returned to their conversations and champagne. Behind her, the harbor waters beckoned like magic.

Holding on to David's arm, she stepped onto the beach.

"I want to wade in the water," she said.

"On your wedding day?" David asked.

"Absolutely on my wedding day."

"But what about our guests? Dinner should be served soon."

"David, look at our guests. They're happily guzzling fabulous champagne and being served delicious canapés."

"Well," David said. "You continue to be an unconventional woman."

Alison lifted up her wedding skirt to a few inches above her knees. She smiled at David.

"I suppose I need to be an unconventional man," David said, and leaning over, he untied his black dress shoes and slipped them off, then removed his black socks and rolled up his trousers.

Hand in hand, Alison and David waded into the water until it was up to their knees.

"It's cold," Alison said.

"It will feel warmer in a minute," David assured her. He put his arms around her. "Maybe if I hold you, you'll warm up."

"Maybe if you kiss me, I'll warm up faster," Alison said.

David kissed her, a slow, deep, satisfying promise of a kiss.

"Hey, Grandma! Granddad!"

Alison and David turned to see who had called them. Five grandchildren held their phones high, snapping shots of Alison and David, radiant and joyful, in the gleaming blue water. These would be the photographs they would frame in silver and set on their mantel and in David's office and in their kitchen.

They waded out of the water onto the shore, and walked barefooted among their guests, and toasted each other with champagne, and went into the enormous white tent with its King Arthur banners flying, and sat at the head table for dinner. Later, there were speeches and toasts and wedding cake.

Even later, the band filled the tent and the lawn and the air with music. They played a mix of their own gypsy jazz and the traditional favorites, starting with "God Only Knows" by the Beach Boys. Alison slipped her shoes on for the first dance with David. Soon other couples joined. The party spilled out on to the grass, almost everyone dancing. The moon was a crescent and the night was brilliant. At midnight, they were still dancing. David danced with his daughter and new stepdaughters and his granddaughters. Alison danced with Ethan and then with Patrick, who surprised her by morphing into a fabulous John Travolta when the band played "Night Fever." Jane danced with Noah and *accidentally* trod hard on his foot. Felicity told Scott he was so sweet for letting the children draw flowers and balloons on his cast; weren't children wonderful! Heather and Cecil sat while surreptitiously slipping Henry and Charlie nibbles of wedding cake. Ethan danced with Canny, Alice, and Daphne all at the same time. Esmeralda danced with Hunter, who came away with stars in his eyes. Luke performed his own hyperactive version of break dancing. Ethan and Esmeralda quietly vanished. Scott and Noah and Patrick sat at a table, talking about real estate prices on the island. Jane and Felicity danced together like wild women under the starry sky, and on an impulse, they each took one of Poppy's hands and pulled her up to dance with them.

It was after one in the morning when everyone yawned and kissed goodbye and slowly, some carrying their shoes, left the party. Some drove home, some went up to their rooms in the hotel. The band packed up, the crowd left. Alison and David hugged their daughters and sons and grandchildren and friends. The newlyweds were staying in a special cottage on the hotel grounds, so they stood on the grass waving their loved ones off.

When everyone else had gone, Alison and David lingered for a while, catching their breath, whispering and yawning and blissfully tired but, like children on Christmas night, unable to surrender to their sleepiness and go to bed.

Behind them, the harbor glistened, the waves whispering of seasons of sunshine and sensuality, cool water, warm sun, the busy rush of days, the deep, sweet sleep of night.

In front of them, the future unfolded like a sparkling trail of moonlight on water.

A NANTUCKET WEDDING

nancy thayer

A READER'S GUIDE

NANTUCKET WEDDINGS

nancy thayer

I unabashedly admit it: I *love* weddings.

They are so hopeful. They are a visual manifestation of all our best wishes for ourselves and everyone we know.

Weddings remind us of our deepest spiritual commitments, the belief that *the very couple* taking their vows in front of us will actually do it—will love each other whether rich or poor, healthy or ill, through good times and bad.

Weddings are the embodiment of dreams. The bride's luscious gown, our own Sunday best, the flowers, the music, the adorable little flower girls carrying baskets of petals—all that lifts our hearts. The whispers and smiles as the guests are seated, the hush that comes over the room before the ceremony commences, the splendid music, the romantic setting, whether in a church or on the beach with waves sparkling in the background—all these elements combine the brilliance of theater with the solemnity of the sacred.

Over the years, Nantucket has become a wedding mecca. I've

attended many weddings of young people. Recently I've attended weddings for the Second-Time-Arounds. These can be the most fun of all. Sometimes a marriage ends in divorce or because of the death of a spouse. These second marriages are the most hopeful, I think.

Because after the first time around, we know that weddings are fantasies but marriages are hard work. When a young person marries, she imagines choosing the perfect furniture for their perfect house where they'll have perfect children.

And then they learn, as we all do, how real life is not perfect.

I grew up in Kansas. The first time I married, I was twenty(!), and my head was full of dreams based on too many Doris Day movies. I had to elope because no one in my family liked my husband-to-be. The second (and last) (and BEST) time I married was in Cambridge, Massachusetts. Everyone in my family was there, except my father, who had passed away that summer. My son, eleven, was an usher, and my daughter, nine, was a bridesmaid. My sister and her family flew from Kansas City so she could be the matron of honor. My uncle gave me away while his sister, my mother, watched. I wore a gorgeous wedding gown, and my husband wore a morning suit. It was perfect.

Except that my little daughter sulked because I got to be the bride. And my son ate too much wedding cake, and you know what happens then. And my mother-in-law brought her long-haired dachshund into the church as her partner. And one of my best friends couldn't come because she was having a baby. And one of my other best friends couldn't come because she was finishing a book—writing, not reading.

Okay, it was almost perfect. Charley and I have been married for thirty-four years, and as the man in that insurance commercial says, "We know a thing or two because we've seen a thing or two." The most challenging years were when—wait. *Every* year was challenging.

Living on an island thirty miles off the coast creates special situations, like the time my daughter, Sam, and I took the ferry to Hyannis on her way to her first year at college, and other travelers who had a suitcase like hers took Sam's suitcase from the luggage rack and drove off with her clothes. And we had their medication. And cell phones didn't exist.

Or the many times Josh and Sam came home for the summer from college and invited their friends to visit, because it was Nantucket in the summer! I spent those days washing beach and bath towels, delivering and picking up kids from the beach/movie/friend's house, and cooking for the masses. Charley and I hardly had a chance to say "Good morning" and "Good night" to each other during those summers.

We always had pets in our home: a curly-haired dog that looked like a sheep, and various cats. We can't really live without a pet. But those sweet animals brought challenges, too, and expenses, like the time we had to take our most vociferous cat Rex on the ferry to the vet in Hyannis because our animal hospital didn't have the right equipment for whatever Rex needed. Rex objected loudly every nautical mile of the way.

Real life can be hard. Weddings can provide a moment of magic. Out of my thirty published novels, eight of them end in weddings. So many of our fables and fairy tales end with the words, *And they lived happily ever after*. They might end more truthfully with the words, *And they lived happily ever after except for the years Zelda hated her job and Albert had to take antidepressants and their son hit a baseball through a cranky old man's window and their daughter sobbed all the time because some boy didn't like her and Zelda couldn't fit into her jeans anymore*.

No one knows what will happen in the future, but we do know we'll do our best to make it happy, and safe and healthy, for the ones we love. I think we believe in weddings and in happily ever after because we know there will be moments through all the years when being married will be worth it, come what may.

QUESTIONS AND TOPICS
FOR DISCUSSION

1. At the start of the novel, it is clear that Felicity and Jane live in different worlds. Felicity is constantly busy with her children, while Jane prioritizes her work as an attorney. Over the course of the summer, they begin to find common ground, confiding in each other about their marital issues and developing a more trusting relationship. Have you ever reconnected with someone you had grown apart from? How did your relationship change?

2. Alison is excited that her fiancé's home on Nantucket can be a place for their soon-to-be blended family to grow closer. Do you have any long-standing traditions in your own family, or have you ever started a new tradition? If so, what makes them meaningful to you?

3. Cynthia, the wife of one of Noah's colleagues, tells Felicity of Noah's affair with Ingrid. Do you agree with this course of action? If you were Cynthia, would you mention the incident to Felicity?

4. Jane is distraught when Scott goes to Wales without her, and their marriage is reaching its breaking point. Yet when she rushes to his bedside later on, Scott tells her that he has had an epiphany and now wants to have children. Have you ever experienced an unexpected event that altered the course of a relationship or friendship?

5. Felicity notes that it is "awkward" watching Poppy discipline Luke, but she brushes off Poppy's remarks to him for the sake of remaining cordial. Think about Felicity's and Poppy's parenting styles. How do you think their personalities dictate the way they approach parenting? How would you feel if another mother chastised your child?

6. When Felicity confronts Noah about his fling with Ingrid, he attempts to justify his behavior, citing the pressures of building his company. How do the standards that Noah sets for himself make him a better or worse partner? Can you sympathize with him on any level, given his actions?

7. Jane and Scott's marriage is based on their common interests: their shared love of the outdoors, their careers as lawyers, and even their initial aversion to having children. Think about the most important relationships in your life. What makes them so significant to you, and how did they begin?

8. Poppy clearly struggles with her father's impending nuptials, not to mention the future of English Garden Creams. When David tells her that he plans to include Alison, her daughters, and her grandchildren in his will, she is appalled. Is her reaction justified? Discuss.

9. For Alison, her marriage to David signifies the beginning of a new life, six years after the death of her husband. Think about finding happiness after loss. What do second chances mean to you?

10. At the end of the novel Felicity and Noah are still at an impasse. She notes that, going forward, she is "free to change. She could leave Noah, but she didn't want to" (page 290). What do you think is in store for Felicity and Noah's marriage?

Read on for an excerpt from

Surfside Sisters

by nancy thayer

Published by Ballantine Books

chapter one

There are two different kinds of people in the world: Those who wade cautiously into the shallows and those who throw themselves headlong into the roaring surf.

At least, that was what Keely and Isabelle thought.

As girls, Keely and Isabelle preferred Surfside to Jetties or Steps Beach, even though that meant a longer bike ride to the water. Jetties Beach was mild and shallow, perfect for children, but Surfside had, well, *surf!*—often dramatically breathtaking surf leaping up and smashing down with a roar and an explosion of spray that caught the sunlight and blinded their eyes with rainbows. Their parents worried when they went to Surfside. People could get caught up by the power of the water and slammed mercilessly down onto the sand. People had their ankles broken, their arms. Once, a classmate of Keely's had broken his neck, but they'd medevaced him to Boston and eventually he was good as new. He never returned to Surfside, though.

Keely couldn't remember a time when Isabelle wasn't her best friend. They met in preschool, linked up the first day, and went on like that for years. They were equally spirited and silly. They played childish pranks, using the landline to punch in a random number; if a woman answered, they whispered in what they considered sultry, sexy voices, "Tell your husband I miss him." Usually they couldn't keep from giggling before they disconnected. At ten, they smoked cigarettes at night in the backyard—until they realized the nicotine only made them nauseous. Once, when they were eleven, they stole lipsticks from the pharmacy, which was really stupid, since they didn't wear lipstick.

Isabelle lived in a huge, marvelous, old Victorian house in the middle of Nantucket. It had a wraparound porch and a small turret. Odd alcoves and crannies were tucked in beneath the stairs, both the formal, carpeted stairs from the front hall and the narrow, twisting back stairs from the kitchen. It was the perfect place for hide-and-seek, and on rainy days, they were allowed to rummage through old trunks and boxes in the attic, piling on ancient dresses as soft as spiderwebs and floppy hats heavy with cloth flowers.

The Maxwell house was rambling and mysterious, a home out of storybooks, and for Keely, the amazing Maxwell family belonged there.

Isabelle's father, Al Maxwell—his full first name was Aloysius, which his children used when he reprimanded them, "Yes, sir, Aloysius!"—was a lawyer, a partner with Perry Dunstan of Maxwell and Dunstan, the Nantucket firm that did mostly real estate law. Mr. Maxwell was larger than life, tall, broad, ruddy-cheeked, and energetic. He didn't talk, he bellowed. He didn't drink, he gulped. He didn't laugh, he roared. His wife, Donna, said the vertebrae of his spine spelled out E-X-T-R-O-V-E-R-T. When he arrived home after a day at the office, Al threw off his jacket, loosened his tie, and strode out to the spacious backyard. He'd join a game of baseball or pick up Izzy or Keely, settle them on his shoulders, and chase the other children, bellowing that he was a wild and angry bull, all the time keeping tight hold on the legs of the child he carried.

Mrs. Maxwell was movie star beautiful. Tall, blond, and buxom, she was the careful parent, the watchful one. She seldom joined in their games, probably because she was busy cooking enormous meals for her family and baking cakes and pies that sold out at church and school fundraisers. She was the mother who volunteered as chaperone on all the school trips, who helped decorate the gym for special occasions, and when her son stomped into the house with most of the high school basketball team, she was ready with hearty snacks like taco bakes and pizzas. She did everything the perfect mom would do, and still remained, somehow, cool, restrained. At least it seemed she was that way to Keely.

There were the two remarkable Maxwell children. The oldest was Sebastian, tall, lanky, blue-eyed Sebastian. How he managed to be so handsome and so modest at the same time was always a curiosity to Keely. She thought that it must be because he grew up in a house where everyone was gorgeous, so it seemed as normal to him as breathing. He played most of the school sports—baseball, basketball, soccer—and he was on the swim team.

After Sebastian, two years younger, came Isabelle. Mr. Maxwell often bragged, "I hit it out of the park with her!" At which Mrs. Maxwell would respond, "Not by yourself, you didn't." Such casual remarks alluding to sex made the Maxwell parents urbane and superior in Keely's eyes.

Isabelle was a beauty like her mother, only willowy instead of voluptuous. Unlike Sebastian, she was aware of the power of her looks, and she was a friendly girl, but deep down inside not really a team player. She liked secrets, liked sharing them with Keely and no one else. She liked plotting and disobeying and sneaking and hiding. She liked mischief. She was often in trouble with the school or her parents, but she was also almost genius smart, so she got good grades and she knew when to rein in her wild side.

The Maxwell house was always crowded with kids of all ages, playing Ping-Pong in the basement, doing crafts at the dining room table while Donna baked cookies, or giggling in Isabelle's room while trying on clothes. Fido, their slightly dense yellow Lab, roamed the house looking for dropped food. He always found something. Salt and Pepper, their long-haired cats, gave the evil eye to all humans that tried to remove them from whatever soft nest they'd made, but if they were in the right mood, they'd accept gentle stroking and reward the human with a tranquilizing purr.

Keely was fiercely, but secretly, jealous of the entire family. It wasn't that her parents weren't rich like the Maxwells—well, it wasn't only that. It wasn't that the Green house was a small one-floor ranch outside town. It wasn't that Keely was an only child with parents who were allergic to animals. She never even had a damn hamster!

But she wouldn't have traded her parents for anyone. Her father was a car mechanic, and her mother was a nurse. Mr. and Mrs. Green were well-liked in the community, and they loved Keely with all their hearts.

Isabelle loved hanging out at Keely's house because she could escape her noisy family, and Keely loved being at Isabelle's house because she loved being around that noisy family.

Secretly, painfully, Keely had a crush on Sebastian. She didn't tell Isabelle. She couldn't. It was too humiliating. She knew she was a child to Sebastian, if she was anything to him at all.

Sebastian was two years older than Keely. She was ten, he was twelve. The end.

Still, Keely lived in a dream, a bubble of yearning, almost an obsession. When she was at Isabelle's house, she locked the bathroom door and picked up his toothbrush. It was like a holy icon. *Sebastian* had touched it. Sometimes she saw his boxer shorts in the bathroom laundry basket. Seeing something so intimate made her heart pound.

She hid her hopeless childish love from Isabelle, who had sharp edges when it came to her brother. Isabelle was constantly confiding to Keely about how Sebastian was so perfect she felt she could never measure up. She carried a massive inferiority complex on her slender shoulders. It didn't help that half the girls in town, older and younger, sucked up to Isabelle, acting all sweetie pie—best friends only because they wanted to get into the Maxwell house and flirt with Sebastian.

That wasn't the case with Keely. She had chosen Isabelle first and hoped they would always be best friends. She couldn't even *imagine* life without Isabelle. And often, she felt as if she were truly part of the Maxwell family. When they went to the fair in the summer or a Theatre Workshop play in the winter or out in the Maxwells' Rhodes 19 sailboat for a day at Tuckernuck, Keely was often invited along. They even kept a life jacket just for Keely hanging on the hook in their back hall. When grades were given at school, Mr. Maxwell always held out his hand for Keely's, read the sheet carefully, and asked Keely questions as if he really cared. The fifth chair at the dining room table was called "Keely's chair," no matter who sat in it. Mr. Maxwell made Keely feel bigger, better, more worthy of simply being on the planet. Keely adored him, but she kept this to herself as much as she hid her infatuation with Sebastian. She was an only child, good at keeping her own confidences.

"My parents are boring," Keely confessed one day when she and Isabelle were idly dangling on the complicated swing set in the Maxwells' backyard. They were ten, too old to play on the swings, young enough to enjoy their joke: "hanging out."

"You're nuts!" Isabelle said. "I'd give anything to live your life. No big brother flicking my ear and forcing me to play catch. I could lie in my quiet room reading and reading."

"Or writing and writing," Keely said.

In fifth grade, they confessed to each other they wanted to become writers. They were already best friends, but this shared, slightly eccentric hope bonded the two girls like superglue. They spent long summer hours writing scenes and stories, reading and discussing them with each other. They'd phone constantly to suggest new plot ideas, to mention a cool new word (*quixotic, ethereal*) they'd learned. They planned their glamorous new lives. They'd have their books published at the same time. They'd have apartments across from each other in New York. On the island, Isabelle would drive a Porsche convertible. Keely decided on a Mercedes SUV so she'd have room for all her children.

But they weren't snobs or freaks. They did stuff with the other girls. They went to all the home football games, to slumber parties, and even the occasional day trip to the Cape with friends to shop and eat at the mall.

But they treasured their secret ambition. They felt like super-heroes, masquerading as silly girls secretly aiming for the stars.

The summer the girls were ten, the Maxwells went off on their European "jaunt"—as Mrs. Maxwell called it. One afternoon in the middle of August, they returned. As always, even before she unpacked, Isabelle phoned Keely. "I'm home!" Then she biked to Keely's house as fast as her legs would pedal.

Keely was out on the lawn, waiting, jumping up and down with excitement. The girls screamed with joy when they saw each other. Keely and Isabelle hugged and whirled around and fell down on the soft green grass, laughing like hyenas.

"I missed you SO much," Isabelle cried.

"I missed you more," Keely insisted. "You have to tell me everything."

Keely's mother came out of the house. "Isabelle. Let me look at you. Oh, honey, I think you're two inches taller."

Isabelle jumped up and hugged Mrs. Green. "I know. I'm a giraffe," Isabelle said, fake mournfully.

Keely's mother laughed. "You're a beauty. Now tell me if I'm correct. You girls like a large pizza with onions and pepperoni and a Pepperidge Farm chocolate cake."

"Yay, Mom, you remember!" Keely stood up, brushing grass off her shorts. Every time Isabelle returned from the Maxwells' European trip, Isabelle and Keely celebrated by eating on the back patio, just the two of them, stuffing themselves with pizza and cake and laughing and whispering and eating more cake until two or three in the morning when Isabelle, groggy with jet lag, said she had to sleep. They'd bring the mostly empty boxes of food into the kitchen and quietly tiptoe to Keely's bedroom. Without even brushing their teeth, they would collapse on the twin beds and sleep until noon the next day.

This summer, when Keely woke, Isabelle was gone. Keely wandered into the kitchen. Both her parents were at work, but her mother had left a note for her.

Isabelle has an appointment with the orthodontist. I drove her to her house at nine this morning. She said she'll call you.

Also, Sebastian wants you to call him.

Poor Isabelle, Keely thought. To have to spend the morning getting fitted for braces—*tragic.*

She ran a glass of cool water and drank it down. She felt like a blimp, bloated with pizza and cake. She wished she drank coffee, because she'd seen its magic work on her parents, but they told her she was too young.

It felt so good to brush her teeth, she decided to take a shower. After that, she pulled on one of her bathing suits with a Kylie Minogue T-shirt over it. The day was hers. Isabelle would probably take a nap after the orthodontist visit. Keely would see her this evening. Until then, she could read the latest novel from the library, or—

Someone was pounding on the door. Keely opened it and found Isabelle's brother standing there with steam coming out his ears.

"Sebastian! Hi!"

"Didn't your mom tell you to call me?"

"Um, yes." Sebastian was as beautiful as an angel, but so were all the Maxwells. Keely had gotten kind of used to it. Right now Sebastian seemed older, cooler. She had to remind herself that he was only two years older than Keely.

"The sand castle contest is today. I need your help."

"Okay, sure. Do you know what you're going to do? Do you need, I don't know, bowls for molds or something?"

"I've brought buckets and stuff. I'm not sure what to do. That's why I want to talk to you. Get your bike and let's go."

"I've got to leave a note for my mom and dad."

She scurried into the kitchen and scribbled a note. She shoved her feet into flip-flops, and checked the beach bag she always had waiting, filled with a thermos of water, towels, and sunblock. She pulled the front door shut, stuck her beach bag in her basket, and wheeled her bike next to Sebastian's.

"So what are your ideas?" she asked as they biked toward Jetties Beach.

"Maybe Neptune and Ariel and—"

"No Disney!" Keely shouted. "Everyone will be doing Neptune and Ariel."

"Well, what then?"

"What about a whale? A great big whale . . . smiling."

"That would work," Sebastian said. Keely grinned.

They were late to the contest. All up and down the beach, people were on their knees, shaping and patting the sand. Keely and Sebastian locked their bikes to the stand and raced down the beach to an open space at the far end.

First they carried buckets of sand to their spot. The sand had to be just right, damp enough to hold its shape but not so sodden it crumbled. Sebastian drew an outline in the sand—he was the real artist in his family—and they began molding the gigantic body of the whale. The tail was the most difficult, so Sebastian had it raised and slanted to show both flukes.

"You make the mouth and the eye," Keely called. "You always do it better than I do."

While Sebastian made the finishing touches on the great animal, Keely had an inspiration. She built a baby whale next to its mother.

The sun rose high in the sky. They took quick dips in the water to cool off before setting back to work. At the end of the day, they were exhausted but happy. Their structure didn't win—a group of college guys had built a miniature Mount Rushmore—but their whales did get photographed for the newspaper. Their theme was so Nantucket, and if she said so herself, and she did. The baby whale, with its smile, was adorable.

In the late afternoon, they biked to the Maxwell house. They took turns using the outdoor shower. Keely went around to the back deck to dry off. She collapsed in one of the Maxwells' fancy cushioned chairs.

"You guys!" Isabelle stomped out on the porch, arms folded over her chest, pouting. "Why didn't you call me? I wanted to help."

"You were with Mom at Dr. Roberts's," Sebastian yelled.

"Show me your braces!" Keely demanded.

"Don't have them yet. It's such a major *project.*" Isabelle flopped into a chair next to Keely.

Sebastian came up the back steps, dripping from his shower, his towel wrapped around his waist, the sun gilding his hair. He'd acquired muscles over the summer. His shoulders were broader, his thighs thicker. Keely hadn't noticed when they were on the beach. She'd been too busy working. But now she noticed, and the sight did something funny to her stomach. She looked away.

"You are *so* going to have a sunburn all over your back," Isabelle told her brother.

Sebastian shrugged. "Call me when you start the movie."

It had become a custom for the three of them to spend the Maxwells' second night back with fish dinners from Sayle's and a movie. Keely and Isabelle said it couldn't be too scary and Sebastian said it couldn't be too romantic and it really couldn't be a musical. They agreed on *Dude, Where's My Car?* The girls both had mad crushes on Ashton Kutcher. Keely made sure Isabelle was in the middle of the sofa, between her and Sebastian. If she sat next to Sebastian, her skin might touch his. It made her hot even to think about that.

As always, Keely phoned her parents and got permission to

spend the night at Isabelle's. The Maxwell house had central air. What a lush plush luxury it was to slide into the silky sheets beneath a light down comforter in the twin bed in Isabelle's room.

Life was back to normal, Keely thought, and she was smiling as she fell asleep.

When Keely was eleven, Sebastian did something extraordinary.

The Maxwell family had spent February vacation in Eleuthera, and Isabelle had brought Keely a cute T-shirt, like that could compensate for the difference between their two lives. Yet Keely didn't want to be all pitiful. First of all, that would be lame and icky. She'd keep her self-pity to herself, thank you very much. No one liked a whiner. But second, and really more important, Keely had loved this past week when most of her friends were gone and there was no school and she checked out a big fat pile of novels from the library and she'd spent her days and much of her nights lost in worlds that required as a passport only the ability to read.

And she came up with a totally cool project.

Keely and Isabelle were in the Maxwells' dining room on a frigid, gray Sunday morning. Sebastian had taken over the den to play the videogames he'd missed on vacation. Mrs. Maxwell had gone shopping for groceries, and Mr. Maxwell was, as always, at work.

"So, Isabelle, now that you're all tanned and fabulous, let me tell you what *I* did all week."

"What?"

"I've started a newspaper!"

"We have a newspaper."

"No, the town has a newspaper. The adults have a newspaper. Kids don't."

"How are you going to make a newspaper? You're *eleven*."

"I'll show you." Keely unzipped her backpack and pulled out a sheaf of papers she'd stapled together. "Look."

The first page said simply: *THE BUZZ*

The second page headline read: AUDITIONS FOR THE SPRING PRODUCTION OF *ANNIE*. The column told where and when the auditions were being held, and continued with a short summary of the musical, followed by a brief recap of past productions.

The third page was headlined LETTERS TO THE EDITOR. There was one letter, which read, *Dear Editor, I'm not that fussy about what I eat, but I wish the cafeteria would put real cheese in the macaroni and cheese instead of the orange superglue they use. I'm writing this because I can't talk because my teeth are stuck together. Hopefully, Glenda.*

"Wow, Keely. This is amazing!" Isabelle said. "But we don't have a Glenda on the island. Isn't that the name of the good witch in *The Wizard of Oz*?"

"Silly, this is only a prototype." Keely nearly fainted with pleasure at using the word *prototype*. "I wrote the letter. I made everything up. So I get to be the editor and you can be the assistant editor and since you have your cool camera, you can be the photographer."

"But how can we make copies?"

Keely flicked Isabelle's leg. "Vacation made you dense. We put it online. If it works, we can talk to the school about making hard copies on their printer."

Isabelle squinted her eyes, conveying deep thought. "If the school makes the copies, they'll know what we're writing and they'll be able to edit it."

"Well, Isabelle, it's not like we'll have a lot of scurrilous material."

Isabelle's eyes widened. *"Scurrilous?"*

"It means scandalous. Outrageous." Keely grinned. Isabelle might have gone far away in physical space, but Keely had traveled far in her mind, and brought back souvenirs.

Isabelle tapped her index finger on her lower lip. "Okay. I see the potential. But it needs something else. Maybe a logo? A cartoon? I don't know, something graphic."

"Good idea, but you and I can't draw."

"Maybe we could use a meme?"

Keely shrugged. "I guess."

The girls felt a gust of icy air as Mrs. Maxwell entered the house.

"Kids! Come help with the groceries!"

Keely jumped up and followed Isabelle. The number of bags Mrs. Maxwell filled at the Stop & Shop always astonished Keely. She made three trips to the SUV and back, lugging a bag in each hand.

"Mom," Isabelle said. "I don't see Sebastian helping. He and his friends eat most of the fruit."

"He shovels the walk and the drive," Mrs. Maxwell reminded her daughter.

In the kitchen, they made a kind of game of putting away the zillions of items. Huge bundles of toilet paper, paper towels, tissues. Mountains of fruit. Gallons of milk, pounds of butter, acres of bread.

"Take that toilet paper upstairs, Isabelle," Mrs. Maxwell said. "Then you're done. Thanks, girls."

Keely returned to the dining room table while Isabelle stomped up the stairs.

At her spot, next to the first page of *The Buzz*, was a piece of paper with a loosely but cleverly drawn bee. It was very fat. It had a huge face with a mischievous smile.

"Sebastian." Keely scanned the room, as if he could be hiding behind the mahogany sideboard.

She studied the bee more closely. Under one of its wings were the letters *KG*. Keely's initials. So he wanted people to think Keely had drawn this.

Okay. She could do that. Quickly she picked up a pencil and drew her own versions of the bee on fresh sheets of paper. They weren't as good as Sebastian's bee, but they weren't that different, especially because Sebastian's bee had a slightly wavy outline.

So. Sebastian had been aware of her. Okay, of her and Isabelle. Still. It made her fingers tingle to think that he had overheard and tried to help. As if Sebastian even knew she existed. That thought was overwhelming.

She wondered how she could thank him.

"Done!" Isabelle rushed into the room and pulled her chair close to Keely. "Hey, what's that? It's so cute!"

"Do you think so?" Keely cocked her head, giving the smiling bee a serious evaluation. She waited for Isabelle to say that the drawing looked like something Sebastian would do. "I don't know."

"Well, I do! It's adorable, Keely. Definitely it has to be on our masthead. You are so talented! Now. We need reporters. Then we'll have more news."

They leaned shoulder to shoulder, scribbling lists, chattering away, thrilled with their plans. For a moment, Keely felt . . . *something*, so she looked up. Sebastian was standing in the doorway watching her. Keely smiled at him. He smiled at her.

Sebastian smiled at her.

One afternoon, Keely and Isabelle sat on the rug of the screened porch, designing and cutting out clothes for their Women in History paper doll project.

Keely had labored over an extremely fancy ball gown and was cutting it when it tore.

"Rats!" Keely cried. "It took me forever to make that dress!"

"Silly, just tape it together. On the back. No one will notice."

"Where's the tape?"

"You know, in the kitchen by Mom's address book."

Keely jumped up and went into the living room and through to the kitchen.

"Can't find it!"

"Sebastian probably took it."

Keely headed up the stairs to Sebastian's room. She assumed he wasn't home—he was seldom home, except for dinner—so she hurried down the carpeted hall, threw open the door of Sebastian's bedroom, and stepped inside.

Sebastian was at his desk, a big fourteen-year-old boy with long hairy legs sticking out of his soccer shorts.

"Oh." She scrunched up her shoulders. "Sorry. I need the tape."

"Fine." Sebastian found it on the far side of his desk. "Here."

Keely approached him to take the tape in its black dispenser. She couldn't help noticing the pad on his desk with the intricate pencil drawing of the Nantucket harbor.

"Did you do that?"

Sebastian shrugged. "Yeah."

Without asking permission, she stepped closer, studying the sketch. "This is cool. And I love the whales you put near Great Point." She was so astonished she forgot to be afraid of him, Isabelle's older, and much bigger, brother. "I didn't know you could draw this well."

"No one needs to know." Sebastian pulled a blank sheet of paper over his drawing.

"Oh. Okay." Keely carried the tape dispenser in both hands as she left the room.

"Close the door," Sebastian said. "And don't come in here again without knocking."

As Keely took hold of the brass doorknob and pulled it shut, Sebastian said, "And don't tell my parents. Especially don't tell Izzy. She can't keep a secret."

"Okay." Keely shut the door. Then, on an insane whim, powered by courage she didn't know she had, she pushed the door open again and went into the room. "But, Sebastian, why is that a secret? Is it a present for someone?"

"Ha. Right." Sebastian gave Keely a look that seemed almost friendly. "My parents want me to play team sports. Not sit alone in my room doodling."

"But that's not doodling! That's art!" Keely protested. "And Izzy and I sit in our own rooms all the time. We're writing a book."

Sebastian's mouth crooked up in a half-smile. "Cool. So just keep it a secret for me, okay, Keely?"

He said her name.

Keely went hot all over, pleased and surprised and funny feel-ing. Of course he knew her name! She was such a total dork!

Too embarrassed to speak, she nodded, left the room—pulling the door shut tight. She returned to her paper doll dress with the tape and also with an odd happiness in her stomach. She shared a secret with Sebastian, one that not even Isabelle knew.

PHOTO: © KATIE KAIZER

NANCY THAYER is the *New York Times* bestselling author of more than 30 novels, including *A Nantucket Wedding, Secrets in Summer, The Island House, The Guest Cottage, An Island Christmas, Nantucket Sisters, A Nantucket Christmas, Island Girls,* and more. Born in Kansas City, Missouri, Nancy has been a year-round resident of Nantucket for thirty-four years, where she currently lives with her husband, Charley, and a precocious rescue cat named Callie.

nancythayer.com
Facebook.com/NancyThayerBooks